Cambridge-educated Colin Butler spent many years teaching English and German in schools and universities. He's lived in Germany and Canada as well as the UK and he's published successfully on Shakespeare's plays, so he's no stranger to violence, treachery and malice. "They're always with us," he says. "Their forms change but that's all."

DEATH BY DROWNING

For Tom and Emily – two of the best.

Colin Butler

DEATH BY DROWNING

AUSTIN MACAULEY
PUBLISHERS LTD.

A CIP catalogue record for this title is available from the British Library.

ISBN 978 184963 467 0

www.austinmacauley.com

First Published 2014
Austin Macauley Publishers Ltd.
25 Canada Square
Canary Wharf
London
E14 5LB

Printed and bound in Great Britain

I

1

An East German murder, a New German funeral and a link with London

"If you panic you'll get stuck and drown in the dark."

Manfred Voss, a first lieutenant in the National People's Army, kept his emotions well hidden as he said his piece and the fresh-faced corporal standing on the other side of his desk did his best to do the same. It was midsummer hot in Voss's office but only the corporal was sweating. Voss tapped a sheaf of papers with the butt-end of his fountain pen.

"These," he went on, "describe all the changes to the rock surface. They also set out the fingerholds. If you learn them by heart, you'll survive. If you don't, you're a dead man."

Each sheet had "State Training Camp – Harz Mountains" stamped on it, together with the East German flag. He wrote "Corporal Fritz Forster, for the use of" on the top one and slid them forwards. Forster didn't pick them up. He'd need an order for that.

"This is a new cave for me, Sir," he said, trying to sound confident. "Can you tell me what it's like?"

He wanted to shift his weight from one foot to the other but he knew it'd be seen as weakness so he stayed as he was.

"If you wish. It's quite high when you first go in and there's a watercourse in the floor for you to follow. Be warned, it's on the long side. Eventually the sides of the cave close in and the roof comes down so low, it looks as if the watercourse is blocked off. I say 'looks' because what really happens is that the floor of the watercourse drops at that point to run under a large spur of rock that juts downwards. Then it comes up in the next cave.

The gap between the floor of the watercourse and the spur of rock is where you go through. It's bigger than you are but only just. You get into the water while you've still got some room, turn onto your back, thrust your arms ahead of you and force yourself into the gap with your hands and feet. You'll be head down, you won't see a thing and you'll be in too tight to back out so don't even try. When you feel the tip of the spur be ready to bend your body upwards. Otherwise you won't get past."

"Is there any current?"

"None at all. When it rains a surge builds up and if you're in the gap then, you've had it. But it hasn't rained once since you've been here and that's two weeks now."

Voss had said all he wanted to say. He told Forster to be outside the officers' block at 13.15 hours wearing close-fitting clothing under his top clothes, then he dismissed him with his papers. As soon as Forster was gone, he locked the door, shut all the windows, took a tape recorder out of a cupboard and started a tape. At first, there was only hiss in his headphones. Then, all blurry as if the microphone were hidden in something, he heard a door open and close and two men speaking. One was Fritz Forster, the other was Clemens Forster, a sergeant mechanic and Fritz Forster's elder brother. Voss and Clemens Forster were permanent staff. Fritz Forster was a volunteer trainee from the other side of East Germany.

"So, have they told you why you're crawling through all these caves?" Clemens Forster asked through the sound of chairs sliding on a tiled floor.

"Some caves on our borders go through to the West and certain traitors are taking people through them in numbers. I'm going to be infiltrated into one of these rat-runs to set up an ambush – it's the Stasi's idea and they'll decide when I go."

Voss heard a bottle cap bounce onto the floor, two glasses clinked together and the two men said, "Prost!" but not too loudly.

"But," Fritz Forster continued and he dropped his voice so much Voss had to turn the volume up full, "instead of setting up an ambush I'm going to go through with the others and I can get you taken along. Think of it, Clemmi! No Stasi, no waiting years for a pokey flat and no Stone Age cars. Just money, money, money and all the freedom you want. What do you say? Are you in?"

There was a long pause. Then,

"I'm not sure, Fritz. You're all right, you're single, but I've got a family to think about. I'd have to get leave as well. Can you give me a day or two?"

"You've got till a week tomorrow, that's the end of my time here. But whatever you do, don't tell anyone. Not even a hint."

They were in Clemens Forster's admin room in the back of the Repair Shop for Non-armoured Personnel Vehicles. He'd put a tape recorder under an empty box as soon as his brother had said he wanted to discuss something serious and he'd switched it on every time he saw him come in because to Clemens Forster's mind "serious" had to mean something the state should know about. As soon as his brother had left this time he'd taken the tape to Voss. He knew Voss was as patriotic as he was. They never called their country East Germany, it was always the German Democratic Republic and they were sure it'd last forever.

When Voss heard the tape he went berserk and he went berserk again as he replayed it now. But by this time he'd worked out what to do about it. He'd been caving since his early teens and one of the things he knew was how far and how fast rainwater travels underground. His camp might not have seen rain for some time but unlike Fritz Forster, who was cut off from the outside world, Voss knew that beyond a range of hills fifteen miles to the north-east it had poured relentlessly six days before onto limestone that was already saturated. That water had been on the move ever since and Voss knew exactly where a goodly portion of it would be at 15.00 hours that afternoon.

At 13.15 hours Fritz Forster was waiting in the shade outside the officers' block. He was wearing tennis shoes without socks and under his fatigues he had on thick long underpants and an equally thick button-up vest. He'd put a towel and a change of clothes in a canvas bag. He felt sticky and tense but when Voss appeared in uniform, complete with his Makarow 9mm service pistol, he snapped to attention and followed him briskly to his run-about, a Trabant 601-A. They drove in silence to the repair shop. The camp looked almost empty because most of the training took place out of sight in unmarked buildings. It was completely fenced in, the fencing was topped with barbed wire and there were manned gun towers with searchlights every seventy-five yards. A three-mile exclusion zone completed the job.

Voss parked the Trabant and took the keys for a Barkas B1000 mini-bus plus a smaller canvas bag Clemens Forster had ready for him. Fritz Forster put it in the back next to his own and climbed into the passenger seat while Voss started the engine. As they drove off he glanced at his brother and saw him nod just a fraction. It could only mean one thing, he thought: he was going to escape with him. He had no notion Voss had got in first.

Voss was stopped twice in the exclusion zone and asked to show his papers, which he was more than happy to do. Checking strengthened the GDR, that was his view, so there could never be enough of it. As they moved onto non-military terrain he wound up his window to cut down the noise.

"This afternoon's quite a test for you," he said and he sounded almost friendly for once. "How do you feel about it?"

"I feel fine, Sir." Then, suddenly uneasy at the word "test", Forster found the nerve to ask, "I'm not being sent back to my unit, am I?"

If he went back early Clemmi might have second thoughts. That was the last thing he wanted.

Voss gave him a queer kind of smile.

"No, certainly not, you're staying with us. Longer than you think, in fact. I'm glad you feel fine," he added. "I didn't think you'd let your country down."

They rattled deeper into the Harz Mountains and then they were at the cave Voss had picked out. An armed guard on a bench under a makeshift canvas awning jumped to his feet as they drove up and stood rigidly to attention till Voss told him to stand easy.

"No one is to be admitted till we leave," he ordered as his papers were checked yet again. "Bring my bag, Corporal," he called over his shoulder and led the way inside.

While they were still in the light he stopped and told Forster to put the bags down. The air was already much cooler.

"There should be two lamps in my bag. Get them out and the calcium carbide as well. I'll start them up."

The lamps looked like bicycle lamps, which is what they were sometimes used as in the early days of cycling. They had unglazed concave reflectors that were attached to a vertical cylinder. The cylinder consisted of an upper and a lower container which could be separated as required.

The calcium carbide powder was in an airtight tin and, as usual, it made Voss wrinkle his nose as he eased off the press-in lid with a pocket knife. Taking his time, he parted the containers and shook the top two to make sure Clemens Forster had put water in them. Then he carefully filled the bottom two with calcium carbide and closed the tin. After he'd screwed the containers together again he opened their drip controls to let water onto the calcium carbide and waited for acetylene gas to form. In the middle of the reflectors was a hole with a jet poking through it and next to the jets was a sparkwheel. He spun first one, then the other, with the flat of his hand and the escaping gas caught fire, giving off a wide, bright beam that would last for up to two hours. Forster was glad Voss was finished at last. There was always a wait for the gas to form but Forster had the impression Voss was deliberately stalling. That impression was reinforced when Voss handed Forster one of the lamps and said,

"You can have a look round if you like. We've got the time."

Aha!

"He's trying my nerves," Forster said to himself. "Well, I'll show him."

He was still buoyed up by his brother's nod.

He gripped his lamp firmly and let it dwell on every part of the cave the light would reach. He expected Voss to watch his hands or his face but whenever he risked a glance in Voss's direction he saw his eyes were fixed on what the beam was lighting up. Had he been more experienced he'd have realised Voss was reading the cave like a very precise clock and using him to do it. It wasn't enough that rainwater was on its way - it had to be dead on time.

"All right, that will do," Voss said finally, handing over a rubberised torch in a holster. "You can start now."

Forster swallowed hard and set off along the watercourse. The air was clammy and the water looked lethal. Beyond the beam of his lamp the darkness seemed like something you could sculpt. When he reached the point where everything closed in he set his lamp down without putting it out, folded his fatigues into a neat pile, strapped the torch to his side and, hoping his underwear wouldn't bag out, he lowered himself into the water till his feet touched the bottom. It was chest deep and wintry cold. He was so nervous he was within an ace of going back but he was convinced Voss would use his Makarow if he did, which is what Voss had intended. Of course, he could always pretend he'd gone through the gap but Voss might know of another way to the other side and use it. He couldn't risk that either.

So he started moving forward till the water was up to his chin and the cave roof was scraping the top of his head. Then he backed off till he had room to turn over and extend his arms. Using his hands and the sides of the watercourse he floated himself forward till the cave roof was in his face. Then he took one last breath, shut his eyes and forced himself under water. Almost immediately he was enclosed by rock.

Very soon his ears were ringing, the pressure in his nose was intense and his sense of time was distorted. Then his mind began to drift and just as he was fantasising how much easier it would be if he exhaled just a little and breathed in some cool, fresh water, he felt the rock curve upwards. That refocused him enough to bend his body and work his way to the surface. He was completely exhausted when he broke clear. All he could do, with the roof of the second cave just above his head and its sides still close to his shoulders, was cling to the edge of the watercourse and suck in air out of the darkness. When his breathing had settled down he reset his sense of direction and felt his way along till he had more room, then he took the torch out of its holster and switched it on. The beam was weak and fitful – "typical GDR," he thought – but it was enough to show him the watercourse disappearing into a vast cavern in front of him. His body was a dead weight as he clambered out and all he really wanted to do was stop shivering and go to sleep. He didn't notice a gash on the back of his head nor his lacerated fingers. Voss had said he could rest for four minutes and since he believed Voss would know if he took even a minute longer he passed exactly four minutes lying on his back and looking at his watch by torchlight. When the four minutes were up he reholstered the torch and felt his way back into the water.

It seemed different somehow but he put it down to fatigue and the darkness, and soon he was enclosed in the gap again and forcing himself downwards. But his strength was ebbing faster than it should and as he felt the rock curve he realised why - he was pulling against a current that was getting stronger. It had to be the surge, he thought, even though he didn't understand why it should be there, and that was the moment he panicked. Desperately he tried to pull with his arms as well as his fingers but his elbows were too hemmed in and he couldn't bend his knees to push with his feet. Then his breathing control went and he began to inhale water. When he died, his body jammed fast and plugged the water flow.

Back in the entrance cave Voss was standing next to Forster's clothes. He didn't need his own lamp because Forster's was still burning, and his eyes kept moving from his watch to the watercourse and back. When he saw the water back up his face relaxed into total satisfaction: Forster had to be dead. Methodically he picked up Forster's fatigues,dowsed and cooled his lamp when he could see without it and exited the cave carrying both canvas bags.

"The corporal who came with me has drowned," he told the ramrod-straight guard, carefully avoiding the word "accident". "I'm returning to camp to make the necessary arrangements. You will not contact anyone and you will not let anyone in unless authorised by me or the Camp Commandant. Do I make myself clear?"

He did but before the guard could say so Voss was climbing into the Barkas and setting off, this time driving at speed.

Voss reported directly to the Camp Commandant. He made no secret of the fact that he'd killed Forster intentionally.

"It was my duty as an officer of the National People's Army," he stated flatly. "I executed him because he was planning to desert."

The last thing the Camp Commandant wanted was a court martial since it would reflect badly on him and his camp so he told Voss to wait in the corridor and phoned a senior Party official he was good friends with. What should he do? he asked. Voss was in luck. The East German economy was on its knees yet again, worker discontent was widespread and the hunt was on for a propaganda lift. So, instead of spending time behind bars Voss was turned into a headline hero. Rapid promotion followed, as it did for Clemens Forster, and by the time, to Voss's unmitigated fury, East and West Germany were united he – Voss - had attained the rank of general.

The new Germany pensioned him off, that was routine, but the equally new State Prosecutor had his own sense of duty and soon the yellowing press reports that had talked Voss up were looking as if they could make a murder charge stick. One of Voss's former telephonists was now working in the State Prosecutor's office. She tipped Voss off and Voss straight away contacted a long-time friend and colleague, Colonel Ulrich Steffen. Steffen was as much a GDR fanatic as Voss but he'd also foreseen that the GDR would go belly-up so he'd quietly built up an organisation called Chameleon to help people who, once the new Germany came into being, would probably be on the wrong side of the law - people like undercover assassins, border guards who'd shot escapers and interrogators who weren't too fussy how they got their answers. Chameleon specialised in intimidating and liquidating witnesses, losing documents, setting up new identities and, if need be, fast-tracking whole families out of the country. It was what old comrades were for.

Steffen said he'd help if he could and after a couple of months the State Prosecutor had thrown in the towel. The Camp Commandant, advised by his Party friend, hadn't put anything usable in writing and ten independent witnesses were prepared to swear the Party had simply heard about a caving accident and invented the rest to get a good story. Thereafter Voss was left alone to brood on the GDR's demise and, during his days of decline, to design his tombstone - a lavishly gilded black marble slab bearing the hammer and compasses of the GDR plus the defiant words, "In death as in life, loyal".

He wished to be buried in the small village north of Leipzig where he'd been born - not in the churchyard (he was an atheist) but in the municipal cemetery where his parents lay. And so early one May morning a group of mostly elderly but still stiff-backed men watched respectfully as his coffin was lowered solemnly into the ground. Clemens Forster, now the well heeled president of Forster & Sons, a Volkswagen dealership in Stuttgart, was there, so was Steffen and so was Annett, Voss's widow. Twisted, bent and painfully thin, she was leaning on the arm of her daughter, Lisa Birdsall, who was now a commodities trader in Chicago. Birdsall had married late. She knew her father had gone wrong somewhere and that had got in the way but then she'd met Elmer Birdsall, another trader and a widower with four children, and all the hang-ups had vanished. There was no reception after the burial and when the group dispersed, Annett Voss, scarcely visible through her dense black veil, asked Steffen to drive her home so Lisa could get off to the airport.

The Vosses' flat in Leipzig was crammed with GDR keepsakes but, over coffee, Annett's mind was on the future not the past.

"Manfred owed you a lot and he knew it," she began, her lips waxy crimson against the creamy white of her face, "but he also bore you an immense grudge."

Steffen guessed what was coming but he let her say it anyway.

"Ulrich, our country's destroyed and our people have been left to rot. Manfred said you had a plan to put things right but you haven't done anything with it. Is that true?"

He shifted uneasily.

"I have to say it is. I wish I didn't."

Her hands grasped her easy chair and her eyes bored into him like gimlets.

"When Manfred had to act, he did, and he stood up for what he'd done like the fighting man he was. Where's your pride, Colonel Steffen? Aren't you ashamed you haven't done the same?"

Steffen didn't answer straight away but this crumbling widow, hanging on to life by willpower and medication, had fingered a wound so sensitive he didn't want to feel it any longer.

"Can I use your phone?" he asked after a pause.

She waved her hand towards her aging two-piece.

Steffen didn't like phones, not for Chameleon jobs anyway. He believed they told more tales than fingerprints but even so, he thought he could risk a call on Annett's. He picked up the receiver and poked in a Berlin number. He didn't have to wait long.

"Daski," came down the line.

Steffen pressed the receiver hard against his ear. Years of shooting practice had dulled his hearing.

"Hullo, Werner, Steffen here. I want to reread one of your files, the one on Lesley Carey. Is tomorrow all right? It's urgent."

"Then tomorrow it is. The usual drill, Ulrich. Be at the shop at half past four and I'll drive you over. And be on your own."

He rang off. Steffen replaced the receiver and looked across at Annett, who was breaking a multi-coloured capsule out of a blister pack.

"Manfred killed one person and that was enough," he said. "But a lot more need to be killed nowadays to make any kind of impression."

She swallowed the capsule with the last of her coffee.

"Can you really kill a lot more though?" she queried. "You personally, I mean. Or are you still all talk?"

"I'm beyond that now, Annett. That phone call was the first step."

"Manfred would be pleased. Can I help in any way?"

"Forget the English name you just heard. It's someone I used to know in London. Manfred never knew him at all."

"My memory's not what it was, that's why I take these pills. The name's gone already."

Steffen was in no hurry to leave, there were the old days to talk about and by the time he walked to his car the light was fading fast. What courage Annett had, he thought to himself, she hadn't shed a single tear all day! He drew strength from that. Strength and a cast iron inner resolve.

2

Daski, Carey and Cormorant

When Steffen arrived in Berlin the next day he checked into the same hotel he always did. It was left-over East Berlin and the nostalgia never failed. The weather was muggy but it didn't look like rain so he opted to walk to Daski's shop. A second-hand clothes shop marked his final turn-off, then came a run-down pharmacy, a travel agent's with faded posters, a launderette and, at exactly 4.30, Daski's Security and Surveillance. The bulletproof window was heavily barred and a cracked plastic sign in the fortified door read "Open weekdays 10.00 – 16.30. Closed weekends". Neon tubing spelled out the shop's name in old-fashioned looping pink. Before Steffen could ring, the door swung open. When it closed behind him he heard bolts slide home.

"I saw you coming," Daski said. "I also saw no one was tailing you. Where did you park, by the way?"

"I didn't. I walked."

"I've told you before, that's a dangerous thing to do. When the Wall came down all the baddies moved east. I should know, they keep me in business. Now, come and stand in front of this camera."

Daski was hunched behind the counter next to a bank of screens, his skin loose and wrinkly from years of sitting and snooping. He'd made his career in the Stasi but when the two Germanys came together he'd switched to the West without breaking stride. In line with his change of life he was wearing a Las Vegas t-shirt, a designer leather waistcoat and stone-washed jeans but on the wall behind him was a framed photo of a much younger Werner Daski. His Stasi uniform was immaculate and, smiling at the camera, he was sitting behind a reel-to-reel with headphones over his ears. He'd kept the photo hidden when he'd first opened the shop but once he was sure no one was after him he'd hung it where everyone could see it and trade had jumped twelve percent.

There was no flash to the camera, just a red LED that came on briefly.

"All done," Daski said. "It's my new toy, it's called a Presence Reader. Your data are now in my security system at home. That means I can open my archive with you in the room. If anyone broke in or ambushed me on the way home I couldn't open it because their picture wouldn't be in the system. Pretty good, eh?"

Steffen nodded compliantly and Daski got to his feet.

"OK, let's go then."

They left by the rear of the shop, leaving it fully armoured and alarmed. Daski's glistening Jeep was parked on a barricaded patch that had once been the back yard. Its windows were tinted black.

"Still driving your Lexus?" he needled as they motored west towards Grunewald, a suburb a lot more Berliners wanted to live in than could afford to. "Not very workers-and-peasants, is it?"

"No, but my customers like it."

Steffen owned a bakery and did his own travelling.

"Typical Daski," he thought. "Always trying to catch people out."

He wasn't afraid of Daski, he had too much on him for that, but he couldn't read his loyalties and that made him wary. He'd been a good Stasi man but he'd changed sides just like that so maybe he'd only ever been loyal to himself. Then there was his shop. It looked as if it ought to fold any day but against that there was the Jeep and the big house in Grunewald. So where was the money coming from? His files?

Daski owned four lorry-loads of them. When the GDR was dying the Stasi tried to destroy all its files but the shredders couldn't take it so documents and tapes were trucked to coal-fired power stations and anywhere else that could disappear them in bulk. Daski saw his chance when a four lorry convoy told him it was ready to leave. His uniform gave him all the clout he needed. He climbed into the lead driver's cab and directed the convoy to a friend's empty warehouse on the Warsaw road. When they got there he shot the padlock off the door, told the drivers to dump their loads inside and sent them back to Stasi Headquarters with a warning not to say anything. They didn't. Fear of the Stasi was in their DNA. As soon as they'd gone he put a padlock from one of the lorry's toolboxes on the door, called his friend from a nearby phone box and told him if he tried to get into the warehouse without asking first, he was a walking corpse. His friend was a sensible man so he lived a long life and died in his bed. Daski had seen the files were as good as gold bars. A lot of people in them would pay top dollar for his silence and better yet, they wouldn't stop paying. First, though, he had to sort out who was who amongst the initials and code names and for that he needed help.

He hadn't belonged to Chameleon when he stole the files but his ears were long so that same night he got in touch with Steffen and put a deal to him. If Steffen would let him join he could have unlimited access to everything in the warehouse. It worked. Daski got protection from Chameleon and Steffen, tapping his contacts for information, made sense of the files and tapes. That was how Steffen learned there was a file on Carey in amongst the rest and Carey's file leaped out at him because he knew Carey from the days when he – Steffen - had been the Military Attaché at the GDR's London embassy. He'd read and reread the file during the sort out he'd done for Daski but he hadn't gone back to it since. Now he needed to.

Daski's house, like the other big houses in the quiet leafy street, was fronted by a high wall and a gate that was more for keeping people out than letting them in. As Daski slowed down, he opened the gate by remote control and did the same for the garage door at the head of the gravel drive.

"I'll drop the blinds in the annex from here," he said as he closed the gate and the garage door from inside the garage. "That way not even Mrs Daski will know who's arrived."

That was why Daski had his "usual drill". It let him control who could and who couldn't be seen when they came to his house. His Presence Reader made things even more secure. It didn't seem to worry him it could cost him his life if someone got frustrated.

He led the way through an underpass and they came up in the purpose-built annex Daski kept his files in. The floor was covered with squares of woven rushes. When wear patterns started to say too much new ones were slotted in. The furniture was solidly middle class and a tapestry showing Frederick the Great in battle covered an entire wall. On a table by one of the blanked-out windows were an electric kettle, a coffee percolator, two cheeseboards under plastic covers and some crockery on a tray. Daski waved Steffen towards an easy chair and kept talking while he made the coffee.

"You've heard it before but I'll say it again. If you operate any covert device in here I'll know about it but if I record what you say, you won't. So you'll have to take my word I'm not doing it."

"Understood."

Steffen knew he had no choice.

Once the percolator was glugging nicely, Daski said, "I'll get the file you want."

He unlocked a drawer, pressed his hand onto a palm reader and the tapestry concertinaed upwards to disclose a stainless steel door. As it opened inwards, lights came on and Daski disappeared inside to re-emerge with a scuffed buff folder bulging with typescripts. It had "Top Secret" stamped on it in fading red caps and the typed initials on the circulation list were counter-initialled in aging fountain pen ink. The code name "Benedict" was top right in uneven purplish print. It had been put together using a stamp that was only four letters wide. The letters were on individual rubber bands that could be rotated.

"Here it is," Daski said, holding it out. "Lesley Edwin Carey, British tunnel engineer, code name Benedict. The reporting agents are Cormorant and Bluebird and their base is the GDR embassy in Belgrave Square, London. You can be making a start while I lock up."

Steffen didn't take it.

"Tell me what's in it first," he said. "Then I'll read it."

"Why that?"

"I prefer to listen. I get the patterns better."

"As you wish. You're the one in charge."

Daski had the file dew-fresh in his mind. He'd gone through it that morning trying to figure out why Steffen should want to reread it after all this time.

"How many people have read it since you've had it?" Steffen asked as Daski shut the door and lowered the tapestry.

"Two. You and me. I log the use of every file and they're only read when I'm around. The people on the circulation list were all senior ranks. If they're not dead by now they're close to it."

"And it's incomplete, isn't it? That's how I remember it."

"It's edited, that's why. Meetings with Benedict were spaced out for security reasons but a lot still got said. If it'd all been transcribed it'd have filled a barn so everything was taped but only the intelligence yield got typed up. That's what's in the file, plus some photos."

"Were you ever in on the editing?"

"Not a chance. I was inland and this was abroad so the first I knew about the file was when you showed it to me. Normally I'd have tried to find out more but you warned me off so I let it go."

"You've got the tapes as well?"

"I have. They're slowest speed so they hiss like snakes but you can still hear what's being said. The photos are good as well. I have to say, Cormorant was good at her job. She could have fooled anyone."

"Do you know who she was?"

"She was embassy staff and Stasi as well so I've got a fair idea. You know for sure, though, because she was there when you were."

"Benedict was talking to Cormorant before I turned up but as Military Attaché I had my own interest in Britain's tunnels. Once I'd eased my way in I got permission to talk to Benedict and Cormorant did the rest. Benedict trusted her and when she said I was all right he trusted me as well."

Daski let "trusted" hang in the air, then he launched into the file.

"As it says, Benedict was a British tunnel engineer. He was unmarried at the time we're talking about and he lived in a place called Rochester in the county of Kent. That's the bit of England that pokes out towards France."

"Thank you, Werner. I was in England long enough to know that."

"Of course. Anyway, when Benedict first qualified he rented a flat in London. He wanted to be near the big contracts and he was soon on the up because he was good. After a while he branched into tunnel security and he was good at that, too – good enough to afford his dream house in Rochester. Unfortunately, all men have their weaknesses and Benedict's was money – however much he earned he had to have more. The Stasi found that out, reported it and, in due course, Cormorant was ordered to make contact with him."

"What put the Stasi onto him?"

"The file's preamble says tunnels have strategic importance so the Stasi routinely tapped British tunnellers. Benedict was one of them, he rang false and the upshot was, he sold information till 1989, when the GDR was collapsing. That makes some fourteen years of well-paid treason. The file identifies Benedict as Lesley Edwin Carey and it gives chapter and verse for all the Cormorant and Bluebird payments."

"How was he paid?"

"In cash. It was his choice, apparently. He claimed it'd be hard to trace and it seems he was right. He must have kept it at home in a strongbox or something and when he bought anything I suppose he'd mix our money with some of his own. No one suspected him, not even the tax office."

"Cash payments were normal in those days," Steffen remarked, "even for big-ticket items. They didn't stand out like nowadays."

"You know that better than I do. You were living over there."

"What about after 1989? Did he sell himself on?"

"Not that I'm aware of."

"Not to the Russians? They'd have loved him. They needed all the help they could get."

"True, but there's nothing to say he'd have loved them back. We were fine, we were like next door neighbours. But our Russian comrades, well, they had an aura and it wasn't entirely a nice one."

"So after 1989 Benedict became a dead letter."

"That's what it looks like."

Steffen took a moment to think things through, then,

"I want you to set up a full surveillance on Carey, as we'll call him now. I want a continuous data flow and I want it to cover everything. As of now. Can you do it?"

"What else am I good at? Can you give me any starters?"

"He's still in the same house in Rochester, he's still unmarried and he's closing in on retirement. We've not completely lost touch, you see – I've seen to that."

"Anything else?"

"He's stayed in tunnel security and he's worked on some big jobs, including the Channel Tunnel. But his biggest job is the one he's got right now."

"Go on."

"Since you know so much about England you'll know there's a tunnel under the Thames east of London."

"The Dartford Tunnel. I might even have been through it."

"Then you'll also know it's too small and the relief bridge next to it isn't much help. So now there's a completely new tunnel further downstream. It's called the North Sea Tunnel and it's immense. It's a whole lot longer because it's under the estuary and it's got better lanes as well. Carey got the top security job when it was in planning and he's still got it. His title is Senior Security Officer and he loves it, especially the Senior bit."

"Is he still greedy?"

"I don't know."

"He's still in the same house, you say. Does that signify?"

"I don't think so. According to him, he's simply stayed put over the years. The North Sea Tunnel was a stroke of luck. Its southern end was always going to be near Rochester."

It was time to reread the file. Daski put the cheeseboards on a card table, poured more coffee and ate in silence while Steffen tracked his way through year after year of well paid betrayal. Then came the photos and, finally, he picked out some excerpts from the tapes and Daski played them for him. When he was finished he asked Daski to copy some of the typescripts, photos and tape excerpts onto a CD-ROM. Daski didn't want to but saying no could be dangerous so he gathered everything up, disappeared into his archive and came back with the disk Steffen wanted.

"You haven't said much about Bluebird," he said, fishing as always.

"He's dead, Werner, dead and gone. A hotel fire in Crete got him. He was burned to a cinder."

It was late evening when Daski dropped Steffen off at his hotel. Thanks to the file Steffen could bust Carey any time but he didn't want to do that, he wanted Carey to co-operate with him and the file alone might not be enough for that. He decided he'd let Daski get his surveillance up and running, then he'd have a word with Cormorant. She'd been clever for the Stasi. Now she could be clever for him.

3

Steffen's secret weapon

Daski knew he wouldn't find out everything, not at that short notice, but he soon built up a picture of an ageing bachelor who was set in his ways and lived for his work. If there was any bent money around it didn't show.

"No offshore bank accounts, no winnings at the races and no van Goghs for Christmas," he reported. "I know he's clever but he looks clean to me."

Whenever Daski contacted Steffen he had to use a primitive code that transposed letters according to the date. He hated it like the plague but Steffen refused to replace it. It linked him to the past, he'd say, and no one'd cracked it yet.

One new thing Daski discovered was that Carey used the Anne of Cleves Healthcare Centre in Rochester when he needed to see a doctor and he didn't seem to use anywhere else. He also discovered the Anne of Cleves outsourced its analyses to Miriam Sobart Laboratories, also in Rochester. "Exclusively" it said in the Anne of Cleves literature and he didn't think they were lying: they'd get found out too easily.

"Carey's had quite a few analyses done," Daski added. "He's fussy about his health."

Given Carey's involvement with Sobart, Daski decided he wanted to know more about her so during a face-to-face with Steffen in Berlin he asked Steffen if he had any information. It turned out he did.

"The Stasi recruited Sobart when she was a trainee medical analyst in the British Royal Air Force," he said, "and thereafter everything she saw, heard or overheard came straight to the GDR. She never took any money, she was an idealist. I didn't hear about her till late but when I did, I recruited her for Chameleon and she's still with us."

"What about these labs of hers?"

"When the Cold War ended she left the RAF and Chameleon helped her make a new start. We needed lab work done from time to time and it seemed safer to have it done abroad. In fact she's only got one lab but 'Laboratories' sounds better so that's what it's called."

"And you don't see her as a problem?"

"Why should I? The Stasi ran her, then I took her on. If she'd been shaky one of us would have found out soon enough."

"Maybe, but Carey has lived in Rochester for years, so has she, and Carey checks his test results with her personally. So, Carey and Sobart are close and my suspicious mind asks, do they know *about* each other? That they both worked for the GDR, I mean. They could, couldn't they? Or Carey might know Sobart's working for you."

A thought suddenly struck him.

"Carey's not in Chameleon, is he?"

"No, he's a consumable, that's all. It's what he's always been."

"So he might pressure Sobart in ways you might not like if he had to."

"Why should he want to do that?"

"To protect himself from you."

Daski gave him time but Steffen didn't respond.

"On the other hand," Daski resumed, "Sobart might try blackmailing him behind your back. She must know he's got plenty in the bank."

"Their careers never touched, everything about them was separate. She wouldn't do it anyway, she's as straight as a die. And if Carey tried anything, she'd tell me straight away."

"She sited her lab in Rochester, though. Where Carey was already living. You think that's coincidence, do you?"

"Absolutely. She was born in Rochester, she grew up there, her parents lived and died there and it's a good place for her line of work. You're imagining things, Werner. It's a bad habit."

"So is relying on trust."

"I agree. So if I have to manage them it won't be trust I'll use. You can be sure of that."

Daski let it go. If there was a problem it was Steffen's, not his. But he always liked to find out more so as Steffen was getting ready to leave, he said,

"Carey's computer systems for his tunnel, they're world class. I couldn't get into them and I don't think many people could. But his personal set-up's a joke. A child could hack into it in minutes. How do you explain that?"

"Vanity. He likes applause and the tunnel's where he gets it. He also thinks he can't be harmed and so far he's been right."

Steffen left Berlin with mixed feelings. He believed he could manage anything if he had to but he wasn't happy that the end of June was in sight and he still hadn't contacted Cormorant. When he got home, his wife was asleep in her room so he shut himself in his study to think things through. When the phone rang it made him start. It was Lisa Birdsall.

"I'm back in Germany," she said. "I tried to get you earlier but all I got was a tape. Listen, Mum was taken into hospital two days ago and she passed away this morning. I was with her when she went. She asked me to say to you, 'Don't let Manfred down', which I'm now doing because I feel I owe it to her. I got your home number from Mum's notebook. She had to write everything down, even things she knew by heart."

She broke off, then began again. She spoke quickly and her voice sounded strained.

"I don't know how to put this but I don't want you to come to the funeral. I could see why you were at Dad's, you and he were linked in some way I was never allowed to ask about. But I want Mum's funeral to draw a line. My family will be there, they're American, not German, and they think the GDR's just one more horror story the Europeans are good at. From now on I want to think like that, but if you're there you'll drag me back. So I'm sorry but I have to ask you not to be there."

It grieved Steffen deeply that Annett was dead and he said so. He also said he understood what Lisa was saying and, yes, of course he'd stay away if that was what she wanted. But inside he was white hot. The GDR was his life and if he couldn't bring it back he could at least lift the old East Germany out of the mess it'd been left in. As soon as Birdsall rang off he took his code book out and, resting a single sheet of paper on a metal tray, he began a message to Cormorant. He'd encoded less than a line when he broke off. Cormorant lived mostly in London so the message would take time to reach her even if she was at home, which he couldn't count on. So, stifling his qualms, he picked up the phone and poked Cormorant's number in with his index finger. He heard a few buzzes then,

"It's Ulrich, isn't it? Your number's on my display."

He turned the volume up to hear her better.

"You're right, Heidi, it's me," he said. "Listen, if I drive to Frankfurt tomorrow can you meet me there? I have to talk to you."

"Frankfurt's a big place. Tell me when and where."

"15.00 hours German time. There's a riverside café called The Chalet, your taxi-driver will know it. If the weather turns I'll be inside, otherwise I'll be on the terrace. You can book an evening flight back. I won't keep you long."

"Any problems and I'll give you a call. Otherwise I'll be there."

The next day was bright and sunny and at two minutes to three Steffen sat down at a table for two looking directly onto the River Main. As he'd hoped, the terrace was full and he was just one more customer in the crowd. No call from London meant no problems and at three on the dot a black haired woman carrying a suede holdall made her way casually to his table. He stood up, they shook hands and when the waitress came over he ordered sand cake and coffee for both of them. Heidi Kapner, formerly Cormorant and now a freelance insurance broker, was medium height, slim and fitness-studio fit. Her face was barely lined and her eyes, black-framed by Rodenstock glasses, were like knapped flint. Her tailored two-piece, set off by a large brooch that looked like jade, was black as well. So were her shoes. She was dressed to mislead. Black sticks in the memory so anyone asked about who Steffen had been with would centre on black hair and clothes. But when Kapner left Steffen she'd slip into the ladies', take a powder blue shirt, summer-weight jeans and beige sandals from her holdall, put in the black wig, the plain-lensed glasses and the rest and re-emerge as if whoever the woman in black had been, it hadn't been her.

"What's on your mind?" she asked, pouring for both of them.

"The old country. How it's been treated."

"What again? You've been moaning about that for years. So have I for that matter."

There was talking and clinking all around. He was sure they wouldn't be overheard.

"True, but now I'm going to do something and that's why you're here. It involves someone you knew a long time ago. His name's Lesley Carey."

"Carey!" she flashed out. "I don't want anything to do with him. I'll despise him as long as he lives."

"That won't be for much longer. I'll kill him when I'm finished with him but I need his help first."

"What makes you think you'll get it?"

"I've used him before – we both have – so why not again?"

Kapner was softening up. If Carey was killed she'd dance on his grave.

"Money worked last time," she offered. "Money and sex."

"Money's out, I gather. As for sex, I simply don't know. Blackmail's crossed my mind. He's Mr Security at the North Sea Tunnel these days. I could threaten him with the get-togethers he had with us in London."

She looked at him sharply.

"You've got records of them?"

"There are two different sets and I own one of them. It's of me as Military Attaché talking to him."

"How on earth did you get it?"

"When the GDR collapsed the NPA had a panic clear-out just like the Stasi. Someone in Chameleon saw my file, kindly sent it to me and, equally kindly, made sure the Stasi's copy was destroyed. The other set concerns you directly. It's mostly Benedict and Cormorant, you see. It's locked away in Berlin but I can access it."

"But Ulrich, if any of that stuff came out it'd wreck your bakery and my insurance business overnight."

"I only said 'threaten', Heidi, and anyway, I need a carrot as well as a stick because I don't think fear is enough. Carey can be very obstinate when he feels like it."

She gave it some thought.

"You promise you'll kill him as soon as you've done with him?"

"Certainly. It has to be."

"And where's he living now?"

"In Rochester. He's never moved house. Why do you ask?"

"It wasn't just sex that kept him wanting to see me, he was head over heels in love with me. Look, I'm not magic, but as soon as I think of something you'll hear about it. Now, are you going to tell me about your grand plan or are you keeping it to yourself?"

He took a digital camera out of his jacket pocket, lit the display up and handed it to her.

"Look at these three photos. They come from mass circulation newspapers. I've got a lot more at home, I've been collecting them over the years. Keep the display under your hand, though. Pretend you're keeping the sun off."

The first one showed a boy's bike locked into a stand. It was the only one there and the caption read: "Timmi will never come back."

"The boy was killed in a coach crash," Steffen explained. "He was on a school trip. Everyone else survived."

The next one showed a woman's face in close-up. She was screaming with grief.

"She's just learned her husband's been killed in an air crash. She'd been waiting for him in Arrivals."

The third one showed a man sitting on some rubble with his face in his hands.

"He's lost his family in an earthquake. How do they strike you, Heidi?"

"They're terrible, Ulrich. I mean, I don't know these people but I can't help it. I feel very sorry for them."

"Which one hurts you most?"

"The one with the bike, I think. Yes, that one, definitely."

"A lot of people would say that. It's because a child's involved."

For a millisecond her eyes had moistened, now they were flint again. There were more useful things in life than sympathy. He took the camera back, switched it off and put it in his pocket.

"I call my plan my distress bomb," he explained matter-of-factly, "and my thinking is this. If I can create enough anguish in enough people I can pressure the government into giving our part of Germany its pride back. The key is to get a huge lot of people to suffer and I've worked out how to do that. You'll guess what's coming next, Heidi. I want more than good ideas from you, I want you fully involved. So I'll ask you now: are you with me on this?"

She didn't answer straight away, then she said,

"Of course. One hundred percent. Trust me and you'll see for yourself."

After they'd cleared their plates and drunk the coffee she stood up and headed for the ladies' while Steffen paid the bill. There was a payphone inside the restaurant with a change machine next to it. He'd seen it from where he was sitting. No one looked twice at him as he passed between the tables and when he had Daski on the line, he kept himself brief.

"I want the Carey surveillance called off right now," he said. "I also want a written report on everything you've found out so far. Encode it and get it to me by courier. If I find out you've kept a copy, I'll destroy you, so don't do it. As far as you're concerned, we've never talked about Carey or anyone connected with him."

He felt better after that. Daski had a fair idea who Cormorant was, he'd said so himself. Now she was activated he had to stop him taking that further.

4

Kapner spies on Carey

Steffen thought he'd made a convert when he left Frankfurt but for Kapner things weren't so straightforward. She'd gained an inside track on what Steffen was planning and that was a plus but she hadn't a clue how to put the bite on Carey again. She'd had to leave him at crash speed the first time round and that'd hurt him badly so simply turning up on his doorstep could easily blow up in her face. And they were both a lot older now: he might look at her, wonder what he'd seen in her and that'd be that. Time passed and she did her best but the ideas wouldn't come.

Then, during the first week of July she had to sign an agreement in Oxford and she opted to go there by train. On the station she bought a copy of *What's On* and she was idly skimming the pages when she saw Carey's name staring at her out of a boxed ad put in by the Royal and Imperial Institute of Tunnel Engineering. Beginning Monday August 17th he was giving a series of weekly lectures in London and they'd be open to the public. As soon as she was home again she sent Steffen a message: could she tap into this? He said she could and yes, she had a free hand how she did it.

The Institute, as tunnellers round the world fondly call it, was founded in 1375 by Edward III. It acquired its present-day name in 1851 when Queen Victoria confirmed its royal charter and opened new headquarters for it near the Houses of Parliament. To be elected a Fellow was the highest honour a British tunneller could hope for. Carey had been elected just a few days before Manfred Voss had died – a fact not picked up by Daski - and one of a freshman Fellow's duties was to give the year's public lectures on tunnelling. The lectures traditionally began in mid-August, they ran for six consecutive Mondays at five o'clock and they were always packed out.

So, well before starting time Kapner had selected a seat that was mostly behind a pillar and at five o'clock sharp, with a flare-up of virulent hatred, she watched Carey step onto the dais from a side door, lounge arrogantly against the portable lectern Isambard Kingdom Brunel had once graced and announce a Powerpoint journey through some of the world's greatest tunnels. It would include the Holland Tunnel between New York and New Jersey, the Channel Tunnel between England and France and, in the sixth and last lecture, the North Sea Tunnel under the Thames Estuary.

When the lecture was over Kapner waited outside to see where Carey went next. She hadn't wanted anything to remind him of her so she'd lightened her dove-grey hair and put on the mousiest clothes an Oxfam shop in Fulham had had on its racks. She had to kill an hour before he emerged through the ornate neo-Gothic entrance. On his own and with a briefcase in his hand he made his way to nearby St James's Park, where he sat lost in thought on a weather-stained wooden bench near the lake. Kapner couldn't believe it. That bench – it'd been new and clean back then – was where she'd first made contact with him. He'd known her as Sophie in those days, Sophie Osterloh, and he'd never learned it wasn't her real name.

After a while he looked at his watch, heaved himself to his feet and, with Kapner still distance-tailing him, set off for Charing Cross railway station, where he caught the stopping train that ran out of London south of the estuary. Kapner guessed he was going to his house in Rochester. She'd heard about it *ad nauseam* but she'd never seen it because they'd always used what he believed was her London flat, though it was really part of a Stasi safe house. From the concourse side of the ticket barrier she watched him get in and that made her decide to see his house for herself. She'd do it after the second lecture. It'd bring her closer to the man she wanted dead. When she got home she sent an update to Steffen. By return Steffen said a) she still had a free hand and b) he wanted her in Frankfurt at 15.00 hours on the Thursday after the second lecture. This time they'd meet in a crêperie called Alesssandro's. It was near the Deutsche Bank.

The way things were going Kapner was wanting to bring an old friend in to help her but before she could ask Steffen if that was on she needed to confirm that St James's Park meant as much to Carey as it seemed to. So the following Monday she trailed Carey again and saw him repeat everything she'd seen the week before, despite a drizzle that was threatening to turn into rain. She had a day return ticket to the end of the line in her purse so when he caught his train she was able to slip onto it as well. She picked a seat two carriages away and discreetly checked the platform each time the train stopped. When, as expected, he got out at Rochester he made things easy for her by leaving the station on foot. She did the same, using the drizzle and the approaching dark as cover.

He lived in a dimly-lit terrace of early Georgian houses called Beale's Row. Samuel Beale was a long-dead minor cannon and a plaque on the first house showed where he'd lived. All the houses in the terrace had slate roofs, large symmetrical windows and small front gardens with iron railings. Staying on the opposite side and keeping well back, Kapner watched Carey unlock his front door and let himself in. After he'd switched some lights on and drawn the downstairs curtains she moved up till she was level with the door he'd just passed through and stood staring at it till she felt she was part of his life again. Then, saturated with malice, she walked determinedly back to the station. Outwardly she hadn't done very much but inwardly she'd forged the link she needed. On the platform she checked the times of the London to Rochester trains, including the last one. It left Charing Cross at 00.12 seven nights a week.

It was late when she got back to London but she knew Steffen didn't sleep much so she phoned him straight away. She was convinced now, if money couldn't trap Carey, sex and passion still might and that had strengthened the idea she'd need some help. When Steffen answered she ran through what she'd done and added,

"I'm phoning because I want Klaus Guderius in on this. Can you ask him to our meeting this Thursday?"

Guderius was an old friend of Steffen as well as of Kapner. They'd both been in the NPA and when Steffen was getting Chameleon off the ground, Guderius had been his so-called Second Officer, which he still was. Guderius was a doctor and while Steffen was carving out a standard career as an officer, Guderius was learning all he could about infections and how to prevent them in places like barracks. He became so good at it, he was appointed Medical Officer to Karl Marx House, a rural retreat for the Party's top brass. When the GDR collapsed Guderius went to the Dominican Republic to make a new start there but when he came back after just three months Karl Marx House was still standing empty because no one wanted to invest in the old East Germany. So he banged in a business plan and took it off the state's hands at no cost to himself. He also got a starter grant on the understanding he'd pay it back when he was in profit. The outcome was the Guderius Residential Wellness Clinic and because the Germans like their wellness clinics it couldn't stop making money. He now had "Medical Director" on his door and the grant was a distant memory.

Steffen didn't agree to Kapner's request straight away. He could see Guderius could make a difference but he lived with the feeling there was something ominous between Kapner and Guderius and that made him hesitate. It might be just that they'd grown up in neighbouring villages but there seemed more to it than that: it was as if they shared a secret he didn't know about and wasn't meant to. If Kapner were more like Guderius he might not have felt that way but she wasn't. Guderius had been NPA and for Steffen that was good enough. But Kapner had been Stasi and there was no doubt about it, she had a shadow side. That didn't stop him keeping her in Chameleon and when his bakery business took him to London he was happy to call on her and sometimes even stay with her. But his sense of a shadow side never left him. He wondered what Kapner would do if he said no and decided he couldn't afford to find out. So he said he'd ring Guderius in the morning.

Guderius's clinic was situated to the north-east of Dresden in a tiny village called Bad Sollmer, which in turn was on the fringe of a national park called Saxon Switzerland. The park was a holidaymaker's paradise but when the haze from the pines made the air thicken it could seem brooding and menacing. When Steffen's call came through, Guderius was in the office of his founder manageress, Hanna Gannisch. They'd been going through the "New Arrivals" files but now it was time for a break. A waitress from Catering had just set out coffee in a flask, porcelain cups and cream in a matching jug. They were on a table near the window.

Guderius and Gannisch had spent most of their adult life together. When he'd arrived at Karl Marx House she was already the manageress. She'd only been in her twenties, it'd been a dream promotion and the room they were in now had been her office back then. When the Party top brass had been consigned to history she'd been asked to stay in the building to keep an eye on it which was why she'd been there when Guderius had gone to, and come back from, the Dominican Republic. If things had worked out differently she'd have joined him over there but they hadn't so they were together in Bad Sollmer instead. They'd never been in love but they'd grown close while he was the Medical Officer. It'd take a lot to separate them now.

When the phone buzzed Gannisch answered it. It didn't surprise her Steffen was on the other end. His bakery wasn't too far away and she, Guderius and the Steffens were all good friends.

"It's Ulrich," she said, holding up the phone. "I'll wait outside."

Gannisch had made it a way of life never to know more than was put right in front of her. It had kept her safe in the old days and it also kept her on the right side of Guderius. She knew he kept things from her – he'd never told her about Chameleon for a start – and that was exactly what she wanted.

When Steffen had finished Guderius called her back in.

"This coming Thursday," he said, "I need to be in Frankfurt by lunchtime. I've got an afternoon meeting. I'll come back the same evening."

"I'll book your flight and get an airport taxi for you. I'll get your absence covered as well."

That was Gannisch. She knew what to do and got on with it. It made for a happy life.

Alessandro's drew most of its customers from the Deutsche and other nearby banks so no one so much as looked at two men and a black-haired lady huddled round a table with papers in front of them. Plenty of other tables had people huddled round them, some with papers and some with laptops, and the waiters were trained to keep their distance. Steffen's papers were Daski's final report on Carey. Steffen had printed it up *en clair* and snipped Daski's name off with a pair of scissors. They all had crêpes in front of them but only Guderius was serious about eating. While he was ploughing through his crêpes Kapner read the report. It wasn't long and when she'd finished it she passed it to Guderius, who read it one-handed and gave it back to Steffen.

"So, Heidi, you're going to let Carey have another go, are you?" Guderius asked as he topped up his coffee.

"It worked before. He used to waggle his prick at me, shout, 'Here comes Father Christmas!' and bang in like a stallion. Afterwards, he'd talk his head off and then bang in again."

"That was then but times change and there's nothing in this report about any other women or, indeed, any interest in sex at all. Maybe the stallion's not feeling his oats any more."

"That's one reason you're sitting here now. Can you give me something to frisk him up if I have to?"

"I don't see why not, I do it all the while at the clinic. The wives speak to Hanna and I provide from stock. When do you want it by?"

"That depends on Ulrich. Do we have a timetable yet?" she asked him.

"Carey's lectures end September 21st and there's no guarantee he'll be in London after that. So, Klaus, get your drugs to Heidi before September 21st."

"Not a problem. One of my providers is in London."

He turned to Kapner.

"It's Hutchinson's of Harley Street. I'll have something sent round."

Kapner patted his hand by way of thanks.

"Your distress bomb as you call it, when is it due to go off?" she asked Steffen.

"When the dark evenings come. Monday October 26th is looking good at the moment. I'm calling an Operational Meeting for Thursday September 24th at my place. It'll be at 20.00 hours and I want you both there. If October 26th is still on I'll confirm it then."

Time was pressing. Steffen left first with Daski's report locked in his briefcase. He paid at the till and hurried out to find his car. He had a couple of bakery calls to make before he headed home. Kapner disappeared into the ladies' with her holdall. When she left Alessandro's her mind was on her flight back but then she saw Guderius's portly figure loitering some fifty yards away. He gave her a wave and she caught him up.

"We can share a taxi to the airport," he said. "I want to talk to you."

When the taxi dropped them off they found a seafood bar that was half empty and two high stools with no one near them. Guderius ordered a half bottle of white wine and a lobster salad; Kapner settled for a glass of grapefruit juice.

"I get the impression," Guderius said, squeezing out his lemon slices, "that you aren't too keen on relighting Carey's fire. Am I right?"

"Only partly, Klaus. Ulrich has said he'll kill him once he's finished with him. I'll enjoy that, it'll put a lot of things right. And we all have a commitment to the GDR. I'll ask you not to forget that."

"No chance of that but anyway, I've been reflecting on our tunnelling friend and I think I can add to your options."

"You're an ogre, Klaus, you always were. What have you got in mind?"

He pulled out his diary from an inside pocket.

"Your make-or-break day is 21st September," he said, rubbing his pudgy hand over his chin, "and it so happens I've got to be in London just before then. So why don't I come to your place and bring some home-made goodies with me? I can bring Hutchinson's stuff while I'm at it so forget about the delivery. Ten o'clock on Thursday 17th is OK for me and I'll ask you to keep the rest of the morning free. I'll need to explain what I'm bringing you."

She kissed the tips of her fingers and touched his cheek.

"You're booked in," she said, making a note in her own diary. "Can you tell me any more right now?"

"The bad news is, if you accept my goodies you'll need to have two goes at Carey, one on 21st September and one a week later. The good news is, after the second go we'll have him entirely where we want him. I'll tell Ulrich what I'm going to do and I don't think he'll argue. When I speak, he listens."

"Of course," she smiled and let him finish his wine. Then they said their goodbyes and went to their separate check-ins.

5

Guderius's basement secret

The morning of Sunday September 13th found Guderius at the desk in Gannisch's office once more. His doctor's bag was by his chair. He'd be using it shortly.

Gannisch opened her desk diary and pressed it flat.

"Sedley Franks Medical Supplies faxed you yesterday while you were off site," she said. "10.15 next Friday is when they've put you down for. London time, that is. I've faxed back to say you'll be there. I've also checked your passport and car insurance, bought your sterling and reserved your hotel rooms. You'll be in Hannover tomorrow night, Brussells Tuesday and London Wednesday, Thursday and Friday. You said you'd book your return yourself."

"So I shall. Where am I crossing the Channel?"

"Calais-Dover. I still don't see why you're going by car," she added as she ticked off what she'd just read out. "Why aren't you flying? It's what you normally do."

"The car's brand new, that's why. A long run will do it good."

He'd taken delivery of a Mercedes E-class the previous Thursday. Gannisch didn't show whether she believed him or not as she slid a document case over to him.

"Everything's in here," she said. "You're really going to lease a body-scanner, are you?"

"Could be more than one, the market's expanding fast. There are different types as well."

Gannisch didn't argue. It was the sort of call he was good at.

They talked shop a bit more and then he said he ought to start packing. He was tied up all afternoon and after dinner he wanted to make sure the place was right before he left. He fixed a time for lunch, pulled his jacket on and, with the document case in one hand and his doctor's bag in the other, he stepped out of Gannisch's office into the clinic's pseudo-Greek vestibule, his spray-on smile already from ear to ear. As always, there were new guests to greet, departing ones to wish a safe journey, hands to shake and suitcases to step round. Taking his time, he manoeuvred his way affably towards the front entrance.

The building that was now the Guderius Residential Wellness Clinic had started life as the eighteenth century palace of a minor German duke. It consisted of a central block three storeys high with an entrance in the middle and forward-reaching wings at either end. Largely by luck it had survived fire, bankruptcy, the Second World War and the GDR more or less unscathed.

As manageress when it was Karl Marx House Gannisch had had her own apartment and she'd kept it ever since. Medical Officer Guderius had had one as well and when he'd come back from the Dominican Republic he'd moved into it again since he hadn't had anywhere else to go. It was really just a cramped bedsit with a cooking area and an undersize bath tub but he hadn't minded because he knew where he'd be living once his clinic was up and running. Separate from the main building was a smaller edifice that was also three storeys high. The minor duke had kept his horses and his servants in it, in that order of importance, but since that time it had been allowed to fall apart inside. Nevertheless, the shell had stayed strong and Guderius had converted it into his private villa with a massive double front door, an entrance hall with a black-and-white chequered marble floor and a grandiose carved oak staircase. His brand new Mercedes was locked away in the double garage he'd had built onto the side nearest the clinic. It didn't need running in and the thought of a return drive to England gave him nightmares but he was one hundred percent convinced security on ferry ports was less tight than security on airports so the car it had to be.

The entrance hall was strikingly cool after the September sunshine outside. As always when he was on his own he stole in silently and once he'd relocked the front door he stood his bag down and soft-soled his way towards a steel door to his right. A metal sign on it read "Lift: Authorised Personnel Only" and at eye level in the wall to its left was a lockable steel flap some eighteen inches above a push button. Only Guderius had a key to the flap and he stealthily opened it now to expose a red warning light. As he'd expected, it was out. Satisfied, he relocked the flap, fetched his bag, put his thumb on the button to open the lift and got in. Facing him was another door. It was the one he'd exit through.

Like most German dwellings the villa had a basement and the lift took him down to it. Its barred windows were frosted so when he stepped out he switched on the lights. He also switched on the temperature control and the ventilation. Both of these had been made to run soundlessly and the ventilation was unusual. He'd designed it himself and had it installed by technicians he'd worked with when he'd been a bugs specialist.

The basement took in about half the villa's floorspace and because Guderius's hobby was restoring antique furniture he had a fully equipped workshop down there. Chairs, tables and stools from the past lay about in various states of repair and a buff workcoat dangled above a piano dolly he used for heavy items. Because the ventilation had only just come on the air still smelled woody but it'd soon clear. He laid his document case on a high stool but he kept his bag in his hand. Then he turned round as if he was going back into the lift. Except he didn't.

The space between the lift and the basement's outer wall was taken up by two wide built-in cupboards that reached from floor to ceiling. They had locked sliding doors and they looked as if they might contain timber. However, when Guderius unlocked the one nearer the lift and slid it open it was empty. Instead, in the wall in front of him was a broad steel door painted grey. Stepping into the cupboard, he unlocked this door and pushed it open. It made no sound on its well oiled hinges and in the darkness beyond was a second room. Pilot lights and illuminated dials glowed inside it and although it took up the rest of the space under the villa, it had no windows to say it was there. Guderius locked the cupboard door behind him, stepped into the darkness and switched the lights on by feel. The temperature control and the ventilation were already on since they were coupled to the ones in the workshop. If he chose to, however, he could operate them separately.

This second room was a fully fitted laboratory. The single clue it was there was the lift, which was oversize and which only ran between the ground floor and the basement. Whenever he showed guests round his villa – which he was always keen to do – he'd take them down to his workshop in the lift and say it was for moving furniture, that was why it was so big. That stopped them wondering what else it might be for – like moving lab equipment. He could've had the lift open directly into the lab but that would've been too risky. As a result, anything bulky had to be trolleyed or carried from the lift into the workshop and then through the broad steel door. When that happened he only used ex-GDR people and he watched them like a hawk. Over the years Gannisch had noticed delivery vehicles either bringing or removing large items that were carefully covered with wraps. But she hadn't been allowed in while the villa was being renovated, Guderius never said anything about the deliveries and so what she knew was zero.

If Guderius had opened the second of the floor-to-ceiling cupboards and passed through the door *it* concealed he'd have found himself in a kind of booth that looked into the laboratory through one-way glass. It was part of his defence against intruders. So was the warning light upstairs, which was connected to a movement sensor in the lab. If it'd been on when he'd checked it he'd have crept down the emergency staircase next to the lift shaft, let himself into the booth and neutralised whoever was on the other side of the glass from a purpose-built console.

This time, however, there were no unwanted visitors so he replaced his jacket with a white lab coat and peeled on a pair of rubber gloves. A digital clock directly above an incubator told him time was on his side. Lunch was still some way off and he'd done his packing already. It was all in the boot of his car.

Once his hands were protected he put his bag on a work surface and snapped it open. His old-fashioned stethoscope came out first. It was followed by the equally old-fashioned sphygmomanometer he used for taking people's blood pressure. It had no electrics, just a wrap-round cuff and a rubber ball. He knew non-medical people were impressed by such things. When he repacked his bag, they'd go on top and if it was searched they'd be seen first.

Next he took out some ampoules of adrenaline, some disposable syringes and some blister packed screw on needles. He laid them out and counted them: there were six of each. He didn't need the adrenaline for London and he only needed three syringes plus needles but he was certain that when he got to Calais, he'd need a fireproof reason for having syringes in his case because saying he was a doctor wouldn't be enough. Well, he had one. He'd say all doctors carried adrenaline, it was standard for allergy emergencies and he needed the syringes to inject it with. If anyone cared to verify that, they could.

Bayer aspirins in a plastic pot came out next. He stood them in front of the syringes and reached down a bottle of isopropyl alcohol from an open shelf. Then he bent down to a heavily-armoured safe near his feet and undid the combination lock. The interior lit up as he swung the door open and fetched out a small glass bottle of tablets labelled "Ophrene/Ten" in black felt-tip. It went next to the aspirins. The Ophrene was followed by a bottle of colourless fluid labelled "Cytofane – Highly Toxic". That was all he needed from the safe so he swung the door to. Finally he opened a storage cupboard and took out two seal wrapped pipettes plus an empty clear glass bottle. It had a leakproof cap and millilitres marked up the side. One pipette went straight into his bag; he was sure no one would ask about it. He unwrapped the other one and removed the glass bottle's cap. He was ready to go.

Using a pair of tweezers he took three Ophrene tablets from their bottle, put them in with the aspirins and turned the pot over a few times to mix things up. The Ophrene tablets looked exactly like the Bayer ones right down to the Bayer cross. They weighed the same as well. The pot and its mix of tablets went into his bag. Then he gingerly unscrewed the bottle of Cytofane, drew off 200 millilitres with the pipette and poured them into the glass bottle, checking carefully that the fluid reached 200 millilitres precisely on the bottle's scale. The used pipette went into a papier mâché tray. With the remaining Cytofane re-capped and put where he couldn't knock it over he took a funnel and poured 100 millilitres of isopropyl alcohol into the plastic bottle to top it up. Then he re-capped it as well, labelled it "Isopropyl Alcohol", put it into his bag and secured it with an elasticated strap to keep it upright. That was it. The stethoscope and the sphygmomanometer went on top of everything else, the remaining Ophrene, Cytofane and isopropyl alcohol went back where they came from, the safe was locked and the used pipette, the funnel, the rubber gloves and the papier mâché tray disappeared into a bright yellow sealable bag. At some point during his after-dinner check he'd slip it into a clinical waste bin and from there it'd be taken, unopened, to the clinic's on-site incinerator.

6

Guderius explains his drugs

Guderius had overestimated his guile and underestimated Calais security. He was interrogated about everything in his bag and then his car was gone through inch by inch. The trouble was, the Mercedes was so new it might've been bought - or stolen - just to service a crime and the stethoscope and sphygmomanometer were so old they could easily be just window dressing. He was terrified the aspirins or the alcohol might be taken away for analysis and when, with seconds to spare, he boarded his ferry his mouth was bone dry and his bladder was full to bursting. His nerves didn't settle till he reached mid-Channel and even then his fingers shook as he put his watch back an hour. As Dover's white cliffs came closer, terror swept through him again but the British were targeting lorries, not cars, and he was waved straight through. Then he was off down the M2/A2 – the Dover to London motorway – taking care to keep to the left and comply with all speed limits.

After two hours or so he was grinding through London's traffic towards Park Lane and the Dorchester Hotel. After he'd unpacked he phoned Hutchinson's, placed his order, idled about till it came and idled about some more till dinner time. He opted to eat in his room and while he ate, he forced his mind back to his terror attacks because terror was a weakness he never knew he had. Did he have any others, he brooded, and he had to admit he didn't know. Gradually, however, the food and the wine cheered him up again.

"The real point is," he concluded, "I didn't collapse. Ulrich should be glad I'm his Second Officer. I might bend but I don't break."

It was a conclusion he liked, it restored his self-respect and if he had any other weaknesses – which he very much doubted – he was certain he'd master them too. He'd have called

Gannisch to let her admire him if it hadn't meant telling her too much but he had to do something so he had two bottles of Laurent-Perrier Cuvée Grand Siècle sent up and worked his way through them. Towards the end of the second one, the day caught up with him and he started to fall asleep. More unconscious than conscious he fumbled his pyjamas on, heaved himself into bed and passed out.

Because he forgot to draw the curtains he woke up with the sun the next morning and it took a river of coffee with his multi-course breakfast to get him more or less functional. While he was eating he decided to go home via Brussels and Frankfurt. Brussels he could do without but he was planning a second wellness clinic near Weimar and in Frankfurt, Germany's financial capital, money opened doors all day and every day. So he'd phone to say he'd be arriving Sunday. He could book his ferry and hotels at the same time. But he'd let the doorman get him a taxi when he was ready to see Kapner. He liked the rituals of five-star hotels, especially the taxi one.

Kapner's flat was in Orange Street, between the National Gallery and Leicester Square. It occupied the ground floor of a late 1940s duplex and it was completely self-contained. When Guderius arrived she sent him into the living room while she made some tea. When she brought the tray in he'd settled down in the largest chair in the room, a russet easy chair with a matching antimacassar. She set the tray down on a Scandinavian coffee table and brought a pouffe across to sit on. All the window gauzes were closed - they always were - the venetian blinds were down and although it was ten o'clock in the morning virtually all the light was artificial. As soon as he'd downed his first cup Guderius opened his bag and, using the rest of the coffee table, lined up the Bayer pot, the bottle labelled "Isopropyl Alcohol", three disposable syringes with their needles and the still-sealed pipette. To these he added a ribbed hexagonal bottle with a drops dispenser moulded into the cap. It was labelled "Hutchinson's Elevator Plus". It was what he'd ordered from Harley Street but he didn't want her to use it now. Things had moved on.

"You'll need to take notes," he said. "Destroy them once you've memorised them."

She slipped out and came back with a notepad and biro. As soon as she was ready he tapped the hexagonal bottle with his finger. As the glass caught the light its pinkish tinge came out.

"This," he said, "is an aphrodisiac for men. Two drops start a golden glow, four drops are action stations and six drops are all guns blazing. It tastes vaguely fishy so I always say, put the drops on an oyster then no one will know. It's reliable but it affects some men faster than others, so be warned."

"What's in here," he went on, pointing to the Bayer pot, "is much more precise. Most of the tablets are genuine but three aren't. Those three contain a substance called Ophrene and its category is Ten."

He wrote Ophrene on her pad and added a ten in numerals.

"You might not have heard of Ophrene," he said. "The Stasi used it but it was on restricted issue."

Kapner shook her head. It was news to her.

"Well, it's a knock-out drug and a good one. You dissolve one tablet in whatever your target is drinking and after two minutes that person loses consciousness for ten. That's what the ten means and it's exact. It doesn't matter whether your target is fat or thin, male or female, the stuff hits their brains and out they go. It's tasteless, it doesn't fizz and when they come round, there's just one after-effect which you may well like."

"What is it?"

"No libido. It's killed stone dead and it stays that way for about two hours, male and female alike."

"If it works."

"It will."

"Does it mix with alcohol?"

"It mixes with anything. There's no chemical change, it just blends in."

"And you can't see it's there?"

"No, but you must get your target to swallow all of it so you're best off dissolving it in a small cup of coffee or half a glass of wine. Something like that. Then you can be sure the whole lot gets drunk. I've given you three tablets. Two are for use and one's spare."

Kapner glanced through her notes. Then,

"How do I tell the Ophrene from the real aspirins?"

"No problem. All the tablets have a smooth finish and real aspirins reflect red light. But the finish on the Ophrene ones absorbs red light instead. So, all you do is find a dark place, shine a red light on the tablets and pick out the three dull ones. That's it."

"That's clever. Who thought it up?"

"The Academy of Sciences in Berlin. Our Academy, I should say, and our Berlin as well. The Stasi wanted an accurate anti-personnel drug and the result was Ophrene, graded into five, ten, fifteen and twenty minutes."

Guderius poured himself more tea. His mouth wouldn't moisten up and talking wasn't helping. Then he moved on to the bottle labelled "Isopropyl Alcohol".

"Inside here are 200 millilitres of a chemical called Cytofane and you'll notice the bottle is made of glass."

He wrote "Cytofane" on her pad and added "Danger of Death" with three exclamation marks.

"The rest is 100 millilitres of what's on the label and you'll know its smell when you open the bottle because its other name is rubbing alcohol. The powers that be were supposed to think that was all there was in there which, of course, they did so I breezed through Calais and Dover as well. Now, Cytofane never got past the lab stage so you'll definitely never have heard of it. It's a killer drug but it can be reversed if the target co-operates within a certain time limit. It uses the body's ability to renew its cells to destroy them instead and you'd better take down carefully what I say next.

Cytofane is injected into body fat or muscle in two separate doses of 15 millilitres each with exactly a week between them. After the second dose the target is on a one-way journey to the morgue unless 20 millilitres of a reversing agent called Retrotox are injected in a single dose within 56 days. If the target is told they've been given Cytofane and they've also been told what it does they feel as if a loaded gun is pointing at their head. Only there isn't a loaded gun, there's just the certain knowledge they're dying unless – wait for it! – the Retrotox can be earned in some way. Isn't that beautiful?"

Kapner nodded enthusiastically. It sounded a whole lot better than Elevator Plus, she said and Guderius heaved an inner sigh of relief.

"So," she went on, her mind firmly made up, "at some point in our amorous evening I slip Carey an Ophrene tablet, inject him with this Cytofane and a week later I do it all again. He'll be told what's happened, will he? After the second go, I mean."

"Yes, but probably not by you. Your job is to get the injections in and this is how you do it. If you let the Cytofane and alcohol mix stand overnight the Cytofane will sink to the bottom because it's denser and it doesn't bond with alcohol. If I were you, I'd loosen the cap a fraction before you go to bed – you mustn't jolt the bottle once you're ready to go. And you'll need to wear rubber gloves since Cytofane can be absorbed through the skin. Anyway, with the pipette you draw off the top 120 millilitres, which is all the alcohol plus a small amount of Cytofane just to make sure no alcohol is left. As your maths will tell you, what remains in the bottle is 180 millilitres of Cytofane. That's a lot more than you need but it's better than not enough."

He picked up one of the syringes.

"These little darlings have plastic screw-in plugs in them. You've got two injections to worry about and before each one you unwrap a syringe, remove the plug, screw in a needle in its place, take off its safety cap and draw in 15 millilitres of Cytofane. You'll find you won't be able to reach the Cytofane unless you do something else first though."

"Like what? Tip the bottle?"

"Don't even think about it. If you try to work the syringe and tip the bottle as well you'll spill the lot."

"So what do I do?"

"Cytofane doesn't react with glass so you take some glass beads, rinse them under the tap, dry them with a hair dryer and put enough in the bottle to bring the Cytofane up to where you want it. When you've loaded the syringe, put the safety cap back on the needle and you're ready to go. The third syringe is back-up like the third Ophrene tablet. And one more thing. Keep everything in containers no one can see into. You don't want anyone asking questions, least of all Carey. And speaking of Carey, this Monday is still on, is it?"

"In the evening, right here."

"And here again for the encore?"

"Nowhere better."

"Good. What you do is up to you as long as the Cytofane goes in. Ulrich wants to sort out Carey straight after the second injection and he wants me to be with him. So we'll both be here when it happens. "

"That's fine. It'll be a bit soon for you to be back in England though, won't it? What will Hanna think?"

"Nothing, it's not her business to think. Anyway, I can get the people I'm seeing tomorrow to ask me back, so that solves that. Anything else for the Second Officer while he's here?"

She closed her notepad and smoothed her skirt absent-mindedly.

"These drugs, the Ophrene and so forth, they must be pretty old if they're GDR. I mean, are they still all right?"

"You can't unmake knowledge, Heidi. The Academy ended with the GDR but the scientists, well, they knew what they knew and they took it with them. Some went abroad but a lot found work in the new Germany and if they were in Chameleon, they stayed in touch. So, the formulae come from the Academy but – you'll like this - the ingredients come from the new Germany's pharma-companies and I put the two together. I guarantee they're all right."

"But you said Cytofane hadn't got beyond the lab stage."

"True but it was tested extensively in GDR prisons and it worked every time. So did the Retrotox though for reasons I needn't explain, it wasn't tested so often."

"I must ask you this, Klaus – will Carey get this Retrotox if he co-operates?"

"That's not my decision but I don't see it, not after what Ulrich's told you. But we have to make Carey believe he will and you've got to help with that."

"As long as I know he's dying I'll enjoy it. Has Ulrich told you any more about his grand plan?"

"No, that's for the Operational Meeting. All he's said is, there could be thousands dead and I truly hope there will be. It's time we struck back."

Guderius was moving into departure mode. A furniture auction was coming up at Sotheby's and he wanted to see the lots. He also wanted to go to Harrods and have a surprise present sent to Gannisch – something really extravagant to show how much he was missing her. But before all of that he had to have something to eat and that, he decided, meant the Ritz. He asked Kapner if she wanted to join him but she said no – better not be seen together now things were starting to happen. So they kissed the way old friends do and he trundled off to find a taxi while Kapner went back to pricing insurance.

7

Kapner sinks her claws in

When Kapner sat down for Carey's final lecture she'd completely changed how she looked so she shifted her seat till she was out of sight of the lectern unless – very cautiously - she leaned into the aisle. Fortunately she wasn't the only one with a restricted view. The evening was cool enough for a coat, which fitted in with her plan, and sunset was nine minutes past seven – she'd checked it in advance.

The lecture was followed by the routine hour's delay, then she saw Carey's lanky shape clump down the steps into the street. She was thirty yards away in a dark spot between two street lamps and she was certain no one else was about. Carey glanced in her direction to make sure no one was coming but he didn't see her and then he was off, his briefcase swinging in time with his steps. She was sure he was heading for St James's Park because that was what he always did. She felt tension as she trailed him but what she felt much more was malice.

The park was deserted. The roads round it lit it up a bit and its footpaths had lamps here and there but it was dim and gloomy where it wasn't completely dark. Fortunately for Kapner, there was a brightish lamp by the weather-stained bench. She gave Carey time to subside into his reverie then she shook her hair to give it some bounce and stole up behind him. She'd managed to get her hair to hang straight, parted it in the middle and curled the ends inwards. That was how she'd worn it when she'd been Sophie Osterloh. She'd also blended in some of the deep rich brown it used to be and, to avoid spoiling the effect later, she'd dyed her pubic hair as well. She'd favoured a greenish-grey duffel coat in her Osterloh days and her handbag had had a shoulder strap. The unbelted coat she was wearing now and the handbag hanging from her shoulder weren't exactly the same but they were close enough and anyway, she didn't want to look as if she'd deliberately dressed up. Her brown shoes had crêpe soles and heels that let her close in on Carey without making a sound. She paused, staring at the nape of his neck, then,

"Hello, Lesley. What are you doing?"

Her voice went through him like an electric shock. He spun round and when he saw her it was as if the past had come alive again. Beside himself with excitement he scrambled to his feet.

"Sophie!" he exclaimed. "Is it really you? After all these years?"

Time had treated him badly. His thick straw-coloured hair had dwindled to a few blanched wisps round the edge of his skull, large pouches had formed under his eyes and the skin on his face sagged badly. His clothes, by contrast, were spruce and expensive looking: he hadn't lost his taste for the good life. Kapner just stood there smiling at him, her arms by her sides, as if she were offering herself to him all over again.

"I was thinking of you when you spoke," he babbled. "I like to come here when I'm in London, I can feel you near me again. And now you're really here! Oh, Sophie! It's my dream come true!"

He wanted her to come and sit next to him – "just like the old days" – but she was keyed up and anxious to move things on. She also wanted to be through with him before his last train left.

"I've got a better idea," she said half coyly, half invitingly and wholly the Sophie Osterloh who'd made him fall in love with her. "Why don't we go back to where I live now? It's right near here. It's behind the National Gallery."

He jumped at it. As he snatched up his briefcase and rounded the end of the bench she forced herself to move towards him. Clumsily he wrapped his long arms round her and hugged her so tightly he hurt her.

"Sophie," he gurgled, "I've never stopped loving you, not for a single second. I still can't believe you're here. I feel so happy, I don't know what to say."

Tears were dribbling down his cheeks so, seeing her chance, she eased herself away, took a handkerchief out of her shoulder bag and dabbed at his face to dry it.

"You silly boy," she said as tenderly as she could manage. "Can't you see how it is? I've come back to be with you and this time it's for good."

Her arm was through his as they wandered towards The Mall, then on to the National Gallery. Sometimes she pressed her head against his arm and sometimes they stopped and she let him kiss her on the mouth.

"Where are you living now?" she asked innocently while they were passing through Spring Gardens.

"You won't believe this but I'm still living in Rochester. In the same house, even. I was on my way to the station when you ... when you said my name."

"What, Charing Cross? The one you used to use?"

"That's the one. Charing Cross, the one I used to use. I'm sorry, Sophie, I'm not thinking straight. Part of me is saying I mustn't miss the last train. I'm due at work first thing tomorrow and I'm too important to be late. But, my precious, another part of me is saying all I care about is you."

He squeezed her shoulders lovingly and when he bent down to kiss her his ruined face was luminous with joy.

"When does the last train leave?"

"Twelve minutes past midnight. It's the milk train."

"No worries, then. You can get to Charing Cross in minutes from my place so we've got all the rest of this magic evening together."

She stroked his arm and nuzzled her head against it yet again.

"I've missed you terribly over the years," she cooed, "and then I saw you were giving some lectures right here in London. So I waited and waited and now I've been to them all. I knew tonight was the last one and I didn't want things to break up again so I followed you here. When you sat down on our bench I was so nervous I nearly crept away without saying anything. But I did say something because I had to and here we are, back together again. We've got a lot of catching up to do, Lesley, and I want us to start tonight."

A grin of anticipation rearranged his face. Kapner knew for certain then she could forget Elevator Plus.

When they got near to her flat she stopped, said she needed to get her key out of her bag and surreptitiously pressed two sets of numbers into a mini-zapper. The first one deactivated her silent burglar alarm and the second one released the all-round locking on her door. Then, using a Yale key, she opened the door as if the Yale was all she needed. She didn't want Carey to know about the electronics in case he ever tried to get past them: he wasn't in security for nothing. After the chill in the air outside, the flat was warm and cosy. The curtains were drawn over the gauzes and blinds, and the lights gave off a homely glow. She slipped her shoes off, put his coat and briefcase away and asked him if he was hungry. He'd knotted one of his shoelaces trying to untie it in a hurry and he was picking at it as he answered. Red in the face from bending down he said he'd eaten at the Institute but she could have something if she wanted.

"I can wait," she said. "We've got more interesting things to do first."

When he'd got both his shoes off she showed him into the living room, settled him into the easy chair Guderius had sat in and, wagging her finger sternly, told him not to move. Under no circumstances was he to come into the kitchen after her. He clasped her bottom and rubbed his cheek against her mound of Venus. Before he could slide her skirt up she gripped his head with both hands and kissed it on a liver fleck. Then she went out, closing the door behind her. As soon as she was out of sight she scrubbed her lips on the back of her wrist.

Her first port of call was not the kitchen but one of the bedrooms. Next to the bed was a cabinet with drawers in it. By the light of the lamp standing on it she took off her top clothes, her panty-hose and – after a moment's hesitation - her knickers, then put on the button-up semi-translucent blouse and the loose-fitting floral skirt that were lying ready on the bed. The skirt's zip was at the back. Finally she put her feet into a pair of fluffy slippers, dabbed some perfume on she knew he'd like, laid her wristwatch next to the bedside lamp and checked she had a dressing gown hanging on the back of the door. With her hair brushed at speed to keep it hanging right she dropped the clothes she'd taken off into a lidded laundry basket and went out into the kitchen.

A serving tray and two smallish glasses were waiting for her. One glass was patterned and the other was plain so she could tell them apart. She'd already sorted out the Ophrene tablets from the aspirins and put them into an empty matchbox. As soon as one of the tablets was in the patterned glass she took a bottle of white wine from the fridge, poured some of it, but not too much, into each glass and re-corked the bottle. The Ophrene dissolved straight away and when she held the glass against the ceiling light all she could see was the wine. With the other two tablets locked away she left the kitchen, opened the living room door just a fraction and told Carey to shut his eyes. Then she fetched the tray, tiptoed into the living room and set it down on the coffee table.

"You can open your eyes now," she said, letting him see what she was and wasn't wearing and also smell her perfumed skin.

"Sophie, you look wonderful!" he exclaimed, gleefully rubbing his knees. "And wine as well! Trust you not to forget. It's how we started our best times together."

Kapner sat down in an easy chair opposite his, taking the plain glass with her. Carey's chair was deep and soft and it'd sunk even further under his weight, whereas hers was firmer and higher. As if to make herself more comfortable she eased her skirt up as she sat down – only a couple of inches but he'd seen her do it. She also parted her knees, again not a lot but enough to make it hard for him to keep his eyes on her face. Above his head where he couldn't see it unless he turned round was a narrow mahogany shelf. On it was a Dresden shepherdess, a spray of artificial flowers in a cut glass vase and a sideboard clock with big numbers. The clock, which Kapner could read from where she was sitting, was synchronised with her wristwatch in the bedroom.

She held up her glass like a connoisseur.

"This," she said, "is ice wine from Germany. When the temperature drops below freezing the grapes are picked at dead of night and pressed before the juice has time to thaw. That's why it tastes so special and why it's right for us now. I've also got some oysters and fresh lemon but they're for afters so they're still in the fridge."

As she said "afters" she drew the hem of her skirt up a little more, looked straight at him and did it again.

"But first," she said, and she had to be quick because he was lungeing out of his chair, "we'll drink to us. And in the part of Germany I come from you have to drink the first glass all in one go if you want be happy forever. That's why we've got these smallish glasses and since you're the guest of honour, yours is the one with the pattern. Let's do it now, Lesley. Then, my one true love, I'm going to take all your clothes off, you can take mine off and we can start being happy forever right now."

"You're wicked," he giggled and while she giggled back he pointed to his fly. "Look at me, Sophie, look at me!" he squealed. "Father Christmas is coming back. Do you remember Father Christmas? You were always glad to see him, weren't you? Do you want to see him now?"

"The wine first, Lesley!" she slammed in quickly, afraid it wouldn't get drunk. "Then I'll make him glad he's come, I promise you. So, here's to your good health. What will you drink to?"

She was expecting him to say her fanny, that would've been just like him, but he suddenly went serious instead.

"To us," he said solemnly. "May we never be parted again."

He drained his glass in one go and the lust came back. As Kapner drank hers out she flicked a look at the sideboard clock. If Guderius was right Carey had two minutes to go. It could be a long two minutes. He already had his jacket off and was revved up to get rid of the rest.

8

Erectile dysfunction

She moved swiftly behind his chair, worked his necktie off and began unbuttoning his shirt; but she couldn't see the sideboard clock from there so she kissed his ear and whispered, "I can't stand it any longer, I must let you see me first." She came round in front of him, kneeled between his knees, cupped her breasts upwards and asked him to undo her blouse. The buttons were a mistake – they were small and there were a lot of them – so she had to help him because he was all thumbs in his hurry. When they were undone she let him have a first feel of her breasts through her bra while she sneaked a glance at the time. Then she turned round and, still kneeling, asked him to undo her bra strap; but not being able to see the clock made her nervous again so when her bra was off she turned and said,

"Kiss me, Lesley. I'm burning hot for you but I have to know you love me."

He closed his hands behind her head and, wanting to prove how much he loved her, he squashed her lips against his own lips and teeth. When he let go she reached behind her and raised the tab of the zip in her skirt.

"Do my skirt for me as well," she said. "You always liked that, didn't you? I'll bet you've seen I've left my knickers off."

She let him reach round her and slide the zip down. When she stood up her skirt was round her ankles and she was naked. Anxiously she took in the clock again. The two minutes were just about up but she only had Guderius's word to rely on.

"It's my turn again now," she urged. "Then we can start. The bedside light's on already. It's waiting for us."

He didn't reply, he was totally inert. She had exactly ten minutes.

She pushed back her own chair to give herself room, gripped his ankles and yanked him onto the carpet, banging his head as she did so. Then she dragged him into the bedroom she'd prepared and hauled him face upwards onto the bed. He was cumbersome as well as heavy so, fit as she was, she was breathing hard by the time she'd finished. Rapidly she undid his belt, unzipped his fly and tugged his trousers off. His baggy polka-dot boxer shorts, his socks and his shirt followed one another onto the floor and then, like her, he was naked. She left his watch on and her own was telling her she was on schedule so she allowed herself a moment to take a look at him. He'd always been scraggy and his collar-bones still poked through his chalk-white skin but there was fat on the sides of his waist that hadn't been there before and the muscles in his arms and legs were wasted. She welcomed the disgust they caused, it fuelled her aggression. With a heave she rolled him onto his front and, kneeling on the bed and reaching over him, she fetched a pair of rubber gloves and a prepared syringe of Cytofane out of the cabinet's top drawer, gathered some skin on his right buttock and, with a surge of pure joy, emptied all fifteen millilitres into him and wished it was fifteen gallons. When the syringe was in the drawer again she pulled him onto his back, felt around some more in the drawer and took out a small jar of clear, unscented hair gel. The top was already off. Still wearing rubber gloves she picked up his limp pizzle, drew the foreskin back tight and smeared gel over the glans.

"You're not getting into me this time, Lesley Carey," she muttered, holding his pizzle between her finger and thumb and fixing its gelled pink tip with her flinty eyes. "You made me puke then and you make me puke now."

As rage welled up in her she let his pizzle flop down and straddled the leg nearest to her.

"Feel it, rat," she gloated, pressing and rubbing herself against it. "Feel my fanny on your corpsey skin. It's the sort of thing you go for, isn't it? But you can't feel it, can you, offal? All that Father Christmas crap and now you can't feel it at all."

She got off his leg, picked up his pizzle again, flicked it spitefully several times then let it lie where it fell. The ten minutes were almost up. She put the gel and the rubber gloves back in the drawer, dishevelled her hair, strapped on her wristwatch and draped the dressing gown she'd put behind the door over her back like a cape. Then, lounging back in a plum-coloured chair, she watched the second hand on her watch tick round. Virtually on the dot Carey began to stir. She parted her legs to see what'd happen.

"Welcome back," she said, organising her face into a warm, welcoming smile. "You've been sleeping like a baby."

He showed no sign of arousal, not even when she parted her legs further and then brought her knees up. But she had to be certain his libido was kaput so as she stood up to kiss him she let her dressing gown slide onto the carpet. Not a quiver. Nerving herself, she walked one of her hands slowly down his body and when that had no effect, she stroked the underside of his pizzle with a fingernail. Nil response.

"Well done, Klaus," she thought.

She was safe.

"Lesley," she gushed, "you were fantastic. You were like a ram on amphetamines."

She picked up her dressing gown but she was in no hurry to put it on, not now. He, meanwhile, stretched luxuriantly, making his joints crack. He couldn't remember anything but he could feel something wet and sticky on the end of his pizzle so he was happy to believe what she told him.

"That's exactly right," he agreed. "It was cataclysmic. Did you enjoy it as well?" he asked as an afterthought.

"Did I enjoy it?" she exclaimed, pulling playfully at some strands of his hair. "It was perfect, Lesley. Just how I wanted it to be."

When they were dressed and back in the living room she asked him, probing cautiously, "Have you kept in touch with anyone from the old days?"

She'd moved her chair close to his again. They had a plate of oysters each and there was a dish for the shells on the coffee table. His plate was much larger than hers and he got most of the wine as well. She wanted to keep him talking. She knew oysters weren't an aphrodisiac although she kept telling him they were but she had a lurking fear the Ophrene wouldn't desex him for anything like two hours, in which case his guzzling and prattling might yet be her best protection.

"Not really," he replied, swallowing three oysters in succession with loud slurping noises. "The man who took over from you – Kromm, his name was, Hendrik Kromm – well, when the GDR vanished so did he. In fact, the only link I have now is your old Military Attaché, Ulrich Steffen."

"Ulrich Steffen. Ah, yes, now you mention him I can just about see his face."

"Your embassy did me an enormous favour when it told you to put me his way. He was charm itself and I spent many a happy hour answering his questions. Though I have to say, Sophie, I always wished you could ask his questions for him. I'd have enjoyed it much more if you'd been there instead."

"He had to ask his own questions. I wouldn't have known what to ask."

"Well, he certainly asked a lot but he was talking to an expert when he was talking to me so he naturally made the most of it. Anyway, sometime after the GDR disappeared who should turn up on my doorstep but the same Ulrich Steffen? Apparently he owns a bakery near Dresden, the UK likes his products and he does his own travelling. I was overjoyed to see him, that goes without saying, but as you know, I'm not an easy man to fool. I'd always talked to Ulrich in London, not Rochester, and I couldn't recollect telling him about my house. I might have done, of course – unlike a lot of things I told him, it wasn't classified – but I take a strong line with people on principle so I asked him outright how he'd got my address. He wasn't the least put out. He's like me, you see, he's got character. He just laughed and said, 'You've been in the game, Lesley. You know how these things work' and, of course, that's true. I'm an insider like you and Ulrich, and not many people can say that. After that we sort of became pals. I won't say he's always popping in but he looks by from time to time."

She fetched him some more oysters from the fridge. He was eating on his own now but he didn't seem to mind. He squeezed half a lemon over several more, shovelled them down greedily and then loosened his necktie, which he'd found

69

by his chair without remembering how it got there. The warm room and the food were making him flush. He'd never have guessed it but when Steffen laughed on his doorstep he'd been laughing at him. Carey had repeatedly told him not only about his house but the whole of Beale's Row. When Steffen had wanted to contact him the Rochester phone book was all he'd needed.

"We still talk about tunnels," Carey continued, wiping his mouth. "He's so interested, you get carried away and before you know where you are, you've told him more than you should. It's just as well I can trust him but I always felt that and, of course, his English is as good as ever. There can't be too much wrong with him with English like that. Have you seen him yourself recently?"

"No," she said, as if nothing could have been less likely, "not at all. We were good colleagues but it's all over now. Ships that pass in the night, that sort of thing."

He gazed round her living room as if he were sucking it in.

"And you're a Londoner again, are you?" he asked, draining his glass with a smack of his lips to show he knew quality when he tasted it.

"Some of the time," she smiled. "And some of the time I'm a Liechtensteiner. I've got a place in Vaduz as well."

"Why there? You're not a tax fraud, I hope."

Kapner was under orders from Steffen to make sure Carey knew one or two things about her. "They've got to come out early and they've got to come from you," he'd said. "If he finds out for himself he could turn nasty." As a result she was hoping for the right starter question and here it was.

"Nothing like that, Lesley, but if I tell you about Vaduz I have to tell you some other things and you might not like them."

"Sophie, we're here to start again, not quarrel and sulk. You may hurt me but it'll make things better in the long run. Try me and see what happens."

"Well, here's a sample to test you with. My name isn't Sophie Osterloh, it's Heidi Kapner."

He was dumbfounded. Had he really been deceived for so long? Then he laughed and waved his oyster knife at her.

"You'll have to do better than that, Heidi – there, you see, I'm calling you Heidi already. As Ulrich said, I've been in the game so what you say doesn't surprise me at all. I expect Hendrik Kromm was a made-up name as well. It certainly sounds like it now I come to think about it. But if that was a sample, what about the rest? Come on, Heidi, I can take it. I insist on knowing the worst."

She almost thanked him out loud when he said that. As poignantly as she could, she answered,

"We have to go back to when we were ripped apart. It hurts me even to think about it but if we're starting again, that's what we have to do."

That made him listen closely. It was a wound that had never healed.

"We parted for one reason only, Lesley – I was ordered back to the GDR. The men at the top – they were always men – had this thing about people like me staying in the West for too long. They were afraid we'd be corrupted by Western culture. I should've seen it coming but I didn't because I didn't want to. I loved you too much, you see."

"That's how you explained it when we said our last goodbyes and I'm glad you've said it again. It wasn't your fault the Iron Curtain came down between us. We were love's tragic victims, that's all."

"I was hoping you'd say that, my dearest heart. What I've told you was true then and it's true now."

But it wasn't true at all. She'd been sweet-talking a research evaluator at Britain's Atomic Weapons Research Establishment in Berkshire at the same time as she'd been sweet-talking Carey in London. British intelligence had picked up on her nuclear lover, the Stasi had found that out and she'd been bundled out of the UK before the British press could get to her. She'd been ordered to have one last meeting with Carey to get him to accept a new spymaster, then she'd gone. She'd been furious with the Stasi at the time: it hadn't been her fault her scientist had been found out. Later on she saw that if she'd been denounced by the British instead of being pulled out by the Stasi she'd never have been allowed to settle in London after the Cold War was over.

"I believe you," Carey said. "I don't mind what else you say now so please, I beg you, don't leave anything unsaid."

She took a deep breath.

"Very well. I want you to know I've been married."

She was afraid that might overload him so she ploughed on before he could react.

"I married a West German who was living in Liechtenstein. I met him while I was skiing there."

"When was this?"

His voice was strained. He was finding it harder to be noble than he'd thought.

"After I lost my employer."

"Your employer?"

"The GDR, Lesley. It paid my wages, then it was gone. Like a company gone bust."

"Ah, yes. I'd never thought of it as an employer."

She let that pass.

"The man who became my husband – Bodo Rossler was his name – was a lot older than me. We used to drink in the same bar and he already knew he had cancer when we … when we became close. He owned an insurance brokerage in Vaduz called Cantico Insurance. It was doing well, he had no family and he was lonely. You can see what I'm getting at, I guess."

Carey pursed his lips and nodded like a judge. An unemployed single girl had to look after herself, he could see that perfectly well. That she'd circled Rossler like a vulture circling its dinner never crossed his mind.

"Bodo's dead now," she went on, "and Cantico is mine. I've expanded into London, which is why I have this flat, but Cantico's headquarters are still in Vaduz so I've kept our apartment there as well. I say 'our' because that's how it was but, like Cantico, it's all mine now."

She'd got past the tricky bit. Now to finish on a high.

"My name is all mine as well, I took it back after Bodo died. I'm Heidi Kapner again, Lesley – your Heidi Kapner."

The sideboard clock was saying she'd have to get rid of him soon and there was no way she wanted him back before the following Monday so, thinking fast, she added,

"As it happens I have to go to Vaduz tomorrow. But I'll make sure I'm back by next Monday."

In fact, apart from Steffen's Operational Meeting, which was lined up for the coming Thursday, she'd be in London all week. If Carey caught her, she'd say a windfall deal had brought her back in a hurry. She took his hand in hers and squeezed it gently.

"My dearest darling Lesley," she purred. "Can we please, please meet next Monday and do it all again? I'll have to work all day – that always happens when I get back from Vaduz – but I'll make sure I'm free by six o'clock and we can have the whole evening to ourselves."

He radiated delight.

"You make me happier than any man who ever lived," he burbled. "But be warned! I'll take amphetamines by the box full. Then you'll find out what a ram can really do."

Once he'd gone she tidied up the living room and put the syringe, the rubber gloves and the pot of hair gel into a dark-coloured plastic bag. To them she added the handkerchief she'd dried his face with – she never wanted to touch it again – and a heavy flat iron she'd bought especially. Then she let herself into the room she used as her office and, from a locked steel box in her safe, she took out her code book, a sheet of paper, a pre-cut piece of cardboard and an empty black lipstick holder that had been carefully cleaned. Using the cardboard to rest on and wearing a fresh pair of rubber gloves she encoded, "Part One gone to plan. Part Two set up as required. Will be present after 13.00. Target due 18.00". The message went into the lipstick holder which she wrapped in tissue before she took her gloves off. They and the piece of cardboard went into the plastic bag, which she tied up tightly, making sure no air was trapped inside it. She didn't have to address the message. The pick-up was pre-arranged.

When she went out she headed for Waterloo Bridge. A sharp breeze was blowing off the Thames, the tide was on the ebb and the water was flowing fast. Halfway across she glanced stealthily round then tipped the bag over the concrete parapet. It sank like a stone. She continued on to the South Bank, turned upstream and as she passed a flower tub she let the lipstick container slip out of the tissue into it. She used the Hungerford Bridge to recross the river and as soon as she was on it, a shadow moved from a plane tree near the flower tub and the message was on its way to Germany. The tissue ended up in a Villiers Street litter bin.

She was so exhausted when she got back to her flat, all she wanted to do was crawl into bed. But first, with her eyes half shut, she picked up her dressing gown from the carpet and put it into the laundry basket, then she stripped the bedclothes off the bed Carey had been on and bagged them. Everything, including what she'd been wearing, would go to the cleaner's in the morning. The mattress and pillow she covered with a dust sheet. Her bedroom was across the corridor. The room she'd dragged Carey into was spare. When she finally slid into bed she rubbed herself voluptuously against the crisp, clean sheets, thankful she didn't have to sleep in the bed she'd just stripped. If someone had died of plague in it she couldn't have detested it more. Then she remembered Carey had gone home with 15 millilitres of Cytofane in him and sheer delight relaxed her into a deep and dreamless sleep.

9

Steffen orders his guns

The small town of Johannisbrunn – St John's Well to English-speakers – stood on a low lying plain where the River Elbe wound into Germany from the Czech Republic. The GDR had called it Leninstadt but the new Germany decided the old name was better.

Just about everything about Johannisbrunn was sad. Unemployment was high, anyone with anywhere else to go to had already gone there and whole blocks of empty flats were waiting to be demolished. The people left behind were demoralised and shabby. When the sun shone they leaned on their balconies or sat on chipped concrete benches in the town square. When it rained or snowed they watched television. Young people scarcely existed.

The only place showing signs of life was Steffen's Bakery. The site had seen baking since the Middle Ages but the Communists centralised everything in Dresden and that put an end to that. Thereafter the bakery stood empty, which allowed Steffen to get it the way Guderius had got Karl Marx House – with a plan and a promise. Steffen couldn't bake but his son, Walter, could, so Steffen prised him out of the New American Bread Company in Magdeburg and put him in charge of production while he, Steffen, built up trade with the same efficiency that'd made him top of his year at the Friedrich Engels Military Academy. He made his own contacts and struck his own deals, and Walter often had no idea who he'd been seeing till the orders came in. But come in they did. Lots of them.

Steffen had no interest in becoming rich. His burning ambition was to create work for former East Germans. The outside of the bakery was straight from the history books but everything else was state-of-the-art including the high speed production lines and the freezer block. Further out there were a cold store, a warehouse, silos and a lorry park. A lot of the produce went abroad. Johannisbrunn had a permanent odour of baking in the air but it could as easily mean frozen rolls for Bucharest as fresh rolls for local breakfast tables.

Steffen liked to arrive early and the day of the Operational Meeting was no exception. As always, he walked through every part of the bakery to see that everything was in order. Everyone knew they owed their job to this unyielding, whippet-thin man. If something was wrong they could say so and he'd put it right. Anyone not pulling his weight was fired.

Walter had just arrived when Steffen knocked on his office door and went in. Steffen's GDR thing meant nothing toWalter and he'd never even heard of Chameleon. To Walter, Steffen's Bakery was a business. If it gave people work that was fine but its real function was making money.

"It's about your mother," Steffen said without sitting down. "I'm going to London Sunday. She'll need looking after for a few days."

Walter's mother, Helga-Marie, was mostly wheelchair-bound. She had rheumatoid arthritis and the aging colonel pushing the frail little lady was a familiar sight in Johannisbrunn. When Steffen was away she either had a nurse in or she stayed with Walter and his wife, Ruth.

"She can come to us," Walter said. "Ruth'll fetch her Saturday. If you're out she'll let herself in."

Walter had said what Steffen had wanted to hear but he didn't go away and Walter knew why. He wanted to hear about his grandchildren, Daniela and Robert, two bright-eyed pre-schoolers whose photos were on Walter's desk. Steffen called round to see them every day he could but that didn't stop him wanting to hear about them as well.

So, without having to be asked, Walter told his father what Daniela had said and what Robert had done since the last time he'd seen them and the granite-hard fanatic stood there like any other grandfather and soaked it all up. When Walter finished Steffen took two five-euro notes from his wallet.

"For their piggy banks," he said. "They're good children."

That was something else: he spoiled them shamelessly.

"I'm going off-site shortly," he continued as Walter thanked him and put the notes away. "I'm going to Leipzig. I've got someone interested in our rye bread. Maybe our fruit flans as well. I'll find out."

"What about tonight, Dad? Are you coming round?"

"Not tonight. I'm expecting company."

Walter liked it when his father had company, as he called it. To his mind it didn't happen enough. He knew all about Steffen's friends – or thought he did. Klaus Guderius would be there, he'd put money on that, and if he was, he might well drop Hanna off at his and Ruth's first. Ruth and Gannisch were good friends and whenever Walter came home and Gannisch was there, he'd brew some more coffee and join in the gossip. Heidi Kapner might turn up as well if she was in the country. And there were others, all with one foot in the past and determined to keep it there. Just like Dad.

Steffen made straight for his Lexus when he left Walter's office. He'd parked where he normally did but this time he'd reversed in with the result that when he seated himself on the passenger side of the back seat he was just out of range of the cctv. No one was parked next to him – it was one of the few perks he allowed himself – and no one could see him by walking behind his car because his bay was end-on to a blank wall.

He'd put a sack on the driver's side of the back seat – he could smell it as soon as he opened the door – and a pre-cut length of string was neatly folded on top of it. On the floor on the same side was a plastic snack box with a clamp-down lid. He reached down for the box, snapped the clamps back and took out a piece of raw fish. After he'd unwrapped the cling film round it he laid it on the upturned lid between his left foot and the driver's side rear door, which he opened half way. Then he settled down to wait. Just in case, he made as if he was reading some documents he'd brought with him but he kept his hands low because he was wearing a pair of old leather gloves.

He didn't have to wait long. Like bakeries the world over, Steffen's Bakery had its quota of cats to keep down vermin with a taste for cereal. One of these cats, scenting the fish, was approaching the Lexus. It was a tortoiseshell and not quite fully grown. It took its time thinking about getting into the car and Steffen, watching out of the corner of his eye, kept absolutely still. Finally it jumped in and immediately one gloved hand seized it behind its head, pinched its loose skin and whisked it off the floor so it couldn't anchor itself to anything. The other hand whipped open the mouth of the sack and within seconds the cat was tied inside it. It put a lot of energy into snarling and struggling but it didn't stand a chance. It snarled and struggled some more when Steffen dropped it onto the floor and then it quietened down. Calmly Steffen took his gloves off and walked round to the driver's door with his documents well in view. He looked like a boss who finished his paperwork before he went to see his customers. The cctv picked him up as he drove off but, as he knew it would, it missed the sack.

Steffen checked his watch and calculated his time. He'd been telling the truth when he'd said he was going to Leipzig but he had an appointment to keep first and it involved detouring to a tree-ringed stretch of water called Lake Muschg. The lake, which was a shortish car ride from Bad Sollmer, had a footpath round it and there were mown open spaces for picnics and sunbathing. Sailing had caught on big-time there, especially at weekends, when Dresden's rising middle class liked to show they at least were in the money. The clubhouse had been lavishly refurbished. It'd once been a training centre for sub-aqua saboteurs but there was no trace of that now.

Steffen motored straight to the clubhouse, parked in the shade next to it and checked his watch again. He was on time. He didn't want the cat to die so he let the car's windows down slightly before he got out. A pennant hanging limply from the clubhouse's flag pole said there was no wind for sailing. As a consequence the lake was deserted, as was the hard leading down to the moorings, and the slatted doors to the boat store were rolled right down and code-locked. Steffen pressed the bell by a side door and heard feet clomping down wooden stairs. Then the door opened and he was looking into the veined, crow's-footed face of Linus Steinmeier, once an NPA gunnery officer and now full-time boatman to the Lake Muschg Sailing Club. He was also Chameleon's weapons supplier.

"Good to see you, Linus!" Steffen exclaimed, grasping his hand warmly. "You're looking well. What about Agnes? Is she all right?"

Steinmeier smiled resignedly as he undid his carpenter's apron.

"Thanks, Ulrich, she's bearing up. And Helga-Marie?"

"Not so good. She doesn't complain but everything's pointing downwards."

They were all getting old. It added to the pressure on Steffen – the pressure to act while he could.

Steinmeier hung his apron on a hook inside the door, locked up and led the way to his workhorse Mercedes van. He and his wife owned a cottage in Muschg Village, a fifteen minute drive away. Before they got rolling, he put through a call to say they were on their way.

"Is Agnes still on our side?" Steffen asked.

He'd been keeping in touch by courier so he hadn't seen her lately.

"Of course. She hates the West as much as ever. Nothing'll change that."

It was what Steffen had expected to hear but he liked to be certain. Some people gave up as they got older. Too many, to his mind.

When they arrived Agnes had the coffee cups laid out ready. She'd put on weight, her arms and legs were puffy and she wheezed a lot as she moved.

"Sorry, Ulrich, it's decaff," she said as she poured. "It's all we're allowed these days. Doctor's orders."

A heavy white cloth covered the table, the crockery was sturdy rather than smart and a bulky wall unit dominated one end of the living room. In most German households its shelves would be full of family photos but Agnes was sterile so she and her husband had lived off their hatred of the West and the shelves were blank. Now they could see what the West was really like neither of them wanted to. Steinmeier "went across", as he put it, when he had to but his wife had never left the ex-GDR and was certain she never would.

Steffen drank his coffee quickly and pushed his cup away.

"You know why I'm here," he said. "Can you help?"

Steinmeier took a bunch of keys from his pocket and spread them on the flat of his hand.

"We might be able to. Let's see what we've got in the basement."

The door to the basement stairs was in the hall and it was locked. So was the door at the bottom end. As Steffen and Steinmeier were going down Steffen heard Agnes lock up behind them. It was what she always did when Steinmeier went down there even if he went down on his own.

The floor of the basement was concrete, the walls were plastered-over brickwork and the air smelled of metal and machine oil. By one wall there was a workbench with a vice, a vertical drill and some safety goggles on it. The wall opposite was lined with black-painted steel weapons cabinets, each one padlocked top and bottom. Ammunition was stored in its own double-locked cabinets.

"Four sniper rifles and ten side arms, wasn't it?" Steinmeier asked, sorting through his keys and laying four long rifles side by side on his workbench. Their butt assemblies and hand guards – their so-called furniture – were made of wood polished smooth.

"I bet these bring back memories," he chuckled. "I've got night scopes as well if you want them."

They were Russian Dragunovs – also known as SVDs. They had old-fashioned dependability and were highly accurate.

"There'll be plenty of light about. Ordinary scopes will do."

"I can do better than that. I've got some zoom scopes and they're beautiful. Cheek plates, too, of course."

"What about ammunition?"

"As much as you want. Anything else?"

"I'll need something to keep the barrels steady. And some cleaning gear."

"I've got bipods and I'll make sure they fit. Cleaning gear comes in packs. How many do you want?"

"Three's enough."

Steffen went over the Dragunovs inch by inch, then he asked to see the side arms. Steinmeier laid out ten black 7.65mm pistols. They were Ceska CZ83s. They, too, were gone over minutely.

"These are fine, Linus. I'll need shoulder holsters for five of them. We'll talk about ammunition upstairs with Agnes. I need to say one or two other things as well."

Agnes was sitting in the living room, still breathing sterterously.

"Two of the Dragunovs plus one cleaning pack and five of the Ceskas plus the shoulder holsters are for an operation abroad," Steffen said. "For ammunition I calculate two ten-round box magazines for each of the two Dragunovs and one clip each for the five Ceskas. That should be plenty. I'm not planning a shoot-out."

"How are you going to carry the Dragunovs?" asked Steinmeier. "I've still got the wooden boxes they came in. I could do something with them."

"They'd be too heavy. Can you run up some canvas carriers? With room for the bipods, the scopes and the magazines?"

"You've got some canvas at work, Linus," said Agnes. "You made some gardening bags with it last Easter."

"It'd crossed my mind as well, love. Boats don't use canvas any more," he explained to Steffen, "but I found a whole load in a storage cupboard and there's still plenty left. It's a sort of dun colour so it won't stand out. I'll make them this afternoon in the sail loft. I don't get many visitors up there and when I do, I know they're coming because the stairs creak."

"Sounds good, Linus. Now, transport to the area of attack will be by sea so I want everything in waterproof wrapping.

Make it three bundles altogether. Put the two Dragunovs plus their bipods, scopes, cheek plates and magazines in the first two and everything else in the third one. Then I'll know what's in each bundle just by looking at it."

"The third bundle could be a bit floppy. I'll stiffen it if you like."

"No need. It's not a problem."

"Where do you want me to deliver to? And when?"

"You'll get a coded message in your drop box and the sender will call himself Kestrel. I need to tighten things up as of now."

Like most Chameleon activists the Steinmeiers had a concealed drop box. It was in the side of their cottage and anything put into it fell down a shaft into a locked box in their basement. Daski had recommended drop boxes after Steffen had had a scare with some forged passports he'd left for collection. The boxes were locked and unlocked with a zapper and as soon as he could Daski was doing the resets directly from Berlin. Regular resets make them more secure, he'd explained, and Steffen had given him the go-ahead.

"The other two Dragunovs and cleaning packs," Steffen continued, "plus the other five Ceskas and all the ammunition you can spare go to Jan Schwarzer's shooting range. I want you to do that as soon as you can."

"I'll do it tonight. I'll fetch them back as well if you like."

Schwarzer's shooting range was a bit further north. It put courses on, it ran competitions and it was never short of members. Schwarzer had been an NPA border guard and Chameleon had first call on his premises. They were a good place to practise. No one noticed guns on a shooting range.

"Agreed. Tell Jan so he'll know."

As he drove Steffen back to the clubhouse Steinmeier's mind went back to Helga-Marie.

"She's really that bad, is she?" he asked, genuinely concerned.

"Her medication makes her sleepy but it doesn't do much else. Walter is watching out for new treatments but unless something big happens she'll go on getting worse."

"I'm sorry, Ulrich. She's worth ten of most people."

He pulled up on his parking spot and they both got out. The pennant on the flag pole was still hanging limp and the lake was still deserted. They shook hands and Steinmeier gave Steffen a parting wave as he set off for Leipzig. On his passenger seat were some sandwiches and a carton of juice Agnes had packed for him. At the first crossroads he came to he reached back and jabbed at the sack. The cat didn't move for long but it moved. It'd survive till evening.

10

The end of the cat

Land and labour were cheap in Johannisbrunn so as soon as Steffen had had enough money he'd bought a secluded plot on the town's outer edge and had had a bungalow built on it. It'd had to be a bungalow because of Helga-Marie's arthritis. Helga-Marie had her own rest-cum-sitting room, bedroom and adapted toilet facilities. Steffen had a study, a bedroom and toilet facilities plus a larger sitting room for when he had guests. It was well away from Helga-Marie's rooms and it had a patio door so if he didn't want to, he didn't have to bring anyone through the bungalow. Within Chameleon "the bungalow" always meant Steffen's bungalow. He didn't like the phrase, it sounded too Western, but it was convenient so he lived with it.

It was close on six when he got back from Leipzig. After he'd put his car away and locked his papers in the boot he walked from the garage to a white-painted summer house in the back garden. He was carrying his leather gloves, the snack box that'd contained the raw fish and the sack with the cat in it. The cat writhed briefly when he kicked it but he wanted it more than just alive, he wanted it fighting fresh. He closed the summer house door behind him, untied the sack and tipped the cat with a thud into an empty tea chest. It didn't have a lid so he left a thick piece of chipboard over it while he took the bottom part of the snack box out to a tap in the garden. The cat hadn't had anything to drink all day so it soon stopped attacking his glove when he lowered the water down next to it. With the chipboard back on top of the tea chest he walked round to the bungalow's front door, leaving everything he'd been carrying in the summer house. He'd go back for what he needed later.

Helga-Marie was in the kitchen when he let himself in. He'd phoned her from Leipzig and a cold meal for two was waiting on the table. She was having one of her "ups" as she called them, meaning she was feeling good. She'd been getting about with just a stick.

They kissed lovingly and she said,

"The caterer's been. The snacks are in boxes in your sitting room and the drinks are in the fridge. I'll make coffee for you nearer the time. Is it still five people coming?"

"Five it is. Did I tell you I was going to talk about my army days?"

Steffen kept Helga-Marie out of Chameleon as totally as Guderius did Gannisch.

"More than once. You said they'd asked you to."

"It's true. A lot of people still take pride in the NPA only they don't like to say it out loud."

He washed his hands under the tap and opened the fridge door to see what the drinks were. They had a commercial-size fridge and Helga-Marie ordered for it on-line. It was Steffen's idea. It meant Helga-Marie was in charge of something even though she couldn't get out and about on her own.

"I've asked people to come to the front door so you can say hullo," he said, satisfied with what he saw, "but I'll let them out through the patio door so they don't disturb you when they go."

She looked at him sadly.

"You never stop looking after me, do you? I wish you didn't have to."

Steffen kissed her again but he didn't say anything. He knew what he felt but he couldn't bring out the words.

"You said Klaus was coming," she went on. "Is he taking Hanna to Walter and Ruth's?"

"I've no idea. That's up to him."

"Well, I hope he is. They love having her round. She's so warm-hearted, she always cheers people up."

Helga-Marie gossiped all the way through the meal and Steffen couldn't hear enough of it. Her ups brought back the live wire army typist he'd married when he was just out of

Military Academy. When they finished eating he fondly held her hand for a moment and then they cleared away.

At a quarter past seven Steffen set the coffee things out to give Helga-Marie a start. The coffee was Rondo, the GDR's favourite brand. It was still roasted in Magdeburg, not far from where Walter had worked, and Helga-Marie made sure there was always some in stock. When Steffen had helped all he could he went into his sitting room where he emptied the boxes onto a sideboard, drew the curtains and pulled five easy chairs into a semi-circle facing a flip-chart. A table bearing a large oblong object under a thick cloth was already standing near it. Like the flip-chart, they'd been there all day. He didn't mind if Helga-Marie looked under the cloth though he didn't think she would. It was a birthday present for Robert he'd fetched down from the loft. If she asked about it he'd say he was testing it, which in a way he was.

To make things complete he took a GDR banner from a cupboard and hung it from the picture rail behind the flip-chart and the table. Some of the room's lighting came from spotlights. When he directed them onto the banner its black, red and gold seemed to glow with inner fire.

When everything was ready he went back into the summer house via the patio door. It didn't have mains lighting so he rummaged around in a drawer till he found a torch, which he set on a shelf and tilted with a cushion and some bits of wood. The edge of the shelf blocked some of the light but a lot of the beam landed on the chipboard and when he inched it to one side, the light caught the cat's eyes as it rose on its hind legs and stared at him. The water had given it a new lease of life. It arched its back, hissed angrily and then tried to get out. But before it could get a purchase on the rim of the tea chest Steffen reached a gloved hand in, dragged it out by the throat and tied it in the sack again. As before, it struggled hard at first and then went slack. When Steffen went back to rewash his hands he dropped it outside the patio door and tossed his gloves on top of it. He was ready now. His guests could arrive when they liked.

Guderius came first. No, he hadn't brought Hanna, she was covering for him at the clinic. Then Kapner arrived. She'd come straight from Leipzig-Halle airport in a rented Opel and she'd hardly got out when a Bentley swung into the drive and parked behind her. It was Michael Lederer, a ship owner from the Baltic port of Rostock. Lederer was followed by Frank Zimmermann, who was a generation younger than the others. He was brought by his father, Kurt Zimmermann, an ex-NPA colonel like Steffen who was inducting his son into Chameleon. The Zimmermanns owned a road haulage company headquartered in Leipzig. Last to arrive was Brigitte Danzig, a former Stasi interrogator who was now a Commerzbank investments manager. She divided her time between Frankfurt, where she lived, London and New York. She and Frank Zimmermann were Chameleon's two best shots, which was why they were there. Leaning on her stick, Helga-Marie greeted them all as they came in and told them where to hang their coat if they were wearing one. Steffen had put bottled beer, soft drinks and glasses on the bottom shelf of the trolley so all she had to do was put the coffee on top next to the cups and cream and, using the trolley like a Zimmer frame, wheel everything into his sitting room with her stick crooked on her arm. When she'd done that she left them to it. While everyone was helping themselves Steffen caught Kapner's eye.

"I want you to buy some things when you get back to London," he said. "Some are for you and some are for me but I don't want the ones for me in my luggage when I come over. Buy two waterproof hold-alls while you're at it. Buy them last and make sure they're big enough to take the other things."

He gave her a piece of paper with a list on it. It included "Two black wetsuits plus thermals for me and you." At the bottom he'd put "My Body Size: Medium". He'd also put his shoe size in UK and European.

"Don't use a credit card, use cash," he told her, "and don't buy everything in the same shop. And I'll need to stay with you when things peak. Is that all right?"

"I'll make it all right."

She read through the list.

"Where do I get black waterproof greasepaint?" she asked.

"Any war-games or paintball shop. It comes in tubes. You can get the remover there as well. It's a solvent and it's fast."

He looked at his watch. It was time to start.

"You all know now about my distress bomb," he began, the GDR banner in full glow behind him. "To make it work, you'll be killing fathers, mothers and children by the many hundreds and I want you to realise what that means. So watch this."

With his jacket off and his sleeves rolled up he opened the patio door and put his gloves on. Carrying the sack in his left hand he re-shut the door with his right and tugged the cloth off the oblong object on the table to reveal an aquarium about one third full of water. Next to it were a folded towel and a pair of scissors. He snipped through the string round the neck of the sack and hauled the cat out by the throat. It meowed and scrabbled while he held it in the air but when he gripped its hind legs it quietened down. Taking his time Steffen lowered it into the aquarium and forced it against the bottom with both hands. Frantically it tried to free itself, looking wildly through the glass as it struggled for its life. Finally it sagged, its limbs subsided and it was dead.

There was more than one kind of silence in the room as Steffen pulled his sodden gloves off and dried his hands and forearms. He'd kept his watch on. It was an East German Ruhla. It wasn't Swiss chronometry but it was tough enough for most things. He only took it off when he had to.

"Could you drown a child the way I've just drowned this cat?" he asked as he refolded the towel. "Trap it under water and watch it die? Because that's what you'll be doing many, many times over."

He looked at them one by one. As he did so he noticed Kapner and Guderius were sitting next to each other. Strange how they always made a pair.

"I could," Frank Zimmermann said but it didn't sound right. It was too loud and too eager.

His father, a widower who'd refocused all his love onto his son, touched his arm.

"What Ulrich means is, sometimes we have to do things in war that would normally upset us," he said, steadily and sincerely. "And this is a kind of war, isn't it, Ulrich?"

"Of course. That's exactly what it is."

Steffen repeated his question, this time putting it to each of them by name, and they all said yes, they could personally trap a child under water and watch it die. Kapner was just flinty hard this time – she wasn't going to be caught out twice. And Danzig, the one-time Stasi interrogator, didn't even try to hide her joy.

Just in case Helga-Marie came in Steffen re-covered the aquarium with the cloth, leaving the dead cat in it and his gloves and towel next to it. Certain everyone in the room was now with him he was eager to move on to the flip-chart.

11

How to kill a lot of people

Brisk and business-like, Steffen wrote OPERATION NEW HOPE in black caps, underlined it twice and added everyone's code names underneath. They were all birds because birds were what he was used to from the GDR. As his felt-tip squeaked across the paper he said them out loud. It was like a memorial:

Steffen – Condor
Guderius – Heron
Kapner – Falcon
Danzig – Osprey
Zimmermann, F. – Goshawk
Zimmermann, K. – Raven
Lederer – Kestrel

On the next sheet of paper he drew a sketch map of south-east England. Where the Thames broadened out to join the North Sea he wrote Thames Estuary. Below the estuary he wrote County of Kent and above it he wrote County of Essex. Where the Thames was still narrow he put a big round blob for London. Dropping below the Kent shoreline he ran a connection from London to the coast and labelled it the M2/A2 motorway.

"The M2/A2 hits the coast at Dover," he said and wrote in the name of the port.

Finally he drew a small circle just above the Kent shoreline and half way between London and the North Sea. That was the Isle of Sheppey, which he connected to the mainland with a road bridge. The bridge he simply labelled Flyover, saying its name wasn't important. The road he extended down the sheet of paper to the M2/A2 and labelled it Sheppey Link Road.

"Most of this will be familiar to you," he said. "But now watch closely."

He took a bright red felt-tip and drew a line that began on the Kent mainland, passed under the Isle of Sheppey and terminated on the Essex mainland. This line he labelled NORTH SEA TUNNEL, again in caps and double underlined. Above where the tunnel terminated he wrote "Easy access from here to London Orbital and rest of England".

"The British know all about terrorism," he said when he'd finished, "and as you can see, the North Sea Tunnel's ideal for any terrorist wanting to enter or leave England fast. To counter that the government's had a Rapid Response plan developed. It's based on something the public mustn't know and it's this: the tunnel can be flooded."

"That," enthused Danzig, "sounds like many hundreds dead all right."

She was really attending now.

"There are five tubes in the tunnel," Steffen went on. "Two from Kent to Essex, two from Essex to Kent and a service tube in the middle. These tubes carry around 250,000 vehicles a day. We're going to flood them at peak time and drown everyone in them. A lot of them will be parents heading home from work and the impact will be immense."

"How will people know it's us that's done the flooding?" Kurt Zimmermann asked. "And why we've done it, come to that?"

"The internet will tell them why. One of our colleagues is hiding in São Paulo right now. When she gets my signal our message will go world-wide and I've made sure our government, not the British one, will get the blame. Regrettably our names won't be on it and nor will the name 'Chameleon'. We have to protect ourselves in case one act of mass destruction isn't enough."

"You mean to say," Kurt Zimmermann persisted, "that the British government would drown any number of its own citizens, not to mention foreign nationals, just to stop a few terrorists? I don't believe it."

"The British government isn't as squeamish as ours, Kurt. Of course, the official hope is to get the traffic out before the water goes in but the tubes don't have to be empty for the pumps to be started. That's why we can flood them while they're still full of traffic."

He paused to see whether anyone else wanted to say something but no one did. They were waiting to hear the rest.

"Our target area is the Isle of Sheppey," he continued. "I'll draw it big for you."

He flipped to a fresh sheet of paper, drew the Kent shoreline about a quarter up from the bottom then leaving a gap, he filled most of the rest of the sheet with a circle. That was the Isle of Sheppey.

"Sheppey is a genuine island," he said. "It's inhabited mostly by sheep but right at the top there's an international container port called Sheerness."

He put a blob top left of the circle and wrote Sheerness next to it.

"Sheppey's only route to the mainland is the Sheppey Link Road and it's a six-lane highway. Three lanes run south from Sheerness to the M2/A2 motorway and three lanes run north. After we've made our attack, getting over the flyover before the police seal it off is a must. If we're fast we can do it. If we're not we'll be trapped."

He let that sink in. Then,

"We're targeting Sheppey because it's where the tunnel's control centre is. Right here, in fact, just left of the island's dead centre."

He placed an index finger on the middle of the island and next to it he drew a black oblong like a coffin seen sideways on.

"Because of the flooding mechanism," he continued as he labelled the oblong, "the control centre is deliberately kept isolated. A narrow road runs between it and the Sheppey Link Road but that's its only connection with the outside world. To get an idea of what it's like think of a high security compound with a tall wire fence round it and just one well guarded gate for getting in and out. The fence bothered me at first but Sheppey isn't the flattest place on earth and behind the control centre there's a hill that's tailor-made. The sight lines are perfect and the bushes and trees are just right for cover. It's easy to get to as well. Just before the Sheppey Link Road reaches Sheerness, a B road branches off and runs behind the town to a picnic area. From there a footpath goes out to our hill which is where you, Brigitte, and you, Frank, will be sniping from. You'll be using Dragunovs."

"What sort of scopes?"

It was Frank Zimmermann.

"Daylight zoom scopes. You'll be shooting after dark but the control centre's lighting is daylight bright. You'll also have Ceska CZ83s for emergencies. So will Klaus and Kurt and so will I. Your weapons will be got into England for you and Michael will tell you how in just a moment. But first I'll say that two more Dragunovs and five Ceskas are on their way to Jan Schwarzer's range and you're all under orders to practise till you can hit anything first time. That includes you, Klaus, and it also includes me."

"What about Heidi?" Kurt Zimmermann asked. "Isn't she in on this?"

"She is but she's got a gun of her own in London."

"It's a Beretta Compact, Kurt, and don't worry, I'm in good practice. When you live on your own, you take precautions."

"It's security guards we'll be shooting, is it?" Frank Zimmermann asked again.

"Yes and no. The flooding mechanism is housed in a blockhouse inside the control centre compound and it's got its own wire fence round it. There's just one locked gate in that fence and it's guarded twenty-four hours a day by pairs of armed soldiers. I repeat, armed soldiers. They wear body armour but they don't wear helmets so your job and Brigitte's will be to shoot them through the head. Then I can get someone in to start the flooding."

"When's this all going to be?" asked Danzig.

"Monday October 26th at 18.00 hours, when the guards change shift. That's a confirmed date now. I can also confirm it'll dark by then. Now I'll hand over to Michael. He'll tell you how he'll get your guns in."

Lederer's purpley face glistened with pride. He'd been a captain in the National People's Navy and he'd sunk quite a few of his fellow East Germans as they tried to get out via the Baltic. Now he was rich and respectable and Lederer Maritime, a Rostock-based container fleet, could compete with anything out of Hamburg.

"One of my ships, The Lord of Cathay, does a regular run from Rostock to Sheerness," he said. "She's next due in Sheerness on October 25th at 19.00 and your guns will be on board. No one will see them go on, I can guarantee that, but getting them off, well, it looked tricky at first but not any more.

The thing is, the quays in Sheerness run out from the shore like teeth in a comb and my ship always ties up at the bottom one. That means any vessel berthed there after dark is lit from one side only and the water on the unlit side is in shadow.

So, just before The Lord of Cathay docks, Ulrich and Heidi will set out from further down the coast in a rowing boat. Rowing boats are quiet and Ulrich knows where he can get one. They won't have time to row all the way before the tide picks up so I'm helping there as well. There's an old NPN tow-behind on my ship. It's a sort of mini-platform with a battery-driven propeller and the driver controls it from behind in a frogman's suit. I keep it for inspecting hulls. Anyway, while The Lord of Cathay is docking the captain will keep the pilot occupied and a couple of crew will strap your guns to the tow-behind, let it down on the shadow side and pull the ropes up before anyone sees. The driver will go down at the same time and he'll meet the rowing boat half way out. If Ulrich and Heidi get their timing right I don't see any problems."

"What colour's your tow-behind, Michael?" Guderius put in. "Not orange or yellow, I hope."

"No, it's a dull greeny-grey." He looked towards Steffen. "You won't see it in the dark so the driver will carry a torch to signal with. You'll need one as well. Who's supplying the guns, by the way? Linus?"

"That's right. I said you'd get a message to him to arrange delivery. And sign yourself Kestrel. That's what he's expecting."

He turned to Kurt Zimmermann.

"You, Kurt, you'll be watching the Kent end of the tunnel to tell me the flooding's actually taking place," he said. "There's a vista point near it called Spade Hill. You won't find much up there, just some parking spaces and benches, and no one will be around at the end of October. As I understand it, when the flooding starts an automatic alarm kicks in which you'll see and hear straight away. You'll also see the northbound traffic stopped at the toll booths. That's how you'll know the flooding's started.

I'll be behind the control centre with Brigitte and Frank. When the alarm goes off you'll send me the message 'Mars is red' and we all get away, you included. You'll have your own transport so you won't have to wait for anyone. On the other hand, if I don't hear from you punctually, I'll send you the message 'Full moon' to say the operation's aborted and again, we all make our getaway."

"We'll be using our mobiles, will we?"

"They're too dangerous, Kurt, even switched off. So, no one will have one and that's an order. I'll get some long-range walkie-talkies instead. And we won't go back to Germany straight away. We'll go to London to keep our appointments as if what's happened's got nothing to do with us. At some point I have to get your gun back, Kurt, but you see how easy it is."

"So we'll all be leaving London, driving down the M2/A2 to the Sheppey Link Road, then turning north towards the island. And I'll peel off before I get there and head for Spade Hill."

"Correct. Brigitte will bring Klaus; you, Kurt, will bring Frank; and Heidi will bring me. Frank will transfer to Brigitte's car along the way, leaving you with a car to yourself."

"Who will these cars belong to?"

"They'll be hired."

"But Ulrich, British highways have surveillance cameras on them just like German ones. They're also lit up at night so even if you travel after dark your hired cars will be recorded and that means they can be traced back to whoever hired them."

"I'm ahead of you there, Kurt. On the morning of New Hope you and Brigitte will have cars waiting for you on your hotel car parks and envelopes with their keys in them will be at Reception. Those envelopes will also contain slips saying what make and colour the cars are, what their registrations are and which bays they're standing in. There'll be cars for me and Heidi as well – one for when we pick the guns up and another one for New Hope itself. They'll be left near Heidi's flat. When we're finished the cars will be collected and returned for us and that will complete the cut-out because the only people connected with those cars will be Chameleon agents using false identities."

"And if one of us gets pulled over and has to show his papers? Or has an accident? What then?"

Steffen turned to Danzig.

"Have you ever been pulled over in England, Brigitte?"

"Never."

"Heidi?"

"Not once."

"Neither have I. The risk is there, I know, but it's too small to stop us and if we should get arrested we'll use the trial to tell the world what we wanted to do and why. Don't forget, when we reveal the British government is prepared to drown perfectly ordinary citizens in a perfectly ordinary road tunnel media interest will go through the roof. It won't be as good as doing the flooding because there won't be any distress but it won't be a long way short."

It was a shrewd combination of heroics and risk assessment and it worked.

"Can we go to Sheppey and see the site for ourselves?" Danzig asked, entirely content with what she'd heard so far.

"No, someone might remember seeing you there. I'll have to show Heidi and Klaus round because they'll be getting you, Frank and me off the island in the dark. But you and Frank will be shooting from fixed positions and Kurt won't be doing that even."

But Frank Zimmermann wasn't as used to slotting into a system as the others. It was the generation gap. How could he function properly if he didn't know where he was, he asked. It looked as if there could be trouble but Kapner, after a stab of anxiety she only just managed to conceal, headed it off.

"Frank's right," she put in quickly. "He needs to see the site for himself. But he doesn't have to go there to do it."

"Google Earth, I suppose," Guderius grunted, brushing crumbs off his lap.

"Not the internet, Klaus," Steffen snapped. "I forbid it absolutely."

Kapner began again.

"Try this then, Ulrich. When I've got extra-special clients I sometimes use a helicopter company called London and County Sky Rides. One of its routes is called Scenic Kent. It goes out to the White Cliffs of Dover and on the way back – wait for it - it flies up the estuary, over the Kent end of the North Sea Tunnel and over the Isle of Sheppey. So all Frank has to do is fake a holiday in London with Kurt and book onto this route like any other tourist. The only thing is, he'll have to book ahead of time because customers are one thing Sky Rides is never short of."

Steffen wasn't happy but he didn't want things to come apart either.

"All right," he said. "I agree. But no contact with Heidi while you're over there and no follow-up car trip to Sheppey. Is that understood, Frank? And you, Kurt?"

Kurt Zimmermann spoke for both of them.

"Understood, Ulrich."

"In that case we'll do the same as with the hired cars. Your tickets will be pre-bought for you using cash. Once the ride's set up your hotel will be booked using cash again. That way round you won't wind up with a hotel booking but no ride.

And we'll keep the room price low," he added pointedly. Then, a little less harshly, "You'll get word as soon as it's done, Kurt."

Steffen promised follow-ups for everyone and then it was time to finish. The air was stale, the food and drinks were gone and Steffen was feeling his age. While they were standing up and stretching he fetched the coats. Danzig and Lederer went first. As the Zimmermanns were about to leave he asked his old friend how business was in England.

"Couldn't be better, Ulrich. There's a massive new hub opened in south-east Kent. It's between the Channel Tunnel railway terminal and the M20 motorway."

"What, Cheriton Broadspace?"

"That's the one. It's generating so much work for us, we're looking to buy some more lorries."

"That's good to hear. Keep me posted."

Kapner and Guderius stayed back, saying they'd help with the clearing up. They reckoned Steffen might want a few words with them on their own. He did.

He locked the patio door, thanked Kapner for her message and told her not to let Carey into her flat before 18.00. He and Guderius would get there between 16.00 and 16.30. He needed to fix some things before Carey arrived.

"I'm flying back tomorrow," she said. "When are you two coming over?"

"Saturday for Klaus and Sunday for me. We'll use different airports as well."

"And where will you be storing the guns, as if I didn't know?"

"It has to be, Heidi. There's nowhere safer."

They tidied the room up, switched the spotlights off and folded the banner away. Steffen wrapped the dead cat and his gloves in a garbage bag and put them in the bin for household waste. In the morning, before Helga-Marie got up, he'd shred his flip-chart sketches and wash the towel through. Kapner washed the aquarium and Steffen rinsed and dried it. It was just fine for Robert's birthday. There wasn't a mark on it and Steffen now knew it wouldn't leak.

"By the way," Guderius said as he pulled on his coat. "Hanna's come across a new treatment for arthritis and I have to say, there might be something to it. Can she tell Walter about it?"

Steffen's grateful smile was spontaneous and warm. Guderius had caught him on his blind side.

"Of course she can and my thanks to her, Klaus. But she's not to tell Helga-Marie. She's not good at disappointments any more. She's had too many."

After Kapner and Guderius had gone Steffen made himself some iced water and lay back in one of the easy chairs. He hadn't realised how exhausted he was. It was only New Hope that was keeping him going. A lot of people were going to die but it had to be and he wouldn't be to blame. Blame lay with the cowards who'd capitulated to the West, not with him. He finished his water and went into Helga-Marie's bedroom. She'd taken her sleeping tablets and was out to the wide.

"Good night, precious," he whispered as he kissed her silver-white hair. "I wonder what Hanna's found for you. If love could make you well you'd have been better years ago."

He eased the door to and went into his own bedroom, hoping he'd dream of Helga-Marie walking without a stick. Or perhaps he'd dream of playing games with Robert and Daniela and everyone having to shout because they were laughing so loudly. They were his favourite dreams. He never dreamed of New Hope and he didn't want to. New Hope was for when he was awake.

12

Carey returns to Kapner's flat

On Monday September 28th there was rain in the air. Kapner did her chores, ran some errands, dyed her hair and had a snack lunch in the kitchen. Then she prepared a syringe of Cytofane, safety-capped it and stowed it in the same bedside drawer as before. An opened pot of hair gel was already in there and so was a pack of tissues. Finally she made the bed and drew the curtains. Whatever might happen she wanted to be ready for it.

At ten past four the doorbell rang. Next to the clothes cupboard in the hall was an oil painting of a Scottish glen. She pressed the frame towards the wall and slid the painting sideways on concealed runners. Behind it was a monitor. It showed Steffen waiting outside. He had a laptop in one hand and a box-like container in the other. A document case was clamped under his arm. Without bothering to slide the painting back she let him in and he stood his things down. When she took his coat it was dampish but not actually wet.

"Don't put it in there," he said as she went to hang it in the cupboard. "If Carey sees a man's coat in there it could make him wonder. The same goes for Klaus's coat when he comes."

As he spoke the doorbell rang again and the monitor showed Guderius. After Kapner had let him in she slid the painting back and put their coats away in her bedroom. Like Steffen, Guderius ignored her hair. Being cautious by nature she made them both wait in the hallway while she checked the blinds and drew the curtains in the living room. Guderius was staying at the Dorchester again. Steffen had told him to take the underground to Leicester Square and walk from there to Orange Street. As he passed the theatre ticket outlet in the Square a zip-up grip with three parcels in it found its way into his hand. Steffen took it from him and unpacked it onto the floor.

"Hide these somewhere," he told Kapner as he unwrapped three pairs of long-range walkie-talkies and looked them over. "And make sure the batteries stay good."

Kapner looked them over as well then put them back in the grip along with the wrapping paper.

"I'll keep them in my safe," she said. "Shall I make some coffee before I sit down?"

"I've got a job to do first. Have you got a small table I can use?"

"There's the serving trolley in the kitchen. Will that do?"

He said it would and then she couldn't help him any more so, getting ready for Carey, she moved the chair she'd sat on the previous Monday back into position and let Guderius sit on it while she sat in the low chair. She didn't want him staring up her skirt just now – she wasn't in the mood. Steffen, meanwhile, had positioned the trolley over a socket in the back wall and brought his things in from the hall.

"You could've used my laptop," Kapner said from her chair. "It would've saved you lugging yours around."

"It's not mine and you don't have the software. It's a bit special."

He placed a standard lamp near the trolley to see better with, brought an upright chair over from the dining table and fetched a sheaf of Steffen's Bakery correspondence out of his document case. Each letter had "Copy made" plus an oversize numeral written under the letterhead as if he'd numbered them to check them through in sequence. Steffen's Bakery had originally had plain black and white letterheads but, thanks to Walter, they were now multi-coloured and fancy.

"Are we allowed to watch," asked Guderius, "or is it all secret?"

"You can watch. It's secret but not from you."

He selected twelve letters from the sheaf and the rest went back into his document case for disposal. Like Kapner and Guderius he eliminated everything he didn't have to keep. Then he borrowed some scissors, cut the letterheads off and put the left-over paper likewise into his document case. Inside the box-like container was a microscope which he stood on the trolley, plugged in and switched on. It had a wide-field lens and its light was unusually bright. The laptop came last. He ran a lead between it and the microscope and brought up the name SpekTrum. Then he tried a test programme.

"Everything seems to be working," he said to himself as he switched the microscope and the laptop off.

In the silence that followed he sorted the letterheads into the order he wanted them in, placed them next to the microscope and looked round the room. An imitation Japanese screen caught his eye and he moved it in front of the trolley. He didn't want Carey seeing what was on it when he came in. He might start asking questions.

"We'll have that coffee now," he said to Kapner and once it was ready he turned to Guderius.

"In the old days, Klaus, microdots were the standard way of smuggling classified documents. You used a special camera and you shrank your images down till they looked like a full stop. Then you stuck this fake full stop over a real one in a book, say, and whoever the book was sent to prised it off, enlarged it and read it. Heidi will know all about microdots from her Stasi days."

Kapner nodded and smiled. Just hearing the word brought back memories.

"Now, all the letterheads I've just been sorting have miniaturised photos printed in them. They're not all in one piece, they're broken up and each fragment is coloured by computer to blend in with what's around it. When I feed them into the laptop from the microscope I can put them together again, take the colouring out and show them as they really are. You'll see for yourselves once Carey's here."

"What's your software again?" Kapner asked. "Did I see the word SpekTrum?"

She spelled it from memory, including the capital T.

"That's what it's called, Heidi. The British developed it for MI6 and the same old friend who slipped Klaus the radios got me a copy. She's also loaned me the microscope and the laptop so all I brought through airport security was the letterheads – which, of course, no one looked at twice."

They had time on their hands till Carey was due so they drifted back to the old days and as the memories flowed, Steffen's hard exterior gave way to an outgoing, friendly personality. In his Military Attaché days he'd turn it on and off as a tactic but now he was just letting it happen.

As six o'clock approached they moved into the kitchen. The coffee cups disappeared into the dishwasher, thin slices of bread went into the toaster and Royal Beluga caviar was spooned into a china serving bowl. A bottle of ice wine was already in the fridge and Kapner stood the same two small glasses next to the menu of a restaurant that delivered gourmet meals. When everything was ready she sent Steffen and Guderius back into the living room, put the lamp on in the spare bedroom and left the door half open. Then in her own bedroom she put on frilly scarlet panties with a button-up flap, a matching see-through bra, a suspender belt and sheer stockings. Never would she have worn them by choice. She pulled a close-fitting frock with a zip down the back over them. It was gauzy enough to let her underwear show through if she didn't wear a petticoat. With fierce and rapid movements she brushed her hair and dabbed some scent on. The fluffy slippers came last. She called Steffen and Guderius through.

"Don't laugh and don't say anything, either of you," she scowled. "Just pay attention. Carey doesn't know this is my bedroom and it's where you'll be when he comes. You can secure the door with this bolt and if you're careful, it won't make any noise. I'll give Carey the Ophrene in the living room soon after he gets here and we'll take it from there. If anything goes wrong I'll get to this door somehow and tap three times. Otherwise you come out when you hear five taps in a row."

"Where's the Cytofane?" Guderius asked.

"In a syringe in the bedroom across the way. It's in the top drawer of the bedside cabinet."

Carey was dead on time. The monitor showed him holding a bunch of flowers and for some reason he'd brought his briefcase. Steffen and Guderius disappeared into Kapner's bedroom and bolted the door. Kapner hid the monitor and opened the outside door.

As Carey came in he shyly handed her the flowers – they were dark red hothouse roses – and as soon as the door was closed he kissed her lovingly. She hung his coat and jacket in the cupboard and waited while he took off his shoes, this time without knotting his laces. She asked him whether he wanted her to take his briefcase as well but he gave her a wily smile and said no, he preferred to hang onto it. When he was ready she ushered him into the living room and he sat down in "his" easy chair.

"I'll put these lovely flowers in a vase," she said. "Then I'll get something nice for both of us."

She came back with the caviar, the toast and the menu on a tray. She said she'd fetch the wine separately. She didn't want to spill it.

"Be having a look in the menu," she said, emptying the tray onto the coffee table. "The main course is in the bedroom but I'm sure we'll want some afters."

She tickled the lobe of his ear with the tip of her tongue and carried the tray back to the kitchen. She'd been afraid he'd behave like a ram on amphetamines if only to show he could but he was strangely subdued and she didn't know whether to be pleased or worried. She poured out the ice wine, added an Ophrene tablet to the glass with the pattern on it and took both glasses plus the bottle into the living room on a smaller tray. Carey's glass and the bottle went onto coasters on the coffee table but she kept her own glass in her hand as she sat down. She hooked her slippers off and touched his toes with hers.

"Here's to us!" she exclaimed but before she could get any further Carey held up his hand to stop her.

"One moment, Heidi," he said with a smile that was both timid and earnest. "I can't tell you how much it means to me, our being together again, so I've brought something to say it for me. Two things, in fact. Let me give them to you now. Then we'll drink to our lasting happiness."

He reached into his briefcase and drew out a brand new photograph album bound in dark brown leather. It had "Heidi and Lesley" stamped on the front in gold letters that were even more lavish than the ones on Manfred Voss's tombstone. In the four corners gold Cupids were aiming at the names with their bows and arrows.

"From now on my home will be yours, my sweet, so I've put these photos together. They show my house in Rochester, which you've not seen yet, and the town around it, which I know you'll like as much as I do. There's a photo of me on the second page" – he turned to it so she could see it – "and the space next to it is for one of you. On the first page I've hand-written 'For Heidi – the end of my loneliness'."

He showed her that as well.

"Lesley, you darling!" she burst out, wondering what the second thing he'd brought would be. "What a beautiful, beautiful thought! You'll get a gigantic reward very shortly, I promise you. I've got the feeling already."

He laid the album reverently on his knees, reached into his briefcase again and took out a small jewellery case covered in time-darkened maroon leather. He opened it carefully and pulled out a gold heart-shaped locket by its chain.

"This locket," he said, holding it up so Kapner could see it, "belonged to my mother. She left it to me when she died. My late father gave it to her when they fell in love and after they married he had it engraved. There's a little stud here on the side of the heart. When you press it the heart springs open and you can see my mother's and father's initials. Underneath it says 'Forever'. It's very precious to me, Heidi, but not as precious as you are. I want you to have it."

He began to get up to give it to her but the chair's low height and its softness made it less than easy to do so he lost control of the photograph album, which he was trying to hold by pressing it against his legs with his free hand. It slipped sideways, landed on the coffee table and turned his wine glass over, emptying it out. As he lunged after it he knocked the bottle over and the wine poured out before he could get to it. Most of the toast and caviar landed on the carpet as well.

Before Kapner could stop him, he'd laid the locket and the album on the seat of his chair and was on his hands and knees spooning the caviar back into the serving bowl and sponging the carpet with his handkerchief, all the while exclaiming how clumsy he was, his mother had said it a million times, and how terribly sorry he was. But Kapner, as she stuffed her feet into her slippers, had only one thought in mind – he'd spilled the Ophrene. If she'd been alone with him in the flat she'd have found a way to mix up some more but with Steffen and Guderius in her bedroom, she suddenly hoped it mightn't be necessary. She'd ask. She reckoned Carey wouldn't let her do any cleaning up, he'd feel compelled to do it himself, so she quickly fetched a pedal bin she didn't use much, a cloth, some cleaner and some bottled water and watched him rub and dab like a skivvy. Before long he'd created a wet patch that smelled of detergent and was appreciably larger than the one caused by the wine. It was time to get to Steffen.

"Give the carpet one last scrub to get the wine right out," she said. "I'll get a fresh cloth to dry the patch you've made."

She closed the living room door behind her and tapped softly three times on her bedroom door. She only heard the bolt being drawn because she was listening for it. The door opened a fraction and she saw Guderius's questioning face. Steffen hadn't heard her. Then Guderius stepped back smartly and she was talking to Steffen.

Quickly she told him what had happened.

"What do you want me to do?" she asked.

"Forget the Ophrene," the reply came back. "Settle him down, keep him facing away from the living room door and get him stripped if you can. We'll take care of the rest."

He closed the bedroom door and as she darted into the kitchen Carey came bustling in clutching the pedal bin and the cleaning things.

"I'm sure the carpet's clean now," he burbled, placing everything on the floor next to his stockinged feet. "All I need is the dry cloth you promised me and you won't know anything's happened. Oh, Heidi," he went on, his mood plunging from jubilant to abject, "I feel I've spoilt everything. All the trouble you've taken and I ... well, I apologise profoundly."

She drew his head down and kissed him on the forehead. It was sweaty from where he'd been scrubbing at the carpet in the warm room.

"Don't be so silly," she tutted as she pulled a cloth out of a drawer. "It's nothing, really it isn't, and to prove it, we'll play the clothes game. That was always your favourite, wasn't it?"

He held the cloth as if it were a prize he'd won and nodded vigorously. She fixed her gaze on the kitchen clock.

"I'll give you five minutes to dry the carpet properly, then I'll come in and we'll start the game. Now give me a big loving kiss and be off with you."

As soon as he'd gone she went back to Steffen and told him what she'd arranged.

"Five minutes," he said, checking his watch. "He won't hold out that long. You'd better get in there now."

He bolted the door again.

"We'll give Heidi time to get her game set up," he whispered to Guderius, "then we'll move in. I'll go first and you hang back a bit. You know where the Cytofane is. Make sure you bring it with you."

13

Steffen shows his killer streak

When Kapner joined Carey in the living room she brought some paper and two biros with her. She watched him mauling the carpet for a bit then told him to leave it, adding,

"Move your chair round so you don't breathe in the detergent. The fumes aren't good for you."

He slid it round till its back was towards the door.

"Couldn't be better. Now pull my chair round so we're still looking at each other. Then you can sit down."

When she sat down herself she was right where she wanted to be: she could see past him to her bedroom door. The photo album and locket were safely on the coffee table. She handed him a sheet of paper and one of the biros.

"Let's see if I've got the rules right," she said, tapping her pen against her front teeth.

She'd had to play the game often enough to know them by heart but checking them would make him forget there was an open door behind him.

"You tell me what you're wearing," she went on, "and I write down what you say. When you're finished I tell you what I'm wearing and you write it down. Then we swap lists and put a secret number next to each piece of clothing. I'm going first so when I call out a number, you take off whatever's got that number next to it. If something's in the way, like if your trousers are in the way of your boxer shorts, you say 'Can't be done' and I call out another number to keep the game going."

She realised how much she was relying on Steffen when she said the next bit.

"When we've both gone through our lists you can ask me to sit on your lap and I'll rub against you the way I did last time."

He had no idea how that was but he winked gruesomely as if he did.

"I suppose you remember my boxer shorts," he chortled, "because they were, well, close to the action, if you see what I mean. That's how I remembered them too and when you get to them this time you'll see how much I've been thinking about you."

"I can't wait," she fluted and blew him a kiss. "I'm good at saying thank you for nice surprises. Now, Lesley, what are you wearing that's about to come off?"

He said his list, beginning with one Institute necktie – he emphasised the word "Institute" – and ending with one right sock.

"Come on, sweetmeat," he gurgled. "It's your turn now. I'm so keyed up I don't know whether I want you to go slow, slow, slow or fast, fast, fast."

She didn't want him to touch her so she took the decision for him. With teasing slowness she started with her stockings, first left then right. But she wasn't wearing enough to make it last and Steffen still hadn't made a move after they'd swapped and numbered their lists so she put on her coy look.

"Would you like to see my suspender belt ahead of time?" she asked. "Just a little peek to get your hormones on the move?"

It baffled her why he should say yes but she knew he would: he could never get enough of suspender belts. She stood up and slowly slid the hem of her frock up. At first he sat there goggle-eyed then, in a hurry, he started to undo his trousers. Panicking, she ordered him to do them up again, shot her frock down and sat down quickly.

"You wicked boy!" she scolded. "We'll play properly or not at all."

He looked suddenly angry and she knew she'd overreacted. She mustn't lose him now, not for anything, so she said,

"I'm sorry, Lesley, really I am but always remember: lovers have tiffs so they can make up afterwards. What's more, when you get to my panties, I'll let you undo the buttons before I take them off."

Lust and infatuation replaced the anger in his face.

"You want to show me your boxer shorts," she went on, eager to keep him in the right mood, "and I can't wait to see them. So I'm going to begin right now and my first number is two."

"Two! That's my left sock!"

He peeled it off and laid it by his chair. His Institute necktie came off next, then his right sock and, at last, his trousers. His boxer shorts were bright orange.

"There you are!" he guffawed, stretching them out for her to admire. "Orange for Orange Street! I told you I'd been thinking about you. Now, my blossom, what's my thank you going to be? You said you'd give me one."

Behind his head she could see Steffen making his way towards them. His face had a look on it that thrilled her. Instantly she understood: Steffen didn't just plan killings, he had killing in his soul. Behind Steffen Guderius trod gingerly across the hallway into the spare bedroom. When he re-emerged he had the Cytofane in his hand.

"You'll get it in just a moment, dearest, but we must finish the game first so listen closely. My next number is four."

"Four!" he squealed and slapped his thigh. "It's my boxer shorts! I'll bet you knew they were four. You must have looked somehow. But I'll still take them off. Just try and stop me."

He pressed his shoulders into the back of his chair and, raising his withered buttocks, forced his shorts down with his thumbs. If he'd not been so excited he might have sensed a swift movement behind him but then it was too late. Before he could get the elastic over his ankles Steffen slammed his hand over his mouth and forced his head against the back of the chair.

"Don't move," he ordered into his ear. "This is Ulrich Steffen talking to you. When I take my hand away don't make a single sound if you want to stay alive."

Carey's eyes shot wide open. Kapner had said she'd lost touch with Steffen yet here he was in her flat. Steffen held him fast till he stopped pulling at his hand. Guderius was waiting just inside the doorway, the uncapped syringe ready to use. Carey couldn't move his head so he had no idea anyone else had crept up on him apart from Steffen. Steffen removed his hand and stepped fully into Carey's view. Carey stayed absolutely still and Kapner automatically withdrew to the side of the room.

"Stand up, Lesley, but don't look round," Steffen told him.

He did as he was told.

"Now move as I direct you but take your time and don't trip over your shorts."

Steffen motioned him sideways till he was clear of the chair. There was no merriment in Carey's face now, only fear and an exaggerated keenness to show willing. Steffen stepped towards him as if he was going to shake his hand but he seized both his shoulders instead, pushed him off balance without letting go and scythed his legs out from under him. As he went down Steffen dropped to his knees with him and pinned him on his back.

"Stay perfectly still," he ordered without raising his voice. "Heidi, hold his feet. Don't let him try to kick."

She came forward, grasped his ankles through his boxer shorts and pressed them into the carpet.

"How do you want him, Klaus?" Steffen called in German. "As he is or on his front?"

"As he is," came Guderius's soft, even voice. "He has to see it happen, doesn't he?"

That was when Carey knew Steffen had someone with him but even when Guderius came into view he didn't see the syringe because Guderius was holding it behind his back. Kneeling down ponderously opposite Steffen he paused for a moment as if he was assessing a piece of furniture. It was the first time he'd seen Carey and he was curious. Then one-handedly he tugged Carey's shirt up above his hip, made a fold of some fatty skin, slanted the needle in with the other hand and depressed the plunger. When the syringe was empty he calmly drew it out, reached into his jacket pocket and safety-capped it.

When the needle had gone into him Carey had assumed he'd pass out within seconds. When he didn't he didn't know what to think. He looked from face to face for an answer.

"He's all over the place," Guderius said to Steffen in German. "Be nice to him. It'll pay off."

"I'll get round to it. But first a drop more fear, I think"

He told Kapner to let go of his ankles then he released his shoulders and stood up.

"You can get up now," he said. "You see, you're alive after all."

Carey laboured to his feet, pulled his shorts up and straightened his shirt while Steffen told Kapner to make some sandwiches along with some tea and coffee. Guderius followed her into the kitchen.

"That photo album marked 'Heidi and Lesley," he said, laying the capped syringe down carefully. "What's it all about?"

She told him. She told him about the locket as well.

"Why don't I bin them in front of him?" she asked. "I might as well get a laugh out of them."

"Hang onto them, Heidi, that's my advice. If we have to, we can bend his soul with them."

It was the answer she'd have given if their roles had been reversed but she still didn't like it so she banged the crockery around in a sulk. But then, like the week before, she brightened up. She'd seen the Cytofane go in and Carey was now under sentence of death. The Cytofane might not go to term – October 26th would get in the way – but that it was in at all gave her one big, big rush. It was wonderful. She hoped it hurt him beyond belief.

"Everything's in here somewhere," she chirped, gesturing round the kitchen. "Make a move on the sandwiches while I get changed."

Guderius reached for her bottom and gave it a full-handed squeeze.

"Why don't I come and help you?" he asked. "Your bum's more interesting than sandwiches."

She grabbed his hand, crooked his little finger and pressed the tip inwards. He grimaced with not-quite-pretended pain then they both laughed.

"Another time, Klaus," she replied and gave him another of her old-friends kisses as she picked the syringe up to put it away.

She knew she was safe with Guderius. One summer's evening in Bad Sollmer when – two girls together – she and Gannisch were making inroads into Gannisch's stock of slivovicz, Gannisch had told her what she knew already: Guderius couldn't do it and what was more, he didn't want to. Gannisch liked him that way. It stopped him wandering off.

When Kapner came back she was wearing a prim denim two-piece with an opaque matching blouse and she felt a lot better for it. Carey, meanwhile, was fully dressed and Steffen had moved some chairs into a tight semi-circle facing the imitation Japanese screen. They ate the sandwiches and drank the tea and coffee in a silence so complete that, despite the drawn curtains and the double glazing behind them, they faintly but distinctly heard Big Ben chiming. Steffen was the first to speak.

"I'm sorry we've treated you like this, Lesley, but we've got something very important on and we need your co-operation. There are one or two things you can tell us and we're also going to ask you to do something."

"You're wasting your time, Ulrich. And you can't buy me either, so don't even try. I don't need your money these days."

Instead of answering Steffen moved the screen away from the trolley and switched on the microscope and laptop. Then he picked up the first of the letterheads and slid it under the microscope. After a bit of searching and adjusting he brought up a black-and-white photo of himself and Carey. It came from Steffen's Attaché file. They both looked years younger but there was no mistaking who they were. In the background was a tiled English fireplace with a print of Tintern Abbey over it, which he enlarged so they could all see it clearly. The photo was grainy, as if it'd been taken with a hidden camera that could've done with a flash.

"Ulrich, that's us," Carey gasped, going chalk white but unable to look away. "We're in your little house in London. It's the house we used when we talked about the tunnels."

"It wasn't my little house, it was the Stasi's. I've got plenty more pictures besides this one. Here, let me show you."

Sometimes he and Carey were wearing jackets, sometimes they were in shirtsleeves, but it was always the two of them, the tiled fireplace and Tintern Abbey.

"Now look at these," he said and his tone hardened.

"These" were three pages from a transcript that had been typed on a ribbon typewriter. Date and place were given at the top of each page. Steffen was asking the questions and his own name was typed in. The person giving the answers was named as Benedict. The transcript didn't seem to be edited very much. It didn't need to be. They were mostly talking data.

"As you can see," Steffen continued, "my name's on the transcript in clear. That's because I didn't have to hide it. But you had two names, Lesley. You were Lesley Carey, the British tunnel expert, but to some people you were also Benedict, the British traitor. Look, here's both your names at once."

He brought up a fresh page from the same file. In the type-writing of long ago Benedict was identified as Carey.

"It's deniable," Carey blustered. "All of it. The GDR was always faking evidence. Everyone knows that."

"Well, perhaps they do but let's look at some more shots first. You English don't say 'snaps' any more, do you? You used to when I was in London but nothing dates like slang."

He showed some equally grainy pictures from Daski's file. This time Carey was with a young-looking Kapner. Sometimes they were dressed as if they'd come in from outside, sometimes they were partly clothed or naked and this time the identifiers were a rubber plant in the living room and a ewer and bowl in the bedroom with "Sunny Blackpool" on them. In both rooms the floral curtains were always drawn.

"Do you know where these were taken?" Steffen asked.

"Heidi's place."

It was all he was going to say.

Steffen screened some more transcripts. This time the questioner was Cormorant and the editing looked heavy.

"If I have to," Steffen said affably but on the alert all the same, "I'll share all this with the British authorities. I can't be touched, nor can Heidi, we were only doing our job, but you can, Lesley, because the files these images come from also detail all the payments you received. And there are tape-recordings too, each one with your voice print on it. You were a traitor under British law and it's provable."

"I'd lose my job, my pension and my fellowship if this came out," Carey burst out. "But I'll say they're all forgeries and that's your goose cooked."

"Let me show you some more photos while you think things over. My own organisation took these - quite recently, in fact, as you'll see for yourself."

They showed Carey entering and leaving the Institute during his lecture series. They were computer-enhanced when the light was bad and they were in colour. So were the ones of him and Kapner in St James's Park and again outside Kapner's flat. Kapner hadn't known they were being taken. It was as if ice over deep water was cracking under her feet.

"The British press can have these for free," Steffen said. "You can imagine the headlines. 'Traitor Trysts In Royal Park' perhaps or 'Bonking Über Alles' – I'm not as good as The Sun but you get the idea. These and the other shots would finish you nicely."

Carey could see that all right but he could see something else as well. Twice he asked to see the Stasi's shots of himself and Kapner, then Steffen's new ones. Breathing hard he compared her hair, her coat and her shoulder bag and saw precisely what Kapner hadn't wanted him to see – that he'd been set up. Rage and grief boiled up inside him and Steffen only just stopped him from grabbing Kapner's throat. His passion flowed through Steffen's arms like a high voltage current, then it gave way to despair and he slumped back in his chair. After a long moment he said,

"You wanted some information from me. What is it? And what do you want me to do?"

Nervously he looked round at the others and his eyes settled on Guderius. That started him up again and his voice got louder.

"But don't answer me yet," he snapped. "I want to know who this man is first. I also want to know what he injected me with and I insist you tell me now."

"That's a lot of questions," Steffen replied easily. Carey hadn't realised the photos and transcripts could damage Steffen and Kapner. That meant Steffen could take his time getting to the Cytofane. "If I may, I'll take the first one first," he said. "Then, when we've talked it through, I'll see about the others."

"Your answers had better be good, Ulrich, or you'll be in big trouble. I'm not just anybody, you know. I know some very important people."

He folded his arms decisively and waited for Steffen's replies.

14

Carey makes his choice

"The North Sea Tunnel's flooding mechanism," Steffen began, "reminds me of a set of Russian dolls. The biggest doll is the control centre with its wire fence round it and inside it is a compound with its own wire fence. Inside the compound is a locked blockhouse and inside that is the flooding mechanism. That's pretty tight security, Lesley, and it doesn't stop there because to get into this inner compound you have to get past two soldiers in armoured guard boxes. That's right, isn't it?"

"It is."

"Do you happen to know what their weapons are?"

"Heckler and Koch carbines plus 9mm Glocks – all loaded, of course. Those soldiers are there to stop people."

"Of course. By the way, I'm not tiring you, am I?"

"Not at all. My stamina's well known. I can outlast anyone if I have to."

"That's good to hear. Now, these soldiers are on two hour shifts so what happens when the shifts change?"

"An army Land Rover brings the new guards over from the mainland and my security people check them in. The Land Rover parks near the inner compound, the new guards get out and the old ones go straight back to base. Too many duties and not enough men, you see. I blame the Socialists. Why anyone votes for them defeats me."

"Do you ever get gaps between shifts?"

"Never. If the Land Rover gets held up the guards on duty stay till it arrives."

"That is, they stay in their armoured boxes. But they're not always in there, are they?"

"Not at first, no. When the new guards come on one of them walks round the outside of the inner compound to check the fencing while the other one watches him or her - we live in

117

enlightened times – on his monitors. When that's done the gate to the inner compound and the steel door on the blockhouse are checked to make sure they unlock and relock on demand."

"So how is the unlocking and relocking done?"

"Both guards have what are called combi-keys. They carry them in a zip-up pocket on their left-hand trouser leg since most people are right handed when it comes to holding a gun. Essentially the combi-keys are zappers with two green and two red buttons on them. One green button opens the gate to the inner compound, the other one unlocks the blockhouse door and the red buttons do the relocking. If anything happens to one guard – he might collapse, say, or get attacked – the other one can control things from where he stands. He doesn't have to go anywhere and he doesn't have to put his weapon down. The combi-keys are handed on at change of shift and, incidentally, if one guard ever does anything suspect the other one can shoot him. It's in their rules of engagement."

"This is excellent, Lesley," Steffen purred and told Kapner in German to give him a smile or two. "Now, if you'll just finish off what the guards do ..."

Carey wasn't far from his public lecture manner now.

"Well, the first guard unlocks the gate to the inner compound, goes in and relocks it from the inside while the second one stands outside and covers him with his carbine. The first guard then unlocks the blockhouse door and checks inside. He knows what to look for, it's part of his training. If everything's in order, as it always is, the first guard relocks the door, lets himself out through the gate and relocks it. After that both guards go into their guard boxes, log what they've done and stay there till change of shift."

"The blockhouse is unmanned, isn't it? There are just lights and surveillance cameras inside."

"That's how it is and the lights are always on. I won't have darkness in there, not at any time."

"And neither you nor the Senior Site Manager nor anyone else apart from the soldiers can enter the inner compound or the blockhouse without an explicit instruction from your Ministry of the Interior. What you call the Home Office."

"No instruction, no entry. Nothing happens without word from the Ministry."

"But the guards go in. Doesn't that make them a security risk?"

"Guards go into Fort Knox but it hasn't been robbed yet. These guards are hand-picked. Take my word for it, they're safe all right."

Steffen had already come to that conclusion. Suborning the guards had never been an option.

"Well, let's move on to the blockhouse. Can you tell us what's inside it?"

Carey hesitated.

"I think you should."

It was a touch of the whip. Carey stopped hesitating.

"Basically it's a console and it's always powered up."

"So the flooding mechanism is always ready to go."

"Of course. How else can it respond rapidly?"

"Easy, Lesley. You forget I'm only a baker these days."

"Ah, yes, you're right to remind me. Anyway, if you want to clear the tunnel before you flood it there are two white buttons to do it with. The one labelled 'On' starts the alarm and stops traffic coming in, and if you need to cancel, you press the one labelled 'Off'. There are five buttons for flooding the tunnel – four for the traffic tubes and one for the service tube. They're all bright red and they're also clearly labelled. You don't have to clear the tunnel to use them and if the alarm isn't running when you press them, it automatically comes on when you do.

Above the console there's a plan of the tunnel plus a bank of monitors that shows every part in real time. Anything can be zoomed in on and an oversize monitor gives you all the detail you need. The camera controls are in their own section of the console and they're all labelled too. In other words, Ulrich, there's nothing a corporal couldn't operate, let alone a colonel."

"Ah, he thinks it's me who's going in there," Steffen said to himself. "Well, I won't put him straight just yet."

"So you can actually watch the water pour in, can you?" asked Kapner, remembering the drowning cat.

"You get a ringside seat, Heidi! The cameras and lighting in the tunnel are all high up so they won't get flooded till the tubes are nearly full. Normally the cameras are operated from Site Security and all the blockhouse gets is a default feed but you can see for yourself, whoever switches the flooding on has to have control of the cameras as well."

"Can the flooding can be switched off once it's on?"

"Yes, there's a big amber button labelled 'Abort Flooding'. There's not much point to it, though."

"I should've thought switching off the flooding had a lot of point," Guderius put in.

"Only if it was started and then stopped straight away. All five tubes have high-pressure inlets built into the roof. They're closely spaced and once the red buttons are pressed, the water pours in like Niagara and the air is sucked out as fast. So, say you started the flooding and I came running into the blockhouse to stop you. Just getting you out of the way would make me too late. Even if I shot you as I came through the door I'd still probably be too late. The abort button's a sop to politicians. In practice no one can use it fast enough."

"Not even in your Home Office?" asked Steffen, who'd heard exactly what he wanted to hear. "You once told me it was permanently linked in. You also said it could override if it had to."

"So it could but by the time it got round to it the tubes would be either full or as good as."

"What happens when they're full?"

"The pumps stop. The tunnel's standard shaped. It slopes down to bedrock, levels out and then slopes up again. All the level bit gets flooded plus half way up the sloping bits. Then back-pressure turns the pumps off."

Guderius leaned forward in his chair.

"If you're drowning, an alarm won't help you very much," he observed in his easy-going way. "So if an alarm always sounds when the flooding starts it can't be for people in the tunnel. It must be for staff outside."

"That's right and they know exactly what to do. The ones inside have no chance unless they're near the ends of the tunnel. It's sad but it has to be."

"Perhaps a memorial plaque would help. But that aside, unless there's something distinctive about this flooding alarm of yours, your staff might think it's just the tunnel being emptied or something completely ordinary like a crash. That could cost some of them their lives."

Steffen was all ears. This was something he'd missed.

"Do you think I haven't thought of that? The toll booths have a mauve light in them and so do all the other front line staff locations. It's as big as a saucer and if it flashes when the alarm goes off it means just one thing: the tunnel's being flooded. My system is foolproof, you see."

"That's something for Kurt," thought Steffen. "I'll get word to him."

It was time to wind things up.

"Thanks for that, Lesley," Steffen said. "Now, if Heidi will get me some A4 and felt-tips I'll ask you to draw me a labelled plan of the whole control centre. Include the floodlights, please. They're important."

"It'd be easier on a computer. It's a lot of information."

"Sorry, Lesley. Computers leave traces. You can use more than one sheet of paper if you like."

Working methodically, Carey spread his knowledge over six sheets of A4. When he'd finished Steffen laid them out on the carpet so Kapner and Guderius could see them.

"Lesley's done his usual good job," he said, keeping to English, "and, as I'd hoped, he's made one or two things very obvious. For example, we don't have to shoot out all the lights. If we take out these here" – he picked out those that lit up the blockhouse and its fencing – "we can dim down the inner compound plus some of the space round it and that will be enough. And if we take out these" – he traced a line from the inner compound to the main gate – "we can create a corridor of twilight for someone to escape down. We needn't bother about the surveillance cameras. It isn't not being seen that matters, it's not being stopped."

"Hence the corridor of twilight," Carey put in with a knowing smirk towards Kapner. "When lights go out and people don't know why, they either react slowly or they don't react at all. You'll be all right, Ulrich, I can vouch for it. You'll have a clear run."

"So will you, Lesley, because it's your escape we're talking about, not mine."

"My escape? How do you mean, my escape?"

His voice sounded tight. His vocal chords already knew what his mind was still shutting out.

"Come now," said Steffen. "You've given me the information I asked for and now you know what I want you to do as well. I want you to flood the tunnel."

Carey went greenish-yellow. One by one he scrutinised their faces as if, just possibly, one of them would signal what he'd heard wasn't true. But no one did and, he could see, no one would.

"You're mad, all of you!" he burst out. "You'll kill thousands of people! Thousands, I tell you!"

"You could be right," Steffen said as he put the plan of the control centre in his document case. "Certainly many hundreds. There's no upper limit."

"But why? What good will it do?"

"We're not prepared to tell you that but please understand this: you will start those pumps because you have no choice. You know some of the holds we have on you but there's one you don't know yet and I don't think you'll argue with it."

Before Carey could speak Steffen gestured towards Guderius.

"You asked me who this gentleman was and what he injected you with. He can answer those questions now. Then you'll understand what I mean."

Guderius gave Carey his big benign smile.

"My name is Klaus Guderius," he began, "and I'm German, as you've probably gathered from my accent. I used to be a doctor in the National People's Army and now I own a wellness clinic near Dresden. While I was in the army our Ministry for State Security caused a drug called Cytofane to be developed. It's administered in two doses by injection and it destroys you cell by cell unless you're given an antidote called Retrotox within fifty-six days of the second dose. What I injected you with was the second dose. Your destruction clock is now running."

Carey stared at him in amazement.

"The second dose?"

The penny dropped.

"Heidi!"

She'd seen it coming and she answered straight away, echoing one of his own phrases.

"It had to be. Ulrich, Klaus and I, we have a higher allegiance. But don't forget, there's an antidote and we'll treat you with it if you do as we ask. Please say you will. I want you to live as much as anyone here."

"I feel as if I'm standing on a trapdoor with a rope round my neck. Just think of it, Heidi. I'm actually dying even as I sit here and speak to you."

"But," Steffen put in, "if you help us, you'll live. All your secrets will stay with us and we'll guarantee your getaway as well."

That aroused a glimmer of hope.

"I won't be rolled over, Ulrich, I'm not the sort and never have been. I'll decide what to do when I know more and not before."

"Very well. On the night we want you to flood the tunnel some of us – I'm not saying who – will shoot the blockhouse guards from the hillside behind the control centre. We'll also dim down the lighting round the blockhouse plus all the lighting in a line back to the main gate. In the confusion you'll take one of the combi-keys, flood the tunnel and escape through the main gate, where a car will be waiting for you with its engine running. A hiding place is already prepared for you and when the heat's off we'll give you a dream life abroad."

"What'll I do for money?"

"Not a problem. If you look after us we'll look after you. On the other hand, if you decide not to co-operate you can order your gravestone now."

It was Carey's life against the lives of possibly thousands. He didn't need to work it out.

"You win, Ulrich. I'll do what you say."

"I thought you'd see it our way. Now, just one more thing before we finish. When you leave the blockhouse after you've started the flooding, pause for a second and give a wave up the hillside to say you've done it. You won't see anything, it'll be too dark for that, but do it anyway because a certain someone might just be looking out for you."

Kapner squeezed his hand and kissed his cheek.

"I knew you were one of us," she whispered. "You've always been a hero to me. Now you're a hero with a cause."

With Carey won over, a sense of anticlimax filled the room. While he lolled exhausted in his chair and Kapner and Steffen tidied up, Guderius fetched their coats and Carey's jacket, which, like a schoolboy's, had a tag in it with his name on in indelible ink. When they were all back in the living room Steffen switched to German and said,

"I'm tied up tomorrow but I'd like us to go to Sheppey on Wednesday to reconnoitre. Can you drive us there, Heidi?"

"Is that safe? Taking my car, I mean?"

He knew what she meant. In his inner ear he could hear Kurt Zimmermann talking about surveillance cameras and cars being traced back. But he didn't hesitate for long.

"Plenty of Londoners take their friends out of town," he reasoned. "Why shouldn't you be one of them? It should be all right. It's not as if New Hope is happening the next day."

"I'll pack lunch for three," said Kapner, doing her best to look convinced. "What time do we leave?"

"08.30 from here and bring your digital camera and binoculars. But no mobiles, either of you, not even switched off. I need you to get into the habit."

As Steffen and Guderius were pulling on their coats Steffen added,

"I'm staying in Knightsbridge so I'll share a taxi with Klaus. That leaves Carey."

He switched back to English.

"How are you getting home, Lesley?"

Carey was about to mumble "I'll catch a train" when Kapner broke in. They couldn't let him loose on late-night public transport, he was too big a risk, she said in German. And if she could drive to Sheppey on Wednesday she could drive to Rochester now.

"I'll drive him back," she went on in English. "He's had a rough time, poor thing. You'll let me do that, won't you, my sweet? And I'll keep the album and the locket in my safe. They're a bond between us now."

He looked at her with red-rimmed eyes.

"Thank you, Heidi," he said but it was scarcely audible.

"If you have any leave coming in the next little while," Steffen told him, "don't take it. And don't worry about your instructions. They'll come by courier."

Steffen and Guderius left first, Guderius carrying Steffen's document case for him. The damp outside had changed to rain.

"Do you really mean to shoot all those lights out and whisk him off to the Copa Cobana?" Guderius asked.

"Of course not. I've given him hope because he needs it but if you remember, I said I'd make it dim round the blockhouse, not dark. We have to do that much to get him to go in but we'll leave enough light to shoot him by when he comes out. The Cytofane can put him under pressure but I want his mouth shut for good right there."

"Did he believe what I said about the Cytofane, do you think?"

"He can't afford not to. He'll check, of course, but in a roundabout way. My guess is, he'll go to Miriam Sobart first thing tomorrow. If he does, she knows what to say."

"You mean she knows about the Cytofane?"

"Certainly not. I've told her Carey's likely to ask for some private tests to be run. He'll give her some cock and bull story and he'll probably be tense. She can run the tests but Carey won't get the results till I say so. I'll get in touch with her late tomorrow to see if I'm right."

"We owe a lot to Heidi. She can twist him round her little finger any time she wants to."

"She's a natural, Klaus. Her Stasi supervisor once told me she was the most complete deceiver he'd ever come across. I wouldn't argue with that."

When they reached the Charing Cross Road they soon spotted a taxi. Steffen waved it down and they melted into the night.

Carey was virtually mute on the way to Rochester but outside his front gate he hugged Kapner tightly in the rain and said,

"I love you so much, Heidi," and then, "Please don't let me die."

"You'll live, I promise. Just do as we ask."

She put out her hand to touch his cheek but he was already through the gate and moving towards his front door. After he'd unlocked it, he gave her one last wave, held up his empty briefcase as a reminder and then he was gone.

When she got back to Orange Street she was as weary as she'd been the previous Monday but once again there was the clearing up to do. She didn't want to go out again so she bagged what she could for the Thames the following night, binned Carey's roses and put his album and locket into her safe. As Guderius had said, they might yet have to bend his soul with them. When she finally went to bed she knew the point of no return was getting close. She ought to be nervous but she wasn't. She was yearning for it as much as she'd yearned for anything in her life.

15

Introducing Miriam Sobart

"We're nearly there, Heidi," Steffen said from the passenger seat of Kapner's Saab. "Get into the inside lane when you can."

They were on the Sheppey Link Road between the turn-off to the tunnel and the flyover. The traffic was mostly lorries and there were plenty of them. A gap opened up, she slotted the Saab in and risked a glance out of Steffen's side window. Lounging in the back, Guderius had a more leisurely view. Everything was drab and wet. A broken-down donkey grazed mournfully by a fence and in a nearby field half a dozen sheep stared motionless in front of them. As the road started to rise, the gap between the mainland and Sheppey came into view. It was typical low tide: a thin trickle of water dividing two expanses of mud. Anyone trying to cross would sink in and stay that way.

"At high tide the mud disappears and you can use a boat," Steffen said, "except you won't find one. High tide or low tide, it makes no difference. You use the flyover or you stay where you are."

The top of the flyover was flat and long, and from it they could see the Link Road stretching up towards Sheerness. Some large drops of rain hit the windscreen and Kapner cleared them off.

"Our turn-off's just ahead," Steffen said as they came down. "Watch for the countdown signs."

The turn-off brought them onto a B road running north-westwards between scrubland and empty fields. A cluster of terrace houses marked the edge of the island and when they reached a derelict quayside Steffen told Kapner to pull up. Several small hulls lay about on the hard, some on their sides and some keel-upwards. They looked as if they hadn't been touched for years. All the rest was mud sloping outwards towards a water channel.

"You can't see them yet but we're not far from Sheerness docks," Steffen said. "We'll leave the car here and head towards them on foot. You'll see deep open water once we get this mud behind us. You'll be surprised how fast it happens."

Kapner parked in a nearby pay-and-display. As they got out they looked like three ageing tourists taking a chance on the weather. Kapner was wearing brogues, jeans and a headscarf; Steffen had opted for corduroys and his favourite walking shoes; and Guderius had city shoes on but he'd taken his necktie off in the car. They were all wearing anoraks and carrying mini rucksacks. There were no other cars about. The place was deserted.

They followed the B road northwards and before long the quayside gave way to a clumpy grass verge. The ground was flatter on the inland side and there was plenty of space for a car to stand on despite the bushes and trees. As they walked on they saw a ramshackle wooden jetty reaching out to the water channel. A good eighty percent of it was rotten, it had no protective railing and its stumpy legs were mostly on mud; but it also had high-sided, high-prowed rowing boats tied to either side of it. These were also on mud and they had their oars inside them. In or near the channel was a scattering of bigger boats. The ones in the channel were riding at anchor. The ones near it, like the rowing boats, were mud bound.

While Kapner was taking photos Steffen said,

"The only way to reach the bigger boats used to be to wait for high tide and row out from the land. Then this jetty was banged together. It's got a sort of hinge at this end made from tarred rope and rollers and those empty oil drums on the underside let it float up and down. The far end's always in water and when the tide comes in it soon reaches the rowing boats. As soon as that happens anyone wanting to go fishing or whatever can untie his rowing boat, row out to his bigger boat and keep his rowing boat astern till he's ready to come back in – the tide permitting, of course. Fishing is usually between midnight and dawn so borrowing one of these rowing boats shouldn't cause us problems."

They set off again and ahead of them the shoreline bent inwards to form a shallow bay, which the road followed round. In amongst some houses on the crown of the bend was a pub called The Castle. It had large picture windows and a rained-on patio. There was no mud in sight now, just water. Beyond the bay was a kind of promenade and at an angle from it across the water were the quays of Sheerness docks.

The promenade was really a flat-topped concrete flood barrier. There were several people on it, one or two with dogs, but its length shrank them down to less than life-size. On the landward side there was more scrubland. Run-down cottages and abandoned workshops punctuated it here and there, and a dilapidated caravan stood on a semi-cleared square it seemed to have made its own. Guderius wondered what sort of person could live in something like that but it was the view over the water Steffen wanted him and Kapner to see. Kapner took out her camera again and handed her binoculars to Guderius.

"Where that ship with the light blue band is," Steffen said, pointing towards the docks, "that's where The Lord of Cathay ties up. Heidi and I'll meet the tow-behind somewhere out in the middle there."

He let Kapner get a good sense of the place, then he said,

"We'll go to the picnic area now. We can eat when we get there then walk out to the hill behind the control centre. Oh, and Heidi, speaking of eating, we passed a service centre on the M2/A2 called the Fare 'n' Square. I want you to stop there on the way back. It'll be before the Rochester turn-off."

"I know it. Any particular time?"

"20.00 hours. We're meeting Miriam Sobart there. I rang her from a call box and Carey's been to see her all right. She wants to talk to us about him."

"We'll be there. It won't take us long."

They didn't say much as they walked back to the Saab. A high was moving in and the sky was clearing. The rest of the day would be fine.

Steffen guided Kapner back to the Link Road and made sure she didn't miss the road behind Sheerness when they came to it. Culley Ditch Road it said on the sign and she and Guderius logged it in their memories. The picnic area was bathed in sunshine but the rain had had its effect: they had it to themselves. Kapner parked the car and they looked all round, taking in all the details.

"On October 26th," Steffen said, "you two will wait here while I take Frank and Brigitte to their firing points. Our escape route is the way we've come – behind Sheerness, down the Link Road, over the flyover and on to the M2/A2. Heidi goes first, Klaus. She's more used to driving on the left than you are and it'll be dark as well."

Sandwiches and coffee gave them the chance to gossip.

"I thought Carey was supposed to be clever," Guderius said while Kapner was running through her shots, "but all those buttons with their Alice-in-Wonderland labels – how witless can you get?"

"In an emergency the Home Office might have to get someone who's totally untrained to work the flooding mechanism so he made that part dead easy and reckoned the military could take care of the rest. I don't call that witless."

"But soldiers can be shot like anybody else. He hasn't allowed for that. And one soldier can always shoot another one even if he's hand-picked. He hasn't allowed for that either."

"True but his really big problem is, the soldiers don't have any back-up and that's a money problem. You heard him say it himself: when the new guards come on the old ones get sent somewhere else. Not that I'm complaining. It gives us a weakness we need."

The ground rose and curved, there was a scattering of trees above the footpath and then Kapner and Guderius had their first view of the control centre. It struck them there were a lot of helicopters about.

"They're there for the traffic," Steffen explained. "Some are police and some are media. The ones ahead of us cover the Link Road plus the M2/A2 towards London and the ones behind us cover the approaches to the tunnel plus the M2/A2 towards Dover. They won't bother us if that's what you're thinking. They've got designated flight paths and we're not interesting enough."

"Where are they based?" asked Guderius.

"If you turn round you'll see a ridge and behind it is an inlet called Sheppey Bight. That's where their base is. It used to be the coastguards' but the police have got it now and they lease a bit to the media – duly fenced off, of course. You can walk up and have a look if you like. We've got the time."

Guderius didn't like, but Kapner was intrigued now.

"Is there anything else over there?"

"Not much. There's a company called TechMarrish but that's about it."

"TechMarrish? I've heard of them. They make fuel cells."

"They make whole test vehicles as a matter of fact. If I were still a military attaché I'd be very interested in TechMarrish. It makes absolute sense for them to be short of neighbours."

The footpath was firm and clear of brambles: even in the dark it'd be trouble free. When the trees thickened up Steffen said, "Frank will go in here" and led the way into a kind of recess.

The temperature dropped as they crossed from light to shade and the air was suddenly dank. Along the sides and at the back of the recess the trees were close together but they were more widely spaced towards the front and the undergrowth turned out to be less dense than it looked from the footpath.

"You notice how safe it is," said Steffen. "Even if someone walks right past, all Frank has to do is keep still and they won't know he's here."

They walked further along till they came to another recess.

"Brigitte will be in here," he said, "and I'll be at the far end of these trees. The ground's even higher there. It'll give me the overview I need."

When they reached the recess Steffen had picked out for himself, they sat down on a blanket Kapner had brought from the car. Down the hillside the control centre looked exactly as

Carey had drawn it and anyone moving about looked calm and relaxed. They reminded Kapner of a film she'd once seen. It was dusk and a serial murderer was watching his next victim from her back garden. The television was on, the curtains were open and she had no idea he was there till the living room door handle slowly began to turn.

One of the people they saw was Carey. He was on his own and he was carrying a clipboard. He walked purposefully till he was level with the inner compound, openly consulted his watch, wrote something down and walked purposefully back.

"What a fraud!" exclaimed Kapner, who'd been watching him through her binoculars. "He's timing his escape. I'll bet it's not the first time either."

"He's more with us than against us then," Guderius commented. "He wants to live, that's his bottom line."

As four o'clock approached Steffen took the binoculars. The new shift was arriving.

He had a good view of the main gate through a gap between two buildings. A khaki Land Rover was checked in and drove to the inner compound, where the guard was changed exactly as Carey had described.

"We'll see it all again at 18.00 hours," Steffen said confidently. "That's another weakness. They've become predictable."

During the next two hours people routinely left or entered the site and the checks were always thorough. For Steffen they confirmed what he already knew: if no one could get into the centre without being checked an insider had to start the flooding. So, everything turned on Carey. If he cracked up, New Hope would fail, it was as simple as that.

At six o'clock the centre's lighting was taking over from daylight and the incoming guards followed their well worn ritual. They watched it through, waited a little longer just in case, then Steffen said they ought to be getting to the Fare 'n' Square. Kapner rolled up the blanket and volunteered to time them as they went back to the car park.

The Fare 'n' Square would never win a design contest. It consisted of two concrete blocks on either side of the M2/A2 plus an enclosed arch with windows in it that joined them together. The facilities were mostly in the arch. They included a newsagent's, some play stations, an open-plan coffee shop and a short-order restaurant. Kapner parked on the south side. They stood by the car and discussed briefly whether to take their rucksacks with them or lock them in the boot. Steffen opted for taking them so they did.

Once he'd read the menu Guderius, who was wearing his necktie again, said he'd rather not eat in the restaurant so they took a table in the coffee shop where Sobart was sure to see them and bought some filled baguettes to go with their drinks. The heating was on the high side so Guderius unzipped his anorak and Steffen and Kapner took theirs off. When Sobart arrived from the north side they bought more coffee, she bought a baguette and, switching into English, they got down to serious talk. No one was sitting near them and there was plenty of useful noise coming from the play stations.

Sobart was plump, grey haired and looked like everyone's favourite granny. Her clothes were smart without being showy and she didn't wear a wedding ring. She liked to say she was married to her work and leave it at that.

"Carey didn't lose any time," she began. "I open the lab at 8.30 on weekdays and at 8.30 plus one second he was on the phone asking to see me. I gave him 9.00 and as soon as he arrived he said he wanted a full-spectrum blood test and a DNA test but the Anne of Cleves mustn't know about them. He said he'd lost confidence in them. He also insisted I do the tests personally. I told him yes, I'd do the tests if that was what he wanted, in fact I'd add in a few of my own and yes again, no one'd know who they were for. I won't say he was dancing for joy when he left but he looked a mite less ragged than when he came in."

"Do the tests show anything?" asked Guderius, professionally curious.

"He's got a white cell anomaly which might or might not mean something and his DNA isn't finished yet. The thing is, what do I do now? He's called me three times today and I've stalled. He said he'd call again tomorrow and I don't want to say the wrong thing."

Steffen and Kapner looked at Guderius, who shrugged his shoulders.

"Nothing much will show for a while," he said, "then a lot will and anyone he sees will ask some very awkward questions."

"They're the last thing he wants," said Kapner. "That's why he's cut the Anne of Cleves out."

"What's happening to him couldn't happen naturally, could it?" Steffen asked Guderius. "If Carey found out it could he'd feel less tied to us."

"Not a chance. What he's got doesn't exist in nature, not even remotely."

So, Steffen thought to himself, he had Carey right where he wanted him. Carey had no reason to have anyone else do his tests and every reason to have Sobart do them. That meant he could be remote controlled through Sobart and Steffen was sure he had her where he wanted her as well. She couldn't go to the police because he knew too much about her and she couldn't blackmail Carey because he was too panicky to keep his mouth shut. In other words, they were both boxed in and as he'd said to Daski, trust didn't come into it. To be on the safe side, though, he wouldn't tell Sobart more than he had to. He definitely wouldn't tell her Carey was going to be shot.

"When Carey calls tomorrow," he told her, "keep him on edge. Say some of the results need going over again – something like that. But don't make things too scary right now. Can you handle that?"

She said she could.

"Good, because, as Klaus says, a point will come when those tests show he's going downhill fast. He'll probably be feeling it by then but anyway, when it happens I want you to tell him straight out he's dying. He won't like it but it won't surprise him either. Once you've told him that, say you don't know what he's got but there could well be an antidote to it, it's got that shape about it."

"Is there one?"

"Oh, yes," Guderius replied, glancing at Steffen for permission, "and Carey knows I've got it."

"So when I say he's dying he won't feel it's the end of the road but you folk won't rush this antidote his way because you want to keep a hold on him. Have I got that right, Ulrich?"

"That's what it sounds like."

She leaned forward over the formica topped table and, although she didn't need to, she lowered her voice.

"Is this for the old country?" she asked confidentially. "Can you tell me that?"

"Everything's for the old country, Miriam. This included."

"That's what I wanted to hear. I won't let you down."

They stayed a little longer, then it was time to go. Sobart shook hands round the table and headed off towards the north side car park. Steffen and Kapner pulled their anoraks on and Guderius zipped his up. Then they picked up their rucksacks and left in the other direction.

"Miriam never asked what we'd given to Carey," Kapner remarked as she drove out of the car park.

"She didn't ask what we're planning either," Guderius added. "She's the same as Hanna and Helga-Marie. They're three of a kind."

"They set a standard," Steffen agreed over his shoulder. "If I could recruit more like Miriam, I would."

They motored in silence, then Guderius asked,

"What comes next, Ulrich?"

"Cover for when we come back to this country. And don't make your plans for after New Hope too rigid. Keep them flexible. I'll be doing the same."

He turned to Kapner.

"What about you, Heidi? Where are you going to be?"

"London first, then Vaduz. I'm leaving Sunday. If you need me back in a hurry, it's the usual arrangement."

She was concentrating on her speed more than anything else. The one thing she mustn't do was get the Saab noticed. Steffen settled down to watch the traffic. He couldn't help himself, he was trying to see which drivers were on their own and which ones had passengers.

"Perhaps," he told himself, "these are some of the people who'll drown on October 26th. They'll be dying thanks to me. Like the control centre guards."

The thought made his feelings surge upwards. He'd never killed anyone himself yet but this was close to it and sublime in scale as well. New Hope was a political statement, he was clear about that, but it was more besides. It was personal fulfilment.

II

16

A room in Chelsea

Whenever Willem van Piet drove from his manor house in Essex to his place of work in London his vehicle of choice was an aging Ford Mondeo. It wasn't the most elegant car in his garage but one thing was certain: no one would look at him twice in it.

Van Piet was the only son of Joost van Piet, owner of Van Piet Banking, a private bank based in Amsterdam. To learn more about the bank that'd one day be his he'd been guest-appointed to Rothschild's in London and late one Friday afternoon, when most people were thinking about the weekend, a Compliance manager he just about knew by sight had sat down next to him in the tea room. A month later, after a sequence of interviews on a remote farm in Derbyshire, he'd told his father he was leaving the bank to join Britain's Serious Risks Office.

"It does things the government doesn't want to answer for," he'd explained over good Dutch coffee in Amsterdam, "but it's not a government department. It's a Crown office."

Joost could see why. The British Crown is above the law and can never be taken to court.

"So who does it answer to in practice?" he asked.

"The Prime Minister, personally."

"Ah, yes, of course. Well, you're a British citizen, you were born over there, so nationality's no problem. How much will they pay you, by the way?"

Willem told him. It sounded like the milk money.

"Our forebears would turn in their graves," Joost reflected, "if any van Piet had to live on such a sum. I'll appoint you to my advisory council and pay you properly. I don't think your new employer will object. British governments, including the present one, have been glad of the bank too often for that."

The Serious Risks Office was located in the London Borough of Chelsea between the Royal Hospital and the Pimlico Road. The building's name stone said Ashell House and a brass plate next to the glass swing doors read Scrite and Associates: Architects. Scrite and Associates was a genuine firm but it didn't need much of Ashell House. The rest was the SRO's and its entrance was at the back. It was covered by a roll-up door which looked like the entrance to a garbage bay. When the door clanked up, a concealed armoured portcullis glided up with it.

Exactly a week after Carey capitulated to Steffen, van Piet parked his Ford in the underground garage and took the lift to his office, which was two floors from the top. It looked out on the trees of the Ranelagh Gardens and, beyond them, onto the Thames. He was just slipping off his jacket when Tom Garry, his secretary, buzzed him.

"Mr Trilling would like to see you, Sir. In his room in ten minutes' time."

Alex Trilling CBE had been with the SRO all his working life and now he was Director General. He'd got to the top by combining high-yield missions with low to zero casualties. Officially he was due to retire but three expensive headhunts had failed to find a successor so he was still in post. That pleased everyone. No one wanted him to go.

Trilling's room – no one called it his office – was on the floor above van Piet's. It was the top floor in status terms, the real top floor being given over to Signals. The room was dominated by a massive wooden desk. Legend said it was made of oak salvaged from the Great Fire of London. Black smears under the varnish were claimed to be soot marks from the blaze.

When Trilling's secretary showed van Piet in, four files were neatly piled next to the two miniature oil paintings that were always on his desk. Trilling never spoke about them but everyone knew they'd been done from photos and who was on them. One portrayed Denise Trilling, who'd died of septicaemia only a few years after she and Trilling had married. She'd been a UNICEF Operations Chief in Uruguay at the time. The other portrayed Belle Faraday, her Canadian team doctor. Faraday had seen Denise Trilling through her last hours. It emerged from tributes to Faraday that, following a flash flood, she'd had no medicines at the time. Denise Trilling had died childless and Trilling had never remarried. Whenever he went back to the six-bedroom house he never seemed to want he always went on his own and whenever he managed a break in the Ranelagh Gardens he'd be on his own again. Denise Trilling always tried to spend goodbye time with her husband before she went abroad and it was as if he couldn't bring her final goodbye to closure. Only two things got him away from the SRO. One was meetings with ministers and civil servants. He loathed them but, as he said, he had to go to them. The other was a sailing dinghy he kept at Cowes. So far as anyone knew water sport was his only passion. His house was a few miles upriver and when he didn't need his car he came to work in his motor cruiser, a Merry Fisher 695, which, to Security's impotent rage, he tied up at an unguarded mooring near Chelsea Bridge. It didn't help that whenever he went out for a ride he forbade Security to come with him.

Trilling looked bone weary when van Piet went in. The SRO was chronically underfunded, the year had been a long one and it showed.

"Ah, Willem!" he exclaimed, locking the corridor door from his desk. "I'm truly sorry to haul you back to England but something important's turned up and you're one of the few people I've got who's not operational."

Van Piet was all in himself. Trilling had blitzed him out of a secondment to ASIS, the Australian Secret Intelligence Service, and the Royal Air Force had got him back to England the day before. Trilling motioned him to take one of the easy chairs facing his desk and asked him whether he'd heard of an organisation called Chameleon. He said he hadn't.

"Well, you have now. It's an East German leftover. An NPA colonel called Steffen set it up to look after military and Stasi types the new Germany might not take to. It's been suspected of most things, including assassination, but Steffen's clever so no one's ever been charged."

"What do our German colleagues think?"

"They're not sure. They reckon it'll die a natural death in time but they don't want to forget about it just yet so they've graded it low risk and left it at that."

"But you don't think it's low risk otherwise I wouldn't be here now."

"I used to but I've changed my mind and I'll tell you why. The Germans keep an open file on Chameleon, it makes them feel they're doing something. If anything crops up, in it goes, and partner organisations like us are asked to chip in, so we keep a file too. So do MI5 and MI6 and whatever gets sent to Germany gets shared round over here. In Ashell House we also keep sub-files on individual members and there're three in front of you now."

Trilling's secretary brought the tea in through her own door and he poured for both of them.

"Now," he continued, "as you know, we get a lot of our open-file data through computer hook-ups."

"When they work."

"Point taken, but they're getting better. Anyway, those data include arrivals from abroad and it so happens two Chameleon grandees came over here recently at virtually the same time. One arrived a week ago last Saturday. His name's Guderius. The other one was Colonel Steffen himself. He arrived the next day."

"And you think that's significant. Why can't it be coincidence?"

"Guderius and Steffen both come here on business and as a matter of fact, we've managed to get their voiceprints while they've been with us so it can be coincidence. But you know the rule: when in doubt, be suspicious, especially when something else makes you take a really close look at people's comings and goings."

He gestured towards the files.

"This top file is a briefing file I've had done for you. Everything you need to know is in it. The others are sub-files on Steffen, Guderius and – note the name – a certain Heidi Kapner."

"She's your something else, is she?"

"I think so. When the GDR had an embassy in Belgrave Square she was on the staff. She was listed as a copy typist but she was Stasi all right. Unfortunately MI5 was slow to pick her up so not all her contacts are known even now, which is an almighty nuisance as you'll see shortly. One contact MI5 did turn up, though, was a nuclear scientist at Aldermaston. Thanks to him Kapner was bazookaed back to where she came from and she spent the rest of the Cold War there. She's in insurance these days. Her company's based in Liechtenstein but she does a lot of her trading over here and when she's in London she lives and works in an Orange Street duplex. She's got the ground floor flat."

"Does she work on her own?"

"She's got an occasional assistant called Sandra Fassbinder. She's Chameleon like Kapner and she also dates back to Belgrave Square, where she really was office staff. She's British by marriage but her husband's dead and her children loathe her for still being a Communist so she skulks on her own in Bermondsey under her maiden name. Kapner's probably company for her as much as anything."

"That's all very sad but I still don't see what your something else is."

Trilling handed him one of the sub-files.

"Try this then. It's Kapner's and there's a picture gallery at the back. I want you to go through it right now. The pages are numbered one to twenty-seven."

The gallery consisted of scanned-in photos in chronological order. Each one had a location, a date and a time underneath it and the quality improved the closer they got to the present. There was a girlish-looking Kapner just arrived in London and a long shot taken at Heathrow showed she still looked girlish when the Aldermaston business sent her packing. There was only one photo from her time in the GDR. It was blurred and grainy as if it'd been taken from a passing car. Then came Vaduz, the ski slopes of Malbun-Steg and London again. By this time she was looking like the business success she'd become. Her clothes were smart, her fading hair was coiffeured and she'd taken to wearing ornamental brooches.

"The earlier shots come from MI5," Trilling filled in. "MI6 took the one in East Berlin and we took a lot of the later ones. Every so often, if one of our people can make the time, they go over to Orange Street, blend in with the background and see if anything's happening. If it is, it's photographed. The Saab on Page 20 is Kapner's, by the way. She's got a bay outside her flat. It's in her motor insurance."

He peered into the teapot but it was empty and van Piet shook his head so he let it go.

"It all sounds more than a little chaotic," van Piet commented, silently wishing his mind was clearer. "I mean, if people can make the time and all that."

Trilling looked at van Piet with infinite weariness.

"I'd already been having a go at it" – he placed one hand in the other like someone who's lost at cards – "but I simply can't do everything. Anyway we've got the Saab on record and we also know Steffen visits Kapner from time to time."

"Is there something between them?"

"Unlikely. Everything says he worships his wife. She's an invalid, by the way. Rheumatoid arthritis."

"What else do we know about Kapner?"

"She has her flat regularly swept for bugs and when she gets back from Liechtenstein she has it swept again. We know that because someone noticed an unmarked van pull up near her flat and the driver go in. From that we found out she's got a contract with Waveney Screening. I don't suppose Van Piet Banking uses them, does it?"

"No, we do our own security. Why do you ask?"

"Some leverage would be handy. We were lucky with Kapner's contract, someone we know at Waveney got sight of it, but they don't co-operate with the forces of law and order unless they have to. If they find a bug from us, MI5 or the police, they make a point of telling their customers because it makes them look good. In Kapner's case that's caused a problem. And speaking of our Heidi, what about the picture gallery?"

"There's a page missing. Page 26."

Without saying anything Trilling took a sheet of paper from a drawer in his desk and reached it over. It was the missing page and one of the photos was ringed by hand. It showed Kapner leaving her Orange Street flat and its date was September 21st. Van Piet didn't have to look at it long. It was something else all right.

"It's her hair," he said. "She's changed the style back to what it used to be. The colour as well by the look of things. And her clothes. But only in this one shot. Was she followed?"

"Why should she be? Chameleon's been low priority. It took over a week for this shot to reach me. As soon as it did, though, I checked her travel dates along with those of Steffen and Guderius. Guderius came over just days before that shot was taken and stayed till September 19th. He came in his own car via Dover."

"Does that matter?"

"He normally flies so – who knows? – he may have been bringing something in. What I do know is, Kapner flew to Leipzig/Halle on September 24th and came back the following day."

"And Guderius came back on the 26th with Steffen arriving the day after. That's a lot of toing and froing. Are these characters still in London?"

"Guderius and Steffen are back in Germany and Kapner's in Vaduz. I've put a full-time tail on her. It's costing us manpower we don't have but my guess is, any breakthrough will come through her. If you ask me, she's revived a contact for some reason – probably a man if she's leading with her looks – and we might even know who it was if MI5 had done its job properly."

"Has she gone out like this at any other time?"

"No idea. When you're stretched for cash you get these gaps."

"Why not hand on to MI5 and MI6 then? They're rich enough."

"If they take over, German security will have to be informed because German citizens are involved and if that happens this country will lose control. The Prime Minister doesn't want that and neither do I. And between ourselves, there's another reason as well. I want the SRO to be Britain's top security service, not the poor relation, and Chameleon can help us achieve that. So, this one's ours and it's staying that way."

Trilling had been glancing at the grandfather clock at the back of his room and now he looked at it again. It was a George Hardey, it'd been made in 1770 and it'd kept perfect time ever since.

"You'll have to excuse me," he said as he unlocked the corridor door, "but I've got an appointment in Whitehall I'm already late for. I want you to take these files with you, read them through and be back here at 2.30 sharp."

At 2.30 sharp van Piet was duly in the easy chair and the corridor door was relocked. His briefing file was within reach on the floor and the sub-files were on Trilling's desk. Trilling spoke first. Van Piet knew from his secretary he hadn't had time for lunch.

"So, Willem, any thoughts?" he began.

"This Ulrich Steffen, he seems to have been quite a star when he was the Military Attaché. Did he cross your path at all?"

"Not officially, he was MI5's pigeon, but I knew he existed because he never hid up. He'd tell anyone who'd listen he was here to steal our secrets and the result was, he got deluged with invitations to house parties and so forth from crackpots who wanted to say they'd had a Communist spy to dinner. If his wife was in London – she was fit and healthy then – she'd tag along as well. On the other hand, the gossip from MI5 was, he was talking to someone special but they couldn't find out who it was. To this day I can't say whether he was or no but if he was, that's another black mark for MI5."

"Then there's Guderius. He traipsed off to the Dominican Republic and was back three months later."

"There's no extradition treaty between the Dominican Republic and Germany. Maybe that had something to do with why he went. Why he changed his mind I don't know. A lot of ex-pats do it. They get where they want to be and then they don't like it."

"There's a photo scanned into his sub-file. He's sitting in a deck chair grinning at the camera and looking distinctly young. It's marked 'Original unavailable. Location and date unknown'. What's that all about?"

"It came to us from MI6. It's marked 'Original unavailable' because the original couldn't be kept without revealing that someone – namely MI6 – was intercepting East German mail in transit. So MI6 made a copy at the time and ours came from it later."

"Guderius looks full of himself and I doubt many army doctors could afford the suit he's wearing. I wonder what he was doing when that photo was taken."

"So do I. The message on the back is scanned in as well, plus the envelope. Are they any help?"

"Not much. The message is handwritten and translates as 'Good times, good memories – Hanno'. The stamp on the envelope is East German and the postmark says Berlin, meaning East Berlin, but there's no sender's name or address and Hanno, whoever he was, used the NPA's field post to reach Guderius. The deck chair and the suit are more civilian than army and the photo looks as if it was taken by an amateur and processed by a shop. Shall I make a guess?"

"Go ahead."

"Well, let's say Guderius was on some kind of non-military élite assignment with this Hanno and there came a point when they split up. Hanno took the photo, had the film processed and sent Guderius a print as a souvenir. The postmark doesn't mean Hanno lived in East Berlin, he might have been passing through to somewhere else."

Despite his fatigue, Trilling was looking pleased.

"So you think Guderius is worth a closer look, do you?"

Van Piet knew what was coming but he said it anyway.

"No question of it."

"Well, I'm glad we agree because he's also easy to get at, easier than Steffen at any rate, and I've made a start already. We don't have the German-speaking field agents we used to have but I've freed up Dawn Chopine and had her booked into this wellness clinic of his. The earliest they can take her is this Friday and then only for two nights, so it must be doing well. She's booked in as Mrs Alice Carrick, a freelance journalist researching German wellness clinics for the *Sunday Times*. Germans read British newspapers so if anyone says they've never heard of Alice Carrick, Dawn will say she writes under several professional names and, sorry, but she'd rather not say which ones. Alice Carrick will be on everything she takes with her and if anyone tries to find out any more about her, they'll wind up talking to our Response Unit. I've told Dawn not to rock the boat while she's out there but there are two things she absolutely must find out. Has Guderius got any scheduled absences coming up and if he has, are they likely to bring him over here? Knowing that could be priceless."

"And you want me to go with her."

"You'll be her backup. You'll travel separately, you'll stay in the village not the clinic, and your name will be Dennis Richards. You'll both be briefed at ten o'clock tomorrow morning here in Ashell House. One of the things you'll get is a download of the clinic's brochure. There's a site plan in it plus up to date pics of Guderius and his senior staff. If things develop the way I think they will, I'll want you to take this whole Kapner/Chameleon business over from me as soon as you get back."

He looked hopefully at van Piet, who didn't say no, and then at the Hardey clock.

"Just for once I've got some time in hand," he said. "Can I tell you anything else?"

"From what you said this morning you'll be having Kapner's flat watched when she gets back. How will you do that?"

"It's already happening. Across the way there's a shop called Horace Beadman's Copperware. It's been there for donkey's years and its line is upmarket pots and pans. Beadman and the SRO know each other so I've put someone in one of his upstairs rooms to keep an eye on things and when she shows up again, the number goes up to three. They'll monitor who comes and goes and if she goes out, two of them will tag along till a full tail can be set up. We're watching the back of her flat as well. The National Gallery is lending us a top floor room and it's not asking why."

"How many outside doors has she got?"

"Just the one. If she wants to go into the garden she has to go out at the front and round the side. I've called in the builder's plans and according to them there's no french door and no basement either – nothing at all in fact. Annoyingly we can't see into the flat from anywhere. She keeps her gauze curtains drawn and she's got an unhealthy fondness for blinds."

"What about the people upstairs?"

"They've got their own staircase on the side of the duplex. If they have any connection with Kapner we don't know about it."

"And we can't put a bug in because of Waveney Screening."

"Technology laughed out loud when I suggested it. I can't pretend I'm pleased but I still say she needs a broomstick to get in and out without us knowing."

"Well, her Saab's not a broomstick. Are there any company cars she can draw on?"

"Driver and Vehicle Licensing turned up four. Hang on a minute."

He spoke to his secretary on the internal phone. When she came in she had a sheet of A4 in her hand. Van Piet ran his eye down the details.

"The address for all of these is Kapner's flat. She doesn't street-park them all, does she?"

"No, it's a technicality. Her insurance tells us they're garaged in a small block of lock-ups in Old Compton Street, just north of Shaftesbury Avenue. We've located it, it's within walking distance of Orange Street and if she heads in that direction when she gets back to London, we're ready."

All van Piet really wanted to do was sit quietly and think through everything he'd read or heard as the day had gone on.

He was convinced he'd missed something big but his mind was too fuzzy to let him see what it was.

"What are you going to do now?" asked Trilling as he unlocked the corridor door.

"Tom Garry's got some paperwork for me and then I'm going home."

Nevertheless, when he put his hand on the door handle he didn't turn it and Trilling let him say his piece.

"Since you've given me a new assignment," he began, uncharacteristically hesitant, "there's something I ought to tell you. While I was in Australia my wife received a poison pen letter. It had to do with the riding school she runs in our grounds. So far it's been a one-off and Essex Police think it might stay that way but it threatened violence against my daughter so I can't ignore it. I hope you see my position."

Trilling tightened his fists and his knuckles whitened. He'd visited the van Piets over the years and he knew their daughter personally.

"That's awful, Willem. I'm dreadfully sorry. How's Mrs van Piet taking it?"

"Célestine? She's distraught. The riding school's in a lull at the moment but that won't last and then things may happen fast. I've got some extra people staying in the house just in case."

Neither van Piet nor Trilling said van Piet might have to drop out but the thought was there. Van Piet said he'd keep Trilling posted, then he was in the corridor, his briefing file balanced in his hand. Normally he'd have used the stairs but this time he took the lift because it was already there. His interest in paperwork was nil but the sooner he got it out of the way, the sooner he could go home.

17

A doubt about Chopine

Gorris Hall, the van Piets' manor house, backed onto the Blackwater, the next great estuary up from the Thames. The Blackwater had seen plenty of violence but those days were past and the van Piets lived there because it was peaceful. That peace was now under attack. When van Piet was almost home his headlights caught a police car coming from the opposite direction and his heart sank. He could guess what'd brought the police back. He could also guess how his wife was feeling.

Célestine van Piet was the only child of Jeanne and Henri de Valus. *Paris-Match* had nick-named her father the Bauxite King and the name had stuck. Her talent for showjumping had shown itself early and when she retired, instead of counting her trophies, she founded the Célestine van Piet School for Young Riders. Part of the land between the Hall and the Blackwater was levelled and two rings, one for jumping and one for dressage, now stood where once there'd been a meadow and a pond. Near the rings were stables and a storeroom with a provender loft. Closer to the Hall an outhouse had been turned into accommodation for residential courses. Making a profit had never come into it. A lot of children came at reduced rates or for free, and if they couldn't afford their own gear they could borrow out of the storeroom.

Then the first poison pen letter had arrived. It was hand-written in block capitals using jet black fountain pen ink. A police graphologist said it came from a right-handed person writing left-handed but she couldn't say whether the writer was a man or a woman. The envelope was addressed in the same block capitals and the postmark showed the letter had been posted in Chelmsford, Essex's busy county town. Replete with obscenities it said it was "very very cruell" to make horses "do things nature never ment them to do" and it told Célestine to "close your schole you hore. Ill damage your daughters eyes so bad shell never see another horse again if you don't". It was signed "Knifepoint". There was no demand for money.

Célestine had been living alone in the Hall at the time and Jackie, the van Piets' ten-year-old daughter, was at boarding school. When Célestine had read it over the phone she'd added in some of the spelling to give van Piet a better sense of it. He'd told her to call the police and ring him back when she knew more. She was also to call Jackie's school: it wasn't to let her out of its sight. Separately he'd arranged for Stafford and Celia Tyler – one of her riding school instructors and his wife – to move into the Hall till he got back. To Célestine's relief and contrary to what she'd expected the police had taken the letter seriously enough for WPC Janine Tewkesbury from Essex Police's Mounted Division to join the staff of Jackie's school as Assistant Matron.

As soon as van Piet had garaged the Ford he went to find his wife. He knew where to look. She'd be in "her" place, the converted brew house that stood a little way off from the main building. It had uneven flagstones with scatter rugs on them, chipped and scratched wooden furniture and a permanent smell of leather. When he went in the computer was on and she was sitting in front of it but she'd given up trying to concentrate and the riding school logo, which doubled as a screensaver, was scrolling idly from right to left. He stood his briefcase down, kissed the top of her head, pressed his face against hers and kept it there, all his tiredness forgotten.

"I saw the police car," he said. "You've had another letter."

She looked up in anguish. Her face was white and she'd been crying.

"It came just before lunchtime. The address was written the same way as before so I didn't open it, I rang the police straight away and they brought a scientist with them. He took it away as it was. They brought him back about an hour ago, possibly longer, I really don't know, and he and the police all talked to me. I desperately wanted to ring you but I knew you were busy. If you've been rushed back from Australia you must be. And what could you do except come home and hold my hand?"

His mind had been clearing on the way home and he didn't answer directly. Instead he asked what the scientist and the police had said.

"The same as before – there was nothing to go on, everything was as clean as a whistle. The police now think more letters are likely. Oh, Willem, I can't bear it."

"Did you get to read it?"

"The scientist brought me a copy. He brought a copy of the envelope as well."

She handed him a large manila jiffy bag from a tray on her desk. It looked as if it came from old stock that needed using up. It was stamped "Essex County Constabulary" and twine wound round a red fibre disc kept it closed. This was the second time in a day van Piet had had a copied message in his hand only this one affected him personally. He read it in silence. Its obscenities were more intense, its threats to injure Jackie were more brutal and it made the same demand as before.

If Célestine was distressed she was also deeply angry. She'd never give in if it was only about her but Jackie's welfare made everything different. She'd asked the police whether she should do as Knifepoint wanted but they'd said no, this person might wait for everyone to relax then strike without warning to punish her for opening the school in the first place. They called it an Avenging Angel complex and said you could never satisfy people who had one, no matter what you did. Better to keep the school open, take all precautions and give the person time to make a mistake. They usually did in the end.

"I said I'd follow their advice," Célestine went on, determined not to break down, "but only if you agreed. Was I right, Willem, or shall I call them and say I've changed my mind?"

"You were right," he replied. "I'd have said the same. Have you told Jackie?"

"No, it'd frighten her, that's all. What good would that do?"

"What about half-term? It's not far off now."

"She'll come here. It's what she's expecting and she'd be even less safe if we packed her off to friends. I'll cancel my half-term classes but that's all. I'll put an excuse on the website but I'll leave no doubt my school is staying open."

"And WPC Tewkesbury? What will she do?"

"Jackie only knows her as the new Assistant Matron and they've become good friends. Jackie knows she can ride so she's coming here as a house guest and the police have said she'll stay on this duty till things sort themselves out better. She tells me she can bank the overtime against a holiday next summer. I doubt that's true but we'll pretend it is and find a way to thank her if it isn't."

"Some things are working then."

"Some things are working."

She wanted to do something practical to get herself back on track so although she wasn't hungry, she said she'd put a meal together while van Piet showered and got changed. They ate on their own in the kitchen. They didn't expect to see the Tylers, who had their own set of rooms, and they didn't like live-in domestic staff so they didn't have any. Neither of them was up to saying much but there was one thing Célestine had to be told.

"Cissie," van Piet said while they were waiting for the coffee to perk, "I've had to take a decision of my own while we've been sitting here and, like yours, it's not been an easy one. I was given a new assignment today and I'm going to go through with it. It means I have to go abroad again on Friday. It's not as far as Australia and it's only for a few days. I'll ask the Tylers to stay indefinitely before I go in to work tomorrow. Then if I'm away any more I'll know there's someone with you."

Célestine didn't reply straight away. Van Piet never shared his work with her because he couldn't and although Trilling had become a sort of distant family friend, he never said anything either. She knew all about her husband's sense of duty but she also knew, if she really pressured him, he'd put her first and stand down. If Jackie hadn't had Tewkesbury assigned to her she might have done just that. Instead she reached across the table and took his hand.

"I won't ask you whether you want to go on Friday because I know what the answer will be." She caught her breath and went on with, "I know you love me dearly and Jackie thinks you're the best daddy in the world. Take our love with you and keep yourself safe. If you … If you didn't come back …"

She couldn't get to the end. Under the low-hanging ceiling light her face went blurred and she dissolved in tears.

They spent what was left of the evening just being together. Célestine went to bed first but although van Piet was feeling more like an automaton than a human being by now he took his briefcase up to his soundproofed study and locked the door from the inside. On a work surface at right angles to his desk was a console topped by a monitor. It was his secure link to Van Piet Banking. He powered it up, fished his briefing file out of his briefcase and put himself through to Intelligence. All major banks have intelligence departments, they just don't like to talk about them, and Van Piet Banking was no exception. Van Piet was hoping Anke Sweelinck would be about. He wasn't acting for the bank this time so he wanted a personal contact. He and Sweelinck were two of a kind. They could both read data in more than one way and they both liked ferreting things out.

He was in luck. Within seconds, Sweelinck's young-old blonde-fringed face was on his screen.

"One moment," she said in Dutch before he could speak. "I've got people round me. I'll patch you through to my den."

His screen went dark, then brightened up again. Now they could speak freely.

"Anke," he said, staying in Dutch, "don't pull a face. I've got a special request to make but I can't tell you why."

As expected, she pulled a face. They both liked their rituals. They made things run better.

"It's a long shot," he went on, "but I'd like to know whether you can turn up anything on a former East German army doctor named Klaus Guderius."

He spelled the name and gave her all the information he'd either read or been told. He also scanned her the photo of Guderius in the deck chair plus the message and the envelope. He finished by saying,

"Tell my father what you're doing and make clear it isn't bank business. He'll guess the rest."

"I'll see what I can manage. Where do I reply to?"

"This station only. It's exclusive to me."

While they gossiped a bit he made himself a reference copy of Guderius's photo and the message and locked it in a drawer within easy reach. He didn't say anything about the poison pen letters, just Jackie's schooling and the horse riding, and Sweelinck updated him on life in Amsterdam. When he shut down he felt distinctly vulnerable. He yawned profoundly and turned his thoughts to the next day's meeting with Chopine. He'd worked with her before and nothing had gone wrong but this time she'd be separated from him. He hoped it wouldn't make any difference but he had an uneasy feeling it would.

18

Chopine targets Guderius's villa

The SRO's Travel Section had been its usual efficient self. Chopine landed at Leipzig/Halle, where a pre-booked Audi was waiting for her. Van Piet landed in Prague, picked up his pre-booked Skoda and motored to Bad Sollmer via Dresden. He was booked into The Golden Bear, a three star overnighter in the main square. It was filling up with weekend hikers when he checked in. Hot sunshine – probably the last of the year - was forecast for the weekend. It was bringing them out in numbers.

As soon as Chopine checked into the clinic the receptionist buzzed Gannisch so she could welcome her personally. In Gannisch's book journalists needed careful treatment. They'd be having dinner together, she said, and Dr Guderius would be joining them. During the meal Chopine worked hard at her cover and by the time coffee was served she knew the Guderius success story by heart. What was more, Gannisch was going to show her round the next morning. Saturdays were always busy, Gannisch warned, but they could lunch together afterwards if she didn't mind eating early – say, half past eleven. Would that be all right?

Chopine said it was perfect. Would Dr Guderius be joining them, she asked him as if she really wanted him there.

"He's going shooting," Gannisch put in for him. "He'll be out all day."

"Shooting?"

"He started last Saturday and he says this time he's not going to let it slide."

She patted his arm affectionately.

"Once a soldier, always a soldier – that's what they say."

Chopine had to know more.

"Where do you shoot?" she asked him as naïvely as she could. "In the woods? There seem to be a lot round here. I saw them from the plane as I came in."

Guderius and Gannisch both laughed.

"I don't hunt, Mrs Carrick," he said. "I couldn't kill a living creature if you paid me. No, I go pistol shooting. There's a range near here called Jan Schwarzer's and I happen to know the owner. Some of my old comrades are doing the same thing. We veterans like to keep in touch and to be honest, I'm ashamed I've got so rusty."

"That's smart," Chopine thought. "He gives a reason up front and no one suspects there might be another one."

When dinner was over she said she'd like to walk outside for a bit: the travelling was catching up with her. The air was fresh and moist, and the gravel drive glowed softly under hooded lighting but further out, everything was pitch black. At first she hovered near the entrance in case anyone was watching. Then, imperceptibly, she left the light.

When she judged she was safe she called van Piet on her SRO mobile. He said he was in his room and could talk freely. Keeping her voice down she confirmed her room number and told him how to reach it. Then,

"Have you got your blank ready?"

"It's in place."

She held the magnetic strip of her room card against the back of her mobile and successively tapped in the codes for Read and Transmit. Van Piet was holding a blank card against his own mobile. When Task Ended came up his card would open anything hers would.

"I've got some news already," she said and told him about Guderius's sudden urge to get his shooting skills back.

"Jan Schwarzer's, you say? I can't think who'd recognise me there. I'll try for a day ticket. When will you call me next?"

"I'm having lunch with the manageress at 11.30 or so and she'll probably be pushed for time so let's say between 12.30 and 1.00."

"If I don't answer I'll call you when I can. If I haven't called by 1.45, alert Mr Trilling."

Straight after breakfast the next day Chopine presented herself outside Gannisch's office. She'd dressed London-smart and had a reporter's notebook in her handbag. They threaded their way through the maelstrom of guests in the vestibule and finally reached a door marked Quiet Please in large red letters. Gannisch tapped in a code and it swung open.

"The rooms through here are for medical examinations," she explained as they rubbed their hands in germicide.

They walked past rooms for scans, x-rays, ECGs, lung volume tests and urine flow analysis. There were no chairs about: appointments were timed so that no one had to wait. Towards the end of the corridor Chopine asked whether she could see Guderius Sunday morning to say goodbye and thank him for all his kindness. Gannisch raked around in her memory.

"I don't see why not," she said. "Let's look at the duty roster. Then we'll know for sure."

They retraced their steps to a reception bay half way along the corridor. Two nurses in crisp maroon uniforms were drinking coffee with someone whose ID said "Dr Sebastian Rolf: Radiography". They said "*Guten Morgen*" to Gannisch and "How do you do?" to Chopine when she was introduced as Mrs Carrick from England. Gannisch asked the staffer behind the Can I Help You? sign if she could use his terminal and brought up the duty roster.

"It's open access," she explained to Chopine, who was looking over her shoulder. "Dr Guderius is on it, just like everyone else. He insisted on it."

She entered Sunday's date and Guderius's initials.

"Here we are, he's on till one o'clock. I'll ask him if he'll see you but I'm sure he will."

"This is really clever," Chopine enthused, running her eye down the screen to see what else it could tell her. "It must make long-term planning a stroll."

"Oh, it does. Let me show you."

Dr Rolf finished his coffee and checked a whiteboard.

"OK, gang," he said. "One left hip coming up. Let's go."

Gannisch gave them a smile as they left but her eyes were really on the monitor. She'd found what she was looking for.

"Most staff are simply marked 'On duty' or 'Off duty'," she explained, "but Dr Guderius and I are marked 'On site' or 'Off site' as well because we live here. If we're on site but not on duty we're on standby and if we're both off site at the same time, we find a replacement. Now, this is Dr Guderius page by page from now till Christmas Day and you can see the various combinations for yourself. But here" – she scrolled from October 22nd through to October 30th – "he's 'Off duty' and 'Off site' for nine consecutive days. He'll be where you came from yesterday as a matter of fact."

"What, London?"

"That's right. There's a company there markets body scanners and we might be leasing one or two. You could arrange to meet if your diaries would let you. He'd like that."

Chopine needed all her training to stay natural. This was the information she'd come for and there it was, right in front of her.

"Nine days," she improvised. "Isn't that a long while to discuss a deal?"

"Nine days including travel, I should have said. But these scanner deals are complex. In fact Dr Guderius says he might have to stay even longer."

She glanced at the on-screen clock and tutted.

"I'm afraid we have to move on," she said. "Our clinic is bigger than it looks and time is slipping away."

She was used to showing people round so she was able to up the tempo without leaving too much out. Over lunch she reeled off one statistic after another and Chopine wrote them down as if they were gold dust.

"I do wish I could keep you company this afternoon," Gannisch said over a somewhat hurried dessert, "but I really can't. What do you think you'll do?"

"If I don't write my notes up I'll forget what they mean so I'll do that first. Then I might sample one or two of the things I've seen this morning like the saunas or the massages. Or I might just go outside and enjoy your lovely German sunshine.

I'm sorry to sound so hare-brained but you've done such a wonderful job I feel spoiled for choice. Would you mind if I left it open?"

Gannisch was signing the bill.

"Not at all. You're our guest and Reception can always find me if you need me. Have a care if you go outside, though. Our lovely German sunshine is getting very strong."

"That's amazing. How can you tell from in here?"

"The glass we're sitting under is light-sensitive. When it darkens down like now, you know the sun means business."

Once Chopine had shed Gannisch she went up to her room and called van Piet. She didn't get him but he called back afterwards. She gave him Guderius's London dates and said she'd call him again at 5.30. She plucked it out of the air but it sounded about right.

When the call was over she felt at a loose end. She'd been keyed up to find things out the hard way and they'd been handed to her on a plate. She yawned, sighed languidly, laid a pair of lightweight trousers and a fresh blouse on the bed and yawned again. She had half a mind to take a nap but if she didn't, what could she do instead? Not write up any notes, that was certain. Lazily she changed her clothes and ambled towards the window. Maybe the sunshine would tempt her outside.

Her room was on the second floor and the view took in a sandy footpath, a stretch of impeccably mown lawn and Guderius's villa. She knew it was that because Gannisch had pointed it out to her. She tried to imagine what it was like to live in it. It looked ideal for a couple with a family – she was getting married in the spring so a couple with a family was her all-purpose standard – but it seemed altogether too big for one person on his own. She could see part of some scaffolding at the far end. It was enclosed in greenish canvas sheeting and she wondered what was behind it. Her curiosity soon got the better of her. There were no guests about: a lot of them would be eating and the leisure facilities were on the other side of the clinic. She'd find out and she'd do it now.

She left the clinic by a rear entrance. The sun was hot all right and the air was humid. She hadn't gone far when she heard someone open and shut the door she'd just come through. It was one of the handymen. Gannisch had spoken to him that morning and his ID had said "Matti Frisch". He'd seen Chopine look back and she knew it so she stopped and waited for him. Handymen with large bunches of keys on their belts can be useful people to know.

"I'm sorry you have to work while I'm idling about," she said as he caught up with her. They were on the sandy footpath she could see from her room. "What brings you to my side of the clinic?"

He came to a halt as if that'd give his answer more weight. Everything about him was ponderous. She caught his self-importance and sensed she was in with a chance.

"The building we're looking at is Dr Guderius's villa," he said, "and if you look you'll see some scaffolding at the far end."

"Ah, yes, so there is. But why is it covered up?"

She'd responded quickly and laid her hand on his arm as if to thank him. She didn't want him to point in case someone saw him do it.

"Well, behind it a chute comes down from the top floor. It feeds into a skip and the canvas stops the dust going everywhere."

What dust? She had to find out more but she didn't want to seem inquisitive so she tried being indirect.

"And you're making sure it's doing its job, are you?"

It worked. There was more to Matti Frisch than minding dust and he wanted her to register the fact.

"You wouldn't know it, Ma'am, but the window at the top of the chute has been taken out and canvassed over till the men come back on Monday. That's another reason the scaffolding's sheeted in and I know it because I'm one of the few who have to."

"I suppose Dr Guderius has got the decorators in. Poor man! That's something I always dread."

"It's a bit more than that. A storage tank in his attic overflowed the other night. It was the usual thing. The inflow didn't close off and there was muck in the overflow. The water brought down a fair amount of ceiling. A lot of carpet and some of the floor took hits as well."

He glanced round and lowered his voice confidentially.

"Between you and me the water also got into the alarm system so it had to be shut down. Dr Guderius isn't too pleased about that and I don't blame him."

Chopine studied the villa, trying to look amateurish.

"I don't see any alarm system," she said, turning away as soon as she could. "Where are the noisemakers and what not?"

"There aren't any. Dr Guderius doesn't want firemen or policemen smashing into his villa when he's not there to keep an eye on them. He says they do more harm than fire and burglars combined. So he's got this radio link from sensors in his villa to a buzzer on his wristwatch. The problem was – I got this from him personally so I know it's right – the water in the system kept triggering the buzzer. So the drill now is, when he goes out he tips the wink to me or one of the other maintenance staff he can trust and that person walks over to the villa every hour or so to check the doors and windows. Plus where the window's come out and the sheeting round the scaffolding."

"But you said Dr Guderius didn't let people inside when he wasn't there. Or is that only firemen and policemen?"

"No, it's no one. Staff haven't got keys for a start. What we do is, we try the doors from the outside and inspect the windows visually. If we see anything wrong we have to stay where we are and phone Dr Guderius, or Miss Gannisch if we can't reach him. But Dr Guderius first."

Chopine's stomach was knotting with excitement. This was a chance in a million. It might even mean promotion. With Guderius off site and his alarm switched off she could slip into his villa and find out what he was so keen to keep out of the way of the fire service and the police. She wouldn't tell Willem, he'd say she mustn't rock the boat. Well, too bad, he wouldn't get that chance. She flattered Frisch some more and said now she'd been outside for a bit she fancied some jogging in the sunshine to run off her lunch. If he'd excuse her she was going back to get changed while she still liked the idea.

The clinic's grounds were right for jogging. They extended a long way and they were mostly grassed. She'd brought some trainers with her, she could borrow a tracksuit from the gym dispensary – it said so in the brochure - and there was a point on the perimeter she could approach the villa from without being seen from the clinic. She'd have to get a move on, that was all. The afternoon was slipping away and she had no idea when Guderius would get back. "Out all day" could mean anything.

There was an indolent, well fed atmosphere in the clinic as Chopine made her way to the dispensary and she had to force herself not to look in a hurry. She handed over her room card and asked for a tracksuit to take with her. She was going to do a few laps round the grounds and she'd change in her room. What should she do with the tracksuit when she'd finished with it?

"You put it down the hatchway, Ma'am," the attendant answered, nodding sideways.

She'd swiped Chopine's room card and now she was scanning in the tracksuit.

"When it gets to the bottom the laundry scans it again so once it's through the flap you can forget about it."

The tracksuit was maroon like the nurses' uniforms and it came in an ornate GRWC carrier bag. Things, Chopine felt, were definitely looking up. It'd take her no time at all to get changed and then she'd get into the villa while she had the chance.

19

At Jan Schwarzer's Shooting Range

Van Piet meanwhile had motored over to Jan Schwarzer's. There were plenty of vehicles on the tarmacked car park when he got there including, he was pleased to see, the E class Mercedes Guderius had brought through Dover. Its registration had been in his briefing file. The range's entrance was like a fairground crossed with a prison. The fairground part was a painted wooden arch covered with cowboys, GIs and private eyes in slouch hats plus "Jan Schwarzer's Shooting Range" in scarlet light bulbs flashing on and off. The prison part was the densely rolled razor wire that topped the perimeter fence. The only way in was through a narrow turnstile operated from inside a pay booth by a cashier in dark glasses. His head was shaven, he had striking rattlesnakes tattooed on the backs of his hands and a loudspeaker in the safety glass in front of him made his voice sound metallic.

Van Piet held up a flier and speaking German with a heavy English accent asked if he could buy a day ticket and try some lessons. He gave his name as Richards, Dennis Richards, and said he'd found the flier in his hotel lobby, which was true but only because he'd gone down to look for it after he'd taken Chopine's call. The cashier asked him which price slot he wanted. He went for the top one since it would take longest to get through. After he'd handed his money in the cashier told him to wait while he radioed someone called Otto. He'd be Mr Richards's instructor for the day.

Otto was a generation older than the cashier. He was squatly built and his grey-white hair straggled over his shoulders. A pair of personalised ear protectors dangled from his hand and, as van Piet quickly discovered, he knew a lot about shooting. He didn't say he'd been a sniper on the death zone between East and West Germany and van Piet didn't ask him where he'd learned his skills. So all the while they were together there was the faintest of shadows between them.

Once he was through the turnstile van Piet had to admit that for all the razzamatazz Schwarzer's was a good place to shoot. Under Otto's expert guidance he tried still and moving targets at various distances and with different types of gun. There was theory as well. His big problem was pretending to know less than he did but whenever he looked better than he should he blamed it on luck or on shooting rabbits with an air rifle when he was a boy. As the morning wore on he still hadn't seen Guderius and then Otto was saying it was time for something to eat. Spare ribs with black eye peas topped the menu in the American-style restaurant and since they were what Otto ordered, van Piet ordered them as well. He didn't want to stand out even in small things. It was hot in the restaurant so they sat near an open window. There were people eating at most tables and Otto knew them all. He might have a past but no one was holding it against him.

Otto was explaining rifling when out of the corner of his eye van Piet saw a roly-poly pink-faced man come in through the swing doors and make his way to the serving counter. He was wearing highly polished brown shoes, leisure-wear fawn slacks that looked as if they'd just come from the shop and a light cotton jacket. The ear protectors round his neck looked like his own. They also looked very new. Van Piet had no trouble recognising him – it was Guderius – and as soon as Otto saw him he broke off from what he was saying, waved and pointed to a free place at their table. When Guderius came across he was carrying a T-bone steak with vegetables and gravy, a side salad, two oversize bread rolls, a bottle of spring water and a plastic beaker, all squashed onto a plastic tray. After he'd set them out he went back for a double portion of Mom's Apple Pie with whipped cream.

"Much as I like your company," he said to Otto as he hung his ear protectors over the back of the spare chair, "I really must keep one eye on that clock up there."

He gestured with mock despair towards the Uncle Sam clock over the swing doors.

"Why do you say that?"

"I was just driving off when DHL brought me a van full of forms to fill in. If I don't go back early I shan't get through them."

"Can't they wait? Most things can."

"No, they involve money. A lot of it."

Otto performed the introductions and Guderius and van Piet shook hands. Van Piet said he was on holiday. He'd driven over from Prague to Bad Sollmer the day before. He'd wanted to visit the area since he'd read about it last year. Guderius took him at face value.

"I actually live in Bad Sollmer. I own the wellness clinic there," he said but his attention was really on his lunch.

"I'm sorry about those forms," Otto put in as Guderius buttered his second roll. "Your shooting's starting to come good."

"Not as sorry as I am. But time, tide and paperwork wait for no man. Isn't that right, Mr Richards?"

Van Piet asked him please, to repeat what he'd said, then he laughed and agreed. He wished his German was better, he added, but he didn't get the practice.

Guderius did most of the talking but it still didn't take him long to finish. He swallowed the last of his water, wiped his mouth with a serviette then wiped his face, which was heated and sweaty, with another one while he gave Uncle Sam a hard look.

"I think I can cram some more shooting in," he said as he stood up. "I'll see how it goes."

He shook hands, gathered up his ear protectors, wished van Piet a pleasant afternoon in English and disappeared through the swing doors, sliding his tray into a rack-on-wheels as he went.

"What was the gun Dr Guderius said he'd been using?" asked van Piet. "I don't think I've heard the name before."

"A Ceska CZ83. It's not his, it's one of ours, but he seems to like it, which doesn't surprise me. It's a gun I like myself. Come to think of it, there's been a run on Ceska 83s lately. I reckon" – he did a quick mental count – "at least five different people have been using them."

"I suppose people see them on television."

"Or in films. It's hard to explain sometimes but you get these fashions here."

Otto was in Chameleon but only on the fringe. He hadn't been told about Steinmeier's delivery and he hadn't asked where the new Ceskas came from. Van Piet finished his milk shake and tidied his tray. He'd been given a site plan when he came in. He took it out and studied it while Otto was finishing.

"What's this?" he asked, pointing to an X with Long Range printed above it.

"It's a bit too advanced for you, Mr Richards. It's one of the longest indoor ranges in Germany."

"Really? Who would use something like that?"

"Deer hunters, competition shooters – anyone who needs to hit his target from a long way away. That could be you if you take more lessons but not today, I think."

"I'd still like to see it though. Do you think I could?"

"I'll find out for you. You might be lucky."

He took out his radio and asked whether anyone was on the Long Range at the moment.

"Booked for the day you say? Who's got it then? Anyone I know?"

Automatically he said the names out loud as he heard them.

"Frank Zimmermann and Brigitte Danzig, eh? Is Kurt Zimmermann on site by any chance? Not till this evening. That's too bad but thanks all the same."

He terminated the call.

"Sorry, Mr Richards. It's booked all day and the father of one of the people using it isn't around at the moment so I can't ask him to help out. You should've asked while Dr Guderius was here. It's two of his friends have got it so he might've helped as well. As it stands no one's allowed onto the range or into the viewing gallery while they're shooting. Mr Schwarzer's orders."

"That's a bit strict, isn't it?"

"They're probably sharpening up for a competition. They wouldn't want anyone seeing what they can and can't do any more than you would."

"Can you get that kind of range with any sort of rifle?" he fished.

"No. My understanding is they're using Dragunovs."

He said it extra clearly for van Piet's benefit and added,

"They're a lovely weapon. More like a musical instrument. They go back to the Soviet Union but they're still as good as you'll get. I've never used anything better, that's for sure. Up here, I mean," he added, just a bit hastily.

So they're practising with Dragunovs, van Piet reflected. That gives them a killing range of two miles and more. That was useful knowledge and van Piet filed it away with the rest.

It was time to get the lessons restarted but first van Piet made an excuse to go out to the Skoda. He needed to check Chopine had made her call and return it. When he finally said goodbye to Otto he tipped him generously but he didn't say he'd earned it mostly in the restaurant. Guderius's Mercedes had already gone. As van Piet drove off he wondered how Chopine had been getting on since he'd spoken to her. Probably she'd been sunning herself. Or maybe she'd headed for the pool. Now she'd found out Guderius was going back to London she might as well enjoy herself. She didn't have anything else to do.

20

Inside the villa

All SRO field workers could pick locks because Trilling insisted on it. Chopine was better than most, she knew it and she'd brought her picks along in the hope she'd be able to use them. Airport security in London hadn't caught them because she hadn't gone through it. Being SRO had been enough and she expected it to be enough again at Leipzig/Halle when she went back. If van Piet had known about them he'd have taken them from her, she was sure of that. But he hadn't so when she pulled her tracksuit top on it covered a strapped-on case of picks and tensioners. She'd brought a pair of fine cotton gloves as well – they went with the picks.

This time round she left the clinic by the main entrance. As she went she told Reception she was going to do a few laps round the grounds. Then she'd find somewhere quiet and sunbathe till she was ready to come in for a shower. The receptionist believed her because she had no reason not to. The edges of the grounds were deserted as Chopine started padding round them. When she reached her turn-off point she glanced all round, reckoned Frisch was safely back in the clinic and headed for the canvas round the scaffolding.

Behind it was much as she'd expected. On the ground was a beaten-up skip, inside which were slabs of plaster, fragments of wood and carpet, and a sawn-up timber bedstead. A water-stained mattress was in there as well. Above the skip was the chute. It was a broad yellow tube made of reinforced plastic sections. Each section had a pair of moulded handles sticking out and the whole arrangement was fixed to the wall with metal hoops that made it stand out a little way. Let into the top was an oversize hopper and above the hopper was the green canvas where the window had come out. Chopine was sure she could get up there without any trouble. When she reached the hopper she'd release the canvas along its bottom edge and heave herself in.

The handles were rough but she needed clean gloves for inside the villa so she turned the ones she'd brought with her inside out. It felt strange pulling them on in hot weather but she didn't waste time thinking about it. She flexed her fingers till they felt good and strong then she clambered over the top of the skip onto the rubbish. It scrunched a bit but it didn't give way and now the bottom end of the chute was within easy reach. She gave it an exploratory tug. There was some play but nothing disastrous. It'd hold.

Once she was in the hopper she manoeuvred herself into as near a crouch as she could manage and by pressing her face against the wall she could see how the canvas was fixed over the opening. It was too long in fact but some holes had been hacked into it and they'd been passed over hooks let into the wall. Three of these hooks were below the stone sill – one for each corner and one for the middle - and the bottom edge had been lifted up over them, possibly from a ladder lashed to the scaffolding. If the ladder had still been there it'd have saved her a lot of trouble but, not surprisingly – like the rope on a pulley hanging idle and any spare planks – it wasn't, so now she had to find something to hold onto while she reached up to do the unhooking. If she toppled backwards she was dead.

She decided to start on the left and work across. She'd push her right hand up under the canvas between the centre hook and the one on the left, hold onto the sill and lean out to the left hand corner. So she took her gloves off for extra grip, slid her picks towards the middle of her back and, using the upper part of the hopper to help her balance, she worked her right hand up the brickwork. But the sill was too thick and smooth and if she hadn't dropped down quickly she'd have toppled to the ground. She refocused and tried again but the sill was still too much for her. Her only option was to lunge blindly over it and hope for a handhold inside. By now she was getting a feel for the way the hopper wobbled when she moved so when she tried for a third time she was able, by thrusting upwards past her point of balance, to drive her hand into the opening and grab the inside sill which, being thinner and made of wood, was easier to get her fingers round. The side of her head was pressing against the outside of the canvas but she now had the height she needed so, steadying herself with her feet and right hand, she inched her left hand out towards the corner hook, slid the canvas off it then, gingerly changing hands, she slid it off the middle one before leaning out to free the right-hand corner.

The bottom edge was now hanging loose. One-handedly she manipulated it over her head and shoulders then pulling with both hands on the inside sill and pushing her feet against the rim of the hopper she hauled herself into the room and, dry mouthed and sweaty, slithered onto the floor. She took a moment to get her breath back then she eased herself to her feet and lifted the canvas back over its hooks. If Frisch or anyone else came by they'd see nothing to make them reach for their mobiles.

There were no other windows in the room so she had to let her eyes adapt to the dimness. The bedstead and the mattress in the skip indicated the room was once a bedroom but no one would want to sleep in it now. The whole ceiling had been saturated and, to Chopine's right, a large segment had collapsed leaving the joists exposed. Round the hole deals held in place by stanchions were stopping even more of it coming down. Swathes of wallpaper had either soaked off or been pulled off, exposing plaster that was cracked and bowed where it hadn't come away altogether. Some of the floorboards had had sections cut out and those that remained had hacked out squares of carpet on them as if the workmen used them to kneel on. The tilt-and-turn unit that had once been the window leaned against one wall and power tools, caged light bulbs and drums of flex lay about near the door. An electric feed pulled through a gap in the floor signalled the room didn't have its own power any more. Dust with sole marks in it was everywhere and dust was something Chopine didn't want to take into the rest of the villa so she took her tracksuit off and minutely removed all the grime it'd gathered. There were some stains on the sleeves and round the knees. They looked like tar stains and they wouldn't come off.

Stepping in tracks a workman had left and squiggling her feet to make them smeary she crossed the room to the door, picking up one of the squares of carpet along the way. The door was locked and when she peeked into the keyhole she saw the key wasn't in it. That was a bonus. If she had to poke it out from her side it might make a noise as it hit the floor. She unzipped her picks, turned her gloves right side out and in seconds she had the door open. She'd been right about Guderius's house-keeping. She cleaned her soles meticulously on her square of carpet before she stepped out and skimmed her makeshift doormat back in. She didn't have to put any lights on in the corridor, there were skylights for that. Telling herself there was no way back she locked the door and moved on.

The silence in the villa was deep and somehow threatening. The first room she entered was a bedroom-cum-guestroom. The ceiling was stained almost as far as the bed but it hadn't come down, which explained why the bed had simply been covered with polythene sheeting. The curtains had been left up as well. They were open and through the window, which she stayed well back from, she could see some of the trees that made Guderius's heart lift. All the top floor doors turned out to be locked – even one that opened into a lavatory and one with a bathroom behind it.

The corridor terminated in a landing and a staircase led down to the next floor. The last room before the landing was larger than the others and had to be Guderius's bedroom. It had a king-sized bed in it and pink silk was the fabric of choice. A gleaming Rococo table with an inlaid top stood against one wall but if it was hiding anything Chopine couldn't find it. It was the same with the drawers, the closet and the en suite lavatory and bathroom. She couldn't find anything. Puzzled, she relocked everything and crept down the stairs. The windows in the side wall had their curtains drawn shut. They were made of cotton and they glowed from the sunlight streaming onto them.

There were only two large rooms and a smaller one on the second floor, which was dominated by a gallery overlooking the entrance hall below. Like the great staircase leading up to it, it had a balustrade made of carved oak. She decided to begin with the room furthest from her but before she could get to it she heard a noise from the double front door as if someone was about to open it. Her pulse shot up and her senses went onto full alert but although she listened hard she couldn't hear any follow-up. It had to be a security check. The silence dragged on and finally she was convinced no one was coming in. Relief coursed through her but the anxiety stayed. It hadn't been Guderius but it could've been: she was living off her luck. All her training was shouting at her to get out right now but she couldn't do it. Maybe she'd be all right if she raised her speed instead.

The room she'd been heading for was under the one she'd got into the villa through and inside it looked like some kind of drawing room. She stayed in the doorway because the curtains had gone but she could still see some of the ceiling had come away and more deals and stanchions were propping up the rest. The carpet was rolled back and there was a pile of debris on the floorboards. Everything salvageable, including a dust-covered grand piano, had been moved to the other end of the room.

What the middle room was Chopine couldn't figure out at all. Not at first anyway. It looked as if it might be for banquets, except the highly polished table was too small and gauze over the windows muted the light. The flooring was parquet with a band of maroon carpet round the edges and the walls had ornately framed oil paintings on them. Virtually all of them were enormous and suddenly the penny dropped. They weren't there to decorate the room they were what the room was for. They all showed scenes from the same part of East Germany, a stretch of lakes and peat moors near Berlin, and its name – the Havelland – was on most of the captions. Some of the paintings showed wildfowl over open water, others showed woodland paths with sunlight shafting through the trees. The skies were big and where land and water met the division was often blurred.

"It's like a shrine," Chopine thought. "What kind of sense does that make?"

Quite a lot, she decided once she'd got her head straight. Guderius came from the Havelland, she knew that from Ashell House, and these pictures must show what he grew up with – water, sky and solitude. Was he a lonely man inside? Was that why he depended on Gannisch? And was the Havelland the only past he clung to? He liked to be known as ex-army but the NPA and the country it'd defended didn't exist any more. Then there was Schwarzer's and the old-time cronies he met there. And this Colonel Steffen, the man behind Chameleon. All that was past as well. Guderius was coming across as someone who got his bearings chiefly from his memories. It occurred to her that a man like that could do sinister things on the quiet and suddenly she was very afraid. But she still wasn't getting out. Ashell House would eat out of her hand when she told them what she'd seen and there was probably more to come. She looked round one last time, relocked the door and switched her mind to the third room.

In it were a filing cabinet, two desks and a brown easy chair. It had to be Guderius's private office. One of the desks was modern and plain but the other one was breathtaking even to a non-expert like Chopine. It was a secretary desk by the great David Roentgen – the maker had worked his name into the wooden top. The desk had a multitude of drawers but when she unlocked them, they were all empty. The same applied to the modern desk except for one drawer, which was crammed with stationery, paper clips and so forth. In the filing cabinet too the one drawer that was not empty had no more in it than some reams of A4 and an unopened box of wallet files. She was even more puzzled now than when she'd been upstairs. All these rooms and drawers were locked regardless. And while a lot of things had been removed, others hadn't and they weren't all bric a brac. Far from it.

Then the ideas started to flow. The paintings pointed to a locked-in child, the army thing pointed to a locked-in loyalist and all the doors and drawers spelled out a locked-in personality. So far, so consistent. But why had some things been removed and others left, including paintings and superb antique furniture? Guderius was a cautious man, she'd learned that from Frisch, and he must know locks like his could easily be forced or picked. So why had he settled for them? She wasted precious seconds looking for the answer, then she thought she had it.

The way she figured it, he'd been in a hurry to beat the workmen he knew had to come in but for his own murky reasons he'd limited his helpers to one or two trusties. That meant he'd had to balance what was sensitive against what could be easily moved. His files were sensitive so they'd gone, but his antiques, while sensitive in their way, were also more cumbersome so, like the grand piano and the paintings, they'd stayed. That left his personal things and they'd stayed because he needed them.

But was there anything sensitive that was still in the villa because it *couldn't* be moved – like a safe fixed to the floor? If so, where was it? In a room on the ground floor? Or in the basement she'd noticed from outside? If there was a safe she could almost certainly open it and then, as likely as not, she'd have him where she wanted him: pinned to a board like a moth.

On a new high she set off down the great staircase where something even more tempting struck her. Why did it have to be something *in* a room? Why couldn't a room itself be locked away – a room no one was supposed to know about? She was really excited now. When she reached the bottom of the stairs the double front door with its gaol-size lock and iron-ring handle were like a final invitation to get clear. But in the mood she was in she blanked it out.

Guderius, meanwhile, was in Gannisch's office getting himself organised. He'd been in two minds as he drove back from Schwarzer's whether to shower and change in his villa, then fill in his forms in the clinic, or collect what he needed from the clinic and then move on to his villa. In the end the villa had got the nod – he was safe from disturbance there – so he pulled up near the clinic's front entrance, told Gannisch what he was going to do and began piling what he needed into a carrier basket Frisch brought him from Stores. His car could stay where it was. The weather was a joy, he was used to high humidity and the walk to his villa would be good for his varicose veins.

"If you leave your office," he told Gannisch as he tested the weight of the basket, "take your mobile with you. There'll be a lot I'll have to ask you about."

"Isn't there always? Incidentally, Mrs Carrick wants to see you before she leaves tomorrow morning. She seems a very nice young lady, I must say. Not like some bumptious numbers we could mention."

"Put a note in her pigeon-hole. Say she can come to your office when she's ready, I'll be around somewhere. Where is she now, by the way? She could bring a lot of business our way if we play our cards right."

"She told Reception she was going jogging. A few laps round the grounds with some sunbathing to follow. You should do some yourself – jogging, I mean. You're getting far too fat and you know it."

Guderius liked being mothered but he didn't like to show it so he harrumphed "I'm the medical director here, Hanna" and topped up the carrier basket with the parcel of forms. He thought about making two loads but he didn't want to lose any more time so he thought again. He'd overrun at Schwarzer's and time in Gannisch's office always melted like snow in springtime.

"Give Matti a buzz," he said on his way through the door. "Tell him I don't want any more checks on my villa till I say. I don't want doors being rattled while I'm concentrating."

He was scarcely outside when some guests coming in from tennis stopped him to tell him how wonderful the clinic was and then a couple who came every year wanted to discuss their latest ailments with him. It all took time and the basket was getting heavier but he enjoyed being the master of his universe so he spun things out even longer than his guests would've done without his help.

In the villa, however, Chopine's nerves were twanging again. Her belief she'd find much more was waning and panic about Guderius was taking over.

A visitors' lavatory with lots of fluffy towels had been the first ground floor room she'd opened. Then came a utility room smelling of soap and disinfectant. She glanced hastily at the neatly shelved tins and bottles but she didn't see anything to make her look twice except for two wooden cupboards. One was floor to ceiling and the other one, which was padlocked, was mounted at eye level. The floor to ceiling one contained brooms, mops, a vacuum cleaner and some housecoats. The eye level one, which was full of dusters, tea towels and dish cloths, was padlocked because it also had three sets of cleaners' keys hanging from hooks inside it. If she'd been less stressed she'd have laughed out loud when she saw them. All that lock-picking and the room keys had been waiting for her behind a simple-to-open padlock. Guessing correctly that Guderius managed everything with just a few master keys, she helped herself.

A lavishly equipped kitchen and a nearby dining room revealed nothing more than greed and prissy neatness, then a short, dark corridor brought her to the door to the double garage. Her tension eased when she saw his car wasn't there. There was just a row of brand new wheelchairs with arm, back and head supports. The last room on the ground floor was a reception room. There were no mysteries in there either.

So, now for the lift. She'd seen the sign from the staircase but she'd wanted to clear the ground floor before she tried it. She put Guderius's keys back where they came from – as long as she had them she felt like a target waiting to be hit and anyway they didn't open locks like the one in the flap by the lift. When she peeked behind it all she saw was a red light that was out. She supposed it lit up when the lift wasn't on the ground floor but she didn't ask herself why it should be locked away. Her sharpness had just about gone.

She guessed there'd be stairs – probably concrete - to the basement behind the door next to the lift and she felt a sort of relief when she found she was right because to her mind steps, not the lift, were the safe way down. Even so, she had to take a quick look at the lift first, just to leave no stone unturned. She pressed the button in the wall and its door slid sideways.

When she stepped in the first thing she did was jam a finger onto the "Open" button to make sure nothing closed behind her. She saw straight away you got in one side and you got out the other, which made sense, but strangely it only operated between the ground floor and the basement and now she was in it, it seemed abnormally large. Perhaps whatever was down below would explain those things. Gearing up for one last effort she stepped back out and waited till the door closed. Then she moved to the stairs, found a timer switch and pushed it to put the lights on. It gave her a trapped feeling to lock the door behind her but she did it anyway. She couldn't afford not to.

21

Guderius springs his trap

In the basement enough light was filtering in to let Chopine leave the lighting off. She left the ventilation and the temperature control off as well - a change of air would advertise someone had been down there. Seeing the antiques made her angry with herself. She should've thought of a basement workshop, given she'd been briefed about Guderius's hobby.

"So much for the secret room," she muttered self-accusingly. "There isn't one."

She'd take a quick look round now she was down there though, then she'd definitely get out fast.

She began with the drawers and cabinets, then came the first of the big cupboards between the lift and the outside wall. The door slid open as if it had nothing to hide but in the wall in front of her was the grey steel door. Her eyes widened and she breathed in sharply.

"I *was* right!" she exulted. "I've got you, Guderius! I've got you, I've got you, I've got you!"

The darkness behind the steel door reminded her this room didn't have any windows so she could put the lighting on. She groped around inside the doorway, found a switch and lit the room up but she didn't lock herself in because half her mind was on her exit. And the ventilation and the temperature control stayed switched off. She could see she was in a laboratory and she wished she had her notebook and pen with her but she hadn't so she'd have to memorise. She noticed some mirror glass where the wall she'd come through was built out. It had to be one-way but it didn't bother her. She guessed it was there to let Guderius watch his witchcraft from a safe place. She didn't think he could be behind it right now. She didn't know he was opening his front door.

He was focused on his paperwork when he let himself in but he'd stuck a bookcase together before he'd left for Schwarzer's and he wanted to see whether the glue had taken first. He laid the basket on the stairs, went across to the lift and when he saw the red light was on he froze. Someone was in his laboratory.

He stole down the emergency stairs, checked no one was in his workshop then locked the door behind him as he'd locked the one at the top of the stairs. He didn't want anyone getting out by pushing past him. He gently tried the doors of the cupboard and the laboratory and found they were unlocked. That told him his prey was only feet away. Imperceptibly he locked the steel door and, gloating malevolently, he went through the second floor to ceiling cupboard into the inspection booth.

Chopine was memorising a separator, a centrifuge, an incubator and a sputum reader when he saw her through the glass. She had her back to him but he knew straight away who she was.

"You must've been surprised to find all this, Mrs Carrick," he murmured grimly. "But you'll be even more surprised at what comes next."

Using a dimly-lit console and leaving the temperature control untouched he isolated the laboratory's ventilation system and switched it on. It didn't whirr, make the lights flicker or generate a draught, it was too well designed for that, and its inflow and extractor had separate controls. He turned the extractor to low and replaced the incoming air with carbon monoxide till an unlabelled detector he could see from the booth went from green to red. The laboratory was now full of carbon monoxide. He shut the extractor right down, closed off the inflow and watched Chopine closely. He didn't want her dead, that would've created too many problems, but he did want her unconscious. He saw her reach out towards nothing with one hand and put the other one up to her head. Then her legs buckled and she lay staring sightlessly into one of the ceiling lights. Her face was red from the gas she'd breathed in.

As soon as she was still he put the extractor on full and fed clean air in. When the detector turned green he let himself in and dragged her into the workshop, taking care not to bruise her. He peeled her gloves off to feel her pulse, noticed they were dirty inside and stuffed them in his pocket. As he expected, her pulse was high but it'd slow down in time. He rolled her onto her front, took a hand towel off a hook and blindfolded her with it in the belief that if she couldn't see when she came round it'd take the resistance out of her. Then he cut off two lengths of the narrow-gauge rope he used for bundling wood and tied her wrists with one length, leaving enough slack for her arms to remain by her sides. When he'd done that he rolled her onto her back, crossed her ankles so the inside bones wouldn't impact on each other and tied them up with the other length. He'd already discovered her picks but he let them be for now. Finally he drew her sleeves up above her elbows, then he hurried twice into his laboratory. He came out the first time with two full-size gas bottles on a trolley. The second time, he brought an uncapped syringe of Thiopentone. Anything else depended on what Mrs Carrick said or didn't say when she came round.

He put the syringe where he could reach it and waited. Soon her colour was back to normal and she started to move her fingers. It was time to act. He couldn't help himself, he had to model himself on Steffen when he was dealing with Carey. He pressed her hands down and brought his mouth close to her ear.

"Don't move!" he ordered. "This is Dr Guderius speaking. When I take my hands away don't make a sound if you want to stay alive."

Hearing Guderius's name reminded her who she was supposed to be. He took his hands away and paused.

"Who are you?" he asked, satisfied she wouldn't start screaming.

"I'm Alice Carrick," she forced herself to say. "I'm a British journalist. Untie me this instant. You've no right to treat me like this."

"How do I know you're not lying? You could be anyone."

"My name's on my passport, which you can see when you like. It's also on my flight tickets. I defy you to prove I'm not Alice Carrick because I know you can't."

Guderius wavered. He hadn't expected a fight.

"We'll see about that," he bluffed, "but first I want to know what you're doing in my villa. And if I think you're lying, I'll kill you."

Chopine was getting her wits back fast. It helped that the knot in the towel was hurting the back of her head. She really was a journalist, she insisted, but she wanted to spice her story up before she filed it and that was why she was in his villa. She was hoping to find evidence the clinic was in trouble – buried scandal, the law, tax, it didn't matter what so long as it was bad. Horror stories sold better than happy stories and she was out to swell her pay cheque. And the picks? She always carried them. They went with her kind of writing.

It all seemed to hang together but Guderius was afraid he was missing something. New Hope could yet be involved, maybe someone had opened his mouth too wide. Just the thought made him panicky and it didn't help that he'd compared himself to Steffen. What'd he think if he could see him now? Nervously he attacked Chopine's story every way he could but it was useless so he decided, if he couldn't make her crack he'd make her harmless instead. In fact, he told himself, that was the best solution anyway. What was more, Ulrich needn't be any the wiser. It was Calais all over again. He'd bent but he hadn't broken.

He ordered Chopine to count to fifty and, as he'd expected, being blindfolded finally made her compliant. As she approached twelve he reached for his syringe and slid the needle into the median cephalic vein in the hollow of her elbow. Within seconds she was unconscious again and he could get back into his laboratory. He put the used syringe into a sharps box, filled a fresh one from a light-proof bottle labelled Lethenol and injected the full dose into the same vein in her other arm. Because the Thiopentone would soon wear off he covered her mouth and nose with a mask from the bottles on the trolley and gave her a mix of oxygen and enhanced nitrous oxide to keep her out good and long. Then he pulled her sleeves down, took the towel off her eyes, untied her wrists and ankles and rolled her onto her front to stop her choking. When the lift came down he carefully dragged her into it, took her up to the ground floor and, with equal care, dragged her into the reception room.

Down below he'd noticed some stains on her tracksuit and he looked at them more closely now. Immediately they told him where she'd got in – there were some spots of tar on the inner sill where a workman had passed a caulking pot through – and anyone else who saw those stains might reach the same conclusion. They wouldn't know about the sill exactly but they'd know tar was being used up there because when it was boiled the smell went everywhere. That conclusion had to be prevented so the story for Chopine and everybody else would be she'd jogged too much in the heat and collapsed on the grass. That left getting rid of the stains. He drew the curtains so no one could see in and fetched some solvent from the utility room. But the stains wouldn't budge and more solvent might bleach the tracksuit. Then he had a better idea. He'd get her back to her room with the stains covered up and take things from there. He'd need Gannisch's help for that so, taking the basket of paperwork with him, he toiled upstairs to his office and rang her on her mobile.

"I want you here right now," he puffed. "Tell the desk I need help with some forms, then come in through the front door. I'll unlock it for you."

When he went downstairs he had a toothbrush and a small clothes brush with him.

Gannisch didn't take long and when Guderius led her into the reception room Chopine was still out to the wide and the air still smelled of solvent. Impassively Gannisch waited for Guderius to tell her what he wanted her to know.

"She got in where the window's missing," he came out with. "When I caught her she said she was looking for bad news about the clinic. She claimed she'd get more money if she found any."

"Was she telling the truth?"

"I don't know and I don't have to. I've given her a shot to blot out her short-term memory. When she wakes up she'll know who and where she is but she won't know what she's been doing all afternoon. It's like when you've been drunk but without the hangover, which is just as well since the anaesthetic she's under could make her feel pukey. She isn't bruised, I've seen to that, but I've got to make sure neither she nor anyone else sees these stains."

He selected a key for her.

"Go into the garage and get me one of the wheelchairs in there. We're taking her back to her room."

She helped him strap Chopine in so her arms, back and head were fully supported. He twisted the stains on her sleeves out of sight and covered the ones on her knees with one of his fluffy towels. Then they wheeled her out through the garage's rear door.

"We'll go into the clinic the back way," he said while Gannisch did the pushing, "and we'll use the service lift. We don't want more guests seeing her than have to. She looks like death."

When they went in Frisch was in a storeroom unpacking and logging neon tubes. It struck Guderius he'd be exactly the right person to spread the story about Chopine fainting. And if Chopine did her own asking that's the story she'd hear back. Brilliant!

"Sorry to disturb you, Matti," he said. "I saw Mrs Carrick from my window, she'd fainted on the grass. Too much running in the sunshine, I'm afraid."

"Oh, dear me!" he exclaimed as he looked at her closely. "Will she be all right?"

"Rest in a cool place is all she needs. We're taking her up to her room for now but you'll see, she'll be out and about before the day's over."

Once they were in Chopine's room Guderius lowered the blinds and told Gannisch to take the duvet off. Then they heaved her face down onto the bed. Guderius took off her shoes but he asked Gannisch to take off her tracksuit. He felt finicky about touching women if she was about.

"Our little snooper's done us a favour using one of our tracksuits," he said, holding on to her shoes.

Chopine was as still as a corpse. Her watch was on her wrist and her case of picks lay next to her.

"How so?"

"We can get her into a clean one before she comes round, that's how so. Take this towel and tracksuit to the gym dispensary. Give them the fainting story while you're at it. The towel's got my bar code on it so they'll know it's mine. Say I wiped her face with it and now I want it cleaned."

"And the tracksuit? The dispensary will see the stains. So will the laundry come to that."

"Say she picked the stains up when she fell on the grass. The men working on the villa must have spilled some tar there. And we want to put a clean one on her for when she comes round so you want another one in her size, please. You can feed Carrick the same line in case the new tracksuit feels different. And spell out it was you who put it on her. I don't want her having hostile fantasies about me."

He fished the gloves out of his pocket.

"One more thing, Hanna. These gloves are hers and, look, they're dirty inside. If we give them back like this she'll know collapsing onto grass isn't the only thing she's been up to. The dispensary might get ideas as well."

"Lose them then."

"No good, she'll be able to remember packing them. She may even have a list for when she's packing. I've thought about making one myself before now."

Gannisch ignored that and held out her hand.

"Give them here. I'll wash them myself and get them back to her."

"Yes, but she'll wonder why you didn't take them to the laundry with the tracksuit."

"No she won't. Not when I point out they haven't got a bar code."

His face lit up and he kissed her on the cheek.

"Hanna," he exclaimed, "if there were angels you'd be one of them. Now, be as quick as you can. I'll stay here till you get back."

While she was gone Guderius worked the grime out of Chopine's socks with the brush he'd brought, then he cleaned her shoes with the toothbrush and a little water. While he was doing that he thought about her picks. He was sure he could trust the Lethenol but it was still a good idea if she didn't see them when she came round. He wondered where she kept them when she wasn't wearing them. In her suitcase probably. He soon found it. It had a combination lock but Chopine wasn't the only one who could breeze past such things. In a large zip-up pocket he found a passport, some signed credit cards and a packet of travel documents – all bearing the name Alice Elizabeth Carrick. There was a mobile in there as well. He switched it on, found a *Sunday Times* number in the directory and copied it down. He wiped everything he'd touched with his handkerchief as he put it back, took a chance with the picks by putting them in as well and gave the whole case a wipe as he put it away.

When Gannisch came back he told her to stay with Chopine till she woke up. If she threw up Gannisch was to say it was routine for heat exhaustion. Gannisch fetched a vomit bowl from under the sink in the bathroom. Every room in the clinic had one.

"You're going to get on with your forms now, are you?" she asked.

"I've got something else to do first and it's off site."

"Who'll be in charge then? It can't be me if I'm up here."

"I'll find someone. I shan't be gone long."

Gannisch made herself comfortable on a maple-frame settee with low-hanging covers and Guderius took the wheelchair down to the ground floor. He didn't mind who saw it now. One of his senior staff, Dr Torsten Mallik, was in the vestibule chatting to the receptionist. Mallik was the complete opposite to Guderius. He was in his early forties, he was fit and he came from the Rhineland. He knew about East Germany from tv documentaries and he hated everything he saw. His specialism was Sports Medicine. He'd helped Guderius separate a lot of fitness freaks from a lot of money so Guderius had promoted him fast. He wanted to hang onto him.

"Ah, Torsten!" he exclaimed. "The very man! The journalist who's visiting us from London, Mrs Carrick, she's been laid low by the heat. Miss Gannisch is in her room with her and I have to go off-site on an errand. Can you mind the shop till one of us is free again?"

Mallik said it was no trouble at all and asked the receptionist to spread the word. He strolled with Guderius to his Mercedes and helped his employer by putting the wheelchair in the boot.

"Matti Frisch needs to know I've gone out again," Guderius said confidentially as he moved to the driver's door. "One check will be enough."

He didn't want Frisch to think anything connected with his villa had changed. He might link it to the pale Mrs Carrick and tell people more than he should.

Once Guderius was through the gates he headed straight for Dresden's mainline railway station and found himself a pay phone on the concourse. He had a cash call to England to make and all the change from his glove box was in a bag in his hand. He had to know whether Chopine was really from the *Sunday Times*. He tapped in the number from her mobile.

"*Sunday Times*, Travel Section."

He switched into English, gave his name as Schremp and said he was calling from Germany. Could he speak to Mrs Carrick, please? Mrs Alice Carrick?

"One moment, Sir."

It was a high-pitched woman's voice he heard. She spoke slowly with a non-regional accent and clear consonants. The SRO didn't want anyone ringing off because they couldn't understand what was being said to them.

"Yes, I thought so," the voice came back. "Mrs Carrick's not staff, she's contract, and she's on an assignment for us till tomorrow. In your country, actually. Can I take a message?"

"No thank you. My information is confidential. I'll try again later."

He hung up and went back to his car with a big smile on his face. He didn't have to confess anything to Steffen, New Hope was unscathed and his self-esteem was back where it normally was – at the top of the scale.

Trilling was in his room when Response passed the details through. It was Guderius's voiceprint and he'd rung from a pay phone in Dresden. Trilling didn't need to read the transcript twice to see something had gone wrong. Why was Guderius checking Chopine's alias? How had he got access to her mobile? Should he intervene right now or should he wait? He decided to intervene. He'd finish what he was doing, then he'd try to get hold of van Piet.

22

"Do you think he's ever killed someone?"

Chopine surfaced in stages and then she was fully awake. She saw Gannisch smiling benignly at her from the settee and wondered why the blinds were down. Then she wanted to be sick and Gannisch seemed to be expecting it. When she stopped retching Gannisch fetched some water for her, wiped her forehead with a towel and fed her the fainting story. Chopine didn't believe her – she'd never fainted in her life – but what had happened if she hadn't fainted? She couldn't answer that. There was a complete blank in her head.

The gloves thing sounded just as weird. Had she really been wearing gloves in bright sunshine? But if she had, why? She scented danger so she improvised.

"I often wear gloves when I run. My knuckles get dry and gloves stop that happening. Here, let me show you."

She held her hands out in front of her.

"That's incredible," Gannisch smiled. "No dry skin at all."

They lapsed into silence. Chopine continued to perk up but her memory refused to come back. She was anxious as well. She was certain she'd done something wrong but she didn't know what it was. She eased herself off the bed. It made her feel groggy but she forced herself to pretend she was all right. She hoped Gannisch would let something slip if she admitted she'd lost her memory but all she got was soothing noises. Then she said how grateful she was to be looked after so well, she'd write how caring the clinic was in her article. And she could put the duvet back herself, it was no trouble at all. Gannisch knew she was being shown the door but she didn't mind: Chopine's amnesia looked rock solid. When she left she took the vomit bowl and towel with her as if she'd been making a routine call. And she hung on to the gloves.

Chopine checked the corridor in case she'd crept back to listen at the door, then fetched her mobile out of her suitcase. When she saw her picks something told her they shouldn't be there. She had a hazy notion she'd strapped them on. She knew she had to call van Piet at 5.30 and her watch told her there were eight minutes to go. She drank some more water, dragged the duvet onto the bed and sat down heavily on the settee. She'd wait till 5.30 exactly. It'd make her feel she was in control of something.

Sitting still made her realise she was too warm with the tracksuit on but she didn't have the energy to change into something else so she settled for pulling up the sleeves and blowing on her wrists and forearms. As she blew she noticed a pink mark on the inside of one of her elbows as if the vein was healing from a wound. She checked the other elbow, found the same thing and realised straight away: she'd been injected. By Gannisch? No, she wasn't a nurse. By Guderius then! Yes, it had to be him. So that was why she'd passed out and – of course – that was why she had this memory blank. She didn't wait any longer, she called van Piet straight away.

He was in his room in The Golden Bear and Trilling had just been telling him about Guderius's phone call. Had Dawn spooked Guderius or had Guderius just been clever? Van Piet said she was due to call him shortly. He'd get answers.

"I might have to go and see her," he added. "Set me up as another *Sunday Times* freelance. That'll do for Reception and I might meet Guderius again. He could get nosey this time."

Chopine's call came through straight after. She told him about the puncture wounds and the memory blank.

"I'm coming over," he said. "Stay in your room till I get there. If anyone's with you, put your 'Do not disturb' sign out. If I don't see it I'll come in without knocking. You never know who's listening down the corridor."

He tacked on the cover story he'd agreed with Trilling.

There was no sign out when he arrived so he let himself in with his card. She'd already changed out of her tracksuit. It could go back when he left. He asked her to repeat what she'd said on the phone and this time she included her picks and why it bothered her where she'd found them. She also included her gloves. Now she'd had time to think she was afraid to leave anything out.

"We don't know why you've been injected, we don't know for certain where it happened and we don't know if it was Guderius who did it. All we know is, he's involved somehow and so is Gannisch. There could be others as well. Your picks say you might've been in Guderius's villa."

"I truly can't remember. It's as if part of my brain's been cut out."

Van Piet made up his mind. He called Trilling and summarised what Chopine had said. She noticed he didn't mention her picks or her gloves.

"Shall I get her out or leave her where she is?"

"Leave her where she is. If she checks out now it'll make Guderius dive for cover and if he's really teamed up with Steffen, he'll want Steffen to do the same. We can't let that happen, Willem. They have to keep coming towards us so we can flush out what they're up to and they won't do that unless they think no one's looking."

"So you think it's safe for Dawn to spend the night here."

"Anyone wanting to kill her would've done it by now. So, yes, it's safe."

"What about her health? She's had these injections, don't forget."

"The obnoxious part of my job is keeping my priorities straight and top of the list is the national interest. So, sorry, she's got to tough it out. When she gets back we'll look after her. She'll be in a closed ward in Guy's while you're still somewhere between Prague and London. Which reminds me, I want to see you in Ashell House before you go home. Call me when you land."

Chopine had heard it all and when van Piet asked her about staying, she said she hadn't joined the SRO to run away from things. Then her confidence wavered.

"Do *you* think I'm safe?" she asked tremulously.

"I agree with Mr Trilling. Because you're alive now you'll stay that way. Your hole in the head will help as well. Why should anyone kill you if you can't remember anything?"

But something else was bothering her as well.

"What are you going to do with me when we get back? Put me on a charge?"

"What for? I don't know what you've done."

"What about my gloves? No one wears gloves in this weather unless they're up to something. And then there's my picks. I'm pretty sure I strapped them on. I can sort of remember doing it."

She looked at him sharply.

"Why didn't you tell Mr Trilling about my picks and gloves?"

Van Piet chose his words carefully.

"It could be something will come back to you that will get you into trouble if you tell anyone. I don't want you to be in that situation because if you are, you might suppress essential information. So, I'm the senior officer on this assignment. That means if you remember anything at all it comes to me and me only, then it's up to me what happens to it. If you can't reach me directly get a message to Tom Garry and he'll do the rest. If you stick to that, it could help you as well as me. Do we understand each other?"

They did.

"When I leave here," he went on, "I'll take your picks with me and lose them for you. As for your gloves, wrap them up carefully and bring them to The Golden Bear on your way to the airport tomorrow."

"Will do. And thanks, Willem."

She shifted on the settee and looked round uneasily. All the arguments she'd heard said she'd be safe but with van Piet about to leave they suddenly seemed a bit thin.

"That Guderius gives me the creeps," she said. "He likes to come across as Dr Nice Guy but I think he's Dr Nasty. Do you think he's ever killed someone? I wouldn't mind betting he has. I imagine him with another villa somewhere else, only this time with a lake, and when the moon shines you see a dead body weighted down below the surface."

"You should write poetry. Nothing in his file says he's killed anyone."

"What does that prove? He ran away, don't forget. He must have had a reason for that."

"He was back after three months though. Was that running away?"

"All right, I suppose it wasn't." Then, "Can you make any sense of all this, Willem? Any sense at all?"

"I'm doing my best but it isn't easy. I think Mr Trilling's right: we have to let them keep coming towards us. That should make things clearer."

When van Piet left the clinic Chopine was feeling shaky again but she insisted on going down to the vestibule with him.

"If we're seen together," she said, "which we shall be, it'll underline the fact that someone from outside knows about me. That's extra protection for me."

She slept badly that night and several times she woke up thinking she'd heard the door open. First thing next morning she rang van Piet. He thought someone might have been listening in case she talked in her sleep. When she saw Guderius she should emphasise her memory was still defunct.

She'd already breakfasted and packed when she had her farewell chat with him.

"When I go to London," he said, leaning back comfortably, "I like to combine pleasure with business. My hobby – no, my passion – is antique furniture and there's no better place for buying it than your great capital."

He watched her closely but "antique furniture" didn't seem to ring any bells so he added,

"As you know, I'm going to London again shortly. It'd be a joy for me if we could meet while I'm there. For dinner, perhaps?"

"He wants to keep checking," she thought. "If only I knew what I turned up yesterday. It must have been something really big."

"What a lovely idea!" she exclaimed. "I'll give you a contact."

She asked him for a piece of paper and in her neat round handwriting she wrote "Mrs Rosamond Lobell", followed by a phone number and an e-mail address – all courtesy of the SRO's Response Unit.

"Mrs Lobell is my agent," she lied. "You can phone or e-mail her any time and she'll do the rest."

She guessed he wouldn't risk contacting her through a third party but he thanked her all the same. It'd been a long shot and anyway, everything he'd heard told him the Lethenol was doing its job.

"Let me give you these in exchange," he said, taking something wrapped in GRWC paper from a drawer in his desk. "It's your gloves. From Miss Gannisch."

"Oh, she's so thoughtful! I must confess I'd just about written them off."

She took them from him but she left them wrapped and they were still wrapped when she dropped them off at The Golden Bear. In London she was intercepted as she was leaving her plane and was taken by ambulance to Guy's. While she was in transit two arrivals from an earlier flight were grumbling about how long it was taking them to get off the airport. They were Kurt and Frank Zimmermann. There'd been a long queue at passport control and then their luggage carousel had jammed. A polite official was moving through the crowd to apologise for the delays. When he asked, Frank Zimmermann told him no, they didn't have any connections to worry about, they were staying in London. Yes, both of them. They were on holiday.

Van Piet was staying in London too but not, he hoped, for very long. When, frustratingly later than scheduled, he reached Heathrow an armed SRO driver discreetly made himself known. Van Piet asked him to wait while he made some phone calls. Célestine came first. He was back in London, he said, but it'd be some while before he could get home. Had there been any more letters? No, he heard, none at all. And she couldn't praise the Tylers enough. He told her he loved her and terminated the call. He knew she'd wait up for him so he didn't bother to tell her not to. She'd waited beyond sunrise before now. His second call was to Sweelinck. Had she come up with anything? She said she had and she was on duty all night so he could call her whenever he liked. His third call was to Trilling's secretary. He was on his way.

He put his mobile away, pulled out the handle of his case and walked across to his driver. The traffic was light and it didn't take them long to get to Ashell House. Once inside he asked Security to tell Mr Trilling he'd be with him just as soon as he'd put his suitcase in his office. When he opened the door the lights were on and Garry was in a visitor's chair drafting letters on his laptop.

"Welcome back, Sir. I heard you were due. I came in to see if I could do anything."

Typical Garry. He should have been at home in Barnet but that wasn't his way. He'd been assigned to van Piet when van Piet had joined the SRO and he'd stayed with him ever since. Van Piet had seen to that.

"Thanks, Tom. In fact I'm glad you're here. Dawn Chopine's been hurt and Guy's is taking first look. She may want you to get a message to me. If that happens, I want to know straight away. She'll probably be nervous and she won't want anyone else to find out. That may affect how she does it, so be warned."

Next van Piet opened his suitcase and handed him the package Chopine had given him in The Golden Bear. It was taped up where he'd made sure it wasn't booby-trapped.

"This is a pair of lady's cotton gloves," he said. "I want them sent for a full fibre analysis before you go home. Urgent and results to me only. Keep your eyes peeled, Tom. I want those results as soon as they enter the building."

He wheeled his suitcase into a corner, ordered Garry to get back to Barnet as soon as he could and, with no great enthusiasm, adjusted his mind to his meeting with Trilling. The sooner it was over, the sooner he could get to Essex.

23

An identity for Hanno

A half eaten sandwich and a cup of cold tea told their own harassed story but as soon as van Piet was shown in Trilling's eyes lit up.

"Thanks for the update from Prague, Willem. Taken all in all it's been a useful mission."

He moved a ring binder to one side and picked up three manila envelopes plus a note he'd written by hand.

"Briefings for you on Frank Zimmermann, Kurt Zimmermann and Brigitte Danzig," he said as he reached them across. "My little note says Kapner is licensed to own a Beretta Compact. They're the best I can do. Skim through them quickly, then we can talk."

They didn't take long and Trilling, rubbing his hands, spoke first.

"It all hangs together, doesn't it? Steffen and Guderius have been over here, Frank Zimmermann and Danzig connect in through Guderius at Schwarzer's, and Kurt Zimmermann connects in through his son. Your Otto says there's been a run on Ceskas and Zimmermann and Danzig have been working out on Dragunovs. As I see it Chameleon's going shooting and the target's in this country. Kapner's probably been practising as well. It'd fit in with the rest."

"Anything else?"

"Plenty. We know when Guderius is coming back and Steffen's arranged to be over here between October 21st and November 3rd. That gives them plenty of time to get up to mischief. GCHQ's monitoring Steffen for us. You'll find the transcripts on your desk when you go home."

"Will they tell me what he's planning?"

"I wish they would. As you'll see, there are gaps so he could be using couriers for the sensitive stuff. Anyway, I've not finished yet. Frank Zimmermann flew in today with his father. They say they're on holiday in London and they're staying in Wapping Travelodge till Wednesday. I put Delia Blaine and Sean Choule onto them at the airport and they tailed them all the way there to make sure."

"Have they got their own transport?"

"Not yet and possibly not at all. They took a taxi into London. We asked the company where they were heading and by the time they got there, Technology had been in and wired their rooms for sound. Never underestimate the motor bike in London, Willem. I'm tempted to have their bags searched as well. What do you think?"

Van Piet shook his head.

"It's like bugging Kapner's flat –the risk's too great. If we shift even one telltale marker it could blow the whole thing. So, better not."

Trilling didn't argue and, not for the first time, he glanced at his phone. He said he was waiting for a call from Guy's.

"All I know so far," he said as he flipped through his scratch pad, "is that Dawn's had Thiopentone and enhanced nitrous oxide put into her. She must have really put someone's back up."

"Or some people's. Assuming the Thiopentone went into one arm what went into the other one?"

"That's what I'm waiting to find out. Apparently Guy's has asked the CIA for a steer."

They fell silent and the only sound came from the Hardey clock. Finally Trilling drummed his fingers on his desk and said,

"I keep wondering what they want sniper rifles for. Perhaps they're going to liquidate someone. It could be, you know. They've got a lot to hide."

"They must want them out of the way badly. Dragunovs are over four feet long and they weigh 9½ lbs a piece. You can't bring them in with your hand luggage."

"Weapons come apart and parts can be spread about. A bit on a ferry, a bit on a lorry – nothing easier. On the other hand, if we're watching when they and their weapons come together we're in with a chance. It's entirely up to us."

When the phone buzzed it startled them both. It was Guy's. Trilling gave van Piet an earpiece.

"I've just heard from Langley," a woman's voice came through. "We're looking at an amnesia promoter called Lethenol. It's freshly made – a year old at most, quite likely a lot less."

"Can you tell me any more about it?"

"It's an East German invention. It takes out short-term memories and it's irreversible."

"Irreversible you say. Could anything leak into Miss Chopine's long-term memory?"

"I can't rule it out but I wouldn't count on it."

"I see. And how's Miss Chopine generally?"

"She knows what's hit her and she's coming to terms with it. We're hoping to release her within twenty-four hours but that can change. When we do you'll need to treat her gently."

Trilling rang off with his old-fashioned courtesy and van Piet handed the earpiece back.

"That about treating Dawn gently," Trilling said. "I'll do that. She'll have someone with her when she goes home. She won't like it but she'll thank me when she puts the light out. She might remember something as well. We'll need someone there for her to tell it to."

He picked up the phone and rang the Head of Personnel on his home number.

"Dawn Chopine," he said. "Does she live on her own?"

Personnel didn't have to check, he reeled off the answer straight away.

"There's a fiancé," Trilling said as he put down the phone. "He works in Bristol and drives over when he can. Well, we'll save him the trouble for the next little while. She's ours before she's his and so is what she says. I'll get him warned off."

It was time for Trilling to unlock the door and let van Piet out. Even before van Piet was in the corridor Trilling was shuffling paper and all the signs said he was there for the night.

When van Piet stopped off in his office Garry had left for Barnet and the GCHQ transcripts were on his desk. He slipped them into the top of his suitcase along with the briefings and the Kapner note and sped off for his car, hoping against hope no one would call him back. He was glad Trilling hadn't mentioned the poison pen letters. He couldn't forget them but that wasn't the same thing as wanting to talk about them all the while.

When he got home he parked in front of the Hall and, leaving his suitcase in the boot, walked round the back and past the practice jumps to the Blackwater. He needed to get his balance back. If Célestine had heard the car draw up, and she almost certainly had, she'd know why he hadn't come in straight away.

There wasn't a sound to be heard, not from his footsteps on the grass, not from anywhere. The air was cool and watery after the Ford's ventilation and low cloud made the darkness complete. He couldn't see the islands in the Blackwater but he could sense where they were. Particularly Northey Island. Marauding Vikings had camped there once. They'd demanded protection money from the locals but the locals had preferred to fight for their freedom and had been wiped out. So it was. If evil sought you out you could resist and you could lose. But if you didn't resist you'd certainly lose. That was how van Piet saw his present assignment. A lot of it was still in Shadowland but he sensed a deep and ugly evil as real as the hidden islands.

He let the night work on him a little longer, then he went back up the slope. As he neared the Hall a light came on and a curtain was drawn back. It was Célestine. She'd heard the car all right, she'd been listening for it, and she'd given him the time he usually took when he stayed outside. He moved into the splash of light so she could see him and she waved and disappeared. He scarcely had time to shut the front door before she had her arms round him. His suitcase stood like a cast-off next to them.

Once the transcripts and the note were locked away upstairs they had the luxury of time to themselves so they put some cocoa in a flask and went out to the brew house with its homely smell of leather. Jackie had been home on Saturday – she'd been showing Tewkesbury round before half-term – and van Piet heard all about her jumps and falls and saw the pictures on Célestine's computer. Then came one of her discussing bridles with Stafford Tyler and it hurt him acutely she wasn't talking to him. He noticed Tewkesbury hadn't been photographed, not even in the background. Finally Célestine switched the computer off, their chatter died away and they were sitting quietly together on a lumpy settee. Van Piet had his arm round her shoulders and she was leaning her head against him. He wished he could tell her what he'd been doing or at least where he'd been but that was a firewall they had to live with. He turned to give her a kiss and saw she'd nodded off but he kissed her anyway and squeezed her just enough to wake her.

"Time to call it a day, Cissie. I've got a couple of jobs to do, then I'll finish too."

Back in the Hall he plodded up to his study and locked himself in.

"Hullo, night owl," he said in Dutch to Sweelinck's face on the monitor. "You said you'd caught some mice."

She patched him through to her top security room.

"It's your lucky night, Willem. Guderius is known to the bank and Mr Joost says I can tell you how. I've got a lot on paper I'll scan to you but I'll tell you this for now: I think I know where the photo was taken and I think I know who Hanno was. I'm not one hundred percent certain but I fancy I'm pretty close."

"You usually are. So what do you think you know?"

"I'll start with Karl Marx House and then move onto the new stuff if that's all right with you."

"As you wish, Anke. You're doing the driving."

"Well, Guderius's big break came when he got the job as Medical Officer there and he got that job because he'd learned how to control bugs in closed surroundings. Now the GDR chiefs who used Karl Marx House were like a lot of people back then – they were afraid of nuclear war. That meant bunkers were on their minds and one of them had a prototype –

let's call it Bunker One - built north of Berlin. You can see the connection. This person wanted someone to check his ventilation wouldn't breed bugs and who better than the trustworthy Dr Guderius? So he got the job."

"Do you know that for a fact?"

"Yes I do. We have a copy of Guderius's report here in Amsterdam. It's his contribution to a report on the whole bunker, which we also have."

"A lesser man would be surprised. Where did they come from?"

"From the East German government. We funded the bunker, you see. That gave us the right to ask for details."

"*We* funded the bunker?"

"The East Germans were as hard up as ever so they borrowed the money from us to buy in what they didn't have themselves. They used land as collateral since it didn't cost anything."

"And we've made a profit on it since."

"Of course. And the West made a profit at the time. We got good knowledge through that loan and we shared it with certain friendly governments."

"What about the photo? Where do you think it was taken?"

"On the site of Bunker One. Do you want me to tell you why?"

"As I said, you're doing the driving."

"I'll start with Hanno then. Did you notice his handwriting?"

"I noticed it wasn't German."

"So Hanno wasn't German although he was using a German name. Do you accept that?"

"Not at all. Someone else might've written his message for him. He might have broken his wrist or something."

"Point taken but try this anyway. The ventilation engineer named as working on Bunker One was a Cuban called Juán Bakos. There's nothing odd about that. East Germany and Cuba were as thick as thieves. According to the whole-bunker report Juán's father was a Hungarian who'd emigrated to Cuba as a crops specialist. He married a German who was in school-teaching there. That's why Juán has a Hungarian surname, and because his mother was German he probably spoke German as well as Spanish, which would've helped a lot because he was the only non-German on the site. In particular it would've helped him talk to Guderius when he joined the show. Now, 'Johann' is the German version of 'Juán' and Germans often call Johanns Hanno. So, Juán Bakos was Hanno while he was working on Bunker One."

"Could be, you mean. There are a lot of ifs in there."

"Judge for yourself. Bunker One was a success so it was decided to build a second one a few miles further east. We funded that one too so we have a report on it as well and the thing is, while Guderius was involved again, Juán isn't mentioned. That means he must have been somewhere else. So the photo and the message were his fond farewell and the envelope ties in with that."

"You're winning me over, Anke. Do you know where he might have gone?"

"Could be Cuba but that's only a guess."

"And if what he wrote is any guide he didn't see himself going back to Germany for a while, if ever. I wonder why that was. Is his work faulted anywhere?"

"No and it's a good question. He was Moscow-trained to scrub radiation out of contaminated air. People like that aren't let go without a reason."

Van Piet thought through everything he'd heard.

"Thanks for that, Anke, you've told me a lot. I'll e-mail Fred Visser right now and ask him what else he can find out."

Visser was head of the bank's Havana office.

"Good idea. If Juán's still alive you might even get to speak to him."

"That could come in handy. Oh, and thank Mr Joost for his help. Tell him I'm going to contact Havana."

"He wants an update anyway. You've got him interested."

They drifted into gossip and then terminated. Once the e-mail to Visser had gone van Piet took out the Steffen transcripts. He didn't even want to see them, let alone read them, but with his enthusiasm at zero he forced himself through Steffen's bakery dealings and his wife's arthritis. By the time he'd finished he had the impression of a dedicated organiser with an iron will and, somewhere inside him, an immense fund of tenderness. He still couldn't see what he might be planning but the word "Shadowland" had crossed his mind by the Blackwater and Sweelinck's discoveries, on top of the Bad Sollmer business, were making some of the shadows line up. They were dark, grim and murderous.

24

The Zimmermanns go sight-seeing

As the Zimmermanns' taxi neared the Wapping Travelodge Choule contacted the duty manager and told him to keep them at Reception till a fair-haired man in a dark blue car coat came in and stood near the lifts. And get someone out the back to bring in an auburn-haired lady wearing an olive Burberry topcoat. She'd have Delia Blaine on her ID. Get a bedmaker's uniform for her and give her access to the store on the Zimmermanns' floor.

After the Zimmermanns paid off their taxi Choule followed them into the lobby. Unlike the receptionist, who was right in front of them, they couldn't see a middle-aged man in a neat pinstripe suit standing in the entrance to the restaurant. It was Des Khan, the duty manager. Once Choule was leafing through the fliers next to the lifts Khan nodded OK to the desk.

When the Zimmermanns got into one of the lifts Choule got in with them and when they got out he ambled down the corridor in the opposite direction. A drinks machine gave him the chance to sneak a glance back. He saw them putting in their swipe cards as two bedmakers rolled a trolley full of bedding out of another lift. One was Blaine, the other was Ellie Morrison, the duty assistant manager. Like Khan she'd worked with the SRO before but not with Choule and Blaine. Blaine and Morrison trundled past the Zimmermanns' rooms and Blaine confirmed the numbers – 521 and 522 – while in a room on the floor below a pair of German-speaking eavesdroppers made their headphones comfortable and started their recordings. Choule went out through the emergency exit at the end of the corridor. Morrison would join him in Khan's office once she'd got Blaine organised.

"This is for where we are right now," she said, laying a plastic card on the trolley.

They were in the bedding store. It contained enough bedding for a medium-size town. It was also windowless.

"And this one," she continued, "opens all the guest rooms on this floor. When the girls do a room they keep the door open and their trolleys stay in the corridor. If you do the same you'll be able to see right out."

"Are there any empty rooms on this floor?"

"505, 528, 534 and 539 at the moment but always knock first. They can go at any time."

She laid an in-house radio next to the cards. The casing was off-white.

"You're privileged," she said. "Only top people get the off-white ones. They're restricted to four users only."

She started with the red button.

"On-off is here. 01 gets the duty manager, 02 gets the assistant, 03 gets Mr Choule or whoever takes over from him and 04 is you while you're here. I gather your people will handle changes of shift. Enjoy your stay."

While Blaine was keeping watch on the fifth floor Choule was drinking tea with Khan and Morrison, who was dressed like management again. He asked for the names, addresses and phone numbers of all senior personnel so they could be vetted before they came on duty. He also told them the operation came under the Official Secrets Act. Telling anyone about it was a criminal offence.

"You're stuck with me till our Officer in Charge arrives. His name's Mr Challoner and he'll stay for the duration. I'm going to take a walk round now but two quick questions first. They come from my boss so if I forget to ask them I wave goodbye to my job. The first one is, have either of the Zimmermanns stayed here before? And second, did the Zimmermanns book themselves in or did someone else do it for them?"

Khan took the first one and Morrison took the second. She soon had an answer.

"They were booked in twelve days ago by a Mr Wilhelm Risch. He paid for three nights in cash starting tonight."

"Is Mr Risch on your cctv, do you think?"

"Sorry, we erase weekly. It's all gone."

Khan looked up from his monitor.

"I've got better news," he said. "We've had quite a few Zimmermanns in the past but we've never had a Frank and we've had no Zimmermanns at all from the addresses these two have given."

Choule phoned in the answers and started his walk round.

Gradually the surveillance settled down. Choule and Blaine were replaced and the eavesdroppers were happy with what they were hearing. Mostly it was television from Frank's room – his English was better than his father's, whose second language was Russian. Like most of his generation that's what he'd learned at school. They ate together in Kurt's room and when they spoke, it was about road haulage. Then it was television from Frank's room till bedtime. Presumably Kurt was reading.

The next morning they were both up early and Kurt phoned Reception to ask for a taxi to Sky Rides. When they stepped outside after breakfast Ashell House had already been talking to Sky Rides and what looked like a taxi was waiting for them. The driver was the chatty sort. All the way from Germany, were they? Well, fancy that. So where'd they heard about Sky Rides? And was there anything they really wanted to see from up there? The Zimmermanns, Kurt especially, were grateful he spoke so clearly. They guessed he was working for his tip. They couldn't know their answers were going live to Ashell House. When they were asked where they'd heard about Sky Rides Ashell House didn't see them glance at each other but it heard the pause before Frank Zimmermann said he'd seen an ad in a travel brochure. And when they were asked what they wanted to see they said they weren't too sure, it depended on the weather.

Sky Rides' heliport had a tightly guarded entrance and an affluent looking glass and steel terminal. While Kurt was paying off the taxi Frank idly watched a helicopter take off and head for central London. Meanwhile a white Volkswagen Polo pulled into the car park. It'd tailed them from their hotel.

Inside the terminal everything was hushed and reassuring and while they were collecting their tickets from the check-in the middle-aged couple from the Polo came and stood behind them. When their turn came they gave their name as Knight and collected two pre-booked and pre-paid tickets of their own. Sky Rides had re-organised the trips of ten customers so the so-called Knights could travel with the Zimmermanns and, with gritted teeth, Ashell House was paying for the free rides that'd made it work.

The helicopter seated just the four of them and the view was panoramic. They plugged their headphones into their armrests and the pilot, who sounded South African, gave them their route. The weather forecast was good and he'd stay as low as he could. Then the rotor blades picked up and they were off. Kurt Zimmermann had told his son what to do so often it was coming out of his ears. When the pilot talked something up they were to look impressed and work their cameras. Between whiles they were to lean back, enjoy the view and scale back the photo-taking. They had to make it look as if, without the pilot, they wouldn't know what to be interested in.

It almost worked. By the time they touched down they'd seen and photographed a large chunk of Kent, including the Isle of Sheppey, the Sheppey Link Road and the flyover. The pilot seemed to take personal pride in the flyover. He hovered low so they could take in its flat-topped design, its march of support columns where the road climbed up, the four pairs of extra-massive columns that carried it through its flat stretch and its elegant lighting.

"It was opened by royalty," he said through their headphones, "and it's won five awards for architecture."

The one hiccup was the Channel Tunnel terminal. The pilot hovered over it for a bit without saying too much but the view took in Cheriton Broadspace and Frank Zimmermann couldn't resist pointing out the green-and-gold livery of four of their lorries to his father. He also took a lot of photos.

Despite the noise and the headphones the Knights got talking to the Zimmermanns on the way back and Mr Knight – call me Derek – asked them again, as if he'd thought of the questions himself, how they'd heard about Sky Rides all that way away in Germany and what was top of their list. This time the answers came straight away: an ad in a travel brochure and the White Cliffs of Dover. And yes, thank you, they'd be grateful for a lift back to Wapping.

As they drove back Knight kept the Polo linked to Ashell House and when Mrs Knight – call me Molly – asked Frank Zimmermann what they were going to see in London he had some names all ready: Buckingham Palace, Westminster Abbey and the Tower.

"Why not visit one of the places we saw this morning?" she fished. "They're all easy to get to."

They only had one more day, Kurt Zimmermann answered – he, too, was getting the hang of prompt replies – so they wanted to see some famous buildings. Perhaps next time. Then they were getting out in front of the Travelodge while round the back a beige Rover was standing where the Polo had been.

After what they'd seen and photographed the Zimmermanns felt they'd been right to come to England and that made them even more determined not to blemish their cover. For the eavesdroppers it meant an unrelieved diet of television and road haulage gossip but by the time the Zimmermanns flew back to Germany they'd duly seen or visited Buckingham Palace, the Abbey and the Tower, and they'd also had an evening cruise on the Thames. They didn't know they twice passed over Kapner's jettisoned rubbish and their SRO tail didn't either.

25

Chopine makes contact

Between Monday October 12th, when the Zimmermanns took their Sky Rides trip, and Wednesday October 14th, when they flew back to Germany, van Piet was commuting with distinctly mixed feelings between Ashell House and Gorris Hall. He had to keep tabs on the surveillance, that went without saying, but leaving Célestine was a wrench and on the Tuesday Jackie had come home for half-term. The morning of Thursday October 15th found him once more in his office, this time sifting through the surveillance reports and transcripts to check he hadn't missed anything. He was seeing Trilling at two o'clock and Lorraine Patel would be there as well. Patel was a familiar figure in Ashell House. She was Kent Police's Head of Armed Interventions and she'd been asked in because, as Trilling saw it, if anything was going to happen it'd be in Kent. The Sky Rides trip said it all.

At about a quarter to two van Piet was getting ready to go up when his phone buzzed. It was Trilling. He was in his secretary's office.

"I need to arrange something with you," he said, speaking softly. "Mrs Patel is fully briefed but she's not seeing things our way. So I want you to sort out some big points and do a snow job with them. Don't worry, I'll cue you in. And I won't say you're taking over from me till she's with us. I don't want her thinking you're biased."

So, a stitch-up. Van Piet smiled wryly. Some people never change.

When he was shown into Trilling's room Trilling was standing at one of the windows with Patel, who wasn't in uniform. His secretary brought the tea in and as soon as she was gone Trilling chafed his cheeks with the palms of his hands and got started.

"We'll begin with the Zimmermanns, if you'll be so kind, Willem."

"My own sources inform me their haulage company is prospering and they pay themselves accordingly. So, on the face of it we're looking at two wealthy tourists. The trouble is, wealthy tourists don't book into Travelodges in Wapping because Travelodges are budget and Wapping isn't central London. Then there's their reservations: we know they didn't make them themselves. We also know they'd never stayed there before so we can rule out the idea they went back there because it brought back fond memories. I think the ride is what mattered. Someone made sure of two seats then booked rooms that weren't too far away. Budget would do for that."

"Or the Zimmermanns fancied a break and asked someone to arrange something for them," put in Patel.

"Could be, but they both hesitated before Frank Zimmermann said he saw an ad in a travel brochure and my guess is they hesitated because they didn't want to give the real answer. The second time round they were ready and a fake answer came just like that."

"Where's all this leading, Willem?" Trilling asked blandly, refilling the cups.

"I'd say they were on a covert operation over Kent, possibly reconnaissance. That'd explain why their so-called holiday was so short. Once they'd had their look that was it. Buckingham Palace and the rest were just filler."

"So which part of Kent did they come to see?" Patel asked sceptically. "They covered virtually all of it."

"I don't know. If there's a clue to that, I've missed it."

"Let me help you then," Patel came back. "As a banker you'll know euros pour into this country daily and it's not just tourists who bring them in. Because we use pounds the Bank of England has a deal with the European Central Bank to take these euros back so every evening large quantities of them get freighted through the Channel Tunnel on their way to Frankfurt.

Now the Zimmermanns took lots of photos over Cheriton Broadspace. They pretended they were looking at lorries but I say they were really sizing up the Channel Tunnel terminal for a cash heist – quite likely to raise funds for Chameleon. Steffen and his cronies will be in charge, the snipers will shoot the train driver and a pocket army brought in by the Zimmermanns will storm the train. How does that sound?"

"Not bad," answered van Piet. "Do you believe it?"

"Why not? It covers what you know."

"So you could believe it. Well, that's a start because you can't deny *something's* happening, there're just too many straws in the wind. Or can you?"

Patel took her time.

"No I can't," she said finally. "I have to accept you might be onto something between you. I also have to accept it's your operation before it's mine. There, I've said what you want me to say. So what comes now?"

"First, I'm going to ask you to help with the tailing," Trilling said, looking apologetic. "I'm too short of manpower to do it all myself. Second, now you're with us I can tell you Willem is in operational charge as of now and since you're Head of Armed Interventions I want you to be his emergency stand-in. Do you agree to that?"

She said she did. Van Piet remained expressionless.

"She's not up to it," he thought to himself. "That's all there is to it."

But when he spoke he stuck to practicalities.

"Our targets will possibly be driving a lot," he said to her. "What's your surveillance like?"

It was Patel's turn to look apologetic.

"Every main highway's on camera but strictly within these walls, we're replacing the current system and the compatibility's a dog's breakfast. We're getting more real time images than blackouts now but we still can't access old images because the systems won't talk to each other. We're working on it, of course, and we're also working on a brand new IPI system – that's Instant Personnel Identification. It'll come on stream any time now and when it does it'll tell us on demand or from pre-set who's driving and who else is in the vehicle. All we need are the base data."

"We'll share ours with you," said Trilling. "Consider it done."

Now she was committed Patel wanted to get back to Police Headquarters in Maidstone, Kent's county town, and set up an operations room. So Trilling closed the meeting and let them out into the corridor. Van Piet went with her to the way out.

"If you access any traffic images that look relevant," he said as they shook hands with no great personal warmth, "make sure I know straight away even if they're only fragments."

"Will do. By the way, you turned in a good performance in there to get me on side. Was it Mr Trilling's idea?"

"Of course but make no mistake. I'm as convinced as he is something serious is coming together. There's death in the air."

Van Piet was itching to get away even more than Patel. He buzzed Garry from his office to make sure there'd be no hold-ups. No, he heard, there was nothing that couldn't wait. In fact Garry wanted to get away himself.

"My wife's sister is poorly again. And since she's on your way home I was hoping I might beg a lift."

"You know where my car is. I'll look for you."

"I'm sorry your sister-in-law's had a relapse," van Piet said as they pulled out of Ashell House. "It's angina, isn't it?"

"I'm afraid it is. As you know, she's had it for some time."

"I do indeed. I also know angina is a perfectly controllable condition. So, what's your real reason for wanting to talk to me in the privacy of my car?"

Garry was completely unfazed. He'd expected to be seen through.

"I bumped into Miss Chopine this afternoon while you were with Mr Trilling. She'd asked if she could come in for an hour and he'd said yes. I'd heard about it, as one does, and I happened to be passing when she came in so, naturally, I stopped for a chat."

"Why should she ask to come in? She's hardly out of hospital."

"She thought it'd make her feel better. Like flying after a plane crash was how she put it. A colleague from Personnel was with her – Belinda Thackeray. I gather she's staying with her."

"Did she ask after me? Miss Chopine, that is."

"Not a word. Mrs Thackeray would bear me out on that because she was close all the while. Anyway, as soon as Miss Chopine saw me we shook hands of course, and I felt something pass between her hand and mine. Right under Mrs Thackeray's nose, as it were."

"Miss Chopine palmed you a note? That was an enormous risk. You might have dropped it."

"Unlikely, Sir. Miss Chopine is a good teacher. We've often practised in the canteen."

They stopped for traffic lights, Garry took a thin slip of paper out of his inside jacket pocket and read out what it said.

"Tell Mr vP I doze a lot and remember an underground room in Dr G's villa. I haven't told anyone else. DC. Please destroy."

The lights changed and van Piet moved off.

"Miss Chopine may make another contact," he said. "If you get the chance say this message has helped already. She needs to feel she's getting something right."

He took the slip of paper from Garry. He'd destroy it himself. Garry, meanwhile, was taking out a sealed buff envelope with a laboratory stamp on it.

"I intercepted this just before you buzzed me," he said.

"Open it now and tell me what it says."

He read it through.

"The gloves have been machine washed several times," he summarised, "and the detergent was Ariel Liquid. Minute traces of very light lubricating oil were found in the fingers and thumbs of both gloves, mostly in the tips. A footnote says a powder detergent would've removed this oil completely. It would appear someone's slipped up. An amateur, by the look of it. Oh, and there's a question for you. Do you want the gloves returned or incinerated?"

"Get them back," van Piet said as he took the report. "I'll know what's happened to them that way."

He didn't say much after that, then,

"We're nearly there, Tom. You can get home all right, can you?"

"I don't see why not. Getting here was the problem."

"I thought it might be."

He dropped Garry off outside a newsagent's and then his mind went back to the report. It confirmed what he already believed: Chopine had burgled the villa and been caught red-handed. Well, she'd exceeded her brief all right but she'd also been useful and perhaps she would be again.

"So who else could be useful?" he asked himself. "Juán certainly. I wonder where he went when he left Germany. Anke's guess is Cuba but I can't afford to guess. I have to know. Urgently."

26

Kapner gets a recall

The next morning van Piet was the first one up. If a poison pen letter arrived he wanted to get to it before anyone else and, sure enough, there was one. It was sitting like a toad on a film-wrapped cruise brochure he hadn't asked for. Its hand-written address gave it away. Using tweezers van Piet fished it out, took it up to his study on a plate and phoned the police. Yes, they'd send someone to collect it.

When he was back downstairs he put the kettle on and made some toast. Jackie pattered down next, still in her dressing gown but already full of gossip. As she was blowing on her porridge Tewkesbury came down, already dressed. She took longer over her breakfast than Jackie, who was soon upstairs again getting ready for the day.

"Keep Jackie outside," van Piet told her. "We've had another love letter. Someone is coming over from Chelmsford for it. If she's practising jumps she won't know they've been here."

It was drizzling a bit and could get worse but Tewkesbury thought she could manage. There was always the storeroom if it turned really wet.

When Celia Tyler appeared she said Stafford would be along as soon as he'd checked the grounds. It was his first job every morning. She also said she'd look after lunch. Would Mr van Piet be eating with them? Van Piet, who was frying breakfast for her and her husband, said he thought so but he couldn't promise. He was on call.

Célestine came down last and slowly. She'd slept badly again and it showed.

Once the Tylers had left the kitchen the van Piets had it to themselves. Célestine was finishing her coffee and van Piet was by the window loading the dish washer when he heard her chair scrape and felt her arm slip through his. An awning over the window was keeping the panes clear of drizzle and they could both see down to the jumping ring. Jackie was looking intently at Tewkesbury, who was holding a rein and explaining something. Even at that distance they could see how happy their daughter was.

"When we adopted Jackie," Célestine began, "we wanted to fill her life with love and we thought all we had to do was do it. But now…"

Her voice choked but that was as far as it went. She'd cried too much already.

"I kept waking up last night," she said finally, "and I've decided to close the school. I'm sorry but now I've got Jackie close to me I feel her safety must come first."

Van Piet was torn. Part of him agreed with Célestine: Jackie's was theirs to protect as well as to love, they were two sides of the same coin. But he couldn't dismiss the police's warning that if they gave in, Knifepoint might attack her when they'd dropped their guard. And there were other things on his mind as well.

"Closing the school was always for you to decide," he said, treading carefully, "but you can see Jackie's safe right now. Can I ask you to wait a bit longer?"

Fear flickered up inside her but she held back her answer because she sensed he had more to say. As he went on his discomfort was unmistakeable.

"Cissie, I have to tell you, another letter arrived this morning. It's in my study and the police are on their way to collect it. It's important I know exactly what it says but I'll have to wait till forensics have opened and tested it." He paused. "It was posted just a few miles from here," he added.

"Where?"

"In Maldon. Whoever it is is getting close."

She froze and stared fixedly out of the window.

"Is there anything else I should know?"

She sounded remote and hostile but it was the only way she could speak at all.

"Only this. I'm going to ask Eddie Snape to look in as soon as the letter's been processed. I want to talk things over with him."

Snape was the Chief Constable of Essex. He knew van Piet, they'd worked together and they got on well.

"And you want me to wait till he's been."

She could see what was coming: he'd ask her not to close the school. He'd give her a string of perfectly good reasons but behind them there'd be a reason she couldn't get at, which meant he'd be asking her to trust him blindly. Should she do that with Jackie's safety at stake? She had no easy answer to that. Perhaps Snape would say something to help her.

"I'll do as you ask," she said. "I'll wait till Eddie's been." Then, forcing a change of mood: "It's high time I went outside. I can't leave everything to Janine. Are you coming out as well?"

He wanted to say yes, simply that. Instead it was, "The minute the police have been."

Celia Tyler was approaching the kitchen as Célestine left it to get ready.

"I'm expecting a visit from the police," he told her. "Mrs van Piet and Miss Tewkesbury know they're coming but I don't want Jackie to. When they arrive I want you to invent some excuse for going out to Miss Tewkesbury and letting her know. I'll come out when they're gone. That'll be the all clear signal. You can alert Mr Tyler on your mobile."

He went up to his study and phoned Snape's direct number. Snape said he'd try for late afternoon and, yes, he'd come in civvies and in an unmarked car. Jackie knew him but he could see why a uniform wouldn't be so clever.

Van Piet went down to the kitchen window again. It seemed as good a place as any to wait. Celia Tyler was leafing through some recipes but she kept herself to herself. Outside, the drizzle seemed to have come on more and the Blackwater islands were just vague blotches but Tewkesbury and Célestine were doing their best. How would Jackie react, he wondered, if she thought one of her parents – no, both of them – was deceiving her? Ten was a funny age. She might understand they were doing it out of love but she might also feel rejected. She knew she was adopted and the knowledge had strengthened the bond between them. But could it weaken it as well? What if she thought her parents felt free to deceive her because she was *only* adopted? That'd create a gulf they could never close.

"That absolutely mustn't happen," he told himself. "Not ever."

But the way things were going, could he prevent it?

While van Piet had been listening to Jackie over breakfast, Kapner, one hour ahead of UK time, had been walking from her apartment to her office. The weather in Vaduz was bright and she was glad to be a long, long way away from Carey. In the building where Cantico Insurance was lodged all the firms had their letter boxes by the main entrance and some, including Cantico, had two. Several of Kapner's staff could access the mini-safe behind "Cantico Insurance" but only she had the combination to "Cantico Insurance (Proprietor)". When she opened the mini-safe behind it she found the usual pile of mail plus a sealed envelope addressed to Falcon. There was the normal scattering of people in the lobby, including an SRO watcher, but no one saw she'd gathered up anything special.

She shut her office door, took out her code book and slit open the envelope: "Return to London soonest," she read. "Contact MS re unhappy rabbit. Take maximum precautions. Treat as security test. Re my arrival: Oct 21st confirmed. Expect me pm – Condor." Angrily she stuffed her code book into her handbag, ripped the message and its envelope into tiny fragments and flushed them down her private lavatory. Poor Carey was unhappy! Lesley Carey, the great lover with the tacky locket and the birdbrained photo album! But she had to go back, there was too much at stake. She booked an overnight room in the Zurich Hilton and a flight to London the following morning. She also arranged for Waveney Screening to sweep her flat when she got back.

It took her the rest of the morning to clear her desk and then she walked back to her apartment to pack. On her way she stopped off in a brasserie for a cup of coffee and a snack. She knew the owner and yes, of course she could have the morning's paper. When she left it stayed on the table next to her cup and plate. In it was a coded reply addressed to Condor. She also wanted to phone Sobart to find out what was going on but maximum precautions meant what it said so she didn't. In fact she'd already done too much phoning. GCHQ had told Ashell House about her hotel and flight bookings plus the Waveney Screening appointment. When Kapner's personal secretary gave her a lift to Zurich she was ordered to drive steadily and carefully. That made it easier for the SRO to keep her in sight.

Back in Essex, as soon as the police arrived Celia Tyler took out hot drinks and biscuits and passed her message on. Van Piet came out as she was gathering up the used crockery. The break had been in the storeroom but the drizzle was easing off so they decided to stay out and make a morning of it.

After lunch van Piet said he had to work in his study. He also said Mr Snape would look in later for a cup of tea. Célestine said she'd like to join them and, as he'd hoped, Jackie took no notice.

Van Piet's work included a call to Havana. He double-checked the time difference to make sure Visser would be up and put in his codes. Visser had lived in Havana for most of his working life. His hair had gone sparse and the lenses of his glasses had thickened but his skin was still as pink as the day he'd stepped off the plane. Van Piet asked him whether he'd got anywhere with Juán Bakos. Was he in Cuba and could he talk to him?

"He's in Cuba all right but if you want to talk to him you'll have to hire a medium. He's dead and buried."

Van Piet went tense.

"Do you know what he died of?"

"Cirrhosis of the liver. He drank too much."

"How do you know that? It's important."

"He had an elder brother who's still alive. His name's Pablo and he lives not far from here in Santa Clara. Cuba's a small island and I found out Pablo and I have a mutual friend who was prepared to put in a word for me. Apparently Juán spent some time working in East Germany. It was ultra hush-hush but whatever it was, he got a medal for it. For services to Socialism, that kind of thing. Pablo showed it to me. He also told me Juán was one of those people who work hard when they have to and drink themselves comatose when they stop. He was already on the skids when he went to East Germany but he kept pouring the stuff in till he was too ill to stay and when he came back he had about three weeks left. According to Pablo no one thought the worse of him for drinking himself to death. The gossip was, Juán's stint in East Germany had someone big behind it, like Fidel himself. So, Juán was one of Cuba's glories and he died a hero. Everyone said so."

"Who was everyone? Did Pablo tell you that?"

"He did better than that, he showed me. He's got a great wad of press cuttings in a box file and there was one in particular of Juán in his hospital bed looking, I have to say, absolutely terrible. Fanning out on both sides were these bigwigs from the university, the government and the diplomatic corps, all glad to have their picture taken with a son of the revolution."

"Did Pablo say anything about Klaus Guderius?"

"Quite a bit. It seems Guderius was brought in to see whether germs would breed in some pipework Juán had put together. Every night was a drinkfest at first but Pablo says Guderius soon noticed Juán was going under so he tried to slow him down. Unfortunately, drunks can be very determined about staying that way and, as Pablo tells it, Juán was no exception. The rest you know."

"Thanks, Fred. That's helped me a lot. Now, before you go I want to show you something."

He fished his copy of the Guderius photo from his drawer and held it up to the camera.

"This is Guderius before the years caught up with him. Did Pablo have any pictures like this?"

"He had that very one. Or, more accurately, he had the negative plus a print made from it. Juán took it himself and had it processed in East Germany. He showed the print to Pablo just before he died and when he finally succumbed, Pablo inherited it and the negative. When Juán came back to Cuba he knew his days were numbered so he sent Guderius a print from East Berlin as a kind of last goodbye. Juán spoke fluent German and he also liked being called Hanno. It made him feel accepted."

Van Piet was convinced Pablo knew more. He might be keeping something back or, more likely, he hadn't been asked the right questions. Someone had to make that good but he couldn't do it himself because he couldn't get away.

"Fred, this Pablo needs to be talked to again. Is he up to it, do you think?"

"He's as fit as a flea. Do you want me to do it?"

"No thanks, I'll handle it from this end. What was your cover story by the way?"

"I said I'd lived long enough in Cuba to admire the people who'd made it a fine country. Was that all right?"

"Couldn't be better. I'll take it from there."

As soon as the screen went blank van Piet picked up his mobile to see what it wanted. It'd been flashing a green alert – not urgent but not to be ignored for long. It was from Trilling:

"Kapner booked tomorrow (Oct 17th) on 09.25 flight from Zurich Kloten to London City. One way only. – AT."

"Well, that's one heading back. We'll see what happens when the others turn up. Now, two more jobs then Jackie gets her father back till Eddie shows up."

The first job was a message to Joost. He could certainly get the right people to have a word with Pablo but they'd have to know what to ask and that wasn't easy. It took van Piet five versions before he was satisfied with his e-mail, then he sent it.

The second job was a call to Patel. How was the operations room going?

"I had a stroke of luck, Willem," she replied. "I was in our main store last night looking out equipment and I found three large boxes with labels I couldn't make sense of. I asked the stock controller to open them and guess what we found."

"No idea. You'll have to tell me."

"You'll remember I said we had an access problem with our old traffic surveillance system. Well, in these boxes were disks and hard copy from the old one and from the new one as well."

"The missing link, you mean?"

"Could be. When I got my temper back I had the lot trolleyed up to the office I'm organising next to the operations room. You said you wanted anything from the old system that looked relevant. I'll see what turns up."

"Keep at it," he said and she said she would. They talked a little more and he terminated.

He was still convinced Trilling should never have made her his deputy. Everyone said she was a good policewoman but his response was always the same, even if he didn't say it out loud: she's a good policewoman because she's got a good policewoman's mindset. That means her way of thinking and ours don't match and that makes her dangerous. She can tell me what she finds and, knowing her, it'll probably be a lot but I'm still going to ration what I tell her back. What she doesn't know she can't wreck.

He looked at his watch, locked up and scampered down the stairs. If his luck was as good as Patel's he'd be able to get some family time in before Snape arrived.

27

Jackie as a decoy

When van Piet reached the rings they were empty. A mobile farrier had been booked in and Célestine and Tewkesbury were watching him set out his gear near the stables. The sky had cleared, Jackie was waiting with the first of the horses and Tyler was in the loft making space for some provender he'd ordered. If it hadn't been for Tewkesbury van Piet would have felt part of a normally functioning family. He slipped his arm round Célestine's waist and they stood close together as the farrier went about his work. Then his mobile went. It was Celia Tyler. Mr Snape was waiting in the kitchen.

"Time for a cup of tea," van Piet told his wife, smiling as if he'd heard good news. He'd seen Jackie look in his direction. "Eddie's arrived."

Tewkesbury was also in Jackie's line of vision.

"The Mr Snape I mentioned this lunchtime's here," he said to her. "If Jackie wants to come in when the farrier's finished, that's fine. She won't disturb us."

He blew Jackie a kiss and started back to the Hall with Célestine.

"Can we use the brew house?" he asked her. "You might feel happier in there."

She wasn't sure "happier" was the right word but she was grateful for the thought and it was she who led the way after they'd collected Snape.

"I'm sorry you've had another letter," Snape said once the tea was passed round. "I've brought a copy with me. I should warn you, it's not pleasant."

He handed Célestine a sheet of A4 from his briefcase. The letter was at the top and the envelope, reduced in size, was underneath. Her face blanched as she read it and her hand went up to her mouth. When she'd finished she passed the sheet to van Piet without saying anything. He read it half out loud and half to himself. Instinctively he left the obscenities out:

"You have ignored me Mrs Cellestine van Piet and therfore Ive been comanded to punnish you. Before your prescious Jacky is much older she will too dammaged ever to hurt a horse again. I will bide my time and I will strike hard. If you beg on your bended knees I will still punnish you. You are a slave of the devvil!!
Knifepoint."

He reread it silently and his eyes narrowed.

Célestine looked at Snape.

"What can we do?" she asked him desperately. "I want to close the school, I said so this morning, but my husband isn't so sure. Please tell us what you think."

Snape felt he had to begin with the obvious if only to get the ball rolling.

"What we mustn't do is panic," he said. "There's a big difference between making a threat and carrying it out."

"Yes, but it could be carried out, couldn't it? And we haven't the least idea when or where that might be."

"I can't argue with that. 'Before Jackie is much older' means very soon but 'I will bide my time' means the opposite. It looks as if Knifepoint's keeping his or her options open."

"Do you think you know why?"

He shrugged his shoulders.

"To make you frightened, keep you tense, your guess is as good as mine. And while I don't want to help this person, did you see where the letter was posted?"

"Maldon and it terrifies me. Chelmsford was bad enough but Maldon is virtually next door."

She had a handkerchief in her hand. Unconsciously she worked it with her fingers as she spoke.

"What makes it worse is that Jackie can be got at so easily," she went on. "I don't have to remind you she's profoundly deaf. It was why her natural parents rejected her. She's been taught how to lip-read but she hasn't been taught how to hear someone creeping up behind her because it can't be done."

"Whoever wrote that letter doesn't have to live near here. They might have sent it to someone else to post or they might have travelled to Maldon just to make you think they can reach you whenever they want to."

"That's exactly what they can do because if they can get to Maldon they can also get to here. Please don't try to mislead me, Mr Snape. It won't work."

Van Piet sensed they'd hit a wall.

"Were there any forensic clues?" he asked, starting in a new place.

"Not a single one. We know what the envelope's picked up from Maldon to here but take that away and it's spotless. So's the letter. Not a skin cell, not a hair, nothing. All I can say is, it's the same writing paper and ink as before."

They'd hit another wall and van Piet tried another start.

"'I will bide my time' could mean when Jackie's gone back to school. Knifepoint could reasonably assume the police would protect her to start with, but police protection doesn't last forever because it can't."

"Don't say that, Willem!" Célestine broke out. "An explicit threat has been made against our daughter. The police can't just walk away from it."

Snape saw whatever he said to that would only inflame things further so he put in a diplomatic pause, cleared his throat and turned to van Piet.

"You seemed to have something in mind just now. Can you tell us what it was?"

"I was wondering whether we could do a deal."

"What sort of deal?"

"Well, I'm heavily committed at the moment but when the job I'm on is finished I can take over Jackie's protection myself."

Célestine looked at him in surprise. This was entirely new.

"What's your time scale?" Snape asked, feeling off the hook.

"I'm looking at two dates at the moment, October 30th and November 3rd. They're not set in concrete, nothing like, but I'm prepared to take a chance so the deal is this. Today's

October 16th. Jackie stays here and you protect her till November 3rd at the latest. After that, I take over."

"No ifs or buts?"

"No ifs or buts. That includes keeping Jackie out of school. If I have to I'll get tutors in."

Célestine touched her husband's arm. She'd reached her own conclusion and she wanted to say it before, not after, Snape said yes or no.

"Knifepoint presumably knows my website so if it says my riding school is closed it's possible he or she will be satisfied despite what they've written. But if I seem to be ignoring this person that could be like waving a red rag at a bull. And precisely that is what I'm going to do because if I can make Knifepoint feel provoked it should make them easier to catch."

She was sitting very straight and she'd stopped twisting her handkerchief.

"I'm well aware that I'm turning Jackie into a decoy but if you, Mr Snape, and my husband think you can keep her safe I'll do it because it's the least worst choice. I won't pretend I'm not terrified but I'll keep my word."

Snape waited to see whether van Piet wanted to add anything but he didn't.

"I'm grateful to you," he said to Célestine. "I'd already decided to accept your husband's deal. I can do it more easily now."

He looked at his watch.

"I have to get back to Chelmsford shortly," he apologised. "Do you have a plan of the Hall and its grounds by any chance?"

Célestine went over to her computer and printed off a set of scale drawings. She and van Piet were dedicated home-makers and the drawings came from their schedule of works. When she'd talked Snape through them, he said,

"You can see for yourselves, Janine on her own isn't nearly enough. It'd take half my force to cover this lot."

"You're not to take any risks, Eddie," van Piet warned him.

It was a long time since Célestine had seen him so nervous.

"I'm not going to. I'm going to saturate the place with Specials. I know they're volunteers but they're fully trained and they're completely dependable. I'll start things from my car when I go."

He thought for a moment.

"What are you going to tell your daughter though? These people won't be invisible."

Van Piet was about to reply but his wife did it for him.

"We'll tell her the truth, Mr Snape. There's no way round it."

"Won't it upset her? I know it's on someone's mind. I had to come in civvies and an unmarked car."

"It's a risk we have to take. When Jackie sees what we're doing it may well make her afraid. On the other hand, it may increase her trust in us as well and that's what we'll hope for. We'll also tell her who WPC Tewkesbury really is."

"We don't have to do that, surely," exclaimed van Piet, his anxieties rushing to the surface.

"Yes we do. I'd rather Jackie found out now than in the middle of a crisis."

Van Piet bit the bullet. He had his fears, he wouldn't conceal it, but he could see Célestine was right. He'd tell it all to Jackie himself.

When Snape was ready to go van Piet said he'd see him to his car. As they walked through the Hall they passed an open door. Jackie was watching television with Tewkesbury. Jackie had her back to the door and although Snape was talking in a normal voice she didn't look round. Snape saw she didn't and looked at van Piet, who didn't say anything. He didn't have to. Outside the Hall, Snape asked,

"Who was running that meeting just now? I'm certain you had your own agenda."

"I heard someone say something like that yesterday. Let's say we took it in turns. But I want you to know something important before you go. Now I've read this letter I'm convinced there'll be another one and it'll be very much worse than the ones we've had already. If there is, I want you to have it intercepted in the sorting office. The way the address is written makes it stand out a mile so it should be easy to do. I want it opened as soon as possible and I want you personally – no one else – to contact me and read it out. Will you do that?"

"All right, but what if you're wrong, Willem? What if there aren't any more letters – just action?"

"Then we have to hope your Specials are all you say they are. I want my home turned into a fortress. Nothing less will do."

Van Piet stood next to the car's open window while Snape radioed in. When he finally drove away he was stony-faced. He couldn't forget seeing Jackie with her back towards the door. As his car disappeared van Piet locked the main gate by remote control and went back into the Hall. Dinner was on people's minds and Célestine was in the kitchen with Celia Tyler.

"I need a few minutes in my study first," he apologised to both of them. Then to Célestine,

"When shall I tell Jackie what's happening?"

"Not before she goes to bed, that'd be asking too much. Make it first thing tomorrow morning. If you're called out during the night I'll fill in for you."

When he was upstairs he checked his e-mails. As he'd hoped there was one from his father.

"I have a friend in the Banco Central de Cuba who might be able to help with Pablo Bakos," he read. "You also ask whether you can have one of our helicopters and a pilot. The answer is yes but you must do your own booking and bear the cost. Joost."

That was all right then, twice over. It was typical of his father that he'd have to foot the bill for the helicopter and pilot.

Next he called Trilling. Another letter had arrived, he said, and he'd arranged to be told if any more came. He was also hiring one of Van Piet Banking's helicopters so he could scuttle back to Essex if he had to. He hesitated a moment then said he felt he'd become a bad risk. Would Trilling like Patel to take over right now so she'd have time to play herself in. Trilling said he wouldn't.

"Stay with it if you can," he said. "If we move too soon we lose everything."

"I agree but what's that to do with Lorraine?"

He heard an exasperated sigh, then,

"You know as well as I do, managing delay is one of the most difficult things there is. If you move too soon, you lose, but if you move too late, the sky falls in. Experience is vital and the simple truth is, you've got it and Lorraine hasn't. She's your backup for one reason only: I haven't got anyone else. Do you understand me now?"

Van Piet said he still wasn't convinced but he'd see the job through if he could. After he'd terminated he phoned Patel and told her about the helicopter. Could he use the helipad at Police Headquarters? She okayed that. If he could let her have the details she'd put it through. She didn't ask any questions and he didn't invite any.

Last of all he booked his helicopter and pilot. He didn't tell anyone what he'd done till Jackie was asleep and he and Tyler had checked the premises for the night. Then he asked the Tylers and Tewkesbury to join Mrs van Piet and himself in the downstairs sitting room. Over hot drinks and biscuits he explained about the poison pen letters and told the Tylers Tewkesbury was a police officer. It took them completely by surprise, she was pleased to notice. Then he moved on to the Specials and finally said a helicopter from his father's bank would be landing in the grounds the next day. The pilot's name was Geert and he spoke perfect English. He'd tell Jackie about him in the morning when he told her about everything else.

"My wife has said Jackie's a decoy," he said, "but if I say she's a tethered goat in a tiger hunt you'll get a better idea of how things are. We don't know where the tiger is or where it will spring from. We don't even know for certain whether there is one. But if there is and it springs we have to be ready for it. So I'll ask you, please, to remain fully alert. The Specials are good but they can't do everything."

28

Rabbit pie

Although Cantico traded online, when it came to things like sales drives Kapner liked to use real people. So she'd hire temps, rent space, and her Cantico cars took care of the travelling. One of these, a BMW, was for her use only. Her Saab she kept for her private life.

Back from Vaduz her mind was on the lock-ups the cars were in as she pensively ate her breakfast. She'd psyched herself up to see Carey, but Sobart came first and maximum precautions had stopped her phoning her. She hadn't had time to get a message to her either so she was going to take a chance and turn up. Miriam Sobart Laboratories worked every day and she was fairly sure Sobart went in Sunday mornings.

After she'd cleaned her teeth and showered she got kitted out. She'd re-dyed her hair so all it needed was brushing down. The locket went into an empty briefcase along with a change of underwear, a nightdress, some lubricating jelly, her hair brush and a pair of glasses with dimmed-down lenses so the irises wouldn't show. More rummaging in drawers produced a pair of nylons and a suspender belt and they went in as well. Her shoulder bag and near-duffel coat were already on a chair near the kitchen door and her street shoes were underneath it. The briefcase went next to them. All she had to do now was hang on for Fassbinder. She'd asked her to come in for the whole day plus the evening. While she was waiting she remembered something she absolutely mustn't forget. In her office, on a shelf opposite the door, was a set of neatly labelled box files laid on their side. In them were holiday photos. She took a packet of coloured prints out of one marked "S.W. England". They were pre-digital but they'd do. They too went into her briefcase.

When Fassbinder arrived the watchers over Beadman's Copperware photographed her and recorded the time; Ashell House identified her from her biometric data; and her name was logged. Thanks to Waveney Screening Kapner felt she could talk to her freely. She'd be out all day, she said, and she wouldn't have her mobile. If anyone tried to contact her Fassbinder mustn't say she was out, she had to say she was unavailable and could she take a message? And she had to stay till Kapner got back. Fassbinder was happy with that so Kapner led the way into the kitchen.

She'd taken her flat because there were two ways out of it. One was the front door and the other was an underground passage dating from when George III's stables stood where the National Gallery now was. It'd been dug out when Napoleon looked like invading because, understandably, the royals didn't want their horses stolen. In terms of modern London it ran from the back of the National Gallery to Old Compton Street, passing under Orange Street along the way. It'd been forgotten after Waterloo and during the Second World War incendiary bombs had destroyed the plans and drawings. So in effect it'd never existed.

After the war a Scot named Trevor Royce got the contract for rebuilding the Orange Street area. Like many Scots then, he was a doctrinaire Communist so when he discovered the passage and found out about its missing paperwork he knew what to do. He filled in the passage between the National Gallery and Orange Street, constructed a new and undocumented entrance in Orange Street and built a duplex over it. In Old Compton Street he cleared the site of bomb damage, made the end of the passage good and built the lock-up garages over it. Then he made everything safe. He leased the upstairs flat long-term but he kept the ground floor one on short leases "in case the Party needs it" and he only told people he could trust about the passage. One of these was Kapner, who came to know him when she was at the Embassy. When she needed a London base she contacted Royce's daughter, who'd taken over his firm. Melissa Grosvenor-Royce shared her father's politics so as soon as the sitting tenant timed out

Kapner acquired a long-term lease for the flat and lock-ups combined.

The venetian blind over the flat's kitchen window was closed so, confident no one could see in, Kapner took a plasticised magnet off the side of the fridge, passed it over an unmarked part of the wall and put it back where it came from. The magnet activated two concealed switches. One put the lights on in the underground passage. They were low-energy and well spaced out so the meter wouldn't spike too much. The other one started the ventilation, which consisted of slow-turning paddle blades in wire holders hung from the roof. Operating in phases they drew air in through conduits concealed behind air bricks in the duplex's outer walls and eased it out through air bricks in the lock-ups. As a system it'd never win a prize but Royce had gauged it'd support a handful of people at any one time and he'd been right.

The kitchen floor was covered with one foot square checkerboard tiles. With Fassbinder helping, Kapner cleared the middle ones, took her magnet again and passed it over a second place in the wall. Twelve tiles on a backing panel sank down and slid sideways, leaving an oblong hole in the floor. It gave onto a brick collar connecting the underside of the kitchen floor to the top of the underground passage. An aluminium ladder reaching down to the floor of the passage was bolted to its side. While Fassbinder pulled the ladder's top section upwards Kapner changed into her street shoes, tugged on her coat and slipped her bag over her shoulder. Then, holding her briefcase in her free hand, she started the climb down. When she'd got far enough to retract the top section Fassbinder gave her a parting wave and disappeared into the flat.

The passage was square-built and the royal horses would've had to be led since the ceiling was too low for riding. The tarred oak setts were soft underfoot and they soaked up any sound. At the bottom of the ladder Kapner selected a torch from three or four on a shelf and checked it was fully charged. Then she reached out to a button block and closed the hole in the kitchen floor. If there was a power cut she had her torch and at each end of the passage there was a crank for opening the floor manually but she still felt a nibble of fear when the oblong closed. It was like being buried alive. It didn't help that the lights in the passage were feeble and the air was cool and clammy.

The passage's walls and roof varied between original red brick and twentieth century concrete, and wherever the floor was wet she made a detour to avoid being dripped on. To keep her mind out of nightmare territory she walked steadily and counted her steps in thirties.

Eventually another aluminium ladder came into view and as she got nearer she could see the arrangement of rails and pistons Royce had devised to open and close the lock-up floor. It was the one her BMW was in and it was a double one. By just dabbing the button box she opened the floor a fraction at a time in case someone had got in and was still there. When it was completely open she left her torch next to several others on a shelf, climbed into the lock-up and slid the top of the ladder back down. The BMW was dusty from lack of use but it'd stay that way a while longer since she was going to Rochester by train. It was safer. She switched off the lights and ventilation and closed the floor. Then she exited through a side door, walked down a back lane and before long she was in a sparsely filled train that was leaving Charing Cross.

Miriam Sobart Laboratories occupied a Snowcem-covered low-rise on a rolling green site upriver from the cathedral. It looked vaguely Mediterranean in the sunlight and the dinghies moored nearby slapped idly in the breeze. The receptionist was as relaxed as the weather. Yes, Miss Sobart was in. What name should she give, please?

"Stephanie Ulrick. I'll write it down for you."

She wrote "Ulrick, Stephanie", hoping Sobart would get the hint. She did.

"You've come about Carey, have you?" she said when they were in her spotless office. She ignored Kapner's appearance entirely.

"That's right. Ulrich's getting worried. What's the story?"

"Carey's whole attitude's on the slide."

"Do you know why?"

"Something's bothering him and I think it's more than medical. He keeps coming here as if he wants to tell me something – and if he wants to talk to me he might want to talk to others, which is why I sent word to Ulrich. Don't forget, Heidi, Carey lives on his own. He's got no one to take his mind off things."

"His work's not suffering, is it?"

Kapner didn't want to say too much but she had to ask that.

"He's not said anything but he's looking so dreadful the people he works with must be wondering why. Are you going to see him while you're here?"

"If he's in I am but I haven't been able to phone him. Ulrich's ordered maximum security."

"I'll call him for you. I'm sure I can invent an excuse."

"Don't let him suspect we know each other. That could spoil everything."

Sobart used her mobile to call Carey's home number direct and he answered straight away. She said she'd been going through his readouts and she wanted to talk to him about them. She'd come round if he liked. She had a gap in her work and she fancied a change of scenery. She listened a bit, said, "I'll be there in an hour" and terminated the call.

"He's at home," she said. "It's his day off and he's taking it easy."

"Are you really going round then?"

Kapner needed to have Carey not just at home but on his own.

"Not for a pension but we can be sure he'll stay in now. I'll ring him after you've had time to get there. I'll tell him I'm sorry but I can't make it after all. After that, he's yours on a plate."

As Kapner walked into Beale's Row she wondered how Carey would react given all that had happened. Well, there was an easy way to find out. She rang his doorbell and stepped back a pace so he'd see the brushed-down hair, the shoulder bag and the near-duffel coat all in one take. Footsteps clumped down the hall, a newspaper was scrabbled up from the doormat and the door was pulled open. Carey'd been expecting Sobart. When he saw Kapner he was thunderstruck.

"Heidi!" he tried to exclaim but all that came out was a strangulated whisper. "Heidi, my love! Come in, come in!"

It'd worked again.

He closed the door behind her and hugged her tightly, pressing the newspaper into her back.

"I got back from Liechtenstein yesterday," she said, freeing herself as soon as she could and pulling his head down to kiss him. "I've been looking at the photos you gave me. I had to come round straight away. I'm burning for you, Lesley. I can't describe it any other way."

"Why didn't you phone me? I might not have been here. My job's right at the top, you know. It makes demands and rightly so."

"I'd have waited for you. I wanted to surprise you."

He looked as dreadful as Sobart had said. His eyes were red with big bags underneath them and his lank hair hadn't seen scissors or a comb for some while. He hadn't shaved and his trousers showed dried splash marks, as did his slippers. He must be being talked about at work, Kapner thought. What if he got told to rest? That thought alone made her glad she'd come. She had to turn him round.

"Well, you've certainly done that," he burbled. "I was expecting someone completely different."

As he spoke a phone in the back of the house rang. He was annoyed when he broke off to answer it but when he re-emerged, he was grinning from ear to ear.

"You'll never guess, Heidi. That was the person I was expecting. She says she can't come round after all. Something about a rush job out of nowhere and what she wanted could wait. So, we've got the whole day to ourselves."

He hung her coat up while she stood down her briefcase and slipped off her shoes.

"I'm sure we can think of all the right things to do," he smirked, "but let me show you round my home first. I want it so much to be your home too if …"

He was going to say "if all goes well" but he was afraid she'd catch he was losing his nerve so he didn't.

The inside of Carey's house showed he was earning well but nothing looked as if it was shared. In the living room only one easy chair faced the television. It'd worn to Carey's shape and it was the only chair to have a footstool in front of it. On the chimney breast was an ebony-framed black-and-white photo of a couple on their wedding day – the lovebirds of the locket Kapner thought with contempt when she saw it. When she and Carey had toured the house he dropped into "his" chair without thinking about it while she, seeing how things were, sat down on one that was stiff from lack of use.

"So, Lesley," she said, a hint of dominance coming into her voice, "we've got the whole day to ourselves, have we? And how are we going to use it? We could start by drawing the curtains, couldn't we?"

He jumped up, rasped the curtains together and switched on some tasselled reading lamps. They created the safe haven glow of a children's hideaway.

"Shall I take my slippers off?" he asked gauchely.

"There's more to come off than your slippers," she teased. "But first things first and I'm glad I'm here to deal with them. You looked terrible when you opened the door. You haven't shaved and your hair's in a shocking state. So, before we do anything else I'm going to cut it for you."

"Cut my hair? I haven't got any clippers, Heidi. I live on my own, you see."

"Scissors and a comb will do plus your razor for the edges. And when I've finished I'm going to put you in the bath and I shan't want to get my clothes wet, shall I? Then you're going to shave because I don't like whiskery men and after that we'll see. Now, where's my *salon* going to be?"

"In the kitchen. It's bright in there and the floor sweeps up nicely."

He sat bolt upright on a mock-rustic wooden chair while Kapner wrapped a towel round his shoulders and stroked the nape of his neck with her nails. His hair lay in greasy half-curls round the dome of his head and a pimple above the hair line had been scratched open. Cluster by cluster she worked her way round and between snips she kissed the top of his head. When she'd finished she let him admire himself in a hand mirror she fetched from her shoulder bag.

"It's wonderful!" he enthused. "Where did you learn to cut hair?"

"At the Embassy. English doctors, dentists and hairdressers were all taboo. I helped out with the haircuts."

She shook the towel onto the floor and Carey got to work with a dustpan and brush while she flicked her clothes clean. More than anything she wanted to get out of the kitchen and rewarm her feet.

"Now," she said when he'd finished, "get into your bath so I can wash those itchy hairs off. I'm going to use your bedroom."

As she drew his bedroom curtains she could hear the water tumbling into the bathtub. He had a double bed to himself, it was unmade and his pyjamas were dumped on the carpet. He obviously wasn't sleeping, just churning the duvet around. She threw his pyjamas onto a chest of drawers, plumped the pillows, shook the duvet straight and slipped her outer clothing off. She'd brought her briefcase up with her and now she snacked on the suspender belt and pulled on the nylons. At that moment the water stopped running and the house fell silent. She allowed herself a brief victory smile then walked down the landing to the bathroom.

Carey was up to his midriff in water and his clothes were in a bundle on a chair. His eyes lit up when he saw her in her underwear and his big grin threatened to split his face. She let him finger her suspender belt and kiss her thigh above her stocking top. Then she shampooed and rinsed his hair before soaping and rinsing his back and chest. As she reached over him she pressed hard against his shoulder.

"There's one little bit I want you to do for yourself," she said, giving him the soap. "Now, do it properly."

She stood and watched as, with child-like obedience, he soaped his pizzle, rinsed it and looked up for approval.

"Is my Lesley hungry?" she giggled. "I'll bet he have any breakfast, the naughty boy."

He hadn't had anything, he admitted. In fact he'd ra lost interest in food so there wasn't much in the house. I now his Heidi was with him why didn't they go out for a mea There was a pub called the John Jasper off the High Street They could go there and have a traditional Sunday lunch.

"Let's do it," she said with relief. "I don't go out with a handsome young man every day."

"John Jasper," Carey pronounced over roast beef, boiled cabbage and lumpy mashed potatoes, "is in one of Dickens's novels. Charles Dickens, to give him his full name. He's dead now but people still read his books."

"What's it about, this novel?" she asked although she already knew. Dickens had been popular in East Germany. He'd been seen as a friend of the working class.

Carey was thumping the bottom of a bottle of brown sauce.

"I haven't actually read it myself. I don't read much apart from technical reports, I'm far too busy, but I know that much. Dickens was born in Rochester, I believe. And there's a Dickens parade every year."

He wiped his nose on his serviette and fondly pressed his foot onto hers.

"Let's drink to us," he said, raising his pint glass the way he'd seen people in films do.

"To us, Lesley," she said and, hoping no one was looking, she clinked her glass of tonic water against his.

It was his third pint and the beer was getting to him. To show his new mood some more he ordered knickerbocker glories for dessert.

The portions were daunting. There was fresh fruit laced with liqueur at the bottom, then vanilla and strawberry ice cream, Peach Melba sauce and whipped cream topped with a glacé cherry looking like an eye with conjunctivitis. When he was finished he leaned back and watched serenely as she toiled down the layers. The ice cream made her teeth ache but she smiled winningly and thanked him for making her day. After coffee they strolled leisurely back to Beale's Row. Carey,

"Good boy," she said and kissed the top of his ear. "I'll dry you now. When you step onto the mat bend down so I can reach you."

Beginning with the top of his head she slowly dabbed the water off, kissing him as she worked her way down. It puzzled her he wasn't showing any sign of arousal. He was simpering vacantly but that was all. When he was dry she drew him tightly towards herself and kissed him on the mouth but that had no effect either. Not sure what to think she backed off and ran her fingers down his cheeks.

"It's time for your shave, sweetest," she said coyly. "And when you're all nice and smooth I want you you know where."

While his razor was buzzing she went back into his bedroom. She stripped naked, lubricated her vagina with the jelly she'd brought, pulled on her nightdress and sat upright on the bed with the duvet pulled up to her chin. The buzzing stopped, she heard water rinse the whiskers away and then, in too much haste to wrap a towel round himself, he came clumping down the landing, carrying his clothes in his hands. When he reached the doorway he stopped and waited till she called him in. She watched him drop his clothes where his pyjamas had been and smiled him onto the bed.

"Take my nightie off," she said, letting the duvet fall and holding up her arms. "We don't want it getting in the way, do we?"

He wanted to do it with a flourish but she was partly sitting on it and instead of caressing her and easing it free, he tugged at it impatiently and almost tipped her over. Bringing her arms down she released it for him and let him heave it over her head. Then she told him to push the duvet onto the carpet. In the train coming down she'd mentally rehearsed what she'd say when they'd got this far. She'd found it hard not to giggle and she had to be careful now not to overact.

"I can't tell you how much I've ached for this," she said, putting on an in-heat look and pulling him towards her. "Please, please don't make me wait another second."

She'd meant to finish with, "I'm ready for you right now" but his overeager lumbering into position made him pitch forward and press on her face. His pizzle was so soft he had to stuff it in with his hand. Then he pushed against her a few times but that was as far as he got. He tried once or twice more and then rolled off, scarlet with embarrassment.

"I can't do it," he said, looking completely despondent. "I thought I could but I can't. I've been suffering too much."

She wished she could say something soothing and get dressed but she couldn't leave him as he was.

"You're too keen you mean," she cooed, jamming herself underneath him, "and you're rushing too much. We've got all day remember."

He pushed and heaved again but still he couldn't fire. She hoped if she could get him half way he might just manage the rest so she said,

"You have to keep going. You're giving up too soon. Hug me tight while you do it and tell me you love me."

He did as he was told. At first he alternated between thrusting flaccidly and wheezing words of love but as he became short of breath he settled for ramming her with mindless ferocity. Sweat dripped onto her, the veins in his temples swelled and his cheeks coloured alarmingly. When sheer exhaustion brought him to a halt he gasped, "I was nearly there, Heidi, I really was" and flopped on top of her, panting heroically.

Kapner was feeling bruised and sticky but she fluted, "I know you were, buttercup" and waited resignedly for him to recover. "When you're ready," she persisted, dominating herself as much as him. "I want you to try one last time."

Once more he began to pump, slowly at first and then in a frenzy. Sweat coursed off his face and body and he salivated freely. Suddenly he arched his body backwards and shouted as if he'd been struck by a spear. Then, making strange gutteral noises, he slowed down until running a fingertip along her forehead was the only movement he was making. He was faking and she knew it but she also knew he'd reached the end of the line.

"That was atomic," she gushed. Had she said that before? She didn't want to sound phoney. "Nobody does it like you, Lesley. You're in a class of your own."

His colour was still high, a blood vessel in his neck throbbed ominously and she reckoned he wouldn't be volunteering for an encore. So she pushed him onto his back and half lay on top of him to keep him there.

"This is how it's always going to be," she murmured. "Just the two of us and all your worries gone."

"I believe you, Heidi. And now we've reaffirmed our love I'll pull through for your sake. I know I will."

They lay still for a while, each with their different thoughts, but she was lying awkwardly and the side of her neck was ricking painfully. She also wanted to nail down what she'd gained so far so she eased herself away from him, reached for her briefcase and said,

"Don't move, Lesley. I've got something to show you. Apart from me, that is."

She pulled out the photos. She'd taken them in Devon from a hot air balloon belonging to a friend who also owned the white cliff-top mansion they showed. Because the estate and the beach were private she was sure Carey wouldn't recognise them.

"Ulrich sent me these," she said. "They're of one of the places he's lined up for us. I mustn't say where it is but you do like it, don't you? Please say you do."

He wiped his palms on the undersheet and thumbed through them.

"It's the Caribbean," he stated. "No, wait a minute, it's South America. On the Pacific coast. I've seen several of these colonial houses in my time. And Ulrich has lined one up for us, has he? Well, we're worth it, that's for sure. He couldn't manage without us, could he?"

He lay back lazily and thumbed through them again while Kapner wondered how to get him out of the bedroom. When he handed them back his stomach rumbled loudly. Maybe that was the answer. She leaned over him and tinkered with his navel.

who'd been allowed one more pint and who'd followed it with another one, kept lurching into her. She fended him off as best she could and finally they were in his house. He half-sat, half-lay, in his easy chair and she perched on hers. The curtains were still drawn.

"You've made all the difference, my pea-hen," he said and his words were clotted as if his tongue were too big for his mouth. "It takes a good deal to upset me – I'm exceptionally tough, you know - but I have to admit I've been nearly out of my mind. Those transcripts and so on were bad enough but what if I get caught before I can get away? I'll lose my house, my job, my fellowship and all the other things I've worked for all these years."

He looked at her imploringly.

"Come and sit on my lap," he begged. "I need to feel you pressing against me."

She made herself as comfortable as she could on his scraggy thighs. His beery breath rolled over her. She put her arms round his shoulders, nuzzled the side of his face and reminded herself with unqualified thanks he was definitely, but definitely, on Death Row.

"You won't get caught, precious," she purred into the hairs in his ear. "Ulrich will see to that. He's said he'll take care of you and he will. He's probably thinking about you right now."

She kissed him with every appearance of passion. It was time to bend his soul.

"I have a special favour to ask," she said as she took her lips away. "I've brought the locket you gave me, to lend it back to you because when your big moment comes I want you to have it in your hand. It'll make you think of me."

He clamped her tightly to him, bursting with emotion.

"Heidi, you're the most wonderful person in the universe!" he exclaimed. "I love you body and soul."

"I haven't finished yet," she went on, picking at his lapel. "I've lent you the locket but the photo album stays with me. And when we start our new life together I'll bring it with me. It's our pledge to each other."

In fact she was going to destroy it. Nothing about the locket connected her with him but that wasn't true of the photo album so it had to go. He intertwined his fingers with hers.

"If I get low again," he asked hesitantly, "I mean, between now and what you want me to do, can I come and see you?"

"If it were up to me I'd say yes. But Ulrich would never allow it. We're on maximum security now, all of us."

It was an answer he didn't like and his mood dipped. But he was too dependent on her to argue with her so he picked on Steffen instead.

"He'll make sure I get my injection, won't he? If he doesn't I'll have plenty of time to tell people what he's done. I'll have nothing to lose if I'm dying. I'm surprised he hasn't thought of that, but there it is. We can't all be bright, can we?"

"Of course you'll get your injection. Ulrich's a man of honour. The big question is, are you?"

He took his time to answer and when he did, the pompous note was back in his voice.

"You've pledged yourself to me and I make this solemn pledge to you: you can trust me, word of honour."

Once he'd made his grand announcement he became more and more clinging and it was only by insisting she had a train to catch that she was able to get away from him. She said she didn't want him to come to the station with her - she was too overwhelmed, she needed to be alone with her feelings. She also persuaded him not to stand in the doorway as she left but she couldn't prevent him opening a window and waving vigorously. He also pointed to something he was holding in his hand and then made a show of kissing it. It was the locket. She mouthed him a kiss back in case he called out and he remained at the window waving and beaming till she'd disappeared from view.

She had her victory smile on as, wearing her dimmed-down glasses, she boarded her train. An unscheduled stop gave her the chance to encode: "Rabbit pie ready to serve. Your arrival noted. Will be there – Falcon". She simply wrote "Condor" on the envelope. The message she'd received in

Vaduz told her Steffen must have spread their code names amongst the couriers.

On her way to Old Compton Street she stopped off in a round-the-clock convenience store and took her glasses off so her face could be seen clearly. She bought some Paracetemol she didn't need and as the paper bag was handed to her she palmed the message across with her money. It would be in Johannisbrunn before Monday was out.

Fassbinder was watching television when she climbed back into her flat. There'd been a couple of phone calls and Fassbinder had said what she'd been told to say. When Fassbinder finally left, the watchers photographed her with a night camera. The biometric data retold their tale and her departure time went into the log. As far as the SRO was concerned she'd arrived early and left late, and Kapner hadn't gone out at all.

"Good boy," she said and kissed the top of his ear. "I'll dry you now. When you step onto the mat bend down so I can reach you."

Beginning with the top of his head she slowly dabbed the water off, kissing him as she worked her way down. It puzzled her he wasn't showing any sign of arousal. He was simpering vacantly but that was all. When he was dry she drew him tightly towards herself and kissed him on the mouth but that had no effect either. Not sure what to think she backed off and ran her fingers down his cheeks.

"It's time for your shave, sweetest," she said coyly. "And when you're all nice and smooth I want you you know where."

While his razor was buzzing she went back into his bedroom. She stripped naked, lubricated her vagina with the jelly she'd brought, pulled on her nightdress and sat upright on the bed with the duvet pulled up to her chin. The buzzing stopped, she heard water rinse the whiskers away and then, in too much haste to wrap a towel round himself, he came clumping down the landing, carrying his clothes in his hands. When he reached the doorway he stopped and waited till she called him in. She watched him drop his clothes where his pyjamas had been and smiled him onto the bed.

"Take my nightie off," she said, letting the duvet fall and holding up her arms. "We don't want it getting in the way, do we?"

He wanted to do it with a flourish but she was partly sitting on it and instead of caressing her and easing it free, he tugged at it impatiently and almost tipped her over. Bringing her arms down she released it for him and let him heave it over her head. Then she told him to push the duvet onto the carpet. In the train coming down she'd mentally rehearsed what she'd say when they'd got this far. She'd found it hard not to giggle and she had to be careful now not to overact.

"I can't tell you how much I've ached for this," she said, putting on an in-heat look and pulling him towards her. "Please, please don't make me wait another second."

She'd meant to finish with, "I'm ready for you right now" but his overeager lumbering into position made him pitch forward and press on her face. His pizzle was so soft he had to stuff it in with his hand. Then he pushed against her a few times but that was as far as he got. He tried once or twice more and then rolled off, scarlet with embarrassment.

"I can't do it," he said, looking completely despondent. "I thought I could but I can't. I've been suffering too much."

She wished she could say something soothing and get dressed but she couldn't leave him as he was.

"You're too keen you mean," she cooed, jamming herself underneath him, "and you're rushing too much. We've got all day remember."

He pushed and heaved again but still he couldn't fire. She hoped if she could get him half way he might just manage the rest so she said,

"You have to keep going. You're giving up too soon. Hug me tight while you do it and tell me you love me."

He did as he was told. At first he alternated between thrusting flaccidly and wheezing words of love but as he became short of breath he settled for ramming her with mindless ferocity. Sweat dripped onto her, the veins in his temples swelled and his cheeks coloured alarmingly. When sheer exhaustion brought him to a halt he gasped, "I was nearly there, Heidi, I really was" and flopped on top of her, panting heroically.

Kapner was feeling bruised and sticky but she fluted, "I know you were, buttercup" and waited resignedly for him to recover. "When you're ready," she persisted, dominating herself as much as him. "I want you to try one last time."

Once more he began to pump, slowly at first and then in a frenzy. Sweat coursed off his face and body and he salivated freely. Suddenly he arched his body backwards and shouted as if he'd been struck by a spear. Then, making strange gutteral noises, he slowed down until running a fingertip along her forehead was the only movement he was making. He was faking and she knew it but she also knew he'd reached the end of the line.

"That was atomic," she gushed. Had she said that before? She didn't want to sound phoney. "Nobody does it like you, Lesley. You're in a class of your own."

His colour was still high, a blood vessel in his neck throbbed ominously and she reckoned he wouldn't be volunteering for an encore. So she pushed him onto his back and half lay on top of him to keep him there.

"This is how it's always going to be," she murmured. "Just the two of us and all your worries gone."

"I believe you, Heidi. And now we've reaffirmed our love I'll pull through for your sake. I know I will."

They lay still for a while, each with their different thoughts, but she was lying awkwardly and the side of her neck was ricking painfully. She also wanted to nail down what she'd gained so far so she eased herself away from him, reached for her briefcase and said,

"Don't move, Lesley. I've got something to show you. Apart from me, that is."

She pulled out the photos. She'd taken them in Devon from a hot air balloon belonging to a friend who also owned the white cliff-top mansion they showed. Because the estate and the beach were private she was sure Carey wouldn't recognise them.

"Ulrich sent me these," she said. "They're of one of the places he's lined up for us. I mustn't say where it is but you do like it, don't you? Please say you do."

He wiped his palms on the undersheet and thumbed through them.

"It's the Caribbean," he stated. "No, wait a minute, it's South America. On the Pacific coast. I've seen several of these colonial houses in my time. And Ulrich has lined one up for us, has he? Well, we're worth it, that's for sure. He couldn't manage without us, could he?"

He lay back lazily and thumbed through them again while Kapner wondered how to get him out of the bedroom. When he handed them back his stomach rumbled loudly. Maybe that was the answer. She leaned over him and tinkered with his navel.

"Is my Lesley hungry?" she giggled. "I'll bet he didn't have any breakfast, the naughty boy."

He hadn't had anything, he admitted. In fact he'd rather lost interest in food so there wasn't much in the house. But now his Heidi was with him why didn't they go out for a meal? There was a pub called the John Jasper off the High Street. They could go there and have a traditional Sunday lunch.

"Let's do it," she said with relief. "I don't go out with a handsome young man every day."

"John Jasper," Carey pronounced over roast beef, boiled cabbage and lumpy mashed potatoes, "is in one of Dickens's novels. Charles Dickens, to give him his full name. He's dead now but people still read his books."

"What's it about, this novel?" she asked although she already knew. Dickens had been popular in East Germany. He'd been seen as a friend of the working class.

Carey was thumping the bottom of a bottle of brown sauce.

"I haven't actually read it myself. I don't read much apart from technical reports, I'm far too busy, but I know that much. Dickens was born in Rochester, I believe. And there's a Dickens parade every year."

He wiped his nose on his serviette and fondly pressed his foot onto hers.

"Let's drink to us," he said, raising his pint glass the way he'd seen people in films do.

"To us, Lesley," she said and, hoping no one was looking, she clinked her glass of tonic water against his.

It was his third pint and the beer was getting to him. To show his new mood some more he ordered knickerbocker glories for dessert.

The portions were daunting. There was fresh fruit laced with liqueur at the bottom, then vanilla and strawberry ice cream, Peach Melba sauce and whipped cream topped with a glacé cherry looking like an eye with conjunctivitis. When he was finished he leaned back and watched serenely as she toiled down the layers. The ice cream made her teeth ache but she smiled winningly and thanked him for making her day. After coffee they strolled leisurely back to Beale's Row. Carey, who'd been allowed one more pint and who'd followed it with another one, kept lurching into her. She fended him off as best she could and finally they were in his house. He half-sat, half-lay, in his easy chair and she perched on hers. The curtains were still drawn.

"You've made all the difference, my pea-hen," he said and his words were clotted as if his tongue were too big for his mouth. "It takes a good deal to upset me – I'm exceptionally tough, you know - but I have to admit I've been nearly out of my mind. Those transcripts and so on were bad enough but what if I get caught before I can get away? I'll lose my house, my job, my fellowship and all the other things I've worked for all these years."

He looked at her imploringly.

"Come and sit on my lap," he begged. "I need to feel you pressing against me."

She made herself as comfortable as she could on his scraggy thighs. His beery breath rolled over her. She put her arms round his shoulders, nuzzled the side of his face and reminded herself with unqualified thanks he was definitely, but definitely, on Death Row.

"You won't get caught, precious," she purred into the hairs in his ear. "Ulrich will see to that. He's said he'll take care of you and he will. He's probably thinking about you right now."

She kissed him with every appearance of passion. It was time to bend his soul.

"I have a special favour to ask," she said as she took her lips away. "I've brought the locket you gave me, to lend it back to you because when your big moment comes I want you to have it in your hand. It'll make you think of me."

He clamped her tightly to him, bursting with emotion.

"Heidi, you're the most wonderful person in the universe!" he exclaimed. "I love you body and soul."

"I haven't finished yet," she went on, picking at his lapel. "I've lent you the locket but the photo album stays with me. And when we start our new life together I'll bring it with me. It's our pledge to each other."

In fact she was going to destroy it. Nothing about the locket connected her with him but that wasn't true of the photo album so it had to go. He intertwined his fingers with hers.

"If I get low again," he asked hesitantly, "I mean, between now and what you want me to do, can I come and see you?"

"If it were up to me I'd say yes. But Ulrich would never allow it. We're on maximum security now, all of us."

It was an answer he didn't like and his mood dipped. But he was too dependent on her to argue with her so he picked on Steffen instead.

"He'll make sure I get my injection, won't he? If he doesn't I'll have plenty of time to tell people what he's done. I'll have nothing to lose if I'm dying. I'm surprised he hasn't thought of that, but there it is. We can't all be bright, can we?"

"Of course you'll get your injection. Ulrich's a man of honour. The big question is, are you?"

He took his time to answer and when he did, the pompous note was back in his voice.

"You've pledged yourself to me and I make this solemn pledge to you: you can trust me, word of honour."

Once he'd made his grand announcement he became more and more clinging and it was only by insisting she had a train to catch that she was able to get away from him. She said she didn't want him to come to the station with her - she was too overwhelmed, she needed to be alone with her feelings. She also persuaded him not to stand in the doorway as she left but she couldn't prevent him opening a window and waving vigorously. He also pointed to something he was holding in his hand and then made a show of kissing it. It was the locket. She mouthed him a kiss back in case he called out and he remained at the window waving and beaming till she'd disappeared from view.

She had her victory smile on as, wearing her dimmed-down glasses, she boarded her train. An unscheduled stop gave her the chance to encode: "Rabbit pie ready to serve. Your arrival noted. Will be there – Falcon". She simply wrote "Condor" on the envelope. The message she'd received in

Vaduz told her Steffen must have spread their code names amongst the couriers.

On her way to Old Compton Street she stopped off in a round-the-clock convenience store and took her glasses off so her face could be seen clearly. She bought some Paracetemol she didn't need and as the paper bag was handed to her she palmed the message across with her money. It would be in Johannisbrunn before Monday was out.

Fassbinder was watching television when she climbed back into her flat. There'd been a couple of phone calls and Fassbinder had said what she'd been told to say. When Fassbinder finally left, the watchers photographed her with a night camera. The biometric data retold their tale and her departure time went into the log. As far as the SRO was concerned she'd arrived early and left late, and Kapner hadn't gone out at all.

III

29

Walter's plan

Kapner's message landed in the bungalow's drop box late Monday and Steffen read it before he went to bed. Everything was falling into place. Guderius, Danzig and the Zimmermanns were ready to go and now Carey was back on track. The next morning – it was Tuesday October 20th – Steffen took Helga-Marie over to Ruth and Walter's, where she'd stay till he got back from England. To help her settle in he'd arranged for Walter and himself not to go into the bakery. They'd have a family day instead.

For lunch there was spaghetti meat balls followed by caramel ice cream, then out came the drawing pads, the felt-tips and the games. Helga-Marie was made comfortable on a well cushioned upright chair, behind which was the aquarium Steffen had drowned the cat in. It had tropical fish in it now. By evening, when Steffen was due to leave, the children's faces were radiant. They each gave him a big kiss and he gave them ten euros each for being good. He kissed Helga-Marie and hugged her gently.

"You're looking good," he said tenderly. "You like it here, don't you?"

She nodded and smiled but she didn't say anything. She didn't have to. And she stayed back when Walter, Ruth and the children went to the front door to see him off.

"Bye, bye!" they chorused, and they waved vigorously as he pulled away. Then Walter switched off the outside lights and the drive was as black as pitch.

When all the others were in bed he and Ruth made themselves comfortable in the sitting room. All they wanted to do now was unwind. Walter subsided into a magazine on tropical fish and Ruth had a seed catalogue to browse in. A coffee pot and two steaming cups stood between them on a stool. The only sound was the swish of paper when either of them turned a page.

After a while Ruth put the catalogue down, stretched luxuriantly and said, "Helga-Marie was on form today. It's lovely to see her like that."

"It's the children. As soon as she sees them she changes. I must talk to Ulrich about money though," he added, pretending to be stern. "It's a good job the bakery's doing well."

"He won't listen, that's for sure. They do what they like with him."

"He loves it. Have you ever seen him cross with them?"

"Never. I don't think he could be." Then, "He's a wonderful man. He's built up the bakery and now he's building up the family. And he's looked so contented lately. You'd think he'd won the lottery."

"He's getting out more, that's why. He's been going over to Jan Schwarzer's and he's even playing skat, I hear."

Skat is Germany's favourite card game. It bored Steffen rigid but it gave him good cover.

"Is he really? Who's he playing with?"

"Klaus Guderius and Kurt Zimmermann for a start. I think Kurt's son turns up as well and there could be others for all I know. Apparently they play at Ulrich's. Helga-Marie says they liven the place up."

Ruth pressed her lips together. Her mother-in-law was worrying her.

"Helga-Marie really ought to be better than she is. Have you found anything on the internet?"

"Well, since you ask, I might have."

He was one of those people who like to finish things before they say anything.

"What's that supposed to mean? Have you really found something?"

"If I have, it's thanks to Hanna. She rang me at work and said she'd read about an English doctor who might – just might – be the person we're looking for. You know the stuff she fills her head with so I was more polite than interested but she said Klaus was impressed so I went into the website – Dr Garrett's his name – and I also looked through some research summaries. I can't say I understood much but Garrett's name kept coming up and that on top of Klaus's thumbs up tipped the balance. Garrett works in a state hospital in Oxford but he takes private patients as well."

"How do you know that?"

"I asked. In English. You'd have been proud of me."

"So you *are* onto something! But why's this man so special?"

"The treatments on offer at the moment don't cure anything, they just slow things down, and with Helga-Marie even that isn't happening. But Garrett's regrowing damaged joints from basic cells and they aren't arthritic any more."

"But Walter, that's exactly what we want!"

"That's what I thought. The hospital says it'll assess Helga-Marie if I take her over and if she's suitable, she goes on the list."

"So why are we still here?"

"Because, like everyone else, I have to wait for an appointment. I've said I'll take a cancellation so if we're lucky we might not wait that long. I thought we could turn it into a family break. We could take Hanna as well. It'd be a nice way to say thank you."

"I'm for it. We've never been to Oxford and I'm sure Hanna hasn't either. She'll be thrilled to bits. Have you told Ulrich yet?"

"Absolutely not. His hopes would go through the roof. He knows Hanna was going to get in touch but that's all. What I'm hoping is, we can go while Ulrich's in England. If I take my laptop and mobile I can fix things so he won't know I'm not in the bakery. We can contact him after we've seen Dr Garrett, find out where he is and arrange to meet up with him. If we've got good news it'll be the icing on the cake and if we haven't, well, he'll know we're still trying."

"I suppose you haven't told Hanna and Helga-Marie either."

"Nor Klaus but don't rush me, I'm not finished yet. According to Hanna, Klaus is flying to England on Thursday about some body scanners and he'll be over there till at least the 30th. So who knows, maybe we can rope in Klaus as well and – if all goes well – have a mammoth celebration party."

There was the slightest change of atmosphere and he realised why straight away.

"Sorry," he said, "I can see I should've told you before. We may have to leave in a hurry as well. I'm sorry about that too."

"Absolution will cost you a kiss, Mr Steffen. And you're the one who has to get out of his chair."

He stood up and kissed her, once for absolution and once because he wanted to.

"If we have to leave in a hurry," she said, "we've got Helga-Marie right here. You don't think she'll say no, do you?"

"Not with the children going. Try holding her back."

"How'll we get there? By plane?"

"Not unless we have to, we'll have too much luggage. I'll put the roof rack on the people carrier once Ulrich's out of the way."

Ruth wrinkled her nose.

"I don't fancy the Channel at this time of year and I don't think anyone else will either. No one likes throwing up."

"Me included, but I've thought of that. Hanna said Klaus came back via Brussels and Frankfurt the other week and it turned out all right so we'll do the same in reverse."

"And?"

"And when we get to Brussels we'll check the forecast for the Channel. If it's good we'll take the ferry and enjoy the ride. If it isn't we'll use the Channel Tunnel. Any more objections while you're in the mood?"

"London traffic. It's terrible and you know it."

"Which is why we'll take the North Sea Tunnel and miss it altogether. I reckon, if we allow three days to get from here to somewhere beyond the tunnel we can be sure of getting to Oxford on the fourth day without being late. Even if we get a first appointment."

As he spoke, something made him laugh.

"Don't go away," he said and went out to his office. He came back carrying two cardboard tubes and rolled up inside them were strips of tinted plastic foil. Ceremoniously he unrolled them one at a time. The first one said RUTH in big white caps and the second one said WALTER.

"What on earth are they?" exclaimed Ruth.

"A present from Ulrich. He bought them when he filled up the other day. If you stick them to the windscreen they keep the sun out of your eyes. Ulrich thought they'd make the children laugh and I think he's right so we'll take them with us."

"Oh, Walter, do we have to?"

"I don't see why not. We're going to a party, not a funeral."

As he put the foils back his mood dipped a fraction.

"I hope the hospital doesn't keep me waiting too long," he said. "Helga-Marie comes first, that goes without saying, but I'd rather not leave the bakery once the Christmas run-in picks up. I've put a new shift on already and it's still only October."

"Phone Garrett's secretary and see how things stand. Do it tomorrow morning. You're sure Hanna can get away if Klaus isn't there?"

"It's not been a problem yet. She can get people to stand in for her if she has to."

"I wish I had people to stand in for me but since I haven't, I'm going to start my packing list right now. I like my panics well organised."

"The day you panic I'll write it in my diary. Let me finish reading about these fish and I'll give you a hand."

They sat quietly under their standard lamps in two warm pools of light. When Walter put his magazine down Ruth said,

"If Helga-Marie gets better it might stop Ulrich being so backward-looking. Will he ever accept East Germany's gone for good?"

"It's not coming back so he's got to. Why do you ask?"

"Because he'd be happier than he is if he could. And then there's the people he hangs around with. There's – I don't know – something sad about them. Even Klaus sometimes."

"I don't hear you moaning about Hanna."

"Point taken but what I'm getting at is, Ulrich's been buzzing lately, we've both noticed it, and I've sort of hoped the new Germany was starting to agree with him."

"I doubt it. I've said it before, it's difficult for us to understand what he's lost. If we were his age we'd probably be the same."

"But he's gained as well as lost, Walter. And our part of Germany *is* picking up at last. I just think, if he could see that he might fit in better."

"Ruth, you've got a big warm heart and I love you for it. But you can't trade ideals in like a used car. People don't work like that."

"But he's got us and the children. Don't we make a difference?"

"Of course we do. And so, possibly, will Dr Garrett. So I'll do what you said and I'll do it in my best broken English. Now, let's get this list going before we both fall asleep."

30

Van Piet plays hardball

Steffen arrived in Orange Street the next afternoon complete with a raft of genuine bakery business. It was Wednesday October 21st. Danzig was already in London. She'd arrived the day before. Guderius was next, then the Zimmermanns.

Danzig, Guderius and the Zimmermanns had been booked into three different hotels in south-east London. They'd been ordered not to contact each other before New Hope, when they'd rendezvous with Steffen and Kapner at 13.30 on the north side of the Fare 'n' Square. Danzig would bring Guderius and Kurt Zimmermann would bring Frank, who'd transfer to Danzig's car leaving Kurt to drive to Spade Hill on his own.

The SRO picked them up as they landed and an x-ray detected night vision binoculars in Steffen's suitcase. When they were reported to Trilling he passed the word on to van Piet, who by this time was mostly in Maidstone. That was where, on the Thursday evening, he read an e-mail from Garry in emergency code. Garry had sent it from his sister-in-law's pc and it said, "DC in Ashell House again (with BT). Her message reads: 'Separator, centrifuge, incubator, sputum reader in underground room. Saw more, can't remember what.' – TG."

Van Piet focused on each word in turn, then deleted.

"It's like a ship in a bottle," he mused. "Pull the thread and the sails come up. They're not fully up yet but they're getting there."

Like van Piet, Trilling was more out of Ashell House than in it – harassed by hell-hounds was how he described it to his secretary as he rushed from meeting to meeting. But on the Friday he and van Piet were in the building at the same time so as soon as he knew the Zimmermanns had landed he had van Piet sent up to his room.

"It looks," he said urgently, "as if all the villains are now in town. I want you to go back to Maidstone, stay there and be ready for whenever they break cover. I'll tell Mrs Patel while you're getting there."

The office Patel had organised for herself was as makeshift as the operations room it led off but at least it had a door she could close and after Trilling had put in his call she went back to the three boxes she'd found in the main store. She felt she was making progress but she didn't believe it'd make life with van Piet any easier. There'd always been differences between them but this time round he was making a four-course meal of them.

She was just closing off her notes when her phone buzzed: Mr van Piet was in the lobby. As soon as he was in her office she had some tea sent in and they went through what they knew for certain. It didn't take long and Patel was soon saying how hard it was to keep her strike force alert when it didn't know what it'd be doing.

"Snipers shoot to kill. Knowing that should keep them on their toes. Us as well," he added pointedly.

He had a tiny bedsit down the corridor and around ten o'clock he turned in. He was just fading away when the phone called him back. It was Patel and she sounded excited. She'd managed to retrieve Kapner's Saab. It was on the M2/A2 eastbound on Wednesday September 30th. The images were blurry but she'd enhanced the registration and it looked like Kapner driving with Steffen sitting next to her. No, she didn't know where they were going – she only had a few seconds' worth to go on – and, no again, she didn't know when they came back. She didn't even know whether they came back on the same road.

Van Piet was wide awake now.

"They could've filled up somewhere so they might be on video. What do you reckon?"

"Filling stations delete every twenty-four hours so you can forget about them. Service centres are a better bet. The law says they have to store their data for forty-two days and they've got the gear to do it with because they don't want to lose their franchise. They can recover anything and they can do it fast."

"How many service centres are there?"

"There're three on the M2/A2 and they're joined northside/southside. There's one between London and the Sheppey Link Road, one as you approach Dover and one about half way between. What are you going to do? Drive out to them?"

"We both are and we're leaving now. While I'm getting ready get a driver for us – in uniform and in a marked car. Wear your uniform as well. People cooperate better when they see a badge. Hang on a minute."

He broke off to check his fake ID cards.

"You'll need a name for me at some point. I'll be Mr Everett from MI5. And one more thing. Pull strings with the Met to have a uniformed driver bring two people in a marked car from Barnet to – let me think. Coming from London, is there anywhere near the first of these service centres a police car can wait?"

"There's a raised reserve about a mile before you get there."

"From Barnet to this reserve then. They'll need taking back as well so the driver could be with us for a while. Make that clear – and all under wraps, of course."

Van Piet didn't want a Kent Police driver on this errand in case Patel questioned him later.

"I'll call in some favours and see what happens. Can I ask who these people are?"

"One's Tom Garry. You know him from Ashell House. The other one I'll keep to myself. Tom will tell the driver how to get to this person when he gets picked up."

He gave her Garry's address for the Met driver and as soon as he put the phone down he used his mobile to call Garry at his home. He hoped he hadn't woken him, he said, and thanked him for the e-mail as well. Then,

"Ring Stella Janes right now – I may need you both for most of the night. A Met driver in uniform will pick you up and I want you to guide him to near Stella's house. He'll bring you both back as well. Don't tell anyone where you're going or why, don't let anyone except the driver know your name and I don't want even the driver to know Stella's name or exactly where she lives so he'd better pick her up and drop her off on a street corner. I'll be Mr Everett from MI5 and I'll vouch for you both as needed. If Stella can't come call me back. And bring your steno pad and some pencils with you."

He terminated the call, got dressed and headed for Patel's office.

"We'll start with the one near Dover and work our way back. What's its name?"

"The Garden of England. You'll wonder why when you see it but they all have to be called something."

As soon as they were in the police car, the blue lights went on and they sped out into the night.

At the Garden of England van Piet ordered the driver to stand in full view while they told the duty manager what they'd come for. The manager knew Patel but she showed her ID anyway, van Piet did likewise and he took them to Security Records. After he'd shown them how to operate the lock, van Piet asked him to take the driver to the coffee shop and not come back till he was sent for.

The room was unoccupied, its sealed window was heavily curtained, the air was piped and the chairs were tubular steel and canvas. Step by step Patel took van Piet through the equipment.

"Give it a try," she said finally. "I'll talk you through it. Put Kapner's registration in and we'll go."

"Sorry, Lorraine. We'll put in a registration I saw on the car park just now, then I'll ask you to wait outside while I try Kapner's. Anything I find out stays with me unless I decide otherwise."

It took all of Patel's professionalism to stop her coming back at him.

"Very well," she said, tight-lipped and glacial. "You're the boss."

She hoped he wouldn't miss anything while he was in there on his own, she added.

After the registration he'd seen had gone in she helped him look at the car from all angles, track it back to when it first entered the car park, track it forward to when the driver got out and zoom in on him. The images were diamond sharp. He could see the driver's face clearly and read the registration as if he was down there.

"There's data handover as well," she said. "You mark something you want to follow, like this driver's face. Then you can track it for all the time it's on site except in the loo. You can do it in real time, fast, slow, forwards or backwards, it's up to you."

He soon got the hang of it.

"What about round a table? Can you see all the faces?"

"Usually, yes, and you can see them singly or in multiples. Watch."

She fast forwarded the target into the restaurant and then, on a split screen, they saw him ordering from the menu and the waitress repeating the order.

"One more thing," he said. "We've shifted a lot of data since we've been in here. Could someone else reconstruct it? The duty manager for instance? Or you, come to that."

"There's a reset procedure to stop most people, including me and the duty manager, from doing that. I suppose you want me to show it to you."

"Yes please."

When she'd done that he told her to go and wait with the driver. Kapner's registration produced nothing so he reset, locked up and they set off westwards to the next service centre. He didn't need any help there and he had a nil result within minutes. That left the Fare 'n' Square. The duty manageress took van Piet to Security Records, then seated Patel and the driver in the same coffee shop Steffen, Kapner and Guderius had met Sobart in.

"Have what you like," she said obligingly. "It's on the house."

She liked to stay in with the police and MI5 had a menace that made her even keener to fall in line.

As soon as van Piet tapped in Kapner's registration the Saab was in front of him. Captioned with the date and time, it was coming into the south side car park. That meant it'd been travelling westwards. When the front doors opened he verified Kapner was the driver and Steffen was the front passenger. Then Guderius heaved himself out of the back. So, all three together. He fast forwarded them into the coffee shop and as soon as he was certain they'd come to stay he called Garry.

"Where are you?"

"Watching traffic."

"I take it Stella's with you."

"She is."

"Move on to a service centre called the Fare 'n' Square. Bring your driver in with you and be as quick as you can."

While van Piet was waiting he thought he'd take a closer look at his data so he went back to where Kapner, Steffen and Guderius were getting out of the Saab, froze the image and zoomed in. There was definitely something odd about them. It was their clothes and mini rucksacks. Had they really been out for a country walk? And if so, where had they been? He tracked them to the south side doors then slowed them down to see whether they looked round for anyone or picked up anything that might contain a message. They didn't. He slowed them down in the restaurant but nothing again.

"Perhaps this is all they've come for," he speculated as he watched them buy their baguettes.

Frustrated he split the screen and watched them eat and drink in slow motion, hoping their eyes might tell him something. At first they didn't, then they did. They fastened on a neat looking elderly lady who'd come in from the north side. He knew it was Sobart from his briefing file. At that moment there was a knock on the door. He reset and opened up. It was the duty manageress.

"A man and a woman have just come in with a uniformed officer from the Met. They say you'll vouch for them, Sir."

"Can we see them from here?"

She lit up a spare screen and zoomed in on Garry, a policeman and a woman in her mid-twenties. Her hair had been hastily scraped into a bun.

"They're the people I'm expecting. Can you bring them here, please? Then take their driver to join mine and my colleague in the coffee shop."

He warned the Met driver off saying anything to anyone and as soon as Garry and Janes were in Security Records he went back to Kapner parking the Saab and froze her, Steffen and Guderius as they were getting out.

"We'll call the driver A, the thin passenger B and the fat one C," he said.

Garry made a shorthand note on his steno pad. Janes, who was an SRO lip reader on maternity leave, waited patiently. She was bi-lingual English and German, like Garry. German was one reason he'd been assigned to van Piet when van Piet had joined the SRO.

"I'll let them move now, Stella."

He marked Kapner and tracked them into the coffee shop. They were slightly zoomed in on so Janes could see their mouths clearly. As their lips formed words she said them out loud and Garry took them down in shorthand. When Sobart arrived van Piet froze her.

"We'll call this one D. If I remember rightly she lives and works in Rochester. Let's see what she's up to."

He tracked her in reverse to her car and asked Garry to check the registration with Driver and Vehicle Licensing. It didn't take him long.

"Miss Miriam Ethel Sobart," he said and added on her home and work address.

"Now there's a thing," van Piet said out loud. "Why would a person who lives and works in Rochester use this place when they could go straight home?"

"You think this meeting is prearranged then?" Garry asked.

"That we'll find out shortly. But I'll recheck her website first."

He downloaded it onto his mobile and it was distinctly different from the entry in his briefing file. In that she'd been sparsely described as "a known Chameleon member living within 100 miles of London" and there'd been just her full name, her addresses, some career notes and a smattering of photos. It also said her laboratory was probably Chameleon-funded but no charges had ever been brought against her. The website by contrast showed her smiling face in close-up, her Snowcem-covered low-rise, a wide-angle sunny-day shot of the river and the kinds of testing she did. Van Piet memorised the tests without comment. Then,

"Let's hear what they've got to say."

He set them all moving again, quartered the screen and listened impassively as Janes took him through what they said and Garry wrote it down. When they broke up he tracked Sobart out first, then Kapner, Steffen and Guderius. Not until the screen went blank did anyone stir.

Van Piet had already come across Carey. He'd been making a list of targets Steffen & Co might be interested in and the control centre on Sheppey had caught his eye. It'd seemed a long shot at the time but not any more – not with its Senior Security Officer getting so much covert attention. He downloaded an aerial view of Sheppey, located the control centre, then backed off to take in the area around it. It was in open country and Steffen & Co had been dressed for a country walk. Was that a lead? He mustn't rush his fences. Carey was an expert on tunnels in general so maybe there was no connection with the North Sea Tunnel. Or with tunnels at all for that matter. Steffen had said, "Everything's for the old country, Miriam. This included" but that could mean anything. Even so, van Piet had opened up some options and he could always hope Steffen & Co would whittle them down for him. It'd be touch and go though.

"Tom, when you've done the transcript e-mail one copy to Gorris and that's it. No second copy, no copy on disk and no notes kept. And you might want to use the pc your last e-mail came from. Stella, you haven't been here, you haven't seen anything and you haven't said anything. None of this has happened."

She smiled wearily. It was Willem all over.

"Don't worry, I'm out of circulation on maternity leave. I'd be the last person to think you knew that when you decided I and only I would do for this job despite having two insomniac infants in the house."

"What you think is up to you but I want you to forget about claiming a job fee as well. When's the twins' first birthday?"

"August 27th."

He noted it on his mobile.

"Twins can be expensive. I'll see what I can do."

He watched Janes go out to the north side car park to wait by the Met's car, then he told Garry to find the Met driver and go out with him. Patel might just know Janes and he didn't want them coming into contact if he could help it. After he'd seen Garry and the Met driver leave he reset and locked up. All the while he'd been in Security Records he'd had a nagging feeling the room could be bugged. He didn't think it was because Patel hadn't said anything and she was up on things like that. Anyway, he'd had no choice. But now he wanted to make a call that absolutely mustn't be overheard and the best place for that was one of the car parks. He chose the north side one.

The Met's car had gone and the air had a bite to it as he tapped in the personal number of the Permanent Secretary to the Home Office. It was a brutal hour to call anyone but he had to know more about the control centre straight away. The phone at the other end rang four times then a voice thick with sleep said,

"Meacher."

"Simon, it's Willem van Piet. Can we talk?"

"I'll go into another room. Bear with me, I'm doing it now."

The accent was the ruling class accent of Eton and Oxford but over time van Piet had come to know Sir Simon as a selfless public servant even if he did sound like someone on a grouse moor.

"Go ahead, Willem. What's on your mind?"

Van Piet told him and, shivering slightly in the chill, he was talked through how the control centre was set up, how the flooding mechanism was guarded and why the Home Office thought so much of Carey.

"Have I left anything out?" Meacher asked finally.

"I don't think so. And please don't let anyone know we've talked."

"What about my Minister?"

It was the nightmare question – no minister wants to get caught out and Permanent Secretaries' careers rest on not letting it happen.

"Not now. Perhaps later. I'll let you know in time."

He allowed Meacher to return to his bed but before he could go back into the warm himself he had another call to make and an e-mail to send as well. Patel had organised Armed Interventions into sections when she got the top job and each section had its own leader. Van Piet's call went to Joe Smail, leader of Gold Section, who'd also been given a Police Headquarters bedsit for the duration. Like Meacher he'd been sound asleep. Van Piet skipped the niceties.

"Joe, just in case you've forgotten, on this job you answer to me, not Lorraine. I'm out of Maidstone at the moment but I want you in my room in an hour's time. Under no circumstances is anyone to know you've been to see me and that includes Lorraine. That's an order. Is it understood?"

"If it comes from you, Sir, I have to say yes. I don't like it though, as I hope you'll appreciate."

"I'm not asking you to like it, I'm asking you to carry it out. If you leak it, you'll be disciplined. I work for the Crown, not the police, and I don't share your loyalties."

The e-mail went to Joost and requested, with immediate effect, protection for Sobart. He elaborated briefly who she was, attached the smiling face from her website and said she mustn't know what was happening. Rochester had its own airport so one of the bank's machines could land right there. And, yes, he'd foot the bill again.

A number of vehicles had arrived on the car park while he'd been out there – Saturday morning was picking up. Feeling glassy from lack of sleep and chilled through as well he went back in to fetch Patel. She was reading one of the Saturday newspapers and their driver was reading *Autocar*. A book of crossword puzzles and a half-drunk cup of coffee were on the table next to him. She must've worked out Kapner and probably Steffen had stopped at the Fare 'n' Square because he'd been tied up for so long but she didn't know Guderius had been in the back of the Saab and she didn't know Steffen & Co had been pressuring the Senior Security Officer of the North Sea Tunnel with the help of a local lab owner. Good. She'd be curious, of course, but he'd keep things that way for now at least. She wouldn't like it but she'd have to live with it.

The run back to Maidstone was deadly quiet. Patel sat next to the driver staring in front of her and van Piet dozed on the back seat. Back at Police Headquarters Patel said she was going to get some sleep and disappeared. Van Piet could do with some sleep himself but when he reached his bedsit he sat down in a chair to wait for Smail. He was on time and he didn't need to stay long: he was a good listener and when he spoke, he didn't waste his words. After he'd gone van Piet got in a couple of hours of sleep and when he woke up he was, to his own surprise, fresh and ready for the day.

He'd have felt less buoyant if he'd known Patel hadn't gone to her bedsit straight away. Armed Interventions was headquartered in the basement and she soon found who she was looking for amongst the night staff. The idea of a heist at the Channel Tunnel terminal hadn't left her and the way van Piet was treating her made her determined to follow it up. So she ordered a mini-drone surveillance of Cheriton Broadspace and the terminal, Zimmermann vehicles to be especially noted and reports to her only. Only then did she go and get some sleep.

Later that morning a liveried helicopter from Van Piet Banking landed on the Maidstone helipad and Geert was added to the Police Headquarters' guest list.

"It was no distance at all," he told van Piet as he unpacked in the bedsit next to his. "South over Essex, a swing over the Thames and here I am."

During a break after lunch van Piet took an e-mail from his father. A team to look after Miss Sobart had left in one of the bank's Cessnas and Pablo Bakos was being helped down Memory Lane. Facts were still thin but one of van Piet's hunches could be confirmed: Juán Bakos had been well in with Western diplomats in Havana as well as with the comrades. Diplomats from Ottawa included.

31

Steffen commits murder

The next day – Sunday October 25th – the wind was gusty and when it rained it was heavy. Kapner spent the morning indoors while Steffen called on hotel managers in and around New Bond Street. Once an order was finalised he faxed it to the bakery from the hotel he was in and left the follow-up to Walter. He preferred working that way – it gave him space for Chameleon. He had lunch with Kapner in The Colour Sergeant, a pub they knew from their Embassy days. It was chilled lager and clean air now, not warm beer and tobacco smoke, but the memories still came back. When they left Steffen tried his pockets as he pulled his coat on. Sure enough, there was a sealed envelope in one of them. It contained the keys to a red Nissan already parked in one of Kapner's lock-ups. Steffen had told her to empty the lock-up, leave the door undone and use the underground passage to get there and back. When they were in Orange Street again she asked if she could take a nap. She wanted to be fresh for later. Steffen looked at his watch and said he thought it'd be all right. When she woke up the afternoon was in decline and the wind had picked up some more but Steffen still thought it'd be all right.

Steffen's shopping list was ready packed in the two hold-alls he'd asked Kapner to buy. Steffen's was indigo and Kapner's was bottle green so they could tell them apart. Steffen added in his night vision binoculars and Kapner put in a couple of towels. She also switched her ansaphone on and checked all the blinds. The lights in the living room could stay on but she put the ones in the kitchen and bathroom on timers. Finally she worked her magnet and they went down the ladder. At the bottom Steffen took the brightest torch he could find while Kapner shut the floor. Then they headed off down the passage with Kapner counting her steps.

"It's always smaller than I remember," said Steffen, brooding on the number of torches. "Do you bring anyone else through here?"

"Occasionally. Not all of my contacts want to be seen."

"Really? Why not?"

"I've, er, got a sideline. I trade in other firms' secrets and that's best done out of sight."

She sounded evasive but he didn't press the point. He knew it wouldn't get him anywhere.

"By the way," she went on quickly, "I've put a wheelbarrow at the other end to bring the guns back on. I bought some straps as well."

"Thanks. I was going to split the load but your idea's better."

When they came up at the other end Steffen hung onto his torch while Kapner switched everything off and closed the floor. They went out through the side door and round to where the Nissan was garaged. They filtered into the traffic and soon they were on the M2/A2. The rain was hitting the windscreen in flurries so Kapner put the wipers on automatic.

"It's gusting hard," she said, gripping the wheel. "I can feel it more now we're out of town."

Steffen was checking his watch.

"It can't be helped. If we don't collect tonight we don't collect at all."

The Link Road was as busy as ever and because she was driving illegally Kapner was ultra-careful even by her standards. When they reached the B road the Nissan's suspension magnified every bump and dip. Then they were in amongst the houses.

"Don't stop here this time," said Steffen when they reached the quayside. "I'll tell you when."

He let down his window to see out better and the wind came buffeting in. Kapner said she could smell the rain in it. Steffen was checking his watch again.

"It'd smell like that anyway. It's just about high tide."

When they reached the jetty he told her to stop, reverse a bit, then pull off the road on the inland side. Despite the rain the verge was firm. Beyond it was a ditch and then bushes. Steffen got out first, fetched his binoculars out of the boot and walked across the road. The wind tugged at his clothing and ahead of him the water was dark and threatening. He ran his binoculars along the jetty and picked out the rowing boat he wanted. It was closer to the land than the others so it'd be less far to carry the guns. Back at the Nissan he said,

"We'll change in the car. If anyone comes, stay still."

"Can we park here, do you think? I mean, is it allowed?"

"There's nothing to say we can't. And we passed several parked cars on the way. If they can do it, so can we."

Kapner had done her shopping well: everything fitted exactly. Twice a passing car made them freeze but no one slowed down to take a look so they blacked their faces, pulled their headwear and gloves on and got out ready to go. Kapner zipped the keys into a waterproof pouch on her belt. As they set off Steffen was carrying the torch and Kapner had his binoculars looped round her neck.

The jetty was wet and slippery, and they felt it move under their weight. When they reached the rowing boat Steffen gave Kapner the torch, pulled the bow in by the painter and held the boat steady while she got in. He followed and, kneeling on the bottom in some rainwater, had yet another look at his watch.

"We should've got here earlier," he said, annoyed with himself. "Slot the rudder in and stow the torch where you can reach it. When we get going keep the rudder straight unless I tell you. It's easier if I steer with the oars."

He drew the bow into the jetty and, in the fluctuating moonlight, studied the knot in the painter so he could duplicate it when they got back. Then he undid it, coiled the painter neatly in the bottom of the boat and settled onto the crossplank that served as a seat. As soon as he could he arced round the end of the jetty and pulled away in the direction of the docks. There was no undertow to row against but beyond the lee of the land the wind was a problem. When it came from The Castle – now ablaze with light - they could hear singing and laughter and when it swung round it brought the thrum of the docks with it. At least, it brought the thrum to Kapner. It crossed her mind Steffen might not be able to hear it.

"I'm going further out," he said. "The pub's throwing out too much light and the moon isn't helping either. When I tell you, look at the nearest ship through my binoculars. It should have Lederer Maritime on the side."

Once they were in darker waters Steffen straightened up and told Kapner to keep him on course for the docks. She knew where she was from the photos she'd memorised but nothing had prepared her for actually being out there. She was getting near to panic so she was glad when Steffen told her to get his binoculars out: it gave her something to fasten her mind on. Clamping the tiller against her body she focused onto the ship ahead of them. She kept losing it as the boat moved about but then, luminous in the binoculars' greeny light, she made out Lederer Maritime just aft of midships. She tried to see more of the ship and then exclaimed,

"The cranes are moving! We must be really late! The tow-behind'll be down already!"

Steffen dug the oars in and pulled harder.

"Take the torch," he ordered between breaths, "and flick it on three times."

She did as she was told and three flashes came back from near the ship's stern.

"The driver's got an infrared marker as well as night vision goggles," Steffen told her, "so when you look through the binoculars you'll see a red dot when he's about a hundred yards away. Don't use the torch again unless I tell you. Someone else might see it."

He was having to speak in bursts but he showed no signs of flagging - his fanaticism was driving him on. Before long the ship was looking its true size and the quayside lighting was giving it a halo. Suddenly Kapner burst out,

"I can see the tow-behind! It's heading straight for us!"

"Keep tracking it. I'll get as near as I can."

Then the red dot showed: a hundred yards to go. Intermittently the moon came out then the clouds reformed, rain pelted down and everything that wasn't artificially lit went dark.

"It's almost here, Ulrich!"

Steffen rested his oars, looked first over one shoulder, then over the other, but all he could see was black on black. Then the clouds parted and he spotted it. It was veering to approach from the side and it had three bundles strapped onto it, two long ones and a short one. The driver was all in black and his face was blacked as well. Keeping the tiller clamped tight Kapner worked the binoculars back into their case to free her hands.

Once the tow-behind was touching, Steffen shipped his oars, darted into the bow and threw the painter out. The driver had to scrabble for it but as soon as he had it he switched his motor off and held the tow-behind against the boat forward of the rowlocks.

"How many mooring lines have you got?" Steffen called down to him as loudly as he dared. He hadn't realised how high out of the water the rowing boat was till now.

"Two," the driver called back, holding up a gloved thumb and forefinger, "and you're late. I've been wasting juice waiting for you."

"The wind held us up."

"It's been blowing all day. You should've allowed for it."

Steffen knew it wasn't just the wind.

"Sorry," he called, leaning right down, then he darted back to the crossplank, hoping Kapner hadn't heard anything. He put his oars out to steady the boat.

"OK, Heidi. Take my binoculars right off, get into the bow and be ready to take two mooring lines. Pass me on my right, I'll press my oar down as you come by. Quickly now."

He gave her as much room as he could and she clambered past him, stooping to keep her balance as the boat rocked under her. The driver had already passed the painter through a lug on the tow-behind and tied it fast. As she reached down he half handed, half lobbed the first mooring line up. The rowing boat had old cut-to-size Mini tyres along its bow and gunnels. They acted as fenders and they were fixed by ropes to hooks on the inside. Kapner tied the mooring lines to two of these hooks and called out when she'd finished.

"Take the guns now," Steffen ordered. "Use both hands. They'll be heavier than you think."

She pointed to the bundles and the driver freed one of the long ones. Holding on to the tow-behind with one hand he pushed it up to Kapner between two of the tyres and she pivoted it into the bow. As he was freeing the second long bundle a wave successively tipped the tow-behind and the boat and he almost lost his grip.

"That was close," he laughed through the rain that followed. Then, "Are you ready? ... Now!"

He pushed the second bundle up and it, too, was pivoted into the bow.

"One to go, Ulrich," she called over her shoulder. "It's smaller than the other ones. I'll have to reach down for it."

"I'll shift across to balance you."

As he moved the moon disappeared and the wind began to turn the boat. He dug his oars in to hold it then twisted round to see where he was in relation to the docks. As he did so something caught his eye. He'd already noticed a vague smudge of light on the land beyond the promenade but it hadn't struck him as significant. Now it brightened for a moment and then disappeared. From time to time afterwards he glanced towards where it'd been but it didn't come back.

"Be careful!" the driver called to Kapner. "This one's floppy. Reach right down when I hand it up and we'll just about do it. I'll count to three."

By "Two!" he'd steadied himself against the tow-behind but just as he called out "Three!" the wind came sideways on, a wave tipped him and the boat away from each other and Kapner, who'd been holding back from fear of the water, missed the bundle as the driver let go. It slid off the tow-behind into the water and the driver plunged after it. He couldn't see a thing under water but as he flailed around he knocked it with the side of his hand. Quickly he grabbed it and pulled it to him. He was getting short of air but he didn't want to come up under the boat so, guessing his direction, he propelled himself away with his flippers, clawing at his snorkel as he went. When he surfaced the moon was still hidden and he was further away than he meant to be.

"Ulrich, I've lost the bundle!" Kapner called out. Rain was beating into her eyes making seeing next to impossible. "I can't see the driver either!"

Steffen took a decision.

"Come back on my right, get the torch and signal!"

She clambered past him, grabbed the torch, clambered hastily back and played the beam through the rain. The driver saw it and called to her to switch off but the wind carried his voice away so he swam closer and called out again. She heard him but she didn't catch his words so, without thinking, she locked the beam onto his face as he half-raised the bundle and shouted at her. Steffen took the situation in and intervened.

"Switch that torch off!" he rapped. "Do it now!"

Able to see again the driver swam back and, breathing heavily, manoeuvred the bundle onto the tow-behind while Kapner once more got ready to take it. The belt of rain was nearly through and the moon was coming out. Steffen rested his oars and twisted round.

"Don't be anxious and don't snatch," he said to her. "You'll be all right."

He didn't sound angry at all now.

"It was my fault," she replied. "I just wish it wasn't so floppy."

When the driver reached "Three!" again the wind fell away, she didn't hold back and the bundle went safely on board.

"Time to go," Steffen called to the driver. "Thanks for everything."

Kapner released the mooring lines, the driver untied the painter and, with a friendly wave, headed off towards the docks. While Kapner was taking the tiller Steffen turned the boat and began rowing hard because the current would soon pick up. He mustn't let Kapner's morale sag so he stuck to not sounding angry. He also felt guilty about the third bundle – it was his fault it was floppy and he knew it.

"Cheer up, Heidi. We've got what we came for, that's the main thing."

She gave him a grateful smile but it was just show. She'd heard what the driver had called out and she resented being grateful to someone who'd been fingered himself. She'd have been even more resentful if she'd known why the third bundle was floppy.

By the time they rounded the jetty Steffen was all in and he was only just in time as well. If he'd taken any longer the water would've ebbed too much for him to put the boat back where it came from. As it was Kapner had to lift the rudder out early and the bottom scraped ominously as he put in a final pull. When he was in position he shipped his oars, moved into the bow and tied the boat up with a knot exactly like the one he'd untied earlier.

In short order he reached the three bundles and the torch onto the jetty. Then he climbed out and held the boat while Kapner clambered after him, his binoculars once more round her neck. She picked up the torch and went ahead to unlock the car, leaving Steffen to transport the bundles. It wasn't raining so he laid them out below the lip of the ditch and started wiping them with his towel. Kapner meanwhile peeled her gloves off, got her own towel and walked to the front of the car on the passenger side. She wanted to get her boots off before she got in because she knew wet neoprene could be a struggle. She used the bonnet to balance herself and the moon came out so brightly she cast a sharp shadow. When she'd worked her footwear off she went back to the car's boot. Steffen had put the bundles in and was putting his gloves in his holdall. She pushed against him as she reached her boots and gloves in and whispered in German,

"We're being watched. There's someone in the bushes opposite the front of the car."

He straightened up and walked casually along the driver's side, rubbing his hands on his towel. When he was in front of the car he let it fall as if by accident and covertly scanned the bushes as he picked it up. All he saw at first were branches and foliage but then he glimpsed part of a face staring in his direction. Kapner, meanwhile, had come up on the passenger's side. She had her boots on again, the torch was in her hand and under her other arm was her towel. It was rolled up.

"You're on the wrong side," she said loudly in English across the bonnet. "This is the tyre I mean. And it's definitely soft."

Steffen came round to her side. When they squatted down she gave him the torch and whispered in German,

"When I say 'Now!' shine this into his eyes. My Beretta's in the towel. It's loaded and the silencer's on. I'll point it in the same direction as the torch. Are you ready?"

"Ready."

"Now!"

He stood up suddenly and the beam lanced into the bushes while Kapner thrust her gun out in front of her.

"Stay where you are and put your hands up!" she commanded in English. "Try anything and you're dead!"

For a moment nothing happened. Then there was a rustling, crackling noise and two hands in knitted gloves went up.

"Step into the ditch!" Kapner called through the beam. "Do it slowly and do it now!"

With more rustling and crackling an ungainly male figure with his eyes screwed up advanced tentatively into the ditch. He was short and his stubbled face was puffy. He looked in his sixties and, like Kapner and Steffen, he was dressed so as not to be seen in the dark. He was wearing broken black shoes, a charcoal grey suit that'd seen better days, a dark brown V-neck pullover and a black roll-neck shirt that'd lost its stretch. His black woollen hat was pulled down over his forehead and on his back was a tattered haversack. He wasn't swaying or staggering but Kapner felt sure he'd been drinking. She ordered him out of the ditch.

"Now turn round and kneel with your back to the car."

Steffen rounded the front of the car as the man dropped onto all fours and then straightened up on his knees. Kapner, still targeting him with her Beretta, moved past Steffen, got

right in behind him and pushed her gun into his back. He felt it
– he was meant to - but he didn't dare look over his shoulder.

"Keep looking in front of you," she said. "In a moment my
friend will switch his torch off but my gun will stay where it is.
If you try to run away I'll kill you. And if anything comes
along the road you freeze. Nod if you understand me."

He nodded slowly and Steffen switched the torch off.
Tensely they waited to see whether he'd move but he didn't.

"Take your gloves off and tip your haversack out. Then tell
us what your name is and what you're doing here."

It was still Kapner who was giving the orders. Steffen
might have slipped up but she had as well. She had to put that
right.

Sluggishly the man pocketed his gloves, pulled his
haversack off and turned it upside down. Into the moonlight
tumbled a one-litre vacuum flask minus its screw-on cup and a
battered pair of night vision binoculars. Like his clothes the
binoculars were a kind of parody of Steffen's.

"My name's John Tuppen. I've come from my caravan. I
live in a caravan."

His voice was dull and surly.

"Where is it?" Steffen broke in. "Come on, tell us where it
is."

But Steffen had already guessed. It was the caravan he'd
passed with Kapner and Guderius when they'd been on the
promenade together.

"Tell us why you've been spying on us," he persisted.
"And don't lie. We'll know if you do."

"I'd been having a drink in The Castle. On my way home I
saw your torch and then I saw someone else's. When I got
back I went inside and got my binoculars to see what was
going on."

"You can see in the dark with them, can't you?"

"So can your friend with hers."

"Don't try to be clever. And your caravan light was on
because you'd left it on – go on, say it."

"What are you asking for if you know it all? I went outside
again at first but it kept raining so I went back in –"

"– and opened the curtains."

Steffen now knew what he'd seen from the water.

"Then you switched your light off and watched us through the window but that wasn't enough, we were too interesting so you left your caravan and tracked us down to here. That's right, isn't it?"

He was about to answer when Kapner hissed,

"Into the ditch, both of you! Something's coming!"

She shoved Tuppen down the slope and rammed the Beretta back into him as he fell while Steffen, who'd kicked the haversack down, scrambled beside him and pressed his face into the ground. What Kapner had heard was a two-stroke motor bike. Its headlight lit up the Nissan, then it was gone, its L-plate flapping behind it. Whoever it was must have seen the Nissan but, like the cars that had already come past, they'd completely ignored it.

"We passed some parked cars earlier," Kapner thought to herself. "We're parked here too and people are driving past as if they expect us to be here. Plus this ape's got binoculars with night vision. It doesn't take much to work this one out."

Steffen had stood up but she stayed down and kept Tuppen where he was.

"I know what you are," she said quietly. "You're a Peeping Tom and this is your little kingdom. You know every path and clearing in these bushes. And you can move double quick when you have to – double quick and double quiet. You've got a bike, haven't you? And, what's more, you got here before we did, didn't you?"

"All right, so I did. So what?"

"You saw what we did, that's what."

She turned her blacked face up towards Steffen's and switched back into German.

"He's too dangerous to live, Ulrich. He's got to die."

There was that thrill again. She expected Steffen to do the killing since he was in charge but she was the one who'd passed the sentence. In doing so she'd moved closer to an élite she profoundly wanted to join – the life-takers.

"Shooting's too messy," said Steffen, electrified by the prospect of killing someone personally. "Is there anything else?"

"Leave it to me," she replied, acting on a hunch. "Just do as I say."

She stood up and ordered Tuppen to get out of the ditch and then stop. Keeping behind him she followed him out while Steffen climbed out with the haversack and dropped it next to the binoculars and the flask. She ordered Tuppen to kneel down again and moved to where he could see her and her Beretta. He could look at her as much as he liked now. He wasn't going to pass anything on.

"What's in your flask?" she asked, speaking almost gently. "Open it for me."

He unscrewed the stopper and held it out towards her.

"It's whisky," he said.

It was as if he was making an offering.

Steffen flashed the torch into the top and Kapner looked in as well. It was about three quarters full and the whisky smelled neat.

"Drink it," she told Tuppen, reinforcing her order with her gun. "All of it."

Flint-eyed she watched him as he raised the flask to his lips. Whenever he paused for breath she gave him a few seconds, then she got him swallowing again. When he said the flask was empty Steffen checked it with his torch. The whisky was already rising to Tuppen's head as he groped for the stopper and screwed it back in.

"Now," said Kapner, "put your flask and your binoculars in your haversack and put your haversack on your back. We're going over to the jetty."

"Shall I bring the torch?" Steffen asked in German.

"No need. You can bring your gloves though."

She let Steffen lead onto the jetty since she could control things better from behind. When they reached the rowing boat Steffen paused, uncertain what to do, and Tuppen, who was having difficulty keeping his balance, made to stop as well but Kapner snapped, "Not yet! Keep going!" and they carried on till they were over water. Tuppen tried to look down at it but tilting his head made him reel so he forced himself to look up and keep going. When they were almost at the end of the jetty Kapner commanded, "Stop now" and they did. She moved to the downstream edge.

"Come here, John," she called. "I want you to see something."

He lurched towards her and, with the moon disappearing and the wind beating in, Steffen closed up behind him.

"Do it now," she told Steffen and he didn't have to ask what she meant. He placed a gloved hand against the small of Tuppen's back and propelled him into the water. He was too befuddled to cry out and since he slumped as much as fell he didn't splash much. The shock of the water made him flounder but he was so disconnected, he didn't register he was breathing it in. Before long he was still. Kapner and Steffen stood watching where he'd gone in till they felt certain he was dead.

"Are we going to leave him where he is?" Steffen asked.

It disappointed him he couldn't see the body clearly.

"I don't see why not. He's as high as a kite and there isn't a mark on him so it's obvious: he got drunk once too often and paid the price. We don't come into it."

When they got back to the Nissan they changed quickly and cleaned the blacking off their faces. The traffic was light all the way to London and when Kapner garaged the Nissan she left the door unlocked. By the time they set off for New Hope a black Fiat would've taken its place. In the underground passage they loaded the guns onto the wheelbarrow, added the holdalls and secured everything with Kapner's straps. With his self-doubt erased by the killing, Steffen pushed the wheelbarrow while Kapner, likewise rebalanced, demurely padded beside him and counted her footsteps in silence.

Kapner's timers had been doing what they were made for so the SRO watchers let it go when the lights in the kitchen and bathroom came on again – only this time it really was Kapner who was putting them on. There were five telephone messages for her, four genuine and one a trial from Ashell House. They'd all been fielded by the ansaphone. Steffen took a shower and said he'd be going to bed shortly since he wanted to get up good and early. As he ate a sandwich with her and drank some milk he asked her about the silencer on her Beretta. Could he have a closer look? She fetched it from her holdall. It was still screwed on.

"It's almost new, isn't it?" he asked as he unscrewed it and held it in his hand.

"Made for New Hope. Do you like it?"

He looked at it closely.

"It's brilliant. Who made it for you?"

"A gunsmith in Soho who knows how to keep his mouth shut."

"Where have you used it?"

"Where I practise. It works like a dream."

He gave it and the gun back to her.

"Could you use it for real if you had to?"

When she said yes she forced herself to sound matter of fact.

After Steffen had gone to bed she took a shower of her own and, swaddled in a thick dressing gown, she tidied everything up. Although it was late she was too wound up for bed so she made herself some cocoa and settled down to a magazine. Occasionally she heard rain thrashing against the windows so she put the television on and found the next day's forecast. The rain would clear overnight and there was a chance of mist in places. She neither knew nor cared Tuppen's body had drifted quite a way before its clothing had pulled it down. While she sat drinking cocoa it lay in lightless water, a mute portent of deaths to come.

32

Guderius's second weakness

As forecast the rain dispersed overnight and there was mist the following morning. It'd clear during the day and return towards evening. Steffen was unhappy about that. If the mist was thick it could cause problems.

After breakfast he spread an old sheet out on the living room floor and unpacked the guns. First out were the Dragunovs with their bipods, zoom scopes, box magazines and cleaning gear. Then came the Ceskas with their ammunition and shoulder holsters. He could hear Kapner moving about in the bathroom and kitchen but he took no notice. He was focused on the hardware in front of him.

Methodically he cleaned and lightly oiled them, then he tried their firing mechanisms. Nothing even looked like malfunctioning. Kapner meanwhile was in the bedroom he'd vacated packing the holdalls. Gloves, balaclavas, face blacking, his night vision binoculars and two towels went into the indigo one, plus five of the walkie-talkies from her safe and two flasks of sweet black coffee – a large one and a small one. The bottle green holdall was for Kurt Zimmermann. The sixth walkie-talkie went into it plus gloves, a balaclava, blacking, a towel, more coffee and his Ceska, which she fetched from the living room. Finally she put in a pair of binoculars. They had up to X150 magnification and anti-tremble. They didn't have night vision but that didn't matter since the end of the North Sea Tunnel was always lit up. When she'd finished she put her head round the living room door.

"Just to confirm, Ulrich. Klaus and I don't need balaclavas and blacking, do we?"

"No. You'll be in the cars all the while."

They both stayed indoors till it was time to leave. Kapner set the flat up and then they loaded everything onto the wheelbarrow in the underground passage. Their clothes were dark and close-fitting and their mobiles stayed in the flat. The black Fiat was in the lock-up waiting for them. Steffen crouched down behind it, felt underneath and peeled the keys off.

As Kapner threaded her way through London the Fiat was routinely picked up on surveillance cameras and just as routinely ignored. However, while she'd been packing the holdalls Kent Police's IPI had come on stream with the result that, once they crossed the county boundary, Patel's operations room got alerts for both of them.

"That Fiat!" van Piet exclaimed. "It isn't Kapner's and it isn't Cantico's. Get it followed, Lorraine! And get someone to find out whose it is."

While Patel was starting the chase van Piet was talking to Co-ordination at Ashell House. How had Kapner and Steffen got out without being seen? Had a furniture lorry or anything like that parked outside the door? Before he'd finished a Mazda was sitting a couple of cars behind the Fiat, a motor cycle courier was cruising ahead of it and a helicopter marked Traffic Police was flying ellipses overhead. At varying intervals the terrestrials were replaced but the helicopter kept where it was since watching traffic was - supposedly - what it was there for. The operations room had a charge to it now. Near the windows Smail was following the chase on his own array. Next to him was Sal Gulliver, his second-in-charge.

Ashell House called back. No large vehicle had parked near Kapner's door within the last twenty-four hours. Did van Piet want the flat opened up?

"Not yet. The alarm might transmit to Kapner. Keep watching and let me know if anything changes."

When the run-down on the Fiat reached Patel she read it through and passed it to van Piet.

"This vehicle's got no connection with Kapner," he said. "She's not mentioned anywhere."

"Then she's driving illegally. We can pick her up for that. Do you want me to?"

If he hesitated before he answered, it happened so fast she didn't notice.

"Not if you want to feel Steffen's collar. If you stop her now he'll plead ignorance and slide away. That absolutely mustn't happen."

The next alert came from Ashell House.

"Danzig has left her hotel in a Vauxhall she didn't arrive in. We think she's heading for Guderius's hotel. Kurt and Frank Zimmermann have left their hotel in a Land Rover they didn't arrive in. Kurt Zimmermann is driving. They look to be heading for the M2/A2 eastbound."

Then came the registrations, model types and colours. Patel readied up and called for run-downs on the vehicles.

"Same story," she said after they'd read them. "Something big's happening, that's for sure. They wouldn't be taking risks like these if it weren't."

Her words were deliberately vague. In the back of her mind were the mini-drone reports she'd had and there was no doubt about it, Cheriton Broadspace was getting a lot of attention from the Zimmermanns. So, she was wondering, were Steffen and Co *counting* on being watched? Was it all an enormous bluff? She was inclined to think it was. Steffen was a colonel so feints must be second nature to him and as for driving illegally, that just made things more credible. There were plenty of ways out of illegal driving charges and Chameleon would know them all. It was that kind of outfit.

Guderius had been up and about long before Danzig left her hotel. He was wearing a black raincoat over a suit the colour of anthracite, a navy blue shirt and a black pullover with a high crew neck. His mobile was stowed away in the top drawer of his bedside table and he hadn't used it since Saturday. Since he had time on his hands he took it out to check his mail and, sure enough, he had four messages waiting for him. The first two were about scanners, the third was a price from a furniture dealer in Islington and – he couldn't believe his eyes – the fourth was from Gannisch. It'd been sent at 18.09 local time on Sunday October 25th and it was in her usual fire hydrant style.

"*Liebchen,*" it began, "this is STRICTLY between ourselves but I must tell you we – Wltr, Rth, Dnla, Rbt, H-Mrie + yrs ALWAYS – are in Brussels. Yes, Brussels!!! We're in W's pple carrier and are COMING TO ENGLAND ON THE FERRY to see Oxford specialist for H-Mrie. We land tomorrow (Monday). Route: Calais, Dover, North Sea Tunnel, London Orbital (overnight in hotel somewhere) → Oxfd for Tues + afternoon appt. Then hopefully big get-together with you + Ulrich IF WE CAN FIND YOU!! XXXX from me!! PS: Tstn Mallik's in charge. PPS and V. IMPORTANT: W's kept this from Ulrich and so MUST YOU!! Whole bakery sworn to secrecy. Only lies permitted!!! More XXXX. Mmmmm!!"

Guderius felt his innards pull very tight. Monday – that was today, the day of New Hope. But why hadn't she said what time they'd reach Dover? He had to know that! Then he realised there was no reason why she should. She wasn't expecting him to meet them.

"Calm down, Klaus! Calm down and think!"

Back in Calais he'd found a weakness in himself – terror – and he'd coped with it. He'd coped with something similar when he'd dealt with the Carrick woman. Now he'd found a different weakness – his devotion to Gannisch. Well, he'd cope with that too if he did the right thing. But what was the right thing?

It occurred to him he'd seen a glossy new ferry timetable in the "Welcome" folder he'd found in his room. He hadn't cared then whether it was new or old because he wasn't going to use it but now it dawned on him: it was new because the summer was over and the autumn schedules had started. That meant all the times would be up to date, including this Monday's. He grabbed the folder and found the timetable tucked into a pocket at the back. But more than one sailing was listed for October 26th. So, which one was it?

"Wait a minute. I can work it out."

He glanced back to Gannisch's message and, yes, they'd be overnighting somewhere off the London Orbital. Now, Walter wouldn't want to get there late because of the children and Helga-Marie, and the sailings per day were well spaced out because the holiday season was over. So, starting with how long it'd taken him to get from Brussels to Calais in his Mercedes he then checked the sailing and landing times – remembering they were all in British time – and added on roughly how long they'd need to get from Dover to the London Orbital. That was scarcely Einstein-level maths and he saw straight away what he'd feared – they'd be in the North Sea Tunnel during late afternoon. If they weren't held up they could be through it before New Hope started. But if they were – and he had to assume they would be because there were always hold-ups – they'd be drowned.

It was more than he could bear. Walter and the rest, they could die, they were nothing to him, but Hanna – she was his life. Panic bubbled up inside him and once more he ordered himself to calm down and think. Then he had it. He'd call Hanna on her mobile and slow them down some way. Or – that was it! – he'd re-route them so they wouldn't use the tunnel at all. He soon worked out a cover story and his trembling index finger was poised to tap in the first digit when he realised calling Hanna was something he absolutely mustn't do. She never ever asked questions but if the North Sea Tunnel was flooded at 18.00 and she and the rest weren't in it because he'd re-routed them following a text message from her she'd make the connection all right – especially after Steffen's announcement on the internet. She wouldn't tell the police, that was certain, but she could be chatty and she might let something slip to Ruth or Walter and they'd definitely tell the police, they'd think they had to. But if he, Guderius, were banged up he'd be separated from Gannish for the rest of his life and that, too, was more than he could bear. So, with tears prickling his eyes and his forehead sweaty, he forced himself to switch off his mobile and put it away.

There was only one thing for it, he'd have to ignore what Gannisch had said about not telling Steffen. He'd explain everything to him and ask him to put New Hope back a bit. If he didn't want to change the day he could put the time back by a couple of hours, there'd still be plenty of people in the tunnel. And since Steffen knew what the people carrier looked like he could, as a safeguard, tell Zimmermann to watch out for it. Problem solved!

Back into optimism Guderius wanted to call Steffen then and there but using his mobile wasn't such a good idea in the circumstances. He'd just have to wait till they met up on the car park and speak to him there. With that settled he wiped his forehead, took a deep breath and forced himself to relax. He didn't want to look nervous when Danzig arrived, she might smell a rat. She'd spent a large part of her life getting secrets out of people and the interfering bitch might get this one out of him. And, he decided, he absolutely mustn't look nervous when he spoke to Steffen. If Steffen thought he was speaking out of cowardice he wouldn't even listen to him.

The more Guderius thought about it the more he became convinced Steffen would be positively grateful to him because if he did what Guderius wanted he'd be allowing Helga-Marie to live. And Walter and Ruth and his grandchildren. The last two would get to him even if the others didn't, he was half-witted about them. Guderius was so good at persuading himself that when Reception rang up to say his lift had arrived he knew everything would go his way – so he didn't think to hide his mobile in his clothes in case it didn't. In the lobby he turned his bonhomie on full and kissed Danzig on both cheeks. Unimpressed, she led him out to the Vauxhall. He must have overslept, she thought contemptuously. His eyes were still red.

Kent Police soon found tailing the three illegals was child's play. They drove steadily, they respected all speed limits and although cloud was forming, the light was close to perfect.

"They're not trying to hide, that's for sure," van Piet said. "They really must feel they've got it right."

Patel kept quiet. More than ever she felt the whole thing was far too obvious. It had to be a trick.

A tea urn and some cups had just been trolleyed in when two messages – one from a trail car and one from the air – overlapped to say the Fiat was signalling to turn off at the Fare 'n' Square. At the same time the driver of an MG convertible two cars ahead braked hard, signalled late and just about made it onto the Fare 'n' Square slip road. He wove through the north side car park, braked hard again by the entrance and killed the engine. Leaving the top down he and his passenger – both in county-style tweed coats – strode through the automatic doors without a glance behind them and while Kapner was parking in an outlying bay they were already in the Fare 'n' Square's Emergency Room. If an emergency was classed as Schedule A the police could demand to be left in there on their own and this, the duty manager was speedily informed, was a Schedule A. So would he leave right now, please?

It was stuffy in the Emergency Room so one of the first things PC Bob Frith and WPC Ruby Weller did was slip their tweed coats off. They could see the Fiat on monitors and they also saw an aging Citroën pull up a few bays in front of it. Despite its age it had a perfectly good rear view mirror so the driver, who had a hands-free, was able to watch Steffen get out, zip up his windproof jacket and stand by the passenger door with a large-format book of road maps in his hand. Like the Citroën driver Weller was delivering a commentary to Maidstone. If Steffen suspected anything he wasn't showing it, she said.

"Keep your eyes peeled," she heard from Patel. "By the way, your next clothes and transport are on their way. You'll be on two wheels this time."

Patel was looking at an image of the car park that was coming from the helicopter.

"If Steffen looks at those maps any more," she said to van Piet, "the print will come off. If you ask me they're an excuse for standing next to the car. I think he wants to be seen. Probably by the folk just arriving."

It was the Zimmermanns, and Weller and Frith both saw Frank Zimmermann point at Steffen before his father could push his arm down.

"Kurt Zimmermann's driving," Weller radioed in. "They're both wearing dark clothes and Kurt Zimmermann's wearing a scarf."

A dark grey muffler was filling the top of his coat.

"Confirmed," came in from the Citroën.

The Land Rover parked behind the Fiat but neither of the Zimmermanns got out. Kapner opened her door and unhurriedly joined Steffen, apparently to take a look at his maps.

"Kapner's also wearing dark clothes," Weller reported.

"It looks as if whatever's going to happen will happen after nightfall," murmured van Piet. Then, "They've got more than one vehicle so they might split up."

"I'll make sure they can all be followed."

"Warn your people they could be armed. If Steffen and Kapner have got out today without being seen they might have done it before."

Danzig, meanwhile, was entering the car park. While she was parking next to the Fiat a genuine Traffic Police helicopter clattered westwards against a thickening sky. Steffen, who was putting his maps away, didn't give it a glance. If there'd been no helicopters about he'd have asked himself why not. But since there were he saw no reason to worry.

33

"You were trained to heal but I was trained to kill."

As soon as Danzig stopped she, Guderius and the Zimmermanns all got out at once and clustered round the Fiat's boot with Steffen and Kapner. Kapner handed round coffee from the large flask. They looked like a party of friends putting in a travel break. Steffen said their weapons had arrived in perfect condition. Kurt would get his right now and the others would get theirs on Sheppey. When they'd finished their coffee Kapner collected the refuse in one of her usual carrier bags, put it into the Fiat's boot and fetched out the bottle green holdall.

"Everything's in here," she said, handing it to Kurt Zimmermann. "Did you bring any binoculars?"

"Just a small pair, the sort bird watchers use. I thought anything bigger might cause problems."

"Don't worry, you'll find a better pair in the holdall. They're a bit bulky but if I can use them so can you."

She'd told Steffen about them while they were driving through London. She'd also got him to revise Zimmermann's battle orders, as he called them.

"Listen carefully, Kurt," he now said. Zimmermann stopped rootling in the holdall to listen. "There's supposed to be mist about this evening and it could make the guards late so your new battle orders are: watch the toll booths continuously from 18.00 to 18.10. If the mauve lights flash, radio 'Mars is red' straight away but if they haven't come on by 18.10, keep watching anyway in case I decide to hang on. I'll let you know when to stop."

"Understood. I'll use Heidi's glasses. She says they're better than mine."

Before Steffen could step away he beckoned his son over, his face a picture of fatherly pride.

"I must tell you this, Ulrich," he said. "A little while ago Frank snapped up a dozen HGVs from a firm that'd gone bankrupt. He's had them reliveried and they're in Cheriton Broadspace right now waiting to be deployed. Frank sent them there last night."

Steffen took Frank's hand and shook it warmly. Anyone who helped Kurt Zimmermann got the best out of Steffen and anyway, he needed Frank for his shooting skills so he was happy to be nice to him. Then he looked at his watch.

"If we go now," he said to them all, "we can take our time getting there. So let's get started."

They all moved at once and Weller radioed in the running commentary. Itching to get away, Danzig half-opened the passenger door for Guderius but instead of climbing in he moved along the Fiat and knocked on Steffen's window.

"I have to talk to you," he said as it went down. "Please."

He was doing his best to look composed. Steffen could see he wasn't but he didn't even think of not listening to his old friend. He told Kapner to turn the engine off and sit with Kurt Zimmermann, then he got into the back of the Fiat and Guderius got in next to him. Danzig and Kurt Zimmermann turned their engines off and settled down to wait.

Guderius told Steffen about Gannisch's text message and how she and Steffen's family were lined up to be drowned unless he delayed New Hope. He'd do that, wouldn't he? Two hours would be enough.

Steffen stared in front of him as if he were looking into a special reality only he could see.

"It's too late to get new instructions to Carey," he said finally. "At the moment he's primed for 18.00. He'll be told if the mist delays the guards so he won't lose his nerve over that. But if we put things back even by two hours without getting word to him first I'm certain he'll crack up and give us all away. So I have to refuse your request, Klaus. You didn't get back to Hanna I hope."

Guderius said no, he wouldn't do anything like that without permission.

"Well done. We'll continue as planned then."

Guderius was devastated.

"No, Ulrich, no," he pleaded. "Helga-Marie will drown, so will your son and Ruth and so will your grandchildren. But it doesn't have to be. You have the power to prevent it and I beg you, as one friend to another, to use that power. If you can't get word to Carey right now why not wait a day or two? He won't crack up, he's too fixated on Heidi, and he won't talk either, he's got too much to lose if he does and he knows it. What's more, Helga-Marie will get the treatment she needs. Think of it, Ulrich! You won't just have her alive, you'll have her cured as well."

Guderius should never have used the word "power", it gave Steffen a feeling of greatness.

"Like you and like me, Klaus, Helga-Marie was in the army. She understands patriotism and she understands duty. She won't know why she's dying and she doesn't have to. To die for your country is enough."

"And Daniela and Robert, what about them? They weren't in the army, they're only children. You can't play with them one day and drown them the next. You love them too much."

"War and death go together. You were trained to heal but I was trained to kill. When you arrived in this country last week you were prepared to kill many hundreds - including children - because New Hope required it. It still requires it and although I love my grandchildren more than I can say I can make no exceptions. Surely you can see that. We share the same ideals."

Guderius could see Steffen wouldn't budge. If he'd brought his mobile with him he'd have found a way of sneaking a warning to Gannisch but he hadn't. He knew there were phones in the Fare 'n' Square because he'd seen them but he also knew Steffen would come in with him if he made an excuse to go in there and stop him getting to them. His only option was to reassure Steffen and bide his time. Gannisch was his only priority now and somehow he'd save her.

"I can see it and I apologise," he said, grovelling as if he meant it. "I showed weakness and I shouldn't have. But I'm still with you, Ulrich. I'm with you all the way."

Steffen gripped his friend's hand.

"Good old Klaus," he said and emotion made his voice thick. "We'll see this through together. Nothing can deflect us from our purpose."

When they got out of the Fiat they seemed like sunshine after rain. Steffen gestured to Kapner to get back into the driving seat and Guderius, with a fixed smile on his face, joined Danzig and Frank Zimmermann in the Vauxhall. They drove off as ordered, leaving the Citroën behind: Kapner first, then Danzig and finally Kurt Zimmermann. At the same time Patel's tail cars started their patterns and air surveillance added to the chatter.

As Kapner approached the Sheppey Link Road she carefully signalled ahead of time, lost speed and led the way into the turn-off. As far as Patel was concerned it was too deliberate by half. She'd been told about the Zimmermanns' HGVs and to her cops-and-robbers mind they were where the real action was. But she wasn't in charge, van Piet was. Maybe if she played for time something would happen to make him think again.

"We'll lose control if we're not careful," she said, sounding as objective as she could. "I'm going to slow them down."

Van Piet shrugged his shoulders.

"Go ahead," he said. "It's not nightfall yet."

Speaking quickly into a phone she ordered the slow and middle lanes to be blocked between Steffen's cars and the turn-off to the tunnel.

"Make it a swerve and a breakdown, make it immediate and drop the speed limit to 10 mph."

"I've got an unmarked car right there," she heard back, "and a marked motor bike. I'll use them."

"You'll need more than the bike. Send some marked cars up the hard shoulder and put in a performance – blue lights, sirens, the works. And tell the media it's a breakdown only. No fatalities, no ambulances to chase but long delays expected. Ask them to break into programmes to get the word out."

Next she briefed her tail cars and air support. Finally she ordered warnings to be lit up all along the M2/A2 and variable speeds to be posted.

Kapner's turn-off, coming on top of what van Piet knew about Carey and the shooting practice at Jan Schwarzer's, pretty much convinced van Piet Steffen was targeting the flooding mechanism. He still didn't know why but he'd come round to thinking that didn't matter too much because he suspected Steffen was being used without his knowledge by someone as murderous as Steffen himself. That someone also had to be caught and the only way to do it that van Piet could see was through Steffen. That made Patel a problem. He hadn't forgotten how she'd flagged up the Channel Tunnel terminal. Did she know the control centre had a deadly secret? If she didn't, that could make the terminal very attractive indeed. He had to find that out.

"If Sheppey is where they're going," he said casually, "we need to think ahead. We can leave the flyover till the last minute and the same goes for the docks. But the North Sea Tunnel's control centre is another story. Anyone getting in there could cause chaos in seconds. Do you know who's in charge of it?"

"The Home Office. But the MoD keeps part of it under armed guard."

"Armed guard? Why that?"

"I don't know, it's classified. My Chief doesn't know either, that's how tight it is."

"Does anyone who works there know? Someone must, surely."

"The Senior Security Officer does. His name's Lesley Carey. The Senior Site Manager does as well. He showed me round when I made my last official visit. His name's Gough Sallis and he's new. When I asked him he said what his predecessor used to say: he knew but he mustn't tell."

"What about the MoD?"

"Not a word."

So she didn't know. And what she didn't know she wouldn't worry about, she'd leave that to those who did. Then she took him by surprise.

"You could find out though, you're senior enough. You could do it right now."

"I could but I'd have to say why and you can guess what'd happen: the place would be knee-deep in soldiers. Steffen's no fool. If he saw that – assuming the control centre's where he's heading – he'd abort."

"What about warning Sallis on the quiet?"

"He's new. You said so yourself"

"So it's carry on watching, is it?"

She wanted to signal she thought he was wrong but instead he saw a chance to bind her in.

"I don't think so. Frank Zimmermann was in Danzig's Vauxhall when they left the Fare 'n' Square. That brought two snipers together and we both know how snipers work. They take up position and they wait. So, when Danzig and Zimmermann take up position they'll tell us a lot of what we need to know. They'll be in traffic for a while yet so now's our chance to get a jump on them. Call Joe over. And see if the weather forecast's still the same."

As Smail left his seat an officer with "Worrall" stitched onto his shirt pocket caught Patel's eye.

"The army's caught up with your breakdown, Chief. They're worried about the next change of shift at the tunnel control centre."

"We'll get them through, we'll use the hard shoulder. Tell them that."

While she was speaking the weather check flashed onto her screen.

"Still no change," she said, just this side of irritably. "Calm and dry with dense cloud forming. Mist down the East Coast, thick in Essex but patchy in Kent. In other words, early darkness, zero moonlight, mist here and there and no wind."

"Will the mist spoil your plans, Joe?" asked van Piet.

"No, Sir, it'll give them a helping hand. It's six armed individuals we seem to be up against so I've got six attack teams of four on standby with Sal in one of them. Visibility won't be a problem and they'll use acoustic optimisers. Like these."

He held out what looked like a pair of in-the-ear hearing aids.

"They pick up remote sounds in quiet surroundings. Like if you're on a park bench and you want to listen in on people three or four benches away. They've got a cut-out for loud bangs I'm pleased to say otherwise I'd be deaf by now."

He put them back in his pocket.

"Transport is helicopters – six for the attack teams plus a command bird for Mrs Patel and yourself."

"Will you be coming with us?"

"If I have to, I'll join you later. I'm more use in front of a screen."

Worrall had moved up behind Smail.

"Two items, Chief," he said to Patel. "First, the army's moving now. Second, the M2/A2 is jamming in both directions."

"Clear the Link Road and have the limit set at 20. Better still, make it 20 all the way to the tunnel. If I don't do that," she explained to van Piet, "we'll get even more crowding at the tunnel than we'll get as it is."

"What about the M2/A2?" Worrall asked.

"Keep the warnings lit up and the speed limits on variable till the Link Road eases. Then review."

"Speaking of the tunnel," van Piet said, "we need someone on the ground close to it."

"Won't a helicopter do?"

"Not if the villains make mischief in the tunnel."

"There's a maintenance area near the northbound entrance," Smail put in. "Why not use that?"

"I'll send Bob and Ruby in," Patel replied. "They're behind Kurt Zimmermann right now."

"What's the surveillance like in there?" van Piet asked her neutrally.

"There isn't any. Our cameras look out from its edge onto the traffic and they can't be turned round. Tunnel security's got its own cctv and the pictures are normally radioed back to Sheppey. But a bulldozer's damaged the mast and it's not repaired yet. So it's a blind spot."

Van Piet was pleased but he didn't show it. He didn't want Carey seeing something was up.

"We can live with that," he said. "What's in there anyway?"

"Cones, signs, the usual stuff. Plus tools and plant and up to half a dozen workers at any given time. Bob and Ruby can keep them down one end if they have to."

"Get Bob and Ruby in now, then give Eddie Snape a call. Do it on your mobile and make it person-to-person. Give him a quick rundown, tell him his side of the tunnel might be involved and say I'm in charge in Essex as well as Kent. He's not to say or do anything without contacting me first. That's an order, not a request, tell him. And do it fast."

He glanced round the room. No one was listening in, of course, but everyone was hearing. He lowered his voice.

"Call him from your office, it's more tactful. As soon as you're done I'll update Mr Trilling and we go."

He looked at the traffic while he was waiting. The Link Road was starting to move and all the vehicles had their lights on. It was getting dark early. He was wondering when the mist would re-form when Patel came back in and said Snape wanted to speak to him. He went into her office, shut the door and picked up her mobile. When he came out he looked grim. He signalled for Smail to move closer and he didn't waste words.

"I have to tell you," he said tersely, "an anonymous letter writer's been threatening my daughter. Eddie Snape called me this morning. There'd been another letter and this time it threatened her life. Eddie thought he could handle it but now he's saying he can't: the mist and the dark are too much of a problem. My place is at home protecting my daughter, I've got no alternative. Consequently I'm withdrawing from this operation as of now and Mrs Patel is in charge. I'll inform Mr Trilling and then go."

There was no discussion, just a silence from both of them and Worrall took his chance. The Fiat and the Vauxhall were heading for the flyover but the Land Rover was on the turn-off to the tunnel. Patel and Smail confirmed that on-screen while van Piet called Trilling from Patel's office.

"I'm deeply sorry you're taking this step," said Trilling, "but I can see why you're doing it. Now, callous as it may seem, since you're handing on I must have a word with Mrs Patel. We can't let up now."

While Trilling was talking to Patel, van Piet, back in the operations room, called Geert.

"We're leaving right now," he said in Dutch. "Get clearance from Flight Control. I'll meet you at the rear exit. There's a ready-packed suitcase in my room. Bring it with you. You've got the room key I gave you, have you?"

He had.

"Bring it as well, it's forged. Buzz me when you're out the back."

Worrall and Smail were screen-watching and, as if he couldn't let go, van Piet stopped long enough to look and listen. The traffic was still very slow.

"The Land Rover's completed the turn-off," Worrall was saying. "It's heading for the tunnel, I expect."

He zoomed in on it then, as Patel joined them, he went back three vehicles to a marked police car.

"That's one of the ones that came up the hard shoulder when we staged the breakdown. It's doing Bob and Ruby's job."

He pointed to another screen.

"The Fiat and the Vauxhall are on the island. They're between the flyover and the road leading to the control centre."

His eyes went back to the Land Rover.

"Hullo," he said. "This one's signalling. He's going up Spade Hill."

"Tell the marked car not to follow," Patel broke in. "Put a helicopter on instead."

Van Piet watched as Kurt Zimmermann followed his headlights up a spur road to the vista point. The marked car continued on towards the tunnel as if it'd always been going that way.

Van Piet's mobile buzzed. He spoke into it fast in Dutch and turned to Patel.

"Good luck," he said. "Just keep after them and they'll do your job for you."

Then he was gone.

Spade Hill wasn't a natural hill, it was heaped up spoil from the tunnel and the vista point wasn't the dead end it appeared to be because a narrow roadway the earth movers had once used ran down to the maintenance area Frith and Weller had been sent to. The roadway hadn't been used much since the hill was finished and it showed. A weather-beaten sign at the top said "No Entry. Works Traffic Only" but no one'd seen the need for a gate because there was one at the bottom end.

When Zimmermann got to the top he had the place to himself. He unbuckled, put his muffler in his pocket and struggled out of his coat to make himself more comfortable. Under his coat he was wearing the black trousers and tunic he'd worn on night manoeuvres in the NPA. He'd had to let the waist out and move some of the buttons but it'd been worth it. When he switched on the interior light to go through the holdall he saw the collar in his mirror and, with a surge of pride, he saluted it.

The Ceska came out first. He loaded it, put the safety catch on, strapped on his shoulder holster and put it in. Then came Kapner's binoculars. They were bulky all right but if they did the job, he'd put up with that. He put his birdwatcher's binoculars in the holdall. He didn't want them overlooked later. He had more time than he thought he'd have, given all the traffic. What should he do next, he wondered. He could open the coffee or he could make a reconnaissance. He opted to make a reconnaissance – he liked the idea, it went with his uniform. He'd try out Kapner's binoculars while he was at it.

The air was damp and mist was definitely forming when he opened his door. He put his coat back on, propped himself against the railing and began a detailed sweep of the tunnel's entrances and exits. The northbound tailback was vast. There was too much traffic anyway and, thanks to the thick mist in Essex, both tubes were emptying at a crawl. In contrast, southbound traffic was moving normally.

In Maidstone Patel was calling for everyone's attention.

"There's been a change of plan," she said, entirely glad to see the back of van Piet. "All the signs are, we're watching a very clever distraction. In my view the real action will be at 18.32 in the Channel Tunnel terminal. The Zimmermanns' lorries have been massing in Cheriton Broadspace and a raid on the euro-transporter looks set to be launched from there. So, the new plan is, when the attack teams take off they head for the terminal and intercept in strength. Joe – " she gave him a folder full of printouts she'd been keeping hidden in her office – "these are your new deployments. Jim – " she gave a similar folder to Worrall – "you'll be in control here, I still want tabs kept on Steffen and his friends. Do the best you can. I'll be in the command helicopter holding everything together."

She was out of Shadowland at last. She'd kept her Plan B from Trilling in case he tried to stop her but neither he nor anyone else could stop her now. When Worrall slipped in that the helicopter assigned to Spade Hill was having to pull out because of failing hydraulics she simply took it in her stride. She was into real policing again and a single leaky helicopter wasn't going to spoil it for her.

34

A rustling in the murk

"That's a relief," said Kapner as she drew to a halt in the picnic area car park. "I thought we were going to be late but look, we've got plenty of time and then some."

Steffen smiled complacently as if he was never late for anything.

A pair of headlights, haloed by the mist, turned into the car park and swung round in a U-turn. It was Danzig's Vauxhall. She backed up parallel to the Fiat, leaving plenty of space between, and like Kapner she parked facing the exit. Steffen got out first and closed his door quietly. The whole place was eerie in the early dark and that made him ultra cautious. Kapner, Danzig and Frank Zimmermann got out next. When Guderius heaved himself out Danzig gave him the Vauxhall's keys.

"Don't lose them," she rasped. "They're the only ones I've got."

"Brigitte," Kapner said to her, "I'll put some solvent and a towel in your boot for when you and Frank get back."

She was rummaging in the boot of the Fiat as she spoke and Frank Zimmermann happened to be near.

"Be a dear," she said. "Put these in the back of the Vauxhall for me."

He opened the boot and the light sprang on. He moved a warning triangle and a coiled tow rope to one side and placed the solvent and towel right in the middle where people in a hurry couldn't miss them. He squeezed the lid down softly and waited. He too felt the place had a menace to it.

Although time was on their side Steffen was impatient to get moving. Kapner blacked his face for him while Danzig and Zimmermann were blacking each other's. They could just about see what they were doing. Then Steffen, Danzig and

Zimmermann pulled on their balaclavas and made sure they had their gloves in their pockets. Steffen asked them whether they'd brought any torches because he absolutely didn't want that. No one said they had and Kapner was glad she hadn't packed one. No one said they had a mobile either. When Steffen handed the guns out he offered to carry Danzig's Dragunov for her but she said it was all right. He knew Zimmermann would say no for the sake of making a point so he didn't bother to ask him. He was looking edgy anyway. The mist was dulling their voices and the only other noise, also dulled down, came from helicopters. They were coming closer to them than when Steffen, Kapner and Guderius had last been on Sheppey and Steffen, who was checking his walkie-talkie battery, said it was because visibility was down: they were creating more room for each other.

"You're sure you don't want me and Heidi to black up as well?" Guderius asked Steffen.

"I've already told Heidi, there's no need. Just stay in the cars and don't show any lights."

"Do you want to take some coffee with you?" Kapner asked him. "I've got a small flask for you right here."

"No thanks. I'll take my binoculars though. Check your Beretta while we're gone and you, Klaus, you check your Ceska. Brigitte, Frank and me can wait till we're in position."

He said, "Gloves on" to Danzig and Zimmermann, pulled his own on and led them out of the car park. Zimmermann's gloves came from the lorry trade. They had non-slip fingers and palms.

Along the footpath the mist was as patchy as the forecast had said. Sometimes it was hardly there and sometimes it was so thick, water droplets collected on their eyebrows and eye lashes. It was densest towards the higher ground so when the control centre came into view they had no trouble seeing it. The mist hanging over it was wraith-like and its lights shone brightly through it.

Steffen stopped for a moment so they could take it in.

"This is what we've come for," he said, automatically not pointing. "If the mist stays this thin the guards are dead already. And don't forget, Brigitte, when Carey leaves the blockhouse, you shoot first and Frank, you follow up even if you think Brigitte's killed him. I want two bullets through his head, one after the other. We have to be sure no one can ask him any questions."

"There's still time for the mist to get worse," Danzig speculated.

"I don't think so, not down there. It could get thicker higher up though and if it rolls downhill you'll just have to move with it to get your shots in. You'll still be out of sight from down below."

They moved on and as they approached the clump of trees behind the control centre they were in so much murk they could only just see where they were putting their feet. Steffen was glad the footpath was well trodden. He didn't want anyone tripping on the way back.

"Frank, this is your firing point," he told Zimmermann when they reached his recess. "It's through these bushes. Keep the safety catch on your Ceska, we don't want you shooting one of us by mistake. And when you set your Dragunov up use one of the guard boxes to get your range. The guard who checks the flooding mechanism is your target and the other one is Brigitte's. Fire on your own responsibility and aim for the head. And can you remember which lights to shoot out?"

Zimmermann nodded but didn't say anything. It riled him intensely that Steffen kept repeating things. It made him feel like a schoolboy.

"That's good," Steffen went on, unaware of the effect he was having, "because Carey may hardly pause at all when he runs out of the blockhouse. Brigitte, you'll be further up the footpath from here and I'll be watching from the far end of these trees. As soon as he drops we go back together."

"What about my father?" Zimmermann asked and his voice caught as he spoke. "Do you think he's all right? He might've missed his turning or something."

"Why don't I call him and ask him?" Steffen replied, taking his walkie-talkie out.

Danzig looked as contemptuous as her blacking would allow but Steffen took no notice. He guessed Zimmermann was asking after his father because he wanted reassurance. Using code names Steffen asked Kurt Zimmermann how the signal was and held the walkie-talkie so they could all hear him.

"Raven answering Condor and the signal is good," he replied.

In his rock steady way he reported there was mist about but he could see everything he needed to and the tunnel was full in both directions. Steffen told him Goshawk was in place and he was about to move on with Osprey. Did Raven want to speak to Goshawk?

"Duty before pleasure, Condor," the ex-NPA man said. "I need to check something first. But, with permission, I'll call him when I've done that."

Permission was granted and Steffen moved off with Danzig.

"You pamper that boy," she hissed once she reckoned Zimmermann was out of earshot. "He's as weak as maid's water. Why couldn't you have brought someone else?"

"Next to you, he's the best sniper we've got. I know he's not strong but his father's strong for him. Not everyone's like you."

"I'd have opened him up in seconds if I'd ever had him in front of me. He's like a parcel without string."

She was more like an electric charge than a human being. Her chopped sloe-white hair was hidden by her balaclava so the only thing not black about her was the whites of her eyes. Frank Zimmermann would've been zero opposition for her, Steffen knew that, but he couldn't help wondering whether she could have broken *him* and his answer was no. He'd been totally loyal to the GDR, he was willing to drown his own family and he'd actually drowned the Peeping Tom. However tough Danzig was, he was definitely tougher.

When they reached the recess he'd picked out for her he stayed while she got her guns ready. As she calibrated the Dragunov's scope she said the view down the hillside was perfect, she could kill anyone at will. The smell of wet wood was everywhere. Once or twice she thought she heard a rustling behind her. The first time it happened she put her finger to her lips and gestured to Steffen to keep still. But although they waited a good long while there was no follow-up.

"Probably an animal," she said. "Or moisture dripping."

Steffen trusted what she said. Her hearing was better than his.

Once she was satisfied everything was all right he moved on to his own position. He could feel the footpath rising and when he reached the far end of the trees he was a good bit higher than the other two. He couldn't see them from where he stood, the murk was too dense for that, but he knew where he'd put them. As he gazed down at the control centre he felt he was looking at a chess board and all the pieces, the black as well as the white, were his. He had no idea how difficult Kurt Zimmermann had found it to sound rock steady when he'd been reporting from Spade Hill. He also had no idea that when – with permission – he'd called back to his son it hadn't been to give him a morale-booster. And not in a thousand years would he have believed Guderius had given Kapner the slip and was heading his way with the Ceska, now loaded, that he'd given him in the car park. Instead he focused on the inner compound and, with an intoxicating sense of triumph, told himself he was almost at journey's end.

35

Walter enters the tunnel

Walter's ferry had left Calais late and by the time it reached Dover the afternoon was up and running. He didn't say much but Ruth knew what he was thinking.

"We can still get through the tunnel before the rush hour," she said as she put her watch back an hour.

Walter did the same with his.

"I hope so," he replied. "I checked twice on the boat. The mist in Essex could hold us up badly."

But he didn't stay glum for long, it wasn't in his nature, and when he put the dashboard clock back it improved his humour some more. It was like living an extra hour for free.

Outside the ferry terminal he pulled over and asked Ruth to take the wheel.

"And what will you do if I say yes?"

She was niggly. The journey was catching up with her.

"Division of labour. I'll work the sat nav."

As she ground up the cliff road towards the M2/A2 she was eager to find something to complain about so she said,

"I'd take it as a kindness if you'd restore my name to the windscreen. The bottom corner's come off again."

He flattened her name against the glass then, by way of a peace offering, he reached across and smoothed out a wrinkle in his own.

Ruth's hopes of clearing the tunnel before the rush hour evaporated when the alerts lit up and the variable speed limits came on. Walter tackled the sat nav in earnest. He'd rather go a long way round and keep moving than come to a halt and just sit there. They took the first exit they came to and were soon in the maze of country lanes between the M2/A2 and the Thames Estuary. There wasn't much traffic at first but, even so, Ruth couldn't go fast because the roads were so twisty. Then other drivers got the same idea and they slowed her down even more. After endless detours in vanishing light and an eternity behind a tractor Ruth eventually found herself in a winding high-hedged lane that was so narrow, she didn't think she could get the people carrier through. But then – it was like driving through a magic curtain – she was on a road bridge and beneath her was the approach road to the tunnel. Walter had told her it was coming but she'd been concentrating so hard on the car in front she hadn't heard him. He put the sat nav back in its holder and mouthed a silent thank you.

"This bridge is called Friars Bridge," he said and translated the name into German but they were all too tired to be interested. "When we get to the other side we can either turn off and look for somewhere to stay or we can go through the tunnel as planned. Thoughts, Ruth?"

Ruth wasn't a quitter by nature but a lot of stress had caught up with her. While she was weighing the odds she risked a glance past Walter and over the parapet. The toll booths seemed a long way off and the traffic looked solid but when she risked a second glance she glimpsed a car and a lorry move. It wasn't much but it tipped the balance.

"We go through the tunnel."

"What about the children?"

She hunted for them in the mirror.

"They'll nod off soon. They'll be all right. Helga-Marie's asleep already and Hanna's letting her eyes close."

Stopping and starting she rounded the bend at the end of Friars Bridge, ground down to the approach road and filtered into the mega-jam.

"At least I can see what I'm doing now," she thought as she cleared moisture off the windscreen. "I don't want to drive down lanes like those ever again."

She wasn't the only one who could see what she was doing. Just as she'd been able to see to the toll booths, Kurt Zimmermann was able to see to Friars Bridge and after he'd made his reconnaissance he decided to see what Kapner's binoculars could really do. Walter's people carrier caught his eye. He didn't recognise it for what it was, he just thought,

"It's the same colour as Walter's" and zeroed in on it. He saw it was left-hand drive and – he couldn't believe it – it had "Walter" and "Ruth" on the windscreen. Then the car in front edged forward and, thanks to the high magnification and the anti-tremble, he could read the number plate. He didn't know Walter's number but German plates indicate where the vehicle is registered. That was enough and now he knew what he was looking at he recognised Ruth at the wheel and Walter sitting next to her.

"What are they doing in England?" he wondered and then a terrifying idea struck him. What if they were in the tunnel when the pumps started? At first he thought the tailback might keep them safe but then he remembered Steffen had changed his battle orders. 18.00 hours had been extended to 18.10 and even that wasn't final. "Keep watching anyway in case I decide to hang on," he'd said. "I'll let you know when to stop." It was open-ended. The tailback was no protection.

As Zimmermann continued to look, the passenger window came down and he saw Walter crane his head out. Then Gannisch looked out from the window behind him. So they had Hanna with them. And the roof box had a new-looking Mickey Mouse stuck on it. That must be for the grandchildren. And poor dear Helga-Marie? They wouldn't have come without her, surely.

The old soldier's emotions were all over the place. Did Ulrich know his whole family could be in the tunnel when the pumps came on? And did Klaus know Hanna could be in there with them? They couldn't know, he told himself, it wasn't possible, it must be a misunderstanding. He was on the point of contacting Steffen to warn him when his walkie-talkie buzzed and, to his amazement, it was Steffen himself – Condor now – asking him how the signal was. There was something about that self-possessed and metallic-sounding voice that prevented Zimmermann from blurting out what he wanted to say most. Like Guderius he knew his friend had willpower like no one else so what was the best way to get through to him? As he groped for words that wouldn't come he stalled by talking about the mist and the traffic. He was frantically wondering what else to say when Steffen told him Goshawk was in place and he was about to move on with Osprey.

Goshawk, not Frank. And Osprey, not Brigitte. Yet Frank was more than Zimmermann's son, he was his whole family. As soon as he heard Frank referred to as if he were a cipher all the turmoil Walter and the rest had stirred up cleared like sand settling in water and he saw New Hope with new eyes. Steffen had made it seem like soldiering but it wasn't soldiering at all, it was murder. Ulrich's family, Hanna and all the other people down there – they were real people with real lives and they had an absolute right to live them. Why had he been so deluded? And why had his ideals brought him so low? He'd travestied his integrity as a soldier and, as that sank in, he felt the kind of shame only a man of honour can feel. He felt ashamed for Frank as well. He'd made him an accomplice in something so degraded he could scarcely look it in the face.

But look it in the face he had to and to begin with he had to get Frank out of this mess before Frank shot anyone and made things even worse for himself. When he'd said he needed to check something before he spoke to his son what he was really after was the chance to speak to him without Steffen hearing because he wanted Frank to gather up everything and escape while he could. When he'd got that message through he'd run down the disused roadway, keep running through the maintenance area and get between the toll booths and the tunnel. He knew the way from the Sky Rides photos. His Ceska was loaded - as ordered by Steffen, he thought ironically - and he reckoned if he fired into the air it'd bring the police out and he could tell them to alert the control centre before it was too late. It didn't matter that he'd be arrested. The important thing was to stop New Hope in its tracks. So he took his walkie-talkie into his hand and buzzed his son.

Frank Zimmermann jumped when he heard the buzz. The dark, the mist and isolated noises he kept hearing were getting on his nerves.

"Goshawk."

"Raven here," he just about heard.

Kurt Zimmermann was keeping his voice well down.

"Is Condor there?"

"He's gone off with Osprey. I can get him if you like. I've got the time."

He wondered why his father didn't contact Steffen directly. He soon found out.

"No, don't do that. Use your ear piece to listen to me. Put it in now."

"It's in."

"You say Condor's gone off with Osprey. That means there's no one with you and there's no one between you and the cars, right?"

"I suppose so. Does it matter?"

"You can't imagine how much. Listen, Frank, New Hope is a massive mistake. If you carry out Condor's orders you won't be a hero, you'll be a common murderer and you'll spend the rest of your life behind bars. I want you – no, I order you – to pack everything up right now, get back to the cars as fast as you can, take one and drive it straight back to our hotel. Use force if you have to but don't shoot anyone, these Ceskas aren't silenced. Say you'll do it and go."

He couldn't know sheer relief was coursing through Frank's veins. He'd liked the idea of New Hope at first, it'd made him feel as good as his father, but the closer it'd got, the more he'd hated the whole thing. And now his father of all people was telling him to bail out. He felt he should pretend he didn't want to desert but his father was in too much of a hurry.

"Quickly, Frank! Say it and go!"

It was the second time he'd ignored his son's code name, it didn't seem relevant now they were both getting out, but then he had second thoughts.

"If anyone contacts you from now on, including Condor, answer as Goshawk and make out you're still where you should be."

"I'll obey you, Dad – I mean Raven. I don't want to," he lied, "but you're my superior officer. I'm leaving now."

That was enough. Kurt Zimmermann terminated the call, threw Kapner's binoculars down to save weight and set off down the hill with the chopping gait of an old man who hadn't run for years.

The maintenance area was virtually empty when Kurt Zimmermann set off because Frith and Weller had been busy. Leather jackets and dirty jeans had replaced their tweeds, their motor bike had got them through the traffic and after he'd seen their IDs the foreman had called in the three workmen still on site and parked them in a hut at the opposite end from the toll booths. They hadn't complained, not even when they'd had to hand in their mobiles. Drinking tea was in their genes and they liked being part of a police raid. Then the foreman was told to stay in his office and if the control centre contacted him he was to pretend everything was normal. The Official Secrets Act came next and it worked its usual magic.

"Anyone coming back in the next little while?" Frith asked him.

"Not till change of shift. That's at ten."

"And the cctv in here's out of action."

"Not just in here. All our northbound cameras are shut down as far as the tunnel. The electrics are being serviced."

"Anything else?"

"At some point the lights will go out. It's to do with the servicing."

"How long for?"

"How long's a piece of string? The toll booths and the alerts have emergency generators so there's no need to stop the traffic."

The foreman's office was a hut opposite the one the workmen were in so he had no trouble seeing they stayed put. Once he was installed in there Frith and Weller went back to their bike, Frith carrying a set of codes and some duplicate keys. Their bike was next to a storage hut near the gate to Spade Hill and their helmets were on the step. They knew there'd been a change of plan but they hadn't been told what it was. They also knew Spade Hill had lost its helicopter. In short, they were on their own. They decided to make the most of it.

"If anything happens in the tunnel, we'll be told and we've got the bike," Frith said confidently, "so we can afford to hang around here. Something tells me Zimmermann will try this gate, he's only at the top of the hill, and if he does, I'm going to make things easy for him."

He unlocked it and opened it just a fraction.

"You hide one side, I'll hide the other," he said. "We've been warned he might be armed. If he comes through we bring him down first and talk to him second. We don't want to get shot."

The gate was as brightly lit as the rest of the maintenance area and the mist was negligible. Weller took cover behind a dumper truck and Frith disappeared behind a bulldozer with its scraper up. It was the one that'd banged into the radio mast. The traffic noise was loud but it was constant so when a new sound came through it they both heard it. It was footsteps clomping in the darkness beyond the gate and they were getting close. Frith raised his hand and Weller signalled back. The trap was set.

When Zimmermann reached the gate he saw it was too high for him to climb so in desperation he grabbed hold of it and pushed at it as hard as he could. But it was the sort with a supporting wheel under the corner furthest away from the hinges and this particular wheel had been allowed to rust. So while he wasn't brought to a halt he lost a lot of momentum. As he passed through he dug in to get it back but Frith dived for his legs and hauled him down. Almost before he hit the ground Weller was yanking his arm up till his hand was touching the back of his head. The sudden pain beat his soldier's discipline and he yelled out. He was wild-eyed and completely breathless. He was also determined to keep moving.

"No! No!" he shouted in English between gulped intakes of air. "Get out my way! I must to the tunnel!"

If he'd known Frith and Weller were police he'd have surrendered and told them all about New Hope but because they were dressed like bikers his only thought was to get past them. So, as Frith was about to shout, "Police!" in his ear he went completely limp and then squirmed so fast Frith and Weller lost hold of him. It was a trick he'd learned in his army days. On his feet again he scampered behind the hut Frith and Weller had left their bike near. It was one of several and by looking round the edge each time and sprinting across the gap he was able to work his way from one hut to the next towards the toll booths. Frith and Weller knew roughly where he was but that was all. They also believed they could stop a bullet at any time. That made them more cautious than Zimmerman and the gap between them widened.

"I'll see if I can speak to the Chief," whispered Weller as Frith peered round a van full of welding equipment. "We need some help here."

It didn't work.

"Look at this," she said and let Frith see the screen.

"'Electro-fortress on'," he read. "'No in- or outward calls without drawbridge prefix and PIN.' It's to stop thieves talking to each other," he added and shrugged his shoulders. "Too bad. We'll just have to manage without."

He took a final look then darted to the next hut. When he was across Weller joined him. It was the last of the huts and from it they could see where the maintenance area, the approach road to the tunnel and the toll booths converged. Zimmermann should've been out in the open but there was no sign of him. He'd disappeared.

Back towards Friars Bridge Ruth's patience was in the red zone again. The children wouldn't go to sleep and Helga-Marie, who'd woken up, was asking a little too often when they could get out. Gannisch was doing her best but, as long as they were stuck in traffic she didn't stand a chance.

Walter was tetchy as well but he didn't feel able to show it. It was his trip and he felt obliged to do something only he didn't know what. Or did he? When he'd craned his head out of the window he'd seen the toll booths in the distance but a lot nearer to him than to them he'd also seen the amber lights of a tunnel escort vehicle parked on the hard shoulder. He put his hand on Ruth's forearm.

"I'll drive," he said, perking up. "I've got an idea."

The traffic was stopped so she unbuckled and ran round the front while Walter struggled into the driving seat. As Ruth was clicking her seatbelt in, the traffic moved forward again and Walter moved with it.

"What's Daddy doing?" Daniela asked plaintively and Robert stopped grizzling to hear the answer.

"He's got an idea," Ruth answered with a big, reassuring smile, "and if you're good you'll find out what it is."

But they were too tired to be good. Robert lapsed back into grizzling and Daniela started to whine loudly. Then they started tormenting each other. Ruth was about to give them a blast when Walter told her to leave them be. He was alongside the escort vehicle and the traffic had stopped again. He lowered his window, reached out and tapped tentatively.

The driver looked at him phlegmatically and let his own window down. He was used to people tapping when he was on the hard shoulder. Sometimes they wanted change for the toll booth, sometimes they needed a lavatory and sometimes they were heading in the wrong direction and what could they do about it? He wasn't overworked and he helped when he could. It offset the waiting around.

"Having trouble?" he called across but because the people carrier was left hand drive he could hear for himself Walter was having trouble.

"We are come from France," Walter replied, raising his voice, "and we must go through the tunnel. Our children are very tired and we have with us an old lady who is not very well. Can you help us, please?"

The driver could half see Ruth as well. Her face was a mask of fatigue.

"It's possible. I'll find out."

He told Walter's story into his hands-free, listened to the answer and said he'd see to it. He turned back to Walter.

"There's an oversize load at the other end of the tunnel and I've said I'll help bring it through. The good news is, because the traffic is bad I have to go through the maintenance tube and because you've got someone sick with you I've got you permission to drive behind me. The bad news is, I can only take you about a third of the way because at that point the electrics are being serviced and you mustn't go through the repair zone. So, what do you say?"

"We should like it very much and thank you. What do you want us to do?"

"When I pull away, put your flashers on, come onto the hard shoulder and follow me. When we get to the electrics someone will get you into the northbound tube. It's not all the way but it's better than sitting here."

"Thank you again. How is the traffic when we leave the tunnel? We are going to the road round London."

The driver looked at his dashboard clock.

"Put Radio Essex on at six o'clock and listen for the traffic report." He gave Walter the frequency and he jotted it down on the dashboard pad. "You'll be well under the Thames but you'll still be able to hear it."

The traffic in front had moved again and someone behind beeped his horn. The escort driver pulled away and Walter tucked in behind him, screwing up his eyes as the full array of amber flashers came on. The children quietened down now they were moving steadily. Ruth unwound a bit as well.

"Clever Daddy," she said and blew him a kiss. "I thought we'd be there forever."

"We've got the rest of the tunnel to hack our way through but, as the man said, it's better than sitting here."

"You won't forget the traffic report, will you? We need to think about getting the children to bed. And Helga-Marie."

"I won't forget. You'd better tell everyone what's been going on. Say life restarts at six o'clock. If that doesn't cheer them up, nothing will."

36

Frank Zimmermann's demise

Guderius was like a wound-up spring as he watched Steffen, Danzig and Frank Zimmermann leave the car park. He knew once the snipers were in position Steffen would be on his own so all he had to do was get away from Kapner, sneak past Danzig and Zimmermann and put a bullet into his friend. Then he'd tell the others Steffen had been shot by accident and call the operation off. He'd have that authority because with Steffen dead he'd be in charge. He'd chance the noise of one or even two shots if it saved Hanna's life and he could easily stash the body in the trees. It'd be just one more spooky death for the British press to feed off. There was still Carey, of course. If New Hope was abandoned he wouldn't be killed but there were other ways of keeping his mouth shut. He was desperate for his Retrotox and there was his record as a traitor as well. Plus Heidi. Maybe he could see her now and again on condition he behaved himself.

To his intense irritation Kapner didn't get back into the Fiat.

"We've got plenty of time," she said, studying her watch. "Would you like some coffee? I made a flask for Ulrich but he turned it down."

Something about the way she spoke made him wonder whether she had something else on her mind but he was too focused on killing Steffen to follow it up.

"I said, Klaus, would you like some coffee?"

He wasn't the least thirsty but he said, "Yes please" in the hope that, if he drank it quickly she'd get back into the Fiat all the sooner. So they stood in the darkness chatting sporadically and drinking Steffen's coffee. When they'd finished she packed away, closed the boot and locked it.

"I'm going to check my Beretta now," she said and looked at her watch again, this time more furtively. "Ulrich expects you to do the same with your Ceska. He doesn't want any lights in the cars though. Can you manage in the dark?"

Guderius said he knew a Ceska better than his own right hand these days so she got into the Fiat and pulled the door to. As Guderius crossed the gap left by Danzig the interior light died away and from inside the Fiat Kapner heard him open and shut the Vauxhall's door. She also saw the interior light come on and go off but what she didn't see was that Guderius didn't get in. He opened and shut the door from the outside then ducked down out of sight. Assuming life would be hectic when he got back from killing Steffen he left the door unlocked. It'd be one less thing to think about.

Kapner meanwhile had her Beretta in her hands. Working by touch she checked it was fully loaded and the silencer was snugly on. The silencer made the gun too long for a normal holster so, rather than carry the silencer separately, she'd modified the holster so she could draw and kill with the silencer already in place. When she was sure everything was as it should be she re-holstered and zipped her jacket up to her chin.

She had her own reason for reminding Guderius Steffen didn't want any lights on in the cars. Hidden by the dark she took a balaclava out of one of her jacket pockets and tugged it over her head. Then she took some blacking she'd kept back from helping Steffen and covered her face with it. When she'd finished she wiped her fingers on a tissue, took a pre-written piece of paper from another pocket and stuck it to the windscreen with Blu Tack. It read "Condor's sent for me. No cause for concern. Preserve radio silence – Falcon". "Preserve radio silence" was underlined twice – she didn't want Guderius or anyone else contacting Steffen to ask questions. Then she switched the interior light to permanently off, lit up her watch one more time, pulled on some gloves and eased herself out through the passenger door. It was on the side away from the Vauxhall. Keeping low down she shut it so gently it only made a soft click and because, unlike Guderius, she was expecting everything to go smoothly when she got back she felt free to lock it, turning the key instead of using the remote control so the flashers wouldn't come on. She'd already locked the other doors from the inside and she knew the boot was locked because she'd made a point of doing it. She couldn't see into the Vauxhall but she was certain Guderius hadn't seen her get out. Stooping and treading silently she made her way to the footpath.

Frank Zimmermann was putting his Dragunov away when he heard a rustling noise again. He broke off and listened intently but it didn't come back so he finished what he was doing, took the carrying case by the handle and set off for the car park. He'd decided to take the Vauxhall because Guderius was weaker than Kapner. He'd be all friendly, get into the passenger seat and – very quietly, of course – strangle him in the dark. That'd stop him getting in the way. He wondered whether Kapner would chase after him when he drove off but what'd she do if she did? Force him off the road? Shoot his tyres out? Maybe he should kill her on the car park just to be on the safe side. He'd almost thought himself into doing that when it struck him Kapner wouldn't do any of those things for one simple reason: Steffen had told her to wait for him so that's what she'd do. Funny how she always did what Steffen told her. He thought she was tougher than Steffen, which was saying something, but he only had to snap his fingers and she came running. It didn't make any sense he could see and it couldn't be sex, not with Steffen, he was as pure as a monk. Perhaps he had some kind of hold over her, they both went back to the GDR. Not that he cared, not now. He had better things to think about.

When he reached the place where he'd first seen the control centre with Steffen and Danzig a helicopter arced away from him and droned off towards the Link Road. Its noise died quickly in the saturated air and in the quiet which followed he heard yet again, or thought he did, something that shouldn't be there. It came from above the footpath where the visibility was nil. If he heard something once it probably didn't mean anything but if he heard it more often it probably did. He had to make sure. Maybe if he got in close he'd see better.

He left the footpath and trod stealthily uphill till, almost before he saw it, he was touching one of the trees he'd noticed earlier. His mouth was parched and it was as much as he could do not to shake. He leaned the Dragunov against the tree, drew his Ceska and slipped the safety catch off. He could just about make out two more trees nearby. Holding his gun ready he stole first to one, then to the other, but he couldn't see anything beyond them and he couldn't hear anything either. He was on the point of picking up his Dragunov when he sensed rather than saw someone coming from the picnic area. As whoever it was came closer the general shape and then the unblacked face told him it was Guderius. He moved quickly behind the tree, hoping his black clothing and face made him invisible. But Guderius didn't so much as glance in his direction.

"No Guderius, no access to the Vauxhall," Zimmermann thought as he watched Guderius go by, then it struck him he could solve the problem right there. He didn't want to shoot Guderius, he was deadly afraid of making a noise, so he slipped the Ceska's safety catch back on, gripped the gun by its barrel and, holding it high, he soundlessly caught the older man up and smashed the butt-end onto his bare head. It made a dull, chunky sound and Guderius dropped in his tracks. Straight away Zimmermann re-holstered, seized him under the armpits and, using all his strength, dragged him behind the tree he'd just left. He was still breathing but Zimmermann hoped he'd be out for a good long while. He should be, he'd hit him hard enough. He soon found the keys and he thought about dragging him further uphill but he was desperate to get going again so where he was would have to do. He kicked his head twice to make sure he stayed unconscious and was about to kick him a third time when he became convinced he was being watched. He stopped and peered all round and, yet again, if there was anything to see he couldn't see it.

"It's the dark," he told himself. "And all this mist. I'm sure it's getting thicker."

He still had the sense to be cautious though so before he stepped onto the footpath he looked right and left as far as he could and listened hard as well. "All clear" he decided and he was on the point of moving on when an indistinct, scarcely perceptible movement made him draw back sharply. Someone else was coming up the footpath. It was Kapner. He knew it from the way she walked. Silently she emerged from the mist and padded steadily past him. The way she looked terrified him but then he felt elated because with Guderius out cold and Kapner heading off into the dark there wouldn't be anyone guarding the cars. But he had to move really fast now since she knew where he was supposed to be and if she saw he wasn't there she'd be bound to alert Steffen.

With his Dragunov in his hand – he was expecting his father to get rid of his weapons when he got back to the hotel – he left the tree and soon he was behind the wheel of the Vauxhall. His balaclava was off and he was urgently cleaning his face with the solvent and towel from the boot. He'd been surprised to find the Vauxhall unlocked but it was in the car park, that was the main thing, and he didn't spare the Fiat more than a glance. All he wanted to do was get away as quietly as possible. He didn't know how far sound would carry through the mist and he wasn't in the mood for experiments. The whole picnic area was on an incline and through his half open door - it kept the interior light on so he could see to clean his face – he heard a helicopter flying vaguely in his direction. So, to conceal the noise from the Vauxhall's engine he put the gear lever into neutral, took the handbrake off, got out and, leaning against the front door column, pushed the car towards the way out. When the helicopter was as close as he judged it was going to get he jumped in, started the engine, cleared the windscreen and took off as fast as the mist and his dipped headlights allowed. If he was stopped now he'd shoot his way through. The British police didn't expect guns, he knew that from television. The Americans did but not the British. Just thinking about it made him laugh. He'd been taking orders all his life but the one he was obeying now – to get out fast – was the last of the line. Now he was getting away from Steffen his bravado was flowing back. His Ceska was in its holster to keep it out if sight but he made sure the safety catch was off.

There was no traffic till he got to the Link Road and then there was lots of it. But the mist was thinner, the traffic was moving and all he had to do was move with it. Before long he'd passed the control centre turn-off but then he was braking to a halt on the inside lane. It was where the roadway started to go up to the flyover and the signs overhead were flashing "Road Closed Ahead". Boxed in and with no idea what to do he switched the radio on and flipped from station to station till the excited voice of a traffic reporter named Doreen made him listen in. She was telling someone in the studio called Chris she was in the station's helicopter and half the flyover - the southbound half - was sealed off on the mainland side. She could see blue flashing lights across all the lanes and the hard shoulder as well. Eye witnesses were saying the police had been in too much of a hurry to cross to the Sheppey side. As soon as they'd reached the flyover they'd screeched to a halt, poured through a stagger in the crash barrier and stopped the southbound traffic dead. It was just like last Easter when they'd blocked the flyover to catch some drug smugglers who'd landed in Sheerness.

"So it's drugs again, is it?" Chris asked.

"The police aren't saying but that's my guess. My advice to anyone wanting to leave Sheppey right now is, don't bother. Book into a hotel, have a nice long dinner and go to bed early. The police are here in numbers and they look as if they've come to stay."

"Is this hold-up linked to the one this afternoon?"

"I don't think so, Chris. This afternoon's was a breakdown but there's no breakdown here that I can see."

"Drugs?" Zimmermann said out loud. "Well, it could be. It'd be just my luck."

He slammed the radio off and banged the steering wheel in frustration. His escape route was right in front of him and these cretinous British pigs had blocked it off.

"They'll be checking vehicles soon," he thought suddenly. "They might've started already. And there's plenty of them, that cow on the radio said so. I don't stand a chance."

Then he had an idea. He opened his door, ran round to the boot, fetched out the tow rope he'd seen in there and hustled back in. He knew a lot about ropes and he'd seen at a glance this tow rope was longer than usual. Working swiftly, he tied a series of knots in it at about two foot intervals and made one end fast round the passenger seat. Then he pulled his gloves and balaclava on, turned his lights off, stamped the accelerator down and wrenched the car onto the hard shoulder.

The flyover had a concrete balustrade topped by a parapet on both its outer sides. They ran its entire length from ground level through the long flat part to ground level again and they had a crash barrier in front of them. Of the four pairs of columns holding up the flat part two pairs were on Sheppey and two pairs were on the mainland. Not far below the flat part and running lengthways were two concrete beams, one on each side of the flyover. They linked the columns together. When they reached an inner column they didn't stop on one side and restart on the other. Instead they formed a broad flat ring round that column and then continued on. Zimmermann knew all this from his Sky Rides photos. He also knew the outer columns had steel maintenance steps jutting out of them. They were caged in at the top and bottom but in between they were uncovered and they went all the way down from the balustrade to ground level. The maintenance steps on the mainland side were his new passport to freedom. He'd use the tow rope to lower himself onto the beam underneath his side of the flyover. Then he'd crawl all the way along it and climb down the steps on the mainland side. The caging shouldn't be a problem. He'd got past plenty of things like that when he was a boy and he was sure he could do it again.

So, when he was just past the point where the first of the columns merged with the balustrade – he didn't dare drive any further - he jammed on his brakes, yanked the handbrake on, killed the engine and threw the passenger door open. It banged against the crash barrier but his luck was in – it didn't bounce back. Immediately he leaped out, ran round the back of the car, hurled his Dragunov as far into space as he could, then grabbed the tow rope off the passenger seat and slung it over the parapet clear of the caging. Almost before it uncurled he was lowering himself down it. It was soon wet from the moisture in the air but his non-slip gloves did their job and the knots gave him something to hang on to. As his head disappeared below the parapet 999 calls bombarded Kent's emergency centre from drivers and passengers who'd seen what'd happened and two armed police motor cyclists roared down the hard shoulder in case he climbed back up. A lot of callers were struck by the speed of the police's response. They'd hardly finished reporting in and the bikes were already there. It was as if someone else had got in first.

Zimmermann was cornered but he didn't know it. He'd climbed over the parapet in what he thought was a good place and while he couldn't touch the beam yet he sensed it was somewhere near his feet. He didn't want to but he had to look down to see exactly where it was and that was when it sunk in there was nothing beneath him except a very deep void. The parapet was the problem. It was wider than the balustrade, which meant he was hanging not directly over the beam but further out.

He was frightened through and through but he still badly wanted to get away so he started to swing and to lower himself fractionally at the same time. At first he felt nothing, then the soles of his shoes touched the beam. He lowered himself a little further, swung again and when his soles made contact this time he stopped himself in mid-swing and gingerly squatted down, all the while keeping the rope in his hands in case he lost his balance.

He wasn't facing in the direction he wanted to go, he'd turned and was facing northwards. Slowly he twisted his head round to look along the beam behind him. He'd been right, it was wide enough to take him, but if he was to get to the first of the inner columns he had to turn his whole body round. He also had to let go of the rope and the thought of doing that nearly made him pass out. He breathed deeply and summoned up all his willpower then, without giving himself time to think, he turned, let go of the rope and flattened himself face down on the beam, all in one movement. He couldn't get the rope back now, it was dangling just out of reach. All he had to hold on to was the outer edges of the beam and as he pressed these tightly with his gloved hands he began to sob. He'd forgotten about hurrying. All he was interested in now was not falling off.

Blinking away his tears because he didn't dare use his hands he made to move along the beam but within seconds he had to stop, regain his nerve and force himself to get moving again. He was so focused on what he was doing he didn't notice a helicopter descending far enough away to prevent its side-draught from dislodging him but close enough to get a clear infrared image of him. Not at first anyway. When he did notice it, he went rigid. It had to be the police. So they were as close as that. And there had to be more above his head.

He decided his only chance was to get to the ring round the first inner column and shoot at the helicopter with his Ceska. Then the police above him wouldn't know exactly where he was and he could still get away as planned. As he lay there his eyes were so close to the beam it seemed wider than it really was and he'd been on it long enough for it to start feeling reliable. Speed counted now and he thought he ought to be able to improve on dragging himself along on his stomach so, keeping his hands on the beam's outer edges, he worked one leg forward, brought his elbows in towards his body, inched his other leg forward and, for a long terrified moment, held a tucked position. Then, very slowly, he began to straighten up. He never intended to stand right up. He reckoned if he could keep his centre of gravity low by stooping he could scuttle to his target column without losing his balance.

However, as the distance between his eyes and the beam increased, so did his fear and as he took his hands off the beam he panicked and went giddy. He knew he had to get down flat again but even as the thought formed in his mind he was starting to topple and then he was over the edge. As he fell through the misty dark he understood clearly he'd be killed when he hit the bottom. He wanted to call out but although he half-managed to open his mouth no sound came out. Down below, the tide was coming in but even if he'd fallen into water it wouldn't have been deep enough to save him. As it was he plunged into Sheppey-side mud, not far from his Dragunov. In the mud there were some lumps of concrete left over from when the flyover had been built. He struck one of these with the back of his head and was killed instantly.

37

Kurt Zimmermann breaks cover

"I really don't understand this," said Frith.

Under the maintenance area lighting the concrete paving was deserted except for a metal grid in the middle distance that looked as if it'd been randomly dumped there. The nearest exit in that direction was a gate near the toll booths but Zimmermann wouldn't have had time to reach it. Frith and Weller had kept it open in case they had to bike through it but now they wanted it closed. Then, wherever Zimmermann was, he'd hopefully be cornered.

"Cover me while I run to the gate," said Frith. "But don't shoot unless you have to. We want our friend fit to talk."

He was about to dash off when Weller pulled him back because something – it was the top of a head – was coming cautiously out of the ground on the far side of the grid. So that was where he was! The grid was the sort used to cover service dugouts and what Frith and Weller weren't high enough to see was that it hadn't been dumped, it'd been prised up and slid far enough forward for a plumber to climb down and work on a drainage leak. The plumber had been roused out when the maintenance area had been cleared and in his hurry he hadn't slid the grid back. Zimmermann had seen the open dugout and scrambled in, hoping the people chasing him would think they'd lost him and give up. He'd steeled himself not to peek out too soon but pressure of time had got to him and, like a submarine in hostile waters, he'd chanced coming up to take a quick look. He didn't know he'd been spotted so he clambered up the built-in ladder and pounded off towards the open gate.

Frith and Weller were after him as soon as they saw him go. He glanced over his shoulder and Weller thought Frith was going to shout, "Police!"

"Don't yell at him!" she called out. "You'll only make him go faster!"

So he didn't.

They were both soon blowing hard but Weller was in better nick than Frith and Zimmermann was slowing badly so she caught up with him before he reached the gate and grabbed him. He struggled and kept running at the same time and Weller was too exhausted to do more than hang on as best she could. It was a losing battle but it slowed him down enough for Frith to pass them and begin to shut the gate. When he saw that, Zimmermann went berserk. He forced Weller's hands off his coat, threw her back and squeezed through the gate just as Frith banged it shut. It locked automatically and Frith lost valuable seconds punching in the code to open it. Zimmermann was getting close to the toll booths now and he had his gun out ready. Frith saw it and dug in even harder. "I'm safe so long as he doesn't turn round," he thought so once again he didn't shout out who he was.

There was no crash barrier between the toll booths and the tunnel entrances on the maintenance area side, just white road markings that funnelled the traffic towards the two northbound tubes. Frith saw that if Zimmermann got past the toll booths he could get in amongst the traffic with his gun. He didn't know why Zimmermann wanted to do that, he just knew it mustn't happen. But he'd lost too much ground at the gate and it'd be a miracle if he caught him in time. Then the northbound side's lights went out. Some light spilled over from the southbound side but the gloom, where it wasn't offset by headlights, was intense. The lighting in the toll booths was only a percentage of what it'd be normally and an overhead gantry announcing "Controlled power cut. Proceed with caution" did nothing to make things brighter. Frith's anxiety level doubled. While the lights were on he could see Zimmermann's coat but now it was almost invisible.

Zimmermann couldn't see any mauve lights flashing so he knew New Hope hadn't started before it should and he didn't care what else was going on. He was entirely focused on getting between the toll booths and the tunnel to fire his gun.

But he'd overused his aging body and the result was, when he got near the traffic he was stumbly while at the same time those drivers who could were cramming on speed in case the tunnel was closed as well. Zimmermann spotted a gap and piled full tilt into it but before he could get through it he was struck by a BMW as it accelerated forward. He and his gun were thrown clear but he was already unconscious when he hit the ground. Frith, helpless, watched it happen. The BMW braked to a halt, Frith did what he could for Zimmermann in the headlights then radioed for an air ambulance, picked up the Ceska and, touching it as little as possible, dropped it into his pocket. Eventually the air ambulance would whirl Zimmermann off to Maidstone General Hospital where his multiple fractures would be operated on. The anaesthetic would keep him silent even longer and what looked like a fancy dress costume would stay unexplained.

Meanwhile, under the Thames Estuary, Walter was back in scarcely moving traffic and Ruth had a tension headache that was gripping her head like a vice. Walter tried the radio to see how good the signal was.

"Is it much longer to the news?" Ruth asked without opening her eyes. "The radio's annoying if it's just playing."

Walter switched it off. The signal was perfect.

"Not long now," he said and, ever the optimist, he added, "Keep your eyes closed and relax. I guarantee the news will be good."

38

Death in the dark

When Kapner stole out of the car park she reckoned she could find Frank Zimmermann and Danzig despite the dark and mist because when she'd been up on the hillside with Steffen and Guderius she'd counted her steps all the way. As she neared Zimmermann's location she said, "Goshawk, it's Falcon!" in a loud whisper. She had to do that. If she simply confronted him with her face blacked and her balaclava on he might panic and gun her down.

"I must've miscounted," she told herself when he didn't reply but she didn't believe it. It wasn't the sort of mistake she'd make. So where was he? Guderius had been right to sense she had a different time-scale from the rest of them. She had her own agenda and killing Zimmermann was at the top.

She called again but still nothing.

She hesitated over what to do next. Part of her said she ought to look for him in the trees and part of her said she ought to push on: the rest of her plan couldn't wait. She tried one last time even though she knew it was futile. Either he'd abandoned his post or – yes, that was it! – Steffen had put him somewhere else. She should've thought of that before. He knew what Zimmermann was like, he must be wanting to keep an eye on him. She was tempted to radio Steffen to find out for sure but she didn't want him to know she'd left the car park so she let it go. She'd find Zimmermann at some point and take him out then. Danzig was next on her list. She restarted her counting and set off to find her.

As she got near she voiced, "Osprey!" in the same loud whisper. Typically Danzig didn't respond. She let Kapner draw level then out of the darkness she rapped,

"Stop right there! Put your hands up and say your real name."

Kapner did as she was told and waited.

"Put your hands down, come in here and stand completely still."

Kapner parted the sodden bushes and pushed her way through. It was so dark in there it struck her Danzig might've brought a torch after all. She had a mind of her own and she wasn't afraid to use it. Confirmation came when a beam of light shone into Kapner's eyes. Danzig had her Ceska in her right hand and in her left she was holding a torch at shoulder level. The beam was weak and Kapner guessed Danzig had run the batteries down so it wouldn't be seen from a distance. Because it didn't dazzle she could see Danzig's face. It was like an ebony mask. She had to force herself not to shrink back as Danzig came closer.

"You can move now," she said, "but mind where you put your feet."

She pointed the torch at the ground to Kapner's left and lit up the Dragunov. A magazine was clipped on, the zoom scope was in place and the barrel, with its characteristic flash damper, was resting on its bipod. The furniture and metal were dulled by condensation.

"Can I have a look?" Kapner asked. "If I move it you can set it up again. You've got the time."

It was Danzig's turn to light up her watch.

"All right. It's safed so you can't shoot anyone. What are you doing here anyway? I thought you were staying with the cars."

"Ulrich radioed me to check everything was all right. That's why I'm blacked up and wearing this spare balaclava. Now I've seen it is I can go back."

"How's Zimmermann? Pissing himself I suppose."

"He's holding up. I'll cheer him up some more when I go back."

That'd stop Danzig going to see for herself. Or radioing Steffen.

Danzig remained standing as Kapner unzipped the top of her jacket, lay down beside the Dragunov and cradled it expertly against the side of her face. As she looked through the scope someone moved into its field of vision. It was Carey. He was wearing a navy blue mackintosh and a flat hat with a navy blue waterproof cover over it. He was heading for the perimeter fence as if he was having a routine look round and he'd just given the guards a cheerful wave. But he didn't feel cheerful. Sallis had told him the military had taken a decision about the next change of shift. They'd needed police help to bring in the guards who were already there and they didn't want that again so they were bringing the next ones in by helicopter. The trouble was, it was taking a while to get one so they'd still be arriving late. The news had rattled Carey but to keep his nerve he'd projected his anxiety onto Steffen.

"I'll have to get word to Ulrich," he'd said to himself. "If the new guards are late and he doesn't know why there's no telling how he'll react. It's a good job I've got my wits about me."

As Kapner tracked him he reached the perimeter fence and, keeping his back to the guard boxes, he raised his left palm up to his chin and, with exaggerated movements, tapped his watch with his right hand. She knew it was too dark on the hillside for him to see anyone so she guessed he was thinking, "If Ulrich is watching he'll see I'm ready to go." It cost her a lot not to de-safe the Dragunov and shoot him there and then but her schedule said she mustn't. His turn would come soon enough. She looked up at Danzig and saw she'd put her Ceska away.

"Your clothes look waterproof, just like mine," Kapner said. "Why don't you sit down? Put your torch out as well. Someone might see it."

"I doubt it," she replied but she switched it off anyway and the darkness was complete again. "You seem to know your way round a Dragunov," she said as she sat down. "Have you been practising on the sly?"

"Ulrich wanted someone in reserve. Klaus was no good so he asked me. I've been practising at my shooting club but only because I had to."

She jiffled as she spoke.

"Just a moment," she said. "I'm getting pins and needles."

She moved into a kneeling position and half-turned away. When she turned back she had her Beretta in her hand and, savouring the ecstasy, she shot Danzig through the forehead, destroying much of her skull. She died instantly. As always the silencer made a slight phut but she'd allowed for that. She'd reckoned Steffen wouldn't hear anything, not with his blunted hearing, and to stop Danzig hearing Zimmermann being shot she'd been going to garrotte him. The cord was in another of her pockets. She hadn't dared try to garrotte Danzig. Danzig had the strength of an animal and she could easily have garrotted Kapner with her own cord. Had Zimmermann heard her Beretta even so? That was a chance she'd had to take.

She dragged Danzig away from the Dragunov and made sure it was pointing where she wanted. She'd be firing it before long and she wouldn't have time to set it up from scratch. As she pushed through the undergrowth onto the footpath she made a swishing noise. That and a helicopter arcing towards the Link Road were the only sounds she noticed.

Steffen, meanwhile, was studying the control centre through his night glasses. Like Kapner he'd seen Carey point to his watch and he'd drawn the same conclusion she had.

"The sooner he's dead the better," he'd told himself. "He couldn't be more obvious if he hired the town crier."

With better hearing he might have caught the faintest of footfalls behind him but then it was too late. Sal Gulliver's gloved hand clamped tightly over his mouth, his head was wrenched back, his feet were kicked out from under him and he thumped to the ground on his back. He fought like a madman but his attackers were well trained, fit and a lot younger than he was. Gulliver whipped her hand away and someone tore his balaclava off but before he could cry out he had adhesive tape pressed over his lips, his head was jerked up by the hair and the tape was wound tightly round it. Then the rest of the reel was torn free and his head was allowed to fall. Before he could recover he was handcuffed, his ankles were shackled and he was bundled round the end tree of the clump behind him. Gulliver scooped up his night glasses and took them with her. Not a word had been said and nothing remained to show anyone'd been there.

When Kapner reached the same spot she trod extra carefully and she didn't call out. Steffen was next on her list but she didn't want him to know she was coming: the way she looked would've been one big danger sign. And if Zimmermann was anywhere near she didn't want him to know either in case he alerted Steffen.

When she didn't find Steffen she didn't know what to think. Something had clearly gone wrong with New Hope and it was making her own plan, which was geared to New Hope, come apart at the seams. Behind her the murk was so thick it seemed solid and it frightened her even more than the water off Sheppey. But to make absolutely sure Steffen and maybe Zimmermann weren't hiding for some reason she forced herself to push a little way into the trees, her Beretta ready to fire. Zimmermann might have killed Steffen, she knew how much he riled him, but she still hoped Steffen was about somewhere to tell her what was happening before she murdered him. She peered around and listened hard but it was a waste of time so she pushed her way out, re-holstered her Beretta and set off back to Danzig's firing point. It was Carey's turn at last.

When she re-entered the recess Danzig's body lay where she'd left it but it didn't excite her now. Struggling to keep a grip on herself she de-safed the Dragunov, zoomed in onto the guard box she'd preselected then carefully scanned all round it. There was more mist down there than last time – she'd noticed it was moving down the hillside as she'd come along the footpath – but she still had a good view. The guards didn't interest her, it was Carey she was after. He was supposed to be near the guard boxes well ahead of time but he wasn't there.

She tracked as much of the control centre as she could but nowhere could she see the tall figure in the navy blue mackintosh and the hat with the waterproof cover. He must be in one of the buildings, she speculated, but if he was he'd soon be out again. Even if there was some kind of delay he'd still fret around the inner compound, he wouldn't be able not to.

She wished he'd hurry up though, she had to be getting back to the car park. Taut with impatience she tapped her trigger finger on the hand guard and then she saw him. Once more he was passing himself off as a model SSO having a look round. He came out of a low building, gave the guards another cheerful wave and stopped near the perimeter fence with his back to the hillside as if he was making a general survey. Straight away Kapner zoomed in on his hat cover. It was like in a shooting gallery.

"You die this day, Lesley Carey, but please, please don't rest in peace."

She squeezed the trigger between heartbeats, just like a professional, but all she heard was a mechanical tap as the hammer struck the firing pin. She tried a second time, then several times, but still nothing. The gun wasn't working, that was all there was to it. So much for Steffen and his perfect condition. She was now so overwrought, a weird sense of unreality was taking her over. It was as if everything in front of her was on the outside of a transparent plastic globe and she was trapped inside it like a hamster. A helicopter passed over the control centre as she stared down the hill but although she could hear it, it was as if it was silent. As soon as she realised how far gone she was she snapped into action. She stood up, checked her watch, pushed hurriedly through the bushes and, despite the dark, set off briskly towards the car park. Part of her thinking was that Guderius would be there. He was on her list too.

As soon as she was gone the darkness at the back of the recess moved and two figures with GS in raised stitching on their combat tunics were standing where Kapner had been. One of them paused to let her put in some distance then took out his radio.

"Gold Three, Gold Three," he said softly. "Kapner's heading for the picnic area and I've got two people tracking her. She tried to shoot Carey but the rifle failed. Yes, that's positive, I watched her do it. And, no, she didn't radio anyone before she left."

He terminated and turned to his colleague.

"Thanks, Fran, it went like a dream. How did you do it?"

"We'd been briefed to expect Dragunovs so I got myself equipped. Kapner looked as if she was going to do some serious sniping so after she'd killed Danzig and disappeared up the footpath I opened the firing mechanism and put in a shortened firing pin. When Kapner pulled the trigger the hammer struck the pin – that was the tap we heard – but the pin wasn't long enough so nothing went bang. Some things are easy, that was one of them. What happens now?"

"We stay here with the body. Regard it as a reward."

Counting her steps Kapner kept her pace up till she saw the Vauxhall was gone, then she slowed to a crawl. Her first guess was Guderius had panicked and cleared out. Or maybe Zimmermann had made him take him away. Or maybe Guderius, like her, had some scheme of his own. He'd seemed nervy enough. That made three guesses which meant she knew sweet nothing. Or next to nothing because so much had gone wrong she knew she needed to be very, very careful if she was going to leave that pitch dark car park alive.

She'd been expecting another car besides the Vauxhall and the Fiat – it was supposed to be parked so that the Fiat screened it from the Vauxhall – but it wasn't there. That was something else she couldn't explain. Standing on its own the Fiat looked as empty as when she'd left it but she couldn't be sure. With every nerve drawn tight she slid her Beretta out, de-safed it and, bending low to make a smaller target, she slowly made her way towards it. She'd locked it when she went but someone might still have got in. They might be watching her now, they might be waiting for her to get in or they might be hiding behind the car and aiming at her as she crept forwards. All her instincts told her to keep well away from it but she had no choice: she had to go right up to it because that was what was arranged. Holding her gun in front of her she moved in closer and every couple of steps she stopped, looked all round and listened hard. Then she was close enough.

39

Old loves never die

The Fiat was covered in condensation. Tentatively Kapner wiped the windscreen and read "No cause for concern" on the piece of paper she'd stuck there. It was like recalling another life. She couldn't see inside the car and she made no attempt to try the doors, let alone get in. Rather, she stepped back and looked all round her but it was too dark to make anything out. A helicopter was droning somewhere but she filtered it out and strained for sounds that were closer. There weren't any. She seemed to be on her own. Then,

"Over here, Heidi."

It was a man's voice, soft and calm, and the language was English. Because she knew who it was and where the voice came from she thought she could see him sitting at one of the picnic tables nearest the car park. Silently she safed her gun, holstered it and walked towards him. When she reached him he stood up and, still silent, she flung her arms round him and hugged him tightly. Only his eyes and mouth were visible through gaps in a black hood and everything else he was wearing was black as well. He closed his arms round her and kissed her on the lips. An uncanny stillness enveloped them both.

"Can we go now?" she asked when their lips parted. "Just as we planned? I can soon get this blacking off."

"All in good time, Heidi. Things haven't gone well, have they? I need to know what's happened before we leave so we don't get more things wrong."

"Let's sit in my car then. We won't be seen in there."

"We're safer here. No one can creep up on us and we've got a lot to talk about. You see, I've been here for quite a while and I've had several surprises. For example, I saw Guderius head off while you were still in your car. Do you know why? And do you know where he is now?"

She didn't answer, she just shook her head.

"You left exactly as arranged, which was good, but then Frank Zimmermann came back and drove off in the Vauxhall. He had the keys and, as you can see, he hasn't come back either. Tell me, Heidi, how am I to understand these things?"

She looked up at him. There was fear as well as trust in her eyes.

"I don't know," she replied. Then, hesitatingly, she asked, "Have you seen Steffen?"

"You mean you haven't killed him?"

"No. He wasn't where he was supposed to be. I'm sorry. He could be anywhere."

They sat down and she went through what'd happened. As for Kurt Zimmermann, she didn't know whether he was alive or dead. She'd been afraid to contact him as long as she didn't know where Steffen, his son and Guderius all were.

"So Carey's alive and the Zimmermanns, Guderius and Steffen probably are as well. That's not good and nor is this: I've been expecting another car to show up but it hasn't. Did you send for it?"

"Yes."

"Do you know why it hasn't shown up?"

"No, I thought it was certain to. Look, can we go now please? Everything's gone wrong and I'm frightened."

"Of course you are," he said, getting to his feet. "We can go right now. Just give me your Beretta. If there's any trouble I'll need it to shoot with. I'm not armed, you see. And take the safety catch off, please."

He held out his gloved hand and waited. She didn't believe he wasn't armed, that couldn't be true, but she needed him for her getaway and anyway, she loved him so much she always did what he said even if she didn't want to.

"The silencer's still on," she said as she drew her Beretta out and de-safed it.

"That's all right, we may need it. And point the barrel towards me. I shouldn't want to catch the trigger by accident now it's ready to fire."

She turned it round again and reached it towards him. As she did so his right hand moved past the barrel and clamped her fingers so hard against the butt she couldn't move them. At the same time his left hand covered her mouth. He was off-balance at first but surprise was on his side and before she could react he shifted his ground and then he had her. Still blocking her mouth he forced her gun hand till, slowly but surely, the barrel started to point at her head. The blacking on her face made her eyes look large and wild and with her free hand she thrust against the table to withstand the pressure. But while she wanted to live she felt maimed by the power he had over her. She felt his hand move so its index finger could reach the trigger and that made her struggle harder but it wasn't enough. Then, just as death seemed only seconds away the Beretta was half-knocked, half-snatched away and three spectral figures slammed him onto the ground. At the same time something hard and metallic pressed into her spine and a woman's voice said,

"Put your hands behind your back! Do it now!"

She knew it was the barrel of a gun and she wasn't inclined to argue with it. As soon as her hands came together she was handcuffed, then her ankles were shackled as well.

The scuffle on the ground was soon over. Two Gold Section officers kept their prisoner still while a third one handcuffed and shackled him. Then he was hauled to his feet. A clothes search turned up a loaded Walther PPK – old-fashioned but still an ideal killer's weapon. The officer who'd immobilised Kapner switched a torch on briefly and went to where the Beretta had landed to stop it being trodden on. But she didn't stay there long. Someone who'd been keeping his distance stepped forward, peeling his headwear off as he did so.

"I suppose we ought to take his hood off before we do much else," he said casually. "Do it, Sal. I'll watch the gun."

Someone else's torch went on and in its beam Gulliver took hold of the hood by its elasticated hem and exposed the livid face and white hair of Alex Trilling. The torch went off again and Gulliver pocketed the hood to keep it safe.

"Thanks, Sal," said van Piet, removing his acoustic optimisers. "You can arrest and caution him now. When you're finished I'd like a word with him."

He had Trilling taken to a table away from Kapner, who'd also been arrested and cautioned. Trilling's guard withdrew and van Piet found himself alone with the man he'd been closing in on for three nerve-testing weeks. He dried the benches for both of them with his gloves.

"I thought you were in Essex, Willem," Trilling said quietly, "and I thought Mrs Patel was in charge."

"You were meant to. When she took off I was already airborne and waiting. I simply slotted back in and rejigged the organisation. We had to stop you killing Kapner, I'm afraid, but now she knows you wanted to it might loosen her tongue. I hope so. I think I've got most of the facts but it'd be nice to have them confirmed."

"I didn't want to kill Kapner. What you saw was her trying to kill me. So far as I know Danzig's the only one dead and she did that. She told me so just now."

"You'll have to do better than that. We didn't just watch you we heard you as well." Then, "Kapner seems very attached to you. I expect she's known you a long time. Did she know you when she used to comb her hair down, just like in the photo you made sure I didn't miss? That's going back some years, isn't it? And, as we've just seen, she still knows you. Old loves never die, do they?"

Trilling didn't answer. Van Piet shrugged his shoulders and radioed Patel: Trilling and Kapner could be picked up any time. Yes, Trilling. Who else did she think was casting all the shadows? And there was a Beretta for forensics. Apparently it'd killed Danzig.

"From where I'm sitting the sky seems to be getting crowded," he added.

"It's the media. They know something big's going on so they're using all the helicopters they can hire and worse yet, tv's broadcasting live. So far they're focusing on the flyover and the tunnel entrance, which is why you've had a clear run. My Chief is hinting terrorists are involved but he's saying he can't go into detail because the operation's on-going."

"Ask him to keep it that way. If he makes any slips the PM will want to know why."

He terminated the call and went over to Gulliver, who'd gone back to the Beretta.

"You've done well," he said. "You won't catch many bigger fish however long you stay in the force."

"Thank you, Sir. You helped a bit yourself if I may say so. Can I ask you a question, please?"

"If you're quick you can. What is it?"

"Why didn't Trilling get into the car with Kapner? You'd think he would, wouldn't you?"

"You heard what he said. No one could creep up on them if they stayed in the open."

"And that was all there was to it?"

"No, he wanted the best place to kill her in. She was expecting to go away with him and he had every intention of making sure it didn't happen. He knew her Beretta had a silencer on it but, as you know, silencers make guns a lot longer so my guess is, he didn't want to be cramped for space. You see, he had a gun of his own but, without taking his gloves off, he asked her to hand hers over with the silencer on, barrel first and with the safety catch off. Now, no one in his right mind does that unless – "

"Unless they've got total control over the person with the gun and they're going to fake a suicide with no one hearing the shot."

"That's how I read it too. Kapner's mouth would've been shut for good and no one would know Trilling had done it."

He looked at his watch.

"I've got to leave it at that," he apologised. "I'm pushed for time and I want another word with Trilling while he's still off-balance. With luck he'll give something away."

When he got back to Trilling, Trilling got in first.

"I'm not talking, Willem. I've said all I'm going to say."

"You'll talk when you're in prison. In fact you'll look forward to it because you won't have anything else to do. But since you won't talk to me why don't I talk to you?"

Nothing.

"Very well. You may not know it but you've made some very big mistakes. One was letting me see the photo of Guderius. I tracked the message on the back, you see. Another was those Knifepoint letters. You wrote them, didn't you?"

"That's nonsense. I found them as upsetting as you did."

"Right now the police are watching your house. Now you're caught I'll ask Tom Garry to send them in. We'll see what they find."

He opened up another front.

"You were expecting Miriam Sobart, weren't you?"

"I don't know any Miriam Sobart."

"Not the suspected traitor? The known Chameleon member whose lab was probably Chameleon funded? She'd need protection with a record like that and I think it came from you."

"That's fantasy and you know it."

"It's not fantasy you know Kapner, nor yet that Kapner knows a certain Lesley Carey, the security man for the North Sea Tunnel. And it's not fantasy Kapner, Steffen and Guderius have been putting the bite on Carey with help from Miriam Sobart."

"Nothing links me to these people, nothing at all."

"That's just as well since if you knew Carey was involved when you started me on this business I'd have to ask why you didn't tell me about him. The truth is, of course, you wanted me to track Steffen & Co to make it look as if you were doing all the right things but you didn't want me to know where they were heading till the last possible minute in case I set up a full-scale ambush for them. That would've really got in your murderous way, wouldn't it? Or better, your murderous way and Kapner's."

"If you've bungled this operation it's your fault not mine. You were in charge – right to the end, I now see."

"With one hand tied behind my back, thanks to you. But let me ask you this. If you were protecting Miriam Sobart was it so she could tell you things about Chameleon that Kapner wouldn't know?"

Trilling fell silent again.

"Looking back I can see I should've suspected something as soon as I read her briefing file but I have to admit I didn't. It was finding out about Carey that made me think: if she *is* telling you about Chameleon she must have told you what was happening to Carey. And if, for your own devious reasons, you wanted to keep that information to yourself, she might well know more than was good for her. So, last Saturday I arranged some protection for her and I told the people watching her, if they saw her leaving Rochester on her own they were to intercept her and tell her, 'Mr Trilling says someone knows you've been betraying Chameleon to him. Go back to Rochester and stay there. Mr Trilling will contact you as soon as he can.' That happened this afternoon just before she reached the M2/A2 and as soon as she heard your name plus the reason I'd cobbled together she did exactly as she was told without asking any questions. Wouldn't you say that was a link? And you must admit, this picnic area is a very lonely place after dark. Just the place to murder someone who knows too much."

"It was Kapner who asked Sobart to come here, not me. If you could hear so much you must've heard her say it."

"I didn't hear her say Sobart's name. For you to say what you've just now said you must have known it all along. Perhaps Kapner will tell me more when I get round to talking to her."

He brought his face close to Trilling's and looked him straight in the eye.

"Perhaps she'll even tell me about Mrs Trilling's murder. Do you think she will?"

Before Trilling could answer van Piet got a call from Patel. She sounded tense.

"This is it," she said, "and I'm glad it's not my idea. I think it's one big risk."

"That's my worry, not yours, Lorraine. Just make sure it happens."

As he stepped away, Trilling's guard took his place.

"No torches till I give the word," he told them. "We don't want to attract the media. Perhaps one of you could spread the word."

Taking his time he made his way to an empty bench, dried it, put in his call to Garry and settled down to wait. Like Trilling, he was on the sidelines now.

40

Carey does as he's told

Carey was back in Site Security and the disruption to routine was eating him up. It was also agitating him he couldn't see all the tunnel's entrances and he'd further heard the flyover had been sealed off southbound. It was drugs apparently so that was all right, but if the flyover was sealed off how would he get off the island?

"A car will be waiting for you with its engine running," Ulrich had promised and Carey didn't doubt Steffen would be driving it himself. It wasn't a job for underlings. Remembering the escape car had calmed him down but gradually he realised he didn't know much about it. Whose car would it be and how would Ulrich get from the hillside – where he was bound to be – to the gate in time to pick him up?

"He'll run to the picnic area car park and drive across country," he decided. "He's a soldier, terrain's an open book to him. I expect he's hired a four by four. He'll be here in no time."

In fact, Carey mused on, he'll probably not even try to leave Sheppey, not straight away anyway. He'd said there'd be a hiding place but he hadn't said where it'd be and Carey, the insider, knew why: Ulrich was a professional, he only said as much as he had to. Carey reckoned it was in Sheerness, a bland little safe house in a nice quiet street. So, the sealed-off flyover didn't matter at all. He and Ulrich could hole up for weeks before they left Sheppey and Heidi would be all right as well, Ulrich would see to that. And when she visited the safe house Ulrich would discreetly go out. Carey had her locket in his jacket pocket and as he touched it, his heart melted. He had to force himself not to say her name out loud.

He wished he could feel as happy about his health - the Cytofane was destroying him and he could feel it happening.

He hoped he'd be fast enough when the guards were shot. He had to get to the flooding mechanism, then to the gate and then to the escape car. It was asking a lot. He wouldn't have time to see his flooding mechanism working and that distressed him no end. He'd told Ulrich he was mad to think of drowning all those people but the chance to see his dreamchild in action had made him think again. His escape came first however. His escape, his Retrotox and unlimited happiness with Heidi.

How many vehicles would the flood water trap? Strange but he'd never asked himself that before. It was bound to be a number so immense he'd go down in history like – he couldn't remember the name – the man who burned down a temple in ancient Greece. Or was it a library? He was about to request a vehicle count north and southbound when he sensed someone was standing behind him. It was Sallis. Carey liked Sallis. He was highly competent and very ambitious and Carey respected both those qualities. He hoped flooding the tunnel wouldn't damage Sallis's career. If it did he'd get a sincere apology to him somehow.

Guiltily Carey pushed his keyboard away while Sallis wheeled a spare swivel chair next to his and slumped down. In one hand he held his usual wad of papers and in the other he had two pairs of ear protectors.

"Sorry to interrupt," he said, keeping his voice down so as not to disturb anyone, "but I've encroached on your territory. The military are on their way at last but they asked whether they could bring a container with them and I said yes."

"A container? What're they bringing that for?"

"It was supposed to go to a barracks in Essex but visibility is virtually nil up there so the flight was scratched. Then someone said our guards were being brought in by helicopter so why not fly it to here and the barracks can collect it when the weather clears? Joined up thinking, you see, even in the army."

"What's in this container? I've a right to know that. Security can't be skimped, you know."

"I've got a fax of the manifest right here."

He tugged it out of the wad and held it out.

"Bed frames, chests of drawers, chairs upright, chairs easy," Carey read out as he worked his way down the list. "Nothing suspect here. They're refurbishing the place, are they?"

"Part of it. Some of it goes back to Wellington, I gather."

"That's no bad thing. He won Waterloo, you know. Where're you putting this container anyway? We've only got one gate and we mustn't block it. Health and Safety and all that."

Not to mention his escape route.

"The space between the front fence and where our buildings start is plenty big enough. I've told them to put it there."

Carey was starting to shriek inside. He was just about coping with the guards arriving late and now there was this.

"Will the helicopter have to land to let the guards out? I've a right to know that as well."

As he spoke his voice cracked from tension.

"Excuse me," he said and drank some water from a bottle. "I've got a bit of a throat."

"Not a cold coming, I hope. We can't have you off sick. No, the helicopter won't be landing. Once the container's on the ground the guards will be winched down and they'll go to the inner compound on foot."

"They must stay together, I insist on that. We can't allow wandering off."

"You're quite right. I'm glad you thought of it."

He paused for a moment.

"Why don't you go with them? Someone's obviously got to and if I can rely on anyone around here it's you. I happen to know you've checked the bottom end twice within the last little while. Not many SSOs would do that but you've always led from the front."

"All in a day's work as far as I'm concerned."

Carey smirked as he spoke but he wasn't pleased at all. He'd hoped he'd looked so everyday no one'd notice but Sallis had. That wasn't good.

"What about the guards who're being replaced?" Carey continued.

"They'll come up here till the next change of shift. Then they, plus the two we're waiting for now will be taken off site together."

Carey smiled to himself guilefully.

"What you don't know, Mister Clever Sallis, is that it isn't going to happen. You startled me just now but I'm ahead of you all the time."

Out loud he said,

"You say the guards coming off duty will come up here. So who'll come with them? The army isn't what it was, you know. They're quite likely to loiter."

"That's very true. I tell you what, why don't I walk down with you and bring them back myself while you make sure the new ones get stuck in? They'll probably need you standing over them if they come on late."

Carey was more than happy with that but there was one more thing he had to know.

"These off duty guards, will they keep their weapons? We're not MoD property, we're Home Office. I think they should surrender their guns."

"Can't be done, Lesley. I wish it could but we don't have the authority."

Carey was less pleased again. Armed soldiers were the last thing he wanted between him and the gate. Well, if they came running he'd just have to go round them. He ought to be able to do that with the lights shot out, even if he did feel ill. He'd tell himself he was running towards Heidi, that'd speed him up.

"I've made my confession," Sallis went on, " and now I want to make amends. These ear protectors come from Stores. One pair's for you, the other pair's for me."

Carey asked what they were for.

"I thought you'd like to see the container brought in. They're using a Chinook so it'll be slung underneath. It should be quite a show. You'll need that coat you've been wearing

346

and hold onto your hat if you're putting it on again. The downdraught of these things is unbelievable."

His radio buzzed: the Chinook was on its way in.

"I'd better be going," he said. "I'll see you outside."

The Chinook was hovering over the control centre's lights when Carey, still buttoning his mackintosh, hurried out. His hat and its cover were in his coat pocket and so were his gloves. The noise made him glad he had ear protectors and it was about to get louder.

The area for the container was cordoned off and staff had been ordered to stay indoors so in the rooms it could be seen from, the lights were all on and the windows were crowded. The Chinook had the usual four-man crew. The pilot did the flying, the co-pilot managed the mission and two air loadmasters looked after the cargo. Sallis was just outside the cordon and when Carey caught up with him, he was talking to the co-pilot. He had a finger in one ear, his mobile was jammed against the other and his ear protectors were hanging round his neck over a bright red football scarf. That and a matching woollen hat made him look even younger than he was. He'd trampled on a lot of people on the way up but no one'd know it from looking at him.

The container came down first, very gently and precisely. Its seals glinted dully as the lights caught them. Then the new guards were winched down. They were wearing body armour but to Carey's relief they were both bareheaded. Bending low, they fast-walked across to Sallis, who was flashing a torch at them, and to Carey, who'd placed himself next to him. They'd done control centre duty often enough to be known to both of them. When the Chinook roared off they took their ear plugs out and put their soft hats on. One of them saluted Sallis and handed him a beige leatherette pouch.

"Delivery documents for signing, Sir," he said smartly.

Sallis thanked him and tucked the pouch under his arm. The nearby windows were emptying fast as routine reasserted itself.

"Welcome to Planet Earth," Sallis said briskly. "I'm perfectly aware we all know each other but checks are checks and they have to be made. While I'm getting these documents signed Mr Carey will take you into Site Security to have your passes processed. Then he'll escort you to your place of duty. I'll be coming with you to see to your outgoing colleagues. When you're ready, Mr Carey. I'll wait for you outside Site Security."

Carey was jubilant. Not only must he be present when the guard was changed, he had to stay down there and the Senior Site Manager would personally get the off-duty guards out of the way. He wished he could contact Steffen to tell him his vigil was nearly over. He must be a nervous wreck by now.

Thanks to an army clerk who sounded new to the job it took Carey longer to have the guards' passes processed than it should've but eventually they were outside again. Carey was now wearing his hat with its waterproof cover and he'd buttoned his mackintosh up to his throat. Sallis did all the talking. Carey was too wound up to say much and the guards kept themselves to themselves. The hillside was invisible and the mist had rolled nearer. I'm looking into darkness, Carey reasoned, but Ulrich's snipers will be looking into light, so there's nothing to worry about. In fact they'll probably use the mist to creep in so close they'll hit everything first time. His hands were in his pockets to keep them warm – he'd decided against gloves in case he pressed the wrong buttons. He wrapped his fingers round the locket and gave it a loving squeeze.

When they reached the inner compound Carey and Sallis hung back while the new guards took over. As Sallis shepherded the old ones away Carey felt curiously abandoned. He was far from wanting other people around but he also wished he wasn't on his own.

Forcing himself to look relaxed he withdrew to the side of the control centre while the guards went through their routine. When the one in the inner compound was ready to check the flooding mechanism she looked back to the colleague covering her. After he'd gazed all round she nodded to him positively, raised her arm to shoulder level and pressed the second green button on her combi-key. The crack of a single shot split the air. It came from the hillside and the guard doing the covering dropped like a stone. A second shot followed and the other guard dropped as well. Then came a sequence of shots and most of the lights went out. Three surveillance cameras were also hit. Carey noticed none of the lights between the inner compound and the gate had been taken out. Never mind, he told himself, these things happen when you delegate and once he was in Ulrich's car he'd be all right. He felt his tension reaching such a peak, only making a move would release it so, with a supreme act of will, he focused entirely on what he had to do. And he'd do it now.

He squeezed Kapner's locket once more then pounded across to the first guard, tore open his pocket and tugged out the combi-key. Seeing his pistol in its holster he scrabbled it out and thrust it into his coat pocket. The gate unlocked without any trouble. It flashed through his mind the snipers must be using armour-piercing bullets since the guards' heads didn't look damaged. But he could be wrong there. He'd seen plenty of films where someone slid his hand under someone else's head and it came out covered in blood.

Suppressing his doubts he rushed past the second guard and then he was in the blockhouse, panting furiously. He was finding it as hard to move as he'd feared. His mind battened onto the five red buttons and one by one he jabbed them down with his thumb. Outside an emergency siren was starting to wail: he had to get out fast. He whirled round and pulled up in shock. A stocky, black-clad figure with "Police" on one side of his body armour and "Smail" on the other was standing bareheaded between him and the doorway, his pistol pointing straight at him. He must have been in there all the while.

"Stay where you are, Mr Carey," he said placidly and shut the door.

Carey's shock didn't last long.

"Once the red buttons are pressed, the water pours in like Niagara" was what he'd told Steffen and he hadn't been making it up. He had his back to the monitors but he didn't need them: it was his system and he knew exactly what it'd do. He might not get away now, he could see that, but if he didn't and Heidi read about him in the papers or, even better, when she saw him on television, she'd know he'd done it for love. In fact he'd tell the court he'd done it for love and that'd remove all doubt. He didn't want her thinking he'd done it out of fear. And he might yet get away. To take Smail out he flung the combi-key at his face and snatched out the pistol he'd taken from the guard.

"Stay where *you* are!" he yelled, pointing the muzzle at him. "This is a Glock, let me tell you! One false move and I'll shoot you with it! You shouldn't even be in here! Don't you know the rules?"

Carey's practical acquaintance with firearms was just about zero but he was sure he could pull a trigger when he had to. Smail, who'd evaded the combi-key without any trouble, raised his hands in the air. His own gun was pointing at the ceiling. Carey didn't dare tell him to drop it in case it went off in his direction.

"As you see, I *am* staying where I am," Smail said. "But there are one or two things you really ought to know."

"Don't try that with me! It's a trick! I know it's a trick, I've seen it in films a thousand times! You want to stop the pumps, don't you? But it won't make any difference now, you're too late already!"

"They're not switched on, Mr Carey. The Home Office has shut them off and, just for once, the guards' guns aren't loaded. You can pull the trigger because the safety catch is off but all you'll get is a click. However, my gun *is* loaded and since you're a man for the rule book I have Home Office authorisation to be in here, which is more than can be said for you. Now, do we walk quietly out of here or do we not?"

"You can't fool me! This gun's loaded all right, they're always loaded! Look at it, I say, it's your death warrant no less! Whatever happens to me, you go first!"

Carey's mackintosh was still buttoned right up, he still had his hat on with the waterproof covering and his gun hand was shaking so much he had to use his other hand to steady it. But as long as the muzzle was pointing at Smail he looked lethal.

Keeping his eyes fixed not on Carey's gun but on his face Smail began slowly to lower his hands.

"Keep your hands *up!*" Carey screamed but Smail took no notice and when Carey pulled the trigger he discovered Smail had been telling the truth.

"I did warn you," Smail said, bringing his own pistol to bear on Carey's heart. "Now, let that gun fall to the ground, raise your hands, turn round very slowly and look at the monitors."

Carey obeyed and saw for himself: there was no water in any of the tubes. None at all. When he turned back to Smail his face was crumpled and blotchy. Formally polite, Smail placed him under arrest and cautioned him. Then he let him put his hands down.

"It's not your day, is it?" he commented. "Two of your friends are dead, the others are under arrest and now you are as well."

"They aren't my friends," Carey replied dully. "At least…"

He broke off. He could deny Steffen was his friend but Heidi? Could he ever turn against her? And Guderius? He wasn't a friend but he depended on him for his Retrotox.

"Two of them are dead, you say," he repeated tentatively. "If you know my name I expect you know their names as well. Are Colonel Steffen, Dr Guderius or Miss Kapner amongst them?"

He wanted Steffen dead, he needed his silence but not, please, Guderius or Heidi.

"No. Colonel Steffen and Miss Kapner are more or less well. Dr Guderius has a head injury but he should recover in time."

Carey was relieved about Guderius and Kapner but the news about Steffen filled him with anger. He became like a volcano about to erupt.

"I'm a dying man," he declared as if it gave him status. "I've been poisoned by a very rare drug. And I've been betrayed as well," he went on, unable to contain himself any longer. "Yes, betrayed. I must've been if you were waiting for me."

Both of them were ignoring the siren and no one had come in or even banged on the door. Everyone was waiting for Smail to come out but he wasn't going to do that yet. He could see Carey was crumbling, the signs were as clear as day. If he wasn't too aggressive Carey might blurt out something in what amounted to a kind of privacy.

"Do you know who betrayed me?" Carey asked, his tone of voice sharpening as he spoke. "I repeat, do you know who betrayed me? Tell me who it was and I promise you can take me away."

"I'm only a small cog in a large machine. I don't know when you first attracted attention but I do know a certain person on our side asked me to do some contingency planning early last Saturday morning. It revolved round you because it had to. First, you could get into the control centre when you liked and second you had some very special knowledge."

"Where did that person's information come from?"

"He was a bit cagey about that. He said he'd only just got some of it and I had to be very careful who I used it with. On your side the intention was to shoot you dead from the hillside. Your life was saved by a weapons failure but the attempt confirmed we'd been right to take a close look at you."

"Shoot me dead? Who tried to shoot me dead? I demand to know this instant!"

Smail looked straight at him.

"It was Miss Kapner. She aimed at you with a Dragunov sniper rifle which she'd de-safed herself."

For a long minute Carey said nothing, then his eyes brimmed with tears. She'd tricked him into being injected and now this.

"Can I put my hand in my pocket, please? I don't have a gun in there, I give you my word. I wouldn't have taken the guard's if I had."

"Go ahead. But move slowly."

Carey pulled out Kapner's locket and held it in the palm of his hand. He started to raise it to his lips to give it one last kiss, then changed his mind and threw it at the gun on the floor as if he was drawing a line under something.

"I'm ready to go now," he said flatly. "Are you going to handcuff me?"

"I'm afraid I must. I have to shackle your ankles as well but I'll make the chain as long as I can. I don't think you'll try anything but I'll say this anyway. There are too many of us outside for you to escape even if you get past me. We were in the container, you see. I suppose the seals stopped you looking inside, which was bad security on your part, though Mr Sallis would've stopped you if you'd tried. While you were indoors checking the guards' passes with a clerk who wasn't as new as she seemed, Mr Sallis brought me down here and let me in."

"So Sallis was helping you when he was pretending to be nice to me. You'd been talking to him behind my back."

"I had to. You made it necessary."

"In other words, you knew what I was going to do."

"We had a rough idea and it firmed up. We could've taken you in and questioned you, of course, but if you *were* intending to flood the tunnel we wanted to see you press the buttons because that'd make it easier for us in court. Everything you've done's on video and I have to say, it's a good idea keeping the lights on in here, they make it just like a studio."

"How did Sallis let you in? Only the soldiers have combi-keys."

Part of Carey was still the SSO. If his system had a weakness he had to know about it.

"You may remember, one of the guards gave him a pouch and said it contained delivery documents for signing. They were fakes, of course, like the manifest, but there was a preset combi-key in with them. Your zappers are so designed that anyone can operate them and Mr Sallis did just that."

"And the guards being shot? That was another setup I suppose."

"The thinking was, if you were going for the flooding mechanism you'd do it when the guards were out in the open so your sniper friends could shoot them and you could get a combi-key. I have to say you gave us a helping hand there.

353

You came down here twice when you didn't need to and when Mr Sallis gave you the chance to stay near the inner compound you took it with both hands. So, when you went to the side fence, you might've been just supervising the new guards, we couldn't rule that out, but you might also have been waiting for something to happen. So my colleagues and I took a chance with some play-acting we'd arranged. If we were wrong we'd do some minor damage but if we were right we'd catch you red-handed. When the guard in the inner compound looked back and, like her colleague, saw you were still there, she raised her hand, pressed her button very visibly and that was the signal for us to open fire. The first two shots went into the air and the guards dropped because they'd been told to. We were afraid you'd notice no wounds were showing but we reckoned you'd think round that one because you'd want to. It seems we got away with it."

So that was why there was no corridor to the main gate – those oafs hadn't thought that far.

Carey was on the point of asking how Smail knew so much detail but a glance at his radio gave him the answer.

"Someone's been giving you a running commentary!" he surged up again. "Who was it? Was it one of my staff? I've been betrayed all round, haven't I?"

"Some of my information came from the air – you might've noticed the helicopters flying about – some came from the person who asked me to do the contingency planning and some came from someone who was up on the hillside."

"Someone I know?"

"I shouldn't think so. While some of your friends were up there, some of my police friends came through the trees and took over. It was one of them. He started out where Colonel Steffen had been standing before the Colonel was required to be elsewhere, then he moved down the hill with the police snipers who'd replaced your two. He was given the Colonel's night glasses to use. They were better than police issue and the Colonel didn't need them anymore."

"Where Colonel Steffen had been standing…" Standing? That didn't sound as if he was going to run to the car park and drive across country but it did chime with something Smail had said earlier – "the intention was to shoot you dead from the hillside". A ghastly suspicion leaped into Carey's mind: there'd been no car waiting for him because Steffen had never intended to rescue him. He'd intended to use him and then have him killed. But not by Heidi, surely. He'd meant someone else to do it, he must have. Perhaps Smail was lying. He had to clear that up.

"Are you sure it was Miss Kapner who tried to shoot me?"

"There's no doubt about it but you might want to think about this. She'd already killed one of the Colonel's snipers when she pulled the trigger on you and we think she'd have killed the other one only she couldn't find him. Now, if the Colonel had wanted you dead –"

"He did! I'm sure of it! I was far too important to live!"

"– wouldn't it have been simpler to have one of his snipers do it rather than involve Miss Kapner in such a complicated way?"

"But why would Miss Kapner do it then? She loved me, she'd never –"

He stopped short and his jaw dropped.

"You think she was she doing it for someone else. Someone Colonel Steffen didn't know about."

"It could be."

"Was it … was it another man?"

"I don't see why not but you'll have to ask someone better placed than me if you want to be sure."

"If it was I've been betrayed on a scale of epic proportions. Epic, I say. Yet how could it happen, I'm as cunning as a fox?" He took a deep breath. "I've drained life's cup to the dregs, Mr Smail. Not many people have to suffer as much as I'm suffering now but I can assure you of one thing: the taste is as bitter as gall."

"I'm sure it is. Now, if you're ready."

Smail moved towards the door. He'd holstered his gun to handcuff and shackle Carey and he saw no reason to take it out again. Carey shuffled forwards, testing what it was like to walk with his ankles chained together.

"I can't move any faster because, as I've told you, I'm a dying man," he said as Smail let him take his time. "It would take a top scientist to understand my condition so I won't explain it to you. You'll simply have to take my word."

Smail said he'd do his best and radioed to Patel they were coming out. No, there were no problems.

"Before we go outside," Carey said, "I'd be grateful if you'd help me in a small way. Please."

"If I can I will. What is it?"

"I'm still wearing my hat, you see, and it's got a waterproof cover on it. My mackintosh is buttoned right up as well. I thought it'd help me to escape if I made myself dark but now I'm afraid I'll be laughed at. Can you put my hat in my pocket and undo my top coat button?"

Smail did as he was asked. He saw no reason not to. He left the Glock, the combi-key and the locket where they were and Carey ignored them all.

Outside Carey saw the dimmed lighting he'd run through. It seemed a long time ago now. The guards he thought Sallis had taken away were in the inner compound and, as he emerged, they pointed their Heckler and Kochs at him while the guards he thought had been shot stood by their guard boxes, their guns now loaded. Further out, off MoD territory, a line of armed police stood ready. As he shuffled towards the gate a media crew saw a scoop in the making. Its helicopter veered in and lit him up with its searchlight. He knew from television what that meant. When the light struck him he straightened his shoulders and tried to shuffle with dignity. Sallis was waiting on the other side of the gate.

"Thanks for your help, Sir," said Smail when they reached him. "Sorry about the damage. And you won't need the siren any more."

Sallis spoke into his radio and the siren stopped. As Smail and Carey, with a police escort, made their slow way to the Site Security block Sallis took care to stay in the searchlight that was tracking Carey. He wanted to be seen as a big player in his capture. It'd go into his cv as well. The army guards remained where they were, waiting for further orders, while more police cordoned off the control centre's entire bottom end. It was a forensic zone now.

The flooding mechanism had been switched off on Sir Simon Meacher's personal authority. He'd acted on a preemptive alert from van Piet soon after he and Geert had taken off in Maidstone. Whether it'd ever be switched on again was a decision for his Minister - who, as agreed, had been briefed in good time – and for his Minister's opposite number at the MoD. The two politicians soon decided it'd be best if the public didn't know the North Sea Tunnel could be flooded. If it knew one tunnel could be, it'd believe others could be as well. Disinformation from the very top was called for.

41

News from Germany and a Boxing Day letter

Van Piet spent Christmas Day at home with Célestine and Jackie. That was the way they liked it. The de Valus were holidaying in Bermuda and Joost was with relatives in Massachusetts. They'd be coming to Gorris for New Year.

On Boxing Day Jackie had some friends in and Célestine had courses to prepare in the brew house so van Piet locked himself in his study to read an update on Daski, Steffen and Chameleon German Intelligence had sent him. Daski had reacted fast to Steffen's arrest. In time-honoured German fashion he'd turned himself in, confessed in full and got the suspended sentence his lawyers had pitched for. His Stasi files were part of the deal. So were the recordings he'd told Steffen he wasn't making, his secretly copied report on Carey and the details of the Chameleon members whose drop boxes he serviced. He'd always known they were good insurance. That's why he'd suggested them and then volunteered to look after them. Lederer was one of those he shopped and Lederer, likewise suddenly law-abiding, flagged up Steffen's mouthpiece in Brazil. A police raid in São Paulo flushed her out. She was now in Germany awaiting trial and Lederer's lawyers were pitching for a fine in lieu of time behind bars.

The update didn't take long to get through but van Piet had also promised a letter to Luke Benjamin, Trilling's successor, about New Hope. Benjamin, a no-nonsense former field man, had had more things to worry about than Steffen, and van Piet had been spending most of his time in Essex so there were plenty of gaps to plug.

"Trilling's opened right up, which came as no surprise," van Piet began. "Guderius, Steffen and Zimmermann have all been talking as well and Kapner's just plain venomous. Only the other week she told me Steffen murdered a Peeping Tom when they were fetching their guns from Sheerness. The coroner had ruled death by misadventure but Kapner didn't want Steffen getting away with it if she had to go down for Danzig so I got the whole story hot off the line. Carey hasn't said much yet. He's on suicide watch, which he's probably enjoying, and he's permanently under sedation. He didn't turn his Retrotox down when it was offered courtesy of a highly cooperative Guderius. I suppose he can't end it all till he gets his strength up to do it.

But back to Trilling. What you need to remember is, he never cared about the SRO, all he cared about was himself. That made him easy to turn and the GDR duly obliged. He was still low-ranking but he'd wormed his way into operational planning so he knew a lot. Then he got onto a liaison committee with MI6 and that produced a deal: the GDR would protect SRO agents if he betrayed MI6's. It worked like a dream. MI6 got slaughtered, the SRO took a few token hits and Trilling got this reputation as the man who knew how. It took him to the top.

He was already turned when Kapner and Steffen entered his life. He once told me he only knew Steffen because Steffen never hid up but the truth is, he was spilling secrets to Steffen as long as Steffen was in London. He also told me there was someone MI5 couldn't catch and that *was* true. That someone was Trilling.

Kapner came earlier than Steffen. Once Trilling had proved he was worth his GDR money he asked for a bonus and she was it – ready wrapped from Belgrave Square and primed to keep her eyes and ears open. But against all the rules she fell in love with him and that love lasted till he tried to shoot her on Sheppey. Maybe it hasn't stopped yet, she says she's still deciding. She never knew Trilling was talking to Steffen back in London and when I told her, her morale hit the floor of her cell. She could accept Trilling keeping things from her because she'd put him on a pedestal but not clodhopping Steffen. He was just a soldier.

Trilling never loved her back, it was the fun he was in it for and part of the fun was manipulating her when she was supposed to be manipulating him. After the Cold War Kapner's business brought her back to London but Trilling was the icing on the cake and they were soon billing and cooing again. He got into her flat through the underground passage and they left messages for each other in the Ranelagh Gardens, where Trilling took his lonely walks. If she was in town she went there herself and if she wasn't she used a courier.

Now according to Trilling, when New Hope started the two people who knew directly he'd been shedding secrets back then were Kapner and Steffen. The rest were all dead and he was certain of that because he'd made it his business to find out who they were and what happened to them. He also knew none of the GDR's files on him had survived. But as long as Kapner and Steffen were alive they were a potential danger and so was Guderius for a reason I'll come to in a moment. While Trilling was head of the SRO it was a situation he could manage but once he retired it wouldn't be and that worried him a lot. Then Kapner told him about New Hope and he realised he could hijack it to wipe out everyone who was still a danger to him. It was that realisation, not the welfare of the SRO, that made him determined not to let New Hope go to any other organisation.

Now for Guderius. Mrs Trilling was still alive when Kapner came on the scene and she was a very high-minded lady. Both Trillings knew well in advance she was going to Uruguay and they also knew Belle Faraday, who'd worked with Mrs Trilling before, was joining her there from Vancouver. At some point before she left, Mrs Trilling discovered her husband was seeing someone else and Trilling was afraid if she found out it was a Stasi agent, she'd turn him in on principle. That meant she had to die but Trilling couldn't work out how to murder her without getting caught so he asked Kapner about it and she contacted her old friend Guderius, who was working with Juán Bakos as a bugs expert. Guderius said he'd help if he could so Kapner wangled some leave and met him in East Berlin. Faraday's name worked the magic because he'd already heard it from Bakos. Apparently she was a sort of cultural link-person so she was permanently in and out of the Canadian embassy in Havana. Guderius also knew – again from Bakos - she was a Communist hard liner. The upshot was, he spoke to Bakos and Bakos got word to Faraday via a Canadian diplomat in Havana that Mrs Trilling – a lovely lady by all accounts - was a lethal class enemy, but a doctor he was working with had the bugs to kill her off. Faraday messaged back she'd put them to good use. Bakos took the bugs with him when he went back to Cuba, from there they went to Vancouver and Mrs Trilling was injected with them in Uruguay. Mrs Trilling thought it was one more vaccination, the puncture wound looked like an insect bite and Faraday ditched the drugs that would've saved Mrs Trilling, claiming they'd been lost in a flood. She pretended to keep looking after her as best she could but the truth was, she was making sure she died. So, when New Hope was born, who knew about this secret from the past? Not Bakos, he'd died of cirrhosis as Guderius knew he would – he'd been quietly helping it along, in fact. Not the Canadian diplomat either. He'd died a natural death and so had Faraday. That left Guderius and, once again, Kapner for Trilling's hit list. Steffen was completely out of this. He often sensed there was something between Guderius and Kapner but he had no idea what it was.

It suited Trilling down to the ground that New Hope would bring Steffen and Guderius to England but the last thing he wanted was the guards being shot and the tunnel flooded because that would've stirred up a manhunt that could've stopped him slipping from Sheppey. That's where Kapner came in and it helped that she had no political interest in New Hope at all. Like Steffen and Guderius, Carey knew a lot about Kapner so Trilling told her she could make life safe for herself and Trilling – and they could be married as well - if she shot Steffen, Guderius and Carey *before New Hope was due to begin*. Trilling also told her that meanwhile he'd go to Sheppey by boat – remember, he never had security cover - and moor up in Sheppey Bight. After the murders he'd meet Kapner in the car park and take her back to his boat on foot. The Fiat could stay where it was, it wasn't in her name. Danzig and Frank Zimmermann would have to be silenced as well, as would Kurt Zimmermann. A booby trapped pair of sensor-driven binoculars was going to shoot him through his eyes so he was lucky he threw them away when he did. Kapner fell for Trilling's candyfloss in the same way as Carey fell for hers. It wasn't until she was looking into the silencer of her own Beretta she realised she had to die as well because she was the biggest risk of the lot. Trilling's hope was, the police would think there'd been some kind of Chameleon bust-up with Kapner committing suicide at the end of it. Such things are not unknown so he was in with a chance.

You'll think I've forgotten Miriam Sobart but I haven't. She'd been a double since her RAF days. MI6 ran her at first but when the Cold War ended she was surplus to requirements and Trilling snapped her up as another source of information from Chameleon. She passed plenty of goodies on to him, including what was happening to Carey, but what she never knew was, she wasn't working for the SRO at all – just for Trilling personally. She was yet another one who knew too much for Trilling's good so she was on his hit list too. I didn't know for sure she was servicing Trilling in the belief she was helping her country but it was a possibility that fitted the facts so I went with it and I'm glad I did. She's got courage.

You're probably wondering what put me onto Trilling in the first place. Well, the starter was the Knifepoint letter Célestine got while I was in Australia. It was so obviously a fake, there had to be something behind it. It sounded as if an idiot had written it but the way it'd been kept clean suggested someone who was anything but. Trilling didn't enter my head at the time but when I got back to London I was primed to suspect anyone of anything. Then Trilling shoved that picture of Kapner in my face. How, I wondered, could our ramshackle surveillance produce the one shot guaranteed to make me fall in with Trilling's intentions? Was it luck or had Trilling rigged the improvements he'd got round to – suspiciously late in the day, I might add - to make sure that shot was taken? If he'd done that, he must've known when Kapner was going out dressed like that and if she told him that herself he must know her – a one-time Stasi agent - surprisingly well. So how long had that been going on? And why stop with Kapner? Did he know Steffen – a former GDR military attaché? And did he know Guderius, the NPA doctor?

Guderius's spell in the Dominican Republic was also a pointer. Because the Dominican Republic doesn't have an extradition treaty with Germany Guderius might have gone there because he'd been naughty in his GDR days – as he had been in fact. Yet he only stayed for three months and when he came back, he clearly came back for good. So either he was clean all along or he wasn't clean but someone with inside information told him it was safe to come back. Prompted by the Kapner photo I thought Trilling might fit the bill. He'd be taking an enormous risk, of course, and one way I accounted for it was that Trilling desperately wanted Guderius where he could get at him in his own time and for some dark purpose of his own. If that was so, Germany beat the Caribbean and England was better still. So what about Steffen? Did Trilling want him within reach as well? It could well be.

Guderius's suspect return made me ask whether my own was as innocent as it seemed. We were short-staffed, everyone knew that, and Trilling needed someone to take on a new development who wasn't tied up with field work. But especially after the second Knifepoint letter I began to wonder. Trilling knew Jackie's deafness made me very protective of her so perhaps the letters had nothing to do with horses and everything to do with getting me to drop New Hope. Not straight away, there'd be no sense in that, but later on when it'd do real damage. One clue was, the second letter was as clean as the first so there looked like some serious skill behind them. Another was, both letters were bad but they left room for worse to come and that seemed deliberate. So was Trilling employing me or using me? If he was using me he'd likely want me around in the early stages but not when crunch time came, and a really bad letter might get rid of me at that point. It'd be worth a try anyway, especially if he had an incompetent deputy lined up, which he did. With Mrs Patel chaos was pre-programmed and that'd give him extra scope to do his own thing. I'm glad Kent Police has demoted her for doing what she did and I wish Joe Smail well in her job. She asked for it and now she's got it. Trilling, by the way, wrote the Knifepoint letters in a sterile cabinet, the sort you see in labs with gloved sleeves attached to holes in the front. He wore the right clothing, he had the gear to clean everything before it went in and the envelopes were self-sealing so he didn't have to lick them. When he finished a letter he put it into a special bag, took it to the post and tipped it in. He didn't touch it at any time. He didn't even breathe on it.

Another big pointer was the photo of Guderius with the Hanno message on it. I knew Guderius was a bugs expert and Mrs Trilling had died of a bug infection. I also knew Belle Faraday was Canadian and Canada, unlike America, kept its diplomatic ties with Cuba during the Cold War. On top of that Van Piet Banking told me Hanno was a Cuban Guderius knew who moved in diplomatic circles. If Guderius had supplied the bugs that'd killed Mrs Trilling I could see why Trilling would want him out of the Dominican Republic but I could only guess why he might want his wife killed. An affair with Kapner was a possibility and when I saw her snuggle up on Sheppey I knew I hadn't completely lost my marbles. Dawn Chopine helped as well. Trilling set up the Bad Sollmer farce with two thoughts in mind. He wanted to look as if he was doing something but he didn't want to frighten Guderius or Steffen. Chopine's blunder nearly blew that and I have to say, Trilling's damage limitation was a class act. Anyway, Chopine remembered a secret lab with an incubator in it. It wasn't the one Guderius used to culture bugs for Mrs Trilling but the association was a strong one. Speaking of Chopine, I gather you want to give her a second chance. That's a mistake. An agent who lets you down once will do it again. It's just a question of when.

I expect a lot of what I've written sounds flimsy but I figured what I couldn't rule out I had to rule in. As we both know, that's how it is in Shadowland. Since Trilling was Suspect Number One I couldn't let anyone he might contact know what I was thinking in case something slipped out. That applied to Mrs Patel, who was out of place anyway, and it also applied to Eddie Snape. When he called me about the Really Bad Letter that was clearly supposed to get rid of me I said if the day firmed up as I thought it would, I'd ask Mrs Patel to tell him about going into Essex and he was to find a reason for wanting me back here. But I didn't say why. I had to take a chance with Sallis if I wanted to catch Carey in the act but Sallis was new so I thought if Trilling tried to cosy up to him, he'd be able to keep his distance. What Sallis didn't know was, if he'd stepped out of line during the endgame the soldiers would've taken him out. Or Smail's snipers. They'd all been told to watch for anything abnormal.

In general I was stuck with a waiting game very much like Trilling's until I could mount a counter-attack. To do that I had to pretend to quit but I also had to be certain I knew where Steffen was heading. Now, Mrs Patel thought the Sheppey thing was a feint but the *secret* shooting practice at Schwarzer's undermined that and when I learned about Carey I was convinced it wasn't a feint because his roughing up was also done in secret. So, obviously, both of these activities were going to be used for real somehow and after I'd learned the North Sea Tunnel could be flooded it was easy to see what Steffen was after, with two snipers using Dragunovs, three armed assistants and a dependent SSO even if I still couldn't see why.

The rest was organisation. If I was to catch Steffen & Co in the act, Smail's people had to sneak up on them in the dark. Helicopter drops close in would be far too noisy but I happen to know Sidney Marrish, the owner of TechMarrish, through Van Piet Banking and I got him to let me use some of his all-terrain fuel cell vehicles. They're dead easy to drive, they're silent and they don't need headlights. Trilling didn't know Smail at all so I talked through with him how best to fan out from TechMarrish and at least take the key villains if we couldn't take them all. His people weren't to intervene unless they absolutely had to. That cost Guderius a headache and Danzig her life but it paid off because none of these lice knew we were watching them. I discussed Carey with Smail as well and gave him all the leeway he needed. He knew from past experience who Eddie Snape was and if I said I was quitting after I'd had a call from him he knew it wouldn't be for real. He also knew it was my orders, not Mrs Patel's, that counted. When I took over again I kept her in the command helicopter but Smail checked any orders she gave him with me and I was talking to him as well. That's how we wrapped things up.

Here's some gossip to finish with. It comes from various sources, including German Intelligence, which is a lot happier now Trilling's behind bars. Daniela and Robert miss their grandfather a lot. He's sent them a sackful of Christmas presents from prison and they've sent him cards they made themselves. Ruth's okayed the presents but she can't forgive him for being prepared to drown them. Walter thinks different things on different days and Helga-Marie keeps saying how proud she is of him. She's living with Ruth and Walter at the moment. It can't make life pleasant for them. She's also going ahead with her Oxford treatment. The West might be fascist but she'll forgive it this once.

Then there's Gannisch. Guderius still owns the clinic and he's approved Torsten Mallik as the new Medical Director so he obviously doesn't know what's going on. Gannisch is all grief when she phones or writes to him but out of sight she and Mallik are closing in on each other. It's the usual thing. Mallik knows Gannisch is Guderius's sole heir and neither of them thinks he'll last long in prison. So you can see what's in it for Mallik if his stomach's strong enough. As for Gannisch, she's found a man who can do what Guderius couldn't and she's still got time to enjoy it. Mallik's clear of the law of course, he never knew a thing, but Gannisch's habit of never asking questions means she is as well. You might think she'd be in trouble after what happened to Chopine but, no, she was simply helping a guest who'd fallen ill and the State Prosecutor is having to lump it.

Ah, yes, one more thing, Kapner's booby-trapped binoculars. The idea started with Trilling and they were made by the same gunsmith who made the silencer for her Beretta. He's been pulled in and he'll get what's coming to him."

Van Piet signed off with the usual courtesies, leaned back in his chair and stretched till he felt mobile again. The Tylers were coming to lunch and Garry and his wife were driving over for dinner. Garry could take the letter back with him, it was the safest way to get it to Benjamin, but that was for another day. There was still a lot of Boxing Day left and van Piet meant to enjoy it with people who, for once, he could trust unreservedly.